# darjeeling

BHARTI KIRCHNER

darjeeling

ST. MARTIN'S GRIFFIN
NEW YORK

www.stmartins.com

Library of Congress Cataloging-in-Publication Data

Kirchner, Bharti.
    Darjeeling : a novel / Bharti Kirchner.
        p. cm.
    ISBN 0-312-28642-2 (hc)
    ISBN 0-312-31606-2 (pbk)
    1. Darjeeling (India : District)—Fiction. 2. Triangles (Interpersonal relations)—Fiction. 3. Plantation life—Fiction. 4. Tea trade—Fiction. 5. Sisters—Fiction. I. Title.
PS3561.I6835 D37 2002
813'.54—dc21   2001058863

First St. Martin's Griffin Edition: August 2003

10   9   8   7   6   5   4   3   2   1

In memory of my mother:

So we don't forget Darjeeling

acknowledgments

I'd like to acknowledge the following people who accompanied me in the long, arduous journey that became this novel. It was a pleasure collaborating with my editor, Linda McFall, and my agent, Liza Dawson. I couldn't have asked for a better team. Your enthusiasm for the project made the long hours worthwhile.

I extend my loving thanks to my husband, Tom Kirchner, once again, for helping me realize my dreams. Thank you for your patience, understanding, reading, and support, as well as for supplying those missing commas!

My deep gratitude goes to Barbara Galvin, Savithri Machiraju, Leon Billig, and Diane Ste Marie, four writers who have seen me through several of my previous books as well as this one. It was a comfort to know you were there for me. I value your input highly.

I owe much to Barbara McHugh, Laura Fine-Morrison, Nalini Iyer,

Valerie J. Brooks, Gianni Truzzi, Mark Anthony Rolo, and Marjorie Reynolds, who have been most generous with their time and support. Special thanks to Jill Schoolman, whose many words of wisdom kept my spirits from flagging down the stretch.

In India I am indebted to Mr. Sharma, S. M. Changoiwala, and his son Samir Changoiwala, Rajah Banerjee, Srirupa Banerjee, Sujit Bhattacharya, Mr. Prakash, Mrs. Roy, and the staff of the Darjeeling Planters' Club for their hospitality and willingness to share information. This book, in fact, is a tribute to all those in the tea industry who devote untold hours as well as their life energy to produce a product that has made the appellation "Darjeeling" synonymous with fine tea.

Though they are not directly connected with this book, I'd like to acknowledge Shau-lee Chau, Sudha Shetty, and Simmone Misra for the warm light they shed on my life. And I want to thank Nancy Pearl, Frank Miller, and Chris Higashi for their friendship and support over the years.

Though leaves are many, the root is one.

WILLIAM BUTLER YEATS

Tea is nought but this:
First you heat the water,
Then you make the tea.
Then you drink it properly.
That is all you need to know.

SEN NO RIKYU,
SIXTEENTH-CENTURY TEA MASTER

darjeeling

one

Autumn 2000

Aloka Gupta gazed down from the window of her apartment at the gray-brown bustle of Manhattan's Fifty-second Street, her thoughts turning to her childhood home and the family-owned tea plantation in Darjeeling. Urged on by the chill of the short autumn days, the tea plants were now forming their third flush of tender shiny leaves, lending a tantalizing fragrance to the crisp mountain air. Eight years earlier, her life and love, like the bumblebees flitting from bud to bud, had been entwined with those bushes.

The cold jumble of glass, concrete, chrome, and steel before her now stood in cruel contrast to the allure of that idyllic time. As she turned away, the final divorce papers, legal-sized and officiously stamped with the seal of the state of New York and the day's date, stared accusingly from the top of her writing desk.

How was a divorce possible? She had always assumed that she would grow up to be a *pativrata* and remain devoted to her husband for the rest of her life. Having been reared on stories of powerful goddesses, Sita, Savitri, and Sakuntala, examples of devoted Hindu wives, she found it hard to believe that now, at age forty, she would be alone. Sita, Savitri, and Sakuntala would exist only on the pages of scriptures.

She sank down in front of her desk, pushed the divorce papers aside, and picked up the current issue of *Manhattan, India,* published by Girish Enterprises. Three years ago, she'd landed a journalist's position with the publication, primarily because of her master's degree in English and high school teaching experience. The widely read weekly reported news and events of interest to the flourishing Indian-American community scattered throughout New York and its environs. Subscribers devoured the newsweekly from cover to cover, passed it to friends, talked about it over *chai* latte, and sent clippings back home. Aloka wrote feature articles and reveled in the challenge of touching the emotions of the readers.

The first two pages of this week's edition were devoted to the profile of a taxicab driver who'd donated his total savings to his village in India to establish a school for girls, and that of a biochemist who served food to the homeless in her spare time. It also contained Aloka's own piece: an interview with a nutritionist about vegetarian sources for vitamin B_{12}. Aloka enjoyed afresh seeing her work in print.

She flipped to page three. The entire top half of the page was dedicated to an advice column, "Ask Seva," the most popular section of the paper. It was her most important contribution, one she penned under the pseudonym. Nine months earlier, when she'd started the column, her editor hadn't been enthusiastic about its reception. Before long she had surprised him with her knack for sensing the needs, feelings, and concerns of transplants from her old country, and responding to them appropriately. By day the new arrivals, the disoriented *desis,* marveled at the broad avenues, monumental skyscrapers, and well-stocked department stores. By night they longed for the meaningful human contact so lacking in their new homeland. They would huddle in a tiny, dilapidated efficiency, shared with another *desi.* Their faces growing long, their eyelashes dampening, they would moan, "My country, my relatives, my language, my food." They would speculate on whether the migration—most often forced by economic realities—hadn't been a mistake. One lonely man, a "married bachelor," was known to dial 800 numbers just to converse with someone. "The first three to four years is a curse," wiser members of the community would advise them. "Thereafter you stop crying."

Aloka did more than stopping tears. Her column was a skillful merger of optimism, guidance, and practical advice on how to make the adjustment to a new home: where to get a silk sari cleaned, how to locate a Hindu priest for an auspicious family event, how to order a vegetarian meal sans eggs in a restaurant, why must one wear layered clothing during the frigid months, and how to make the first move in a relationship.

"Seva" meant service and, as in much of the vocabulary of Indian languages, carried overtones of devotion. True to the spirit of her assumed name, Aloka didn't deliver a terse reply to a sensitive question, or enlist the help of a team of psychologists for a technically accurate answer. Rather, she dispensed commonsense advice a loving sister might offer. Young and the old, male and female, new arrivals and longtime residents alike read her column and conferred about it at the kebob house, as well as on Internet user groups. They corresponded with her and visited her website, *www.askseva.com*, seeking guidance on all manner of problems but especially those of the heart. They embraced her as a source of hope and wisdom. She was "their own."

This week's column had begun with suggestions of low-cost ways to enjoy the city: the Sunday band at Central Park, the cumin-spiked vegetable juices served by a blind vendor near Rockefeller Square, and the American release of an earlier Soumitra Chatterjee film at a Bronx theater. The column had ended with a plea to help find a missing Tamil-speaking child.

Her upbeat style, clear simple phrasing, and handwritten "Love, Seva" signature, done in a single stroke of the pen, had won hearts. *Manhattan, India* now boasted the highest circulation of all local Indian-American periodicals, some fifty thousand and growing.

But who was the real Seva?

The question was a hot topic of discussion at social and religious gatherings of the community. The current consensus—and it shifted often—

was that the voice belonged to a chain-smoking, elite female novelist, Nandita Pal, who called a choice Fifth Avenue address home. Not even Pranab, Aloka's ex-husband, had suspected it was her. This was the first secret she had kept from him. As her marriage had disintegrated, she had felt a greater need to rely on her own career and identity. She told friends and acquaintances that she worked for a diversified company that counted publishing, music, and importing clothing among its activities. When asked, Aloka would offer, "Oh, I do a little writing and some market research." Seva's real identity remained the paper's closely guarded secret.

Now Aloka reached for the pile of mail she'd brought from work and began sorting through it. She received mostly complimentary letters, along with an occasional diatribe—"truffles and arrows," as she called them. The first card in the batch happened to be from an admirer. It said:

> *Even if it turns out that you're forty and overweight, with rotten teeth and five terrible children, I'd still love you.*

Aloka chuckled and shook her head, tossed the card in the corner waste can, and picked up the next.

> *I am absolutely positive you are a man.*
>   *Your replies are much too intelligent for a* zanana.

Annoyed by the condescending term, which translated roughly as a mere woman, Aloka wadded the note into a ball and flung it toward the waste can, missing it by several feet. Her eyes were already focused on the next letter.

> *Why do women in New York wash their hair so much? The last three attractive women I asked for a date all replied, "I'd love to, but I have to wash my hair."*
>   *I wish I were Breck.*

Aloka smiled to herself. A suitable solution to "Breck's" problem was beginning to form in her mind when she was startled by the sound of footsteps. She turned halfway in her chair.

Pranab was standing in the doorway. In the drab navy jacket of a telephone repair service specialist, he seemed ill at ease. His body emitted a faint oily odor.

"Oh, it's you." Why today, of all days? she wondered. "I wasn't expecting you."

He stepped into the room. At five-foot-ten, he towered over her; but in the deep afternoon shadows he appeared diminished. His deep-set eyes seemed to have retreated even farther behind the habitual tortoiseshell spectacles; his lips were compressed into a thin line, giving his face an icy expression.

"Just came for a book."

He paused uncertainly before the maple bookcase that contained old volumes bound in maroon, literature they had shared. This study, with its cherry-finished desk beneath the window and adjustable reading light, had always been his shrine.

A wayward lock of hair stuck out from the nape of his neck and her fingers trembled with the urge to smooth it. She rubbed them instead over her tight-fitting denim jeans, a cheerless reminder of the pounds gained over the last several months.

"Can I help you find anything?" She spoke in English, glad that they shared a second language. In propitious times, they had conversed in Bengali, or Bangla, their poetic mother tongue, with its mellifluous tones. Not today. Only English, a neutral language bare of emotions, could be trusted to convey the appropriate formality.

His silence knifed through her like a high wind from the Himalayas. She watched him remove a tattered volume with a cracked binding, his favorite treatise written in Sanskrit, musty scent emanating from it. With long tapered fingers he began to leaf through the book. His expression softened when he turned to a page that contained a favorite passage.

He snapped the book closed and gave her a glance. How quickly husband becomes stranger. Not even the hint of a question hung in the air. When there were no questions between them; she knew the marriage was dead.

He half turned toward the door. "I'm moving to my new place tomorrow," he finally said, in a tone that was low, mundane, and devoid of sentiment.

She wanted to ask: Where have you left the voice that once so forcefully exhorted the tea workers in Darjeeling to rise against their oppressor—my father, no less? In those exciting days, Pranab, his robust figure clad in a white *kurta* and his luminous eyes emanating fervor, had commanded like the mythical god Arjuna. She had loved him enough to risk her life for him.

"Here's my new address and phone number in case you ever need it." He dropped the apartment keys on a side table and pressed a blue Post-It into her hand.

How would he manage on his own? He needed a woman in his life. Right now she longed to massage his forehead with a fragrant oil to chase away the day's irritations, like a good Hindu wife would do.

She said, "I'll be sure to forward your mail."

He took a step toward the door. "If I can ever do anything for you, Aloka . . ."

She heard the regret in his voice, witnessed the tentative movement of his legs. Perhaps their ten-year relationship hadn't ended. There were empty pages yet to be written.

She stood motionlessly, staring after his departing figure, hoping for him to swivel around at any moment. His image became smaller and his outline blurred. It was as though she were peering at him through a rain-drenched glass panel. Finally he floated out of the room. She listened to the familiar squeak of his Nikes descending the stairs. Then an ambulance siren smothered that tiny sound, but not her hopes.

two

In the next hour, Aloka furiously cleaned her apartment. Housecleaning had always been her antidote to the blues. In the living room she swept the patina of dust from the surface of the glass-topped coffee table. As she arranged the throw pillows, she noticed, though not for the first time, that the sofas, relics of her moribund marriage, didn't match. In the early days, when they were short of money, she had snapped up the cushiony, roll-armed, mocha-colored sofa from a thrift shop for a few hundred and considered it banditry. From the same shop Pranab had selected the flare-armed, saddle-brown sofa, but for some mysterious reason never sat on it. He would walk around his purchase with a disgusted look on his face and grab a chair instead. She had always meant to ask why but somehow never got around to doing so.

Now, as she waxed the floor, she asked, "Why, Pranab?"

She straightened the frame of a family photograph on the off-white wall. Her attention fell on a print of the Mary Cassatt painting *The Sisters*, hanging right below the photograph. Aloka had fallen in love with that print the instant she'd seen it at a small local gallery. Now she gazed at the guileless eyes of the two winsome children looking out together against a background of bluish green mist. She felt a quiver in her heart.

The discordant jangling of the telephone interrupted her dreamlike state. She answered and recognized the voice of her editor from *Manhattan, India*, and managed to reel herself back into a more businesslike frame of mind. She had been unable to break the news of her divorce to her boss, an expatriate Indian who'd been married to the same woman for thirty-five years. Another time she, an advice columnist, might have appreciated the irony of the situation, but not this afternoon.

"I just heard you went home early today, Aloka. Aren't you feeling well?"

"No, nothing like that. Just some personal problems." Her voice quaking, she told him of the divorce.

Though he mumbled words of apology, she could almost see the happily overweight man shake his head disapprovingly atop a nonexistent neck and mutter to himself, "These young people." Many older members of the Indian community—Mr. Choudhury, Mr. Gopal, and Mrs. Roy came to mind—became numb or overagitated when they received news of a divorce. Marriage, they understood. A wedding ceremony was conducted with much pageantry and was attended by many well-wishers. But the same people wouldn't be around when one's relationship was in tatters. In divorce, a woman stood alone.

"Do you need a couple of days off, Aloka?"

"No. The worst part is over. I'll be back in the office tomorrow."

"Good, good. I can't run the paper without you. The last time you took a few days off and your column didn't come out, we got a hundred frantic calls. By the way, there's a pile of letters sitting on your desk. Do you have any relatives nearby you can call?"

Aloka strained her gaze up at the poster on the wall. Victoria was only three zones away. It was still early enough to make a phone call to Sujata.

"Yes, a sister out in Victoria, British Columbia."

As soon as the words flew past her lips, she saw the irony behind such a fantasy. She couldn't have a soul-to-soul communication with her sister about the divorce, or any other matter. They barely stayed in touch.

"I know you haven't asked for advice, Aloka, but I'd like to offer you some from the perspective of a chap who has lived long enough to make most of life's mistakes. When things get tough, it's always best to turn to your parents, brothers, and sisters. You may have drifted apart, perhaps there are some resentments, unresolved issues, that sort of thing, but in the end blood connections are as strong as the currents of a powerful river, as we say in India. It took me a long time to figure that out, and in the meantime I went through a lot of unnecessary suffering alone. Now I see my family in a different light. They've played a big part in whatever success I've achieved and helped me through some very difficult times, once I finally learned to trust them. They're the ones who've made me who I am. It helps to get in touch with your life source from time to time."

Aloka, grateful for his insight, thanked him and proceeded to consider his advice. After she hung up, she retreated to the kitchen to seek solace in its pampering atmosphere. A fruity fragrance from a half-eaten peach on the table left over from a hurried breakfast clung to the air. The room had once been redolent with the homey smell of milk, sugar, and ghee from Indian pastries bought at the "Little India" section of Lexington Avenue. Now, from her recently acquired health-conscious perspective, they seemed too fatty and cloying. Her eyes caught a crinkled white paper sack on the counter. She opened it and teased a half dozen crescent-shaped cookies called Pleasure Domes out onto a plate. She had purchased them fresh this morning from a patisserie on Fifty-fourth Street. With their powdery, sugar-dusted tops and faint vanilla scent, they were her current weakness. Right now they held scant appeal, serving only as a reminder of a friend's birthday bash tonight.

Drifting back to the study, Aloka went to stand by the window just in time to see the mail carrier leaving the building. Grateful for the distraction, she picked up her key, traipsed down to the first floor, and opened her mailbox. A tinny sound reverberated in the air as if in protest at this intrusion. The minute she saw the reassuring blue envelope postmarked Darjeeling, the only mail of the day, she snatched up her prize and tore it open even as she trudged back up the stairs.

The script was tiny, shaky, and unmistakably Grandma Nina's. A true matriarch, Grandma had dominated the Gupta lineage for three generations, making her presence felt even overseas through letters that arrived in innocuously flimsy blue envelopes.

Aloka extracted a creamy delicate sheet whose rustling folds brought to mind fragments of her girlhood. Mother had died when Aloka was twelve. Father and especially Grandma had raised her and Sujata. At bedtime Grandma would tuck her in, drawing a blanket up to her chin and touching her forehead in a blessing so that she would be cozy and secure for the night.

> *In my last letter I had mentioned how women in the village of Sonagunj were trying to get elected to their community council. As you well know I am all for them. It was our ancient poet Kalidasa who once said, "Look for a land where women are in good spirits, for that is a prosperous country."*
>
> *Now listen to this latest ploy by conniving male chauvinist politicians. Only "obedient" wives are allowed to run for election, so men can continue to rule through them behind the scenes.*
>
> *Can you believe it?*

Aloka smiled. Grandma's letters always began with a commentary on some aspect of social or political life—she had been nicknamed All India Radio by her neighbors. Though she believed word of mouth was the best way to disseminate information, Grandma began her day by scouring the pages of the *Statesman,* an English-language daily flown in from Calcutta, while sipping a cup of Darjeeling tea. Her maidservant would have long since learned that the color of the tea must be "rose blush with a hint of white," from just the right amount of hot milk. After finishing the "flavory" cup, Grandma would begin her letter-writing ritual.

> *My dear child, although it has been nearly eight years, I have never asked you to return, even for a brief visit, remembering full well the tragic circumstances of your departure. Yet, I feel compelled to ask you now. As you are no doubt aware, November 16th is my eighty-first birthday. I would very much like to celebrate reaching that special age with you, Pranab, and Sujata.*

Grandma commemorating her birthday? Why now? She hadn't bothered to do so on her sixtieth, regarded a special age in India. The adult Guptas, especially the womenfolk, had never wanted any fuss made on their birthdays, insisting that such frivolous attention should be lavished only on children. But no, Aloka now realized, this invitation could be different. Nine was a sacred number in ancient India and a symbol of good fortune. Of course Grandma would need to celebrate, having lived to the most auspicious year of nine-times-nine.

At this age, the sun appears a little paler each day. I no longer hear all the sounds in the house. The hours are never too full.

Refusal was clearly out of the question. Aloka's gaze darted to the calendar on the wall: lonely days imprisoned in little square boxes and never enough of them. It was already October 1, which left only six weeks to apply for a visa, book a flight, purchase gifts, and, just as importantly, prepare mentally. But could she?

If you decide to come, as you surely must, please don't forget to send me your itinerary. I'll dispatch a servant to meet you and Pranab at Bagdogra Airport. Give my love to that dear boy.

> With *much* bhalobasa,
> Your affectionate Thakurma

Aloka refolded the page with a heavy sigh: The two references to Pranab in the letter hadn't escaped her attention. Grandma had always maintained a cordial relationship with Pranab and at one point even saved his life. How could Aloka arrive without him?

She could see it now, Grandma sitting in a chair on the front lawn all day, straining her eyes to follow each vehicle as it screeched on the road. Grandma's mind would be whirling with images of them jumping out of the car, slamming the door, and rushing to greet her. She would see them bend down to touch her feet in the Bengali greeting of respect for the elders and they would receive her murmured blessing before saying a word. Grandma would rise and embrace each with equal affection. "Aloka!

Pranab!" she would call out, tears of joy coursing down her creased cheeks.

Arriving alone would devastate Grandma. After a few minutes she would silently blame both Aloka and Pranab for the failed union, and Aloka, being there alone, would bear her disapproval alone. Eyes downcast, Grandma would grimace, as if she had bitten into a young green mango without the customary salt, perhaps reminding herself, with the benefit of hindsight, how she had mistrusted Pranab.

Aloka brushed her fingers across the letter. In the Gupta family, three generations had dwelled under one roof with intimacy, the inevitable clash of personalities woven into the tapestry of communal life. She heard Grandma complaining, "I don't understand, Aloka. I just don't understand. In our household marriage is for a lifetime."

Suppose Aloka told everything. Still, she wouldn't be able to satisfy Grandma. Like the sacred River Ganga with its one hundred active mouths, Grandma would mutter a hundred questions, each requiring a detailed explanation.

And Sujata, who had once had an affair with Pranab? The clumsy girl had even taken up embroidery so she could secretly gift Pranab a handkerchief with his initials stitched on it. Years later Aloka had discovered that handkerchief among Pranab's clothing and experienced all over again the jealous rage that had overcome her on the night her father had informed her of the illicit love. The passing years had diminished the intensity of her animosity toward Sujata, but the episode continued to fester like a scabbed-over wound.

How much did Sujata remember of that period? She was still single. Did she ever wake up in the darkest hour of the night, perspiring, trapped in a fantasy about Pranab?

It was Sujata's reaction that Aloka feared the most; Sujata, who would sit silently, wearing a smug expression. Eyes focused on the mountain peaks, she would act as if she hadn't heard a word.

Aloka stowed Grandma's letter in the decorative straw basket that housed all correspondence from home and copies of her own letters, then went over to the window. In the deepening gloom, multistory office complexes twinkled like a backlit honeycomb. Street lamps cast a pitiless glare on the hurrying figures below. The tumult of the traffic in the background remained undiminished. Evening could never quite subdue the Empire City. Whereas Darjeeling succumbed to the darkness like an obedient child, this gritty giant trod it underfoot.

During the day Aloka reveled in New York, but after dark it seemed ruled by a malevolent force. She hadn't been sleeping well lately, often waking up with a shiver in the middle of the night.

Her boss's remark about his kinsmen in India returned to her: "They're the ones who've made me who I am." Those words sunk in now. The Guptas had made her the woman she was today, one confident enough of herself to offer advice to others.

She forged her decision: She would return to the mountain home of her youth for Grandma's birthday, to renew connections with her family.

Back at her desk, buoyed by a feeling of joyous anticipation, Aloka drew the letter caddy toward her and picked up a fine pen. She wrote a short, pleasant note to Grandma, accepting the invitation. As always, she chose her words carefully, paying close attention to the impact they made both in sound and meaning. But this time she also made a special effort to convey an overall impression of warmth and lightness. It took her some tries to get it right. She omitted any mention of Pranab. Nevertheless, he managed to insinuate himself into her mind as if to remind her that she couldn't edit him out of her life quite so easily. Even as she put the pen away and started to get dressed to attend her friend's birthday party, she couldn't help but daydream. Pranab. Haunted eyes, face drawn with pain. Where was he this evening? What was he doing? Was he also reminiscing about their life together?

Her face flushed. Damn the man! He had stolen the hour from her and left her craving again, just as he had the first time she met him in Darjeeling.

three

1990

As Aloka set off on one of her frequent visits to the family tea garden, she could not have anticipated that an unexpected encounter was about to alter the course of her life. As she picked her way along a narrow trail winding across the side of a precipitous Himalayan foothill carpeted with shiny deep green tea bushes, she heard the tinkle of prayer wheels that someone had spun off in the distance, stopped, and looked proudly over the two-hundred-hectare tea estate that the Guptas had owned for generations. As the oldest child in the family, it would all be hers one day, even though her interest in the farming and marketing aspects of tea was nonexistent. She frowned as it occurred to her that if her younger sister Sujata were standing here, she would be able to identify exactly which fields were dedicated to new tea bushes and which ones currently produced tea leaves for consumption. No matter. When her time came to keep the estate running, Aloka would depend on her father's dedicated staff. Tea, after all, was their life's work.

It was just about quitting time when she reached the tea-processing factory, a long two-story building set into the hillside. At the far corner a tallish young man emerged from her father's office and headed away from her toward the gate. Her father regarded him as an up-and-coming employee.

In one fluid motion he slid through the half-open iron gate, pivoted, and closed it with a somber metallic click. The sunlight through the grillwork limned his refined oval face and deep eyes. He must have noticed her, for he halted and folded his hands at chest level in a *namaskar* greeting.

It was only natural that he would pause and show respect to her. After all, she was the owner's daughter, "tea memsahib." As a rule, the employees bowed obsequiously and scurried away, leaving her feeling isolated, but this fellow was still standing there relaxed, next to a bank of nasturtiums, claiming his due space beneath the purple haze of the hills. She stepped forward.

"We haven't met formally," he announced in Bengali. "I am Pranab Mullick. It's an unexpected pleasure to see you here."

"Thank you. I am Aloka Gupta. My father has mentioned you many times. How do you like your new responsibilities?"

Even though she said it politely, she realized this was an inappropriate question. After all, this man, newly promoted to a coveted management position, worked for her father. How else could he answer except by saying, *Bhalo lagche*—I like it well enough?

"*Bhalo lagche,*" Pranab replied. "But my mother is disappointed. She wanted me to be a professor of Sanskrit."

"So, why didn't you?"

"It's the language of the gods. At this point, I'd rather be an ordinary mortal for whom a good cup of tea is the best bonus of the day."

"I'd studied Sanskrit in high school. It's a difficult language, but the sounds resonated in me. Even ordinary words have big concepts behind them. You could describe everyday sights in a beautiful way."

"If we were speaking Sanskrit, I'd have said the soft lavender sari you're wearing is a swath of the sky."

She fingered her newly purchased Tangail cotton sari, suddenly aware that he had crossed a boundary and become personal. She was single, thirty years old, with marriage proposals in the offing. Marrying late for career reasons had been in vogue, but she had a family reputation to uphold. Her family, after all, was *bonedy*. Blue-blooded. Grandma Nina laughingly called them the "Second Gupta Dynasty," the first being that of Chandra Gupta, who had ruled eastern India in the early years of the fourth century A.D. And even if the luster had faded a bit, the latter-day Guptas had provided her with an excellent education and instilled in her the proper social graces. She turned to go.

"May I have the pleasure of walking you home, Miss Gupta? I was going in the same direction."

She hesitated. Would her father approve of her mingling alone with his subordinate? And what if some tea worker spied them together? Wouldn't they gossip? But then she prided herself for being a modern, college-educated woman who taught in the prestigious girl's school, Loreto. She found herself nodding her assent, pleasantly. "Sure. That would be nice."

They walked along the narrow road that snaked up over a ridge and then down to the Gupta residence. She admired the casual ease with which Pranab negotiated the rutted surface, all the while engaging her in conversation. It occurred to her for the first time that he must have grown up in this mountainous region, too.

A Land Rover rumbled by, scraping up a vortex of dust. While Aloka covered her nose and mouth with a handkerchief, Pranab pointed out that the vehicle was carrying a load of boxed tea to the train station for shipment to an auction house in Calcutta just in time for the holiday season. He'd blended and tasted an assortment of teas from the company stock to produce liquor with the right color and briskness.

"It's been a long twelve hours." Yet his face glowed as he explained how the black currant note of the last mélange was still lingering in his mouth, how much the work meant to him. "No chilis or onions in my food, and I don't ever touch alcohol or tobacco. Nothing that would dull my palate."

Aloka had been taught tea tasting at an early age. She could still recite the procedure: Slurp the tea to aerate it, roll it in your mouth, gurgle, consider, and spit. The palate would register the taste instantly. She didn't much care for the practice. Nor had she ever been particularly enamored of the beverage. At home tea was served at all hours—"the kettle boils overtime," the servants were fond of saying—but she was content simply to drink her daily cup. Even so, she was aware that the tea bushes belonged to various *jats,* or pedigrees, and to assess the quality of the manufactured tea, a taster needed a keen nose, sharp taste buds, and discerning eyes, as well as knowledge of the market. Pranab must be a rare individual who possessed all these qualities.

A tea plucker coming from the opposite direction cut through Aloka's introspection. The woman cast a warm glance at Pranab, who halted and inquired if her husband was feeling better. She shook her head, her anguish evident in that barely perceptible movement, veiled her face with the hem of her sari, and walked on.

Pranab's cheeks seemed to shrink. "The workers need better medical care," he said in a thin voice. "A health dispensary they can afford. Jyotin has had a fever for three days. But I can't persuade him to go see a doctor. He says it'll cost too much money."

"Don't they get a weekly salary, a ration of rice, firewood, and free housing?"

"That's not enough. They need medical care, schools for children, and so much more."

Aloka was well aware that those intrepid souls woke early, battled rain, chilly weather, and precarious terrain to bring in the crop. They were the ones who made the manufacturing of the esteemed Gupta Golden Tip possible. More than sixty percent of the workers were women.

"Especially the women." Pranab had picked up her thoughts. "It's really true when they say, 'You can feel the touch of a woman in a cup of tea.' Whenever I drink a cup, I'm reminded of their miserable existence. They labor so long and so hard without complaint. And what do they have to show for it? Most of them will be old by the time they're forty."

She felt a twinge of apprehension at the implied rebuke of her father. Her personal connection to tea ran much deeper than his, going all the way back to the late 1800s, when her ancestors had arrived on horseback. Darjeeling was only a small hamlet then, a mountain resort where the affluent came to escape the heat of the plains. When her ancestors first tasted the tea, they found it so satisfying that they resolved to buy this choice location and settle down. They announced that henceforth their aim would be "to produce the highest quality brew, fit for the gods." The estate had prospered under the Guptas and it was currently producing a hundred thousand kilograms of premium Darjeeling tea. Grown organically at an elevation of twenty-one hundred meters, which is optimum for the highest-quality tea, Gupta Golden Tip was snapped up at tea auctions in Calcutta. Aloka's father, Bir, who had been running the business for thirty years, had received the Tea Board of India's coveted Award for Quality three times. Well respected by his peers, he received numerous letters of appreciation from his customers, such as this one that arrived only last week: "Thank you for giving an old man a reason to get up in the morning—a pot of your flavorful Golden Tip." Her father not only supervised the cultivation of the crop, but also the construction of service roads on the estate and financial matters. He was a farmer, an engineer, and an accountant rolled into one. The workers addressed him as *barababu,* the big man.

This new man had jolted her out of the sheltered world in which her father had assumed the status of a demigod. This was where she drew her boundary.

"Wait a minute," she said. "My father sees to it that the workers are well treated."

"Please forgive me. I didn't mean to discuss work with you."

The creased lips, the shadowed eyes had distracted her enough that she almost barged into a tree limb that hung across the road. Bending down to avoid being hit, she brushed against the sleeve of his blue-checked shirt. She stepped away in shyness. He glanced at her sideways. She admitted to herself that the proximity and the passionate air about him were impacting her physically, like a persistent knocking on a door. She became aware that they were totally alone on this winding road hemmed in by dense stands of fir, birch, and acacia. The trees muffled any traffic sounds.

"You teach school, don't you, Miss Gupta?" Voice smooth and easy, he had stepped again to her side.

"Yes." The change of topic was welcome. She matched his steps. "Please call me Aloka."

"You can call me Pranab."

Negotiating a steep downhill slope, Aloka only belatedly realized that he had stopped using *aapni,* the respectful "you" in Bengali with which he had started the conversation and had progressed to *tumi*, the familiar "you." In her large circle of friends, such informality of address came only after several meetings. She looked up at him, at the rebellious lock of hair falling down over his forehead like a tassel, and challenged him with, "Do you always feel free to use *tumi* at the first meeting?"

"Usually, yes. When you're surrounded by plants, birds, animals, and insects all day long, you begin to see everyone and everything as equal. I don't consider myself superior to my workers. And by the way, even if I am a few years older, you don't have to do the Pranab-*da* bit. Just call me Pranab."

Again she marveled at how easily he became intimate. "My younger sister calls me Aloka, not Aloka-*didi*. Grandma scolds her, but she doesn't really believe in honorifics, either."

"Who gave you the name, if I may ask?"

She said with deference, "My father."

"I suspect your father's face lights up when you walk into the room."

Her eyes followed his to the light of the setting sun that turned the mist of a cascading waterfall ahead into a shimmering veil of gold. She blushed as she silently acknowledged the compliment, recalling that in Bengali, "*alok*" meant light. From the Hindu myths and stories that Grandma had told her, Aloka had gathered that illumination in all forms signified truth, clarity, auspiciousness, and prosperity. Why, on the upcoming Laxmi Puja day that honored the goddess of hearth and home, she would light tiny terra-cotta lamps fueled by clarified butter. Simply lighting a lamp constituted a form of devotion.

"I don't think of myself as a source of light at all." She forced a laugh to cut through the seriousness. "Oh, no. There are so few lives I touch—my family and close friends and the girls I teach."

She paused as they approached the gate of her family home. Across the fenced yard stood a two-story bungalow with a manicured lawn and a well-tended flower garden. Just above the entrance were engraved the words "Aloka Kutir." The houses around here were usually named after the most beloved progeny. It seemed only natural for her to invite him to come in.

"Wish I could." Pranab's eyes were wistful, even regretful. "But I have to get home. My nephews are waiting for their tabla lesson."

So, he was into music, as well. The hand drums were the instrument of the god Shiva and subsequently of his son Ganesh, Aloka had learned in her childhood. Music had always been a passion of hers and even now she practiced every week. Music helped her come in touch with her many emotions. Her mind went to work. She envisioned a soiree in which her own singing voice would be a delicate counterpoint to the insistent sound of that divine instrument emanating from a pair of sturdy, sensitive hands.

"Perhaps some evening we could play music together." Taking the flash in his eyes as consent, she added, "What about next Thursday?"

"It's awfully nice of you to invite me, but I have an engagement that evening. Maybe some other time."

With that, he waved, and with a "Cheerio" hurried off.

It was far too sudden. She swallowed the aftertaste of disappointment and stood there. The man intrigued her, unbalanced her. She would have to find out more about him.

She closed the gate softly, as though to keep the fragrance about him from blowing away, and entered the house.

four

For the rest of the afternoon, Aloka remained in an exalted mood. She opened the windows in her room and looked out at the wider world, even though the wind outside brought in coolness. Later, humming a classical tune, she drifted downstairs to the kitchen. There she squeezed a fresh lime into a glass of ice water, her father's chosen beverage, despite the fact that the family cook was still around. Bearing a tray, she was about to step into the drawing room when she spotted her younger sister Sujata slipping in through the entrance. Sujata, who worked in Murshidabad, located south of Darjeeling and a long day's journey by train, had come home for a brief vacation.

"Hi, *bontee*." Aloka used the diminutive for a little sister in greeting, though Sujata, four years younger, had grown taller than her. "Haven't seen much of you today."

Sujata looked up briefly, wiggled the toes of her sandaled feet, and fidgeted.

She hadn't changed. Even in her late twenties, Sujata remained shy and withdrawn. Moving to another town, it seemed, had only reinforced her attitude. A sense of loss engulfed Aloka. In their youth they'd been inseparable, playing together in the house and sharing the same pillow in bed. They'd go to Laxmi Puja or to a *mela,* hand in hand, tagging along behind Grandma, dividing up a sweet, or asking a vendor to put two straws in a glass of sweet *lassi.* As a teenager, Aloka had even allowed Sujata to play with her lipstick.

"Why don't you join Father and I?" Aloka tried again. "This week we're reading a novel and discussing its roots in the classic Bengali literature of the last century."

"Thanks, Aloka, but no. I really am more in the mood for a cup of hot tea and a pile of magazines. I don't read novels, I wouldn't contribute much to your discussion. Besides, it's your private time with Father, so I will leave you to it." With that, Sujata flounced away.

"Let's spend some time together tomorrow, then," Aloka called after Sujata. Such long shining hair, still plaited in a tight braid like a schoolgirl's. And that dull beige sari in a limp fabric did nothing to enhance Sujata's dark, slender form. Aloka would have to shop for Sujata soon if she were to have any chance at attracting a suitor. The right outfit, jewelry, and a bright lipstick would make a difference, Aloka was sure.

In the drawing room, Bir leaned back on a couch, eyes closed. He was a portly man with the somnolent air of one who woke at dawn, just as the roosters crowed, then after a light breakfast went to the office and labored till late in the evening. His last act of the day was a staff *darbar,* or court, that he held with his key personnel. As soon as he returned home, he sought Aloka. Her presence melted his cares, he was in the habit of saying. His wife had died when the children were young and he never remarried. Even when she was alive he hadn't spoken much to her. Men of his generation didn't consider their wives their companions.

Aloka took another look at Bir. His coarse skin might befit someone of lesser upbringing, but his prominent nose bespoke an inner resolve. A *gerua* tunic did little to conceal the ample belly that told of advancing years and a shortening life, and which worried Aloka. She always found it curious that *gerua*, a shade of yellow associated with renunciation, was Bir's favorite, for he was far from renouncing worldly pleasure. With little interest in religion, he didn't bow before the bronze statuettes of gods and goddesses that Grandma had scattered throughout the house. And his appetite for fine Bengali dishes was legendary—he demanded double servings of fish fry, *maach bhaja*. He had read a treatise on Bengali cooking and memorized the preparation methods. "Did you change the oil?" he would ask the cook. "Did you turn the fish pieces four times?"

At the sound of footsteps he heaved himself upright. "Ah, there you are, my dearest child. Did I hear you speaking with Sujata?"

"Yes, Father. I tried to persuade her to join us, but she wasn't in the mood. I wish she'd come home for good."

"It would surely help me. I could easily find work for her in the office. But no, she has to show how independent she is. She never did listen to me. I wonder if she'll ever acquire any responsibility toward her folks."

Aloka glanced uneasily at Bir's weary face, now mottled with angry crimson patches. "Father, you mustn't get excited. Have you forgotten the doctor's advice?"

"Are you going to read for me?"

Aloka reached over and picked out a slim volume from the bookcase, a Bengali novel entitled *Mahaprasthaner Pathe* by Probodh Kumar Sanyal, the true tale of a grueling Himalayan pilgrimage. She opened to the last chapter of the old classic and sighed when she realized there were only a few pages left. " 'I'll give you my last words,' " she began to read aloud. " 'In this infinite journey I have lost friendships, love, illusion, and desire. I have dropped my arrogance. Yet the road insists I haven't satisfied its hunger.' " As she warmed to her task, the words of the language with its musical sounds and poetic phrases flowed softly, easily into a fusion of images, meaning, and sentiments. Bir listened quietly, with his eyes half shut.

Before long she reached the end. She snapped the book closed and reflected on the insights she'd gained, with a sense of premonition.

Bir opened his eyes abruptly. "In ten years I'll be ready for the same pilgrimage."

"That's hard to believe. Thakurma can't make you go to the temple even during Durga Puja."

"When you get older you realize the hardest thing to achieve is peace of mind. I don't believe religion will give one that, so I seek it in my own way."

Might he be implying difficulty at work? Aloka grasped that managing a tea estate was no trivial task, even though Bir rarely shared his concerns with her. The weather had been unsettled lately, and as a result both the quality and quantity of the crop were substandard. Foreign demand for Darjeeling tea was down as well. The livelihood of over two hundred employees depended on how Bir dealt with this adversity. To make matters worse, from what Pranab had confided in her, those employees were discontented.

"By the way, I met Pranab Mullick today." Aloka tried to sound casual.

"Ah! I have meant to invite him over but just haven't gotten around to it, what with all the problems at the factory."

She fumbled with her sari border. "He walked me home today. He's a rather interesting fellow, seems to know a lot about tea, and—"

"Let me tell you a little about him, some things he may not have mentioned. He comes from a lower-middle-class family. His father works as a clerk at some trading company. They live in the older part of the town near the train station. For all that, he has a good education. His parents somehow managed to send him to Presidency College in Calcutta. The fellow is a born tea taster. We have a saying in the industry that "when it comes to tea tasting, you are as good as your palate," and he has a brilliant one. He's already the best in the region. But he wanted to be a field supervisor and so recently I decided to let him have a go at it. Otherwise I might have lost him to another tea estate. He seems to be developing rapport with the workers, spends a lot of time with them, I see a good future for him."

A tiny smile played on his lips, glowed his face. Eyes away from Aloka, Bir seemed to ponder his decision with some satisfaction.

Aloka pushed herself from the chair. "It's time for you to rest, Father." She slipped out of the room, a chill stealing over her.

Late afternoon the following Thursday, Aloka found herself in front of a tea worker's residence, situated on a dirt road on the edge of the tea plantation. A longtime family servant whose brother worked in the tea factory had disclosed to Aloka the details of a secret conference between Pranab and the tea laborers and guided her to the location. The one-story brick house displayed a tin roof painted bottle-green. A tangled thicket of wild berries fenced the front, a gossamer prayer flag fluttered near the entrance, and a mustard field, waves of yellow and green, grew on the next plot. With darkness rolling in, the landscape was immobile, almost expectant. From somewhere a hen clucked as if to confirm Aloka's growing feeling of unease.

From her hiding place behind a window, she took in the bare, medium-sized room. Devoid of any furniture, it buzzed with tea workers and their families, nearly fifty of them in all, who sat squeezed together in the matted floor. Their weather-discolored faces and rough hands bore testimony to their hard toil.

Eyes flashing, austere in his white dhoti, Pranab stood erect before them. Lost in his concern for others, unmindful even of himself, he appeared much larger. It was as though his head touched the ceiling. She was elated simply to observe him from afar.

A hush fell. Pranab's voice boomed, "Brothers and sisters!"

The workers looked up prayerfully. And she responded by standing straighter. The idea occurred to her that he sensed her presence and was projecting a little extra with his performance. Despite the throbbing in her chest, she listened with total attention.

"We have gathered together for the first time to address issues of grave concern. You who make Darjeeling tea possible have not received a salary increase in over a decade, not since the time your *barababu,* Mr. Bir Gupta, took over the management of the tea estate. You are still required to pluck a minimum of seven kilograms of leaves every day in order to get paid. Many of you can't afford to buy medicine when you're sick. Your children are poorly educated and thus doomed to a life in the field like yourselves. It can all be summarized in one word: injustice."

She recoiled. How dare he speak against her father in this manner? This was revolting. Yet the words were so full of power and promise and uttered with such sincerity that she was unable to step away.

The workers rose from their seats as one, their clenched fists pummeling the air overhead. Their shouts came in waves. "Better pay! Free medical care!" They stomped their feet as they crooned their slogans in a rising crescendo.

"Your management is unfair to you, but you don't have to take it."

The workers chanted, "Long live Pranab-*babu*!" Their faces had changed from solemnity to fury.

Pranab stood motionless before them, his gaze gleaming with zeal that at once exerted a pull on her and held her off. She wrapped the shawl around her shoulders tighter.

Would they harm her father? She recalled how, just a year ago, the coolies in the neighboring Chameli tea estate had gone on a strike. They had done a *gherao* and trapped the manager in his office for a whole day. As night fell, he tried escaping through a back window, but was caught by the mob and beaten severely, before the police could arrive and save him from an even worse fate.

"More rations! More rice!"

As the voices receded, Aloka overheard a worker in the back whispering to another, "Is he sincere? What's in it for him? Can we trust him?"

How could they question Pranab's trustworthiness? Now Aloka found herself siding with the man who stood against her father.

Pranab began speaking again. Aloka hung on his every syllable. "The Plantation Labor Act was a conspiracy between the government and the wealthy landowners. The excise duty on tea is a poor excuse for ill pay." He went on making more hackneyed political proclamations, then concluded with, "From now on, you will record all your grievances. I will petition the management. And I will personally present the case before the Darjeeling Planters' Association."

Again came an exhilarating singing, this time, "Pranab-*Maharaj ki jai!*"

They had exalted him to the position of a great king. In the commotion that followed, the tea workers began to shriek out their demands all at once. Just as she began to shake in worry about where this frenzy would lead, he extended a hand majestically.

What power that still, authoritative hand exercised. The noise subsided. A young woman stroked the white blossoms on her ponytail; a small child crawled up to Pranab's feet; an old man began sobbing, overcome by the sensations of the moment; and the rest simply stared up at Pranab raptly.

"I am here to serve you, not *barababu*." He said so kindly, yet so firmly.

Aloka tore herself away from the window, crammed with the conflicting emotions of terror, excitement, and guilt. She could never repeat this to her father, for the estate was his life, and in his own estimation he was managing it well. She must leave before someone noticed her.

Had she betrayed him and her family this afternoon? The family she placed above all?

Halfway home, as she passed a dense stand of silver fir and deodar and paused to admire their stately heights, she found her mind becoming lucid. She realized, much to her consternation, that in spite of what she'd witnessed she would seek out Pranab again, take another stroll with him. Her heart and soul would have it no other way. Only next time, she promised herself, she would steer the conversation in a safer direction—Sanskrit, perhaps. Yes, that was it. She'd dust off the old Sanskrit volumes in Father's library and read the lyrics, the *kavya*, of the classic poet Kalidasa. It had once amused her to read about lovesick heroines, how they throbbed and itched and panted in private.

She laughed to herself once again, this time uneasily, as an icy uncertainty gripped her back. For the first time in her life, she'd lost a measure of her self-control. She was faring no better than those miserable heroines of yore.

five

1992

It was now three weeks since Sujata had returned home, this time for good. Six years ago, after graduating from college, she'd taken a job in a bank in Murshidabad to get away from her relations. Life in a joint family seemed confusing and full of compromises. She liked making her own decisions. And unlike her older sister Aloka, Sujata had been, in everyone's opinion, a difficult child. She didn't engage in small talk or sing like Aloka. Nor did she accompany older relatives to the temple or the children to the zoo. Aside from Grandma, no one objected much to her untimely departure.

The bank in Murshidabad had failed. Whereupon her parents, and especially Aloka, had asked her to come home, enjoy some time off, and consider taking a position at the family tea estate. The idea had appealed to

Sujata. As a child she'd frittered hours roaming the tea garden. She still cherished what Grandma had told her years ago.

"You are a 'tea' girl, Sujata. Even before you were five years old you could pluck the leaves with just the right snap of your fingers. You had the knack of figuring out whether the morning mist was just right for the buds to be plucked. You even made an effort to pronounce tea's botanical name." Crisply and clearly Grandma would enunciate the Latin words, *Camellia sinensis.* "I believe a camellia tree bestowed its spirit on you in return."

That spirit had stayed with Sujata even after reaching adulthood. While living in Murshidabad, she'd kept up with the news about the tea industry, a major revenue earner for the state of West Bengal. Her preferred daily newspaper, the *Statesman,* which routinely reported matters of importance to the industry, such as the mounting need for research and development and whether the auction system was still beneficial, kept her glued to the armchair in the evenings. In fact, she often turned first to the newspaper's special "State" section that contained mostly articles on the tea industry. She read up on sprinkler systems that were best suited for irrigating tea plantations, the latest environment-friendly chemical to control tea mites, the ideal labor-to-land ratio, even approaches to controlling damage caused by rampaging elephants. She became increasingly interested not just in tea growing, but also in all aspects of its merchandising. It cheered her to know that giant conglomerates like Brooke Bond, Lipton, and Tata no longer had a monopoly in tea marketing, despite their fancy boxes and catchy marketing slogans. Smaller tea estates were making a mark on the national and international scene with their exclusive offerings.

Now that she'd returned home, she would be able to put her knowledge to work. At least she hoped so. She disagreed with her father, whose mantra was, "Crop, crop, crop." She believed in pruning the bushes more often and fertilizing the soil better, thereby producing quality tea as opposed to expecting larger and larger output.

Toward late afternoon that Sunday, Sujata ambled into the house. The rest of the family had gone to Kalimpong, a hill town seventy-four kilometers to the east, to help with the wedding negotiations for Aloka and Sujata's cousin-sister Kabita. They would iron out the remaining details and finalize the engagement, verbally in Bengali fashion, "ripening the agreement," *paka dekha,* as it was called. The actual wedding date was still two months away. Ordinarily, Sujata would have accompanied the family. She liked Kalimpong all right, especially its yearly fair, but she'd been volunteering as a tutor for a Tibetan refugee boy who was preparing for school examinations. Since the family wasn't expected back for another hour, she was looking forward to solitude.

She had barely stepped inside when the maidservant, who was sweeping the hallway, announced, "Pranab-*babu* is waiting in the drawing room."

Waiting for Aloka, of course. Such patience, such devotion, all in all a trifle insufferable, even if the two had known each other for two years and been engaged for one. Relatives and friends considered them the perfectly matched couple. And from the family's point of view it was heartening that when the time came for Aloka to take over the tea estate, the experienced and capable Pranab would be there to see that the operation ran smoothly. What better person for the job? It rankled Sujata that there appeared to be no place for her in this blissful picture.

In the last three weeks Sujata had had glimpses of Pranab. With Aloka. He didn't seem to notice Sujata much. Pretty Aloka, popular Aloka had him wrapped around her finger and he puppied along.

"I'll be down in a few minutes," Sujata replied to the maidservant.

She hitched up her sari and climbed the stairs to her room on the second floor. Did Pranab still remember the auspicious Bengali New Year's day last April when they'd had their first long conversation? She'd come home for a week's vacation then, missing Aloka, who had left for Patna to visit relatives. One lazy afternoon Sujata was lolling on the front lawn with Grandma when Pranab happened by. She'd already noticed how much time he invested in Grandma, joking and playing cards with her, and debating whether a cup of tea had enough "floweriness." He addressed her as Thakurma, or "elder goddess," like she and Aloka did. Obviously he was trying to impress the old matriarch.

"Namaskar," Pranab had said to Sujata in greeting that day. *"Ki khabar? Kemon achen?"* The polite queries in the Bengali society: What's the news? How are you?

He was glibly pleasant but not engaging. In her mind Sujata was already searching for an excuse to leave, when her gaze followed Pranab's to the periodical *Indian Farmers* that was resting on the grass next to her. Her father subscribed to the magazine and she'd already read it. The cover story in bold letters read, "Is There a Cure for Protein Deficiency?"

"You can't change taste buds," Pranab declared as he took his seat, adding that the answer to the protein shortage lay in the more efficient cultivation of lentils, India's traditional legume.

"No!" Sujata rejoined, relishing the prospect of pulling down this smug boy. "The answer is the soybean. It may be unfamiliar and it does have a strong beany taste, but it's highly nutritious and more versatile."

"Nevertheless, lentils have sustained us since the twelfth century, as you'll know if you've studied *The History of the Bengalis* by Nihar Ranjan Rai." As if considering the subject closed, he began evaluating the cup of tea before him. It was "high fired," he commented, "and scorching-flavored. But interesting."

Sujata fumed, but not for long. "Look at East Asia," she countered, "how they've made wide use of soybeans. Tell me who's better fed."

"Do you always have to argue, Sujata?" Grandma broke in. "Have you forgotten our saying, 'Lentils and rice make a Bengali'? I grew up mostly on *dhal-bhat* myself. Would you care for another cup of tea, Pranab?"

"This is more than an idle argument, Thakurma," Sujata interjected. "It's a matter of survival for the common people."

"May I ask how you know so much about the common people?" Pranab inquired with a trace of sarcasm. Turning to Grandma, he said, "No more tea for me."

"I've spent time in the tea fields talking to the workers and finding out all sorts of things. To them, belly first, taste later. Surprisingly, they're willing to try new food crops, such as soybeans, if someone would show them how to use them."

"It's true, she's always out there." Grandma leaned toward Pranab.

"She does seem to have an inquiring nature," Pranab allowed—grudgingly, it seemed. "I'll have to ask my mother to cook some soybeans for me." With that he smiled at her in a skittish manner. She got up and had started toward the house when she overheard Grandma whispering to Pranab, "You don't seem to mind you lost the debate."

Sujata gave a backward glance and caught Pranab smiling cryptically. "I've lost the battle only, Thakurma."

He remained on her mind for the next several hours—the words he'd uttered, how his shoes had made firm contact with the ground, how his body had made even that wicker chair seem grand. Later the same afternoon, Sujata wandered into Aloka's room in her absence with the excuse that on such a hot day the sea-foam-green walls, Aloka's color of choice, had a cooling effect. Aloka had studied color scheme and spoken of the harmony colors could create. Sujata had never paid much attention to the effect of colors or, in general, to the household. She was merely browsing through the room when her eyes caught sight of the red velvet book with a lock on its side that rested on a side table: Aloka's diary. The book had always held temptation for Sujata, and it so happened that a careless Aloka had finally left the key out in the open. Sujata's fingers reached out with a yearning. Reading her sister's private musings was wrong, she discerned that, but she couldn't help it. As she held the book in her hands, she admired the heft of the book, the smoothness of its cover, and the perfume of its pages. Eagerly she scanned the book for seductive secrets, finally stumbling on Aloka's professions of love for Pranab:

> The moment my eyes fall on him I become as receptive as a pansy opening its petals to the mounting sun. Whenever we are together I feel humbled by his presence and become a grain of dust at his feet, a mere vessel for love that is far greater than I.

How Sujata had snickered at that! She had dropped the diary on the table at that point and cleared out of the room.

In reality a feeling of lack had tormented her. Why didn't she possess secrets worth storing in a bulky diary? Why did Aloka always snag the best? What made her so charming, so desirable?

Now, months later, Sujata pondered the same questions, as she checked her image in an antique hand mirror one last time before going downstairs to receive Pranab. The reflecting surface talked back to her, repeating what

Aunt Komola had so succinctly put long ago: "Sujata is just not as pretty as Aloka." The pretty face of her sister flashed mockingly before Sujata: a fine profile, ivory complexion, eyebrows that arched like the gateway to a palace, and *kajal*-lined eyes that were mysteriously black like a reflective pool. Those peering back at Sujata now from the dulled mirror were amber-brown—the color of quality tea—warm and deep, with a spark of intelligence, but the skin was coarse and dark and the eyelashes were sparse. Sujata used very little cosmetics, as too much would only accentuate her homeliness. Yet without the patina of makeup she also appeared less polished. With a sigh she set the instrument of torture aside.

She stepped into the mahogany-furnished drawing room with its gleaming wooden floor and inhaled the piney fragrance of the recently applied furniture polish that still lingered in the air. The paneled walls were hung with fading portraits of past Gupta generations, as well as pictures of the living members of the family. She considered the silver-framed childhood photograph of her and Aloka: two adolescents, heads touching, their hair plaited in braids, posing against a background of mountains in Tiger Hill. Aloka, an index finger poking through the loop of her earring, had her other arm hooked around Sujata's neck. The photograph almost captured the faint scent of the weeds, wildflowers, and leaves they usually gathered from playing outdoors. Sujata took her eyes away.

Above the mantel sat Grandma Nina's photo, an eight-by-ten framed in natural wood. At birth Grandma had been given the name Nitya-Shobhona, "Eternal Grace," but soon had acquired the less grandiose sobriquet of "Nina." Always a diminutive creature, Grandma seemed to shrink in size over the years, but her inner strength and dignity remained apparent in her strong shoulders and a direct, penetrating gaze. In the photo the pear-shaped body was draped in a soft white sari with no trim. "White connotes simplicity and purity," Grandma had always been fond of saying. From a center parting, her thinning gray hair cascaded down on either side to be loosely tied in a knot at the nape of her neck. Gold teardrop earrings, her only adornment, flashed like fireflies.

Sujata glanced out the window at the soaring ramparts of Mount Kanchenjunga. Only then did she peer down at Pranab. Ensconced on a couch by the window, he was leafing through the pages of an issue of *Desh* magazine. Unable to speak, she tugged at the train of her crepe sari.

At the rustling sound, he looked up and rose to his feet, simultaneously launching into the perfunctory litany, *"Ki khabar, kemon achen,"* and what a surprise it was to see her. "I thought you might be at the tea garden." He half rose from his seat. "Looks like Aloka's late. I won't wait any longer. I'll catch her tomorrow."

She flopped into a chair across from him. "You don't have to leave just because I came in."

He sank back into his seat on the couch and removed his glasses. His eyes were large, steady, and imbued with a splendid light.

"What are you reading?" she asked.

"Oh, this? It's an article on the Suez Canal. At various times in the past, the English, the French, and the Egyptians all fought over that passage between the Mediterranean and the Red Sea." He described ships squeezing through a narrow blue passage, bloody in some places, carved out of a barren landscape. "Suez was most vital."

Sujata was grateful that the family wasn't hovering nearby except in portraits on the wall. "There's also a port town by the name of Suez, as I recall. How fascinating it must be to watch the boats coming and going. To imagine that the most powerful nations on earth were all critically dependent on that little channel. History can be made in the most obscure places."

"You have a lot to say, Sujata. I've been meaning to talk to you alone, but I never seem to get the chance."

"Or maybe you just don't notice me."

He flashed a meaningful grin: a pair of full lips parting to show a perfect set of teeth. She took her eyes away, to the lace edges of the window curtain.

"My mother used to say that as a youngster my eyes never went to sleep," he said. "I knew everything that went on. She joked that I had eyes on all sides of my head."

She simply said, "Oh?" But her thought was a sarcastic: So what have you noticed about me?

He must have read her train of thought, for he glanced at her slyly. "You like to stroll down Chowrasta. Your braid moves back and forth across your shoulders. You pay no attention to who's watching from behind. You're quiet. You love to sit on the back lawn and keep your grandma company.

You have many opinions, but you express them only to her."

Her cheeks burned as it dawned on her that she'd been more than noticed. She lowered her gaze to the rug, to the chaos of black, maroon, and burnt orange hues, the interweaving of the leafy patterns, the knotted edges.

Pranab must have noticed her discomfiture. "We have a new hire at the tea factory. She's from the south and barely speaks Hindi, so she constantly makes up words that are a cocktail of Hindi and Tamil. Her co-workers think it's hilarious, but I find it fascinating. After all, what's a language for, if not to mold the vocabulary to express our opinions and wishes? And express them we must, wouldn't you agree?"

Glory to the goddess Durga that the family was late. As soon as Aloka returned, Pranab would be off with her and this stimulating repartee would end.

"Yes," Sujata said, "but it's not always for lack of words that we fail to speak, mind you. Some of us have thoughts or feelings dying to be expressed, but we can't seem to find the right person, the right situation, or the right occasion."

"How true. Take me, for instance. I have a secret hobby that I haven't told a soul about—I'm learning to dance."

Sanskritist, tea taster, and now a dancer? How unusual. Few educated Bengali men would even consider taking up dancing as a hobby. She leaned forward, her bemusement giving way to ill-concealed enthusiasm. "What type of dance?"

"Bhangra. Not even your sister knows about it. She's so much into classical music and dancing that I can't bring myself to tell her. What little music training I've had is also classical. But recently I have become interested in traditional village dancing. It's less refined, to be sure—even crude, some might say—but it's honest and vibrant and speaks to me."

He went on to describe how a master from Punjab had taught him the hand and foot movements of a five-hundred-year-old dance practiced by peasant men in honor of the new harvest and to please the earth. "When I am dancing," he concluded, "I feel at one with the simplest of people. Too often we look down on them and forget that they're essential to our prosperity; indeed, to our very own survival."

She savored this glorious afternoon and the delicious feeling that by sharing his secret he had revealed a part of himself that even Aloka wasn't permitted to see. Pranab belatedly seemed to realize as much, for his voice trailed off and he looked away.

Sujata made an attempt to get his attention back. "I won't mention this to anyone."

At this, the lurking maidservant, who was dusting a picture frame over and over again, gave them a curious sidelong glance. Sujata, suddenly heedful of the maidservant's presence, ordered her to bring almond milk and a platter of *nimkees*, the puffy, triangular pastries she favored. Embedded in the request was an unspoken invitation for Pranab to linger. The shell of self-control she so prided herself on had begun to crack.

When the maidservant bustled off, Sujata continued, "Would you perform a Bhangra dance for me sometime? I'd really like that."

The words had barely run off her lips when she began to regret her impulsiveness. What if he was clumsy? They'd both be embarrassed. On the other hand, if he was a bold dancer, and he could very well be, should she, a young unmarried woman, watch him alone? His loose-fitting shirt and trousers couldn't conceal his well-muscled body. Grandma would call him *jawan*, using the local parlance for a vigorous young man. Sujata herself would call him a *jawan*.

Shortly, the maidservant arrived, teak tray in hand, interrupting Sujata's train of thought. She looked up at the pinkish white beverage and perfect little triangles of *nimkees* heaped on a platter. Envisioning a deeper conversation to follow, she started arranging the food and beverage on the table.

Pranab glanced at the platter, sprang to his feet. "I'll have *nimkee* some other time. I really must go now."

She lowered her eyes, not allowing them to reflect her disappointment, and, like a proper hostess, followed him to the door.

At the threshold he hesitated. "Why don't you meet me by Senchal Lake at four on Saturday? I'll perform a dance I've been working on. I should have it mastered by then."

She averted her eyes. How could she possibly accept this audacious invitation from her sister's fiancé? Tempting though it might be, it was at odds with the moral standards her father and grandmother had instilled in her since childhood.

"I—I lead a Tibetan children's hike on Saturdays," she stammered, the lie stinging her tongue.

"No, that's on Friday afternoon."

A knowing smile spreading across his lips—or was it a smirk?—he turned without a backward look, as though he had perceived she was blushing three shades of mauve.

"I can't," she replied to his back, a little louder this time, then watched him walk away confidently.

Had he planned this encounter? She couldn't be sure. Would it even matter?

For the rest of the afternoon, as she wandered in a valley behind the house, a thousand bees buzzed in her ears, humming his name.

six

The next morning, immediately following breakfast, Sujata set out on the twenty-minute uphill hike to the tea field. She trekked a narrow winding path that ran along a mountain slope. Several brooks threaded their way through solid plots of glistening evergreen tea shrubs. This, to her, was no mere hike, for she considered the birds, plants, insects, and animals around her as manifestations of the earth mother. The quiet time in their presence never failed to leave her feeling purified.

With the monsoon over, the weather had turned crisp and clear. The tea plants, many over a hundred years old, were eager to flush for the third and last time of the season, and gave off a delicate fragrance. According to a local maxim, smelling tea leaves had an effect similar to drinking tea. How true. Inside, Sujata glowed with a surge of calm energy.

She looked up and saw the colorfully dressed female pickers, scattered in an irregular line across the slope ahead. Hair plaited in thick braids, huge pyramidal wicker baskets on their backs supported by woven trump lines across their foreheads, they waded up an invisible trail through the tightly spaced rows. Gold and glass bangles on their arms jingled rhythmically and glinted in the sun's rays. The women deftly plucked the topmost inch, "two leaves and a leaf bud," from the youngest branch tips, and, without looking up, tossed them over their shoulders into their baskets. It required twenty-two thousand such shoots to produce one kilogram of tea. Kripa, a young tea plucker, looked up at Sujata for a brief second and smiled a silent greeting. Then she went back to making the smooth, rhythmic arcing hand motion, branch to basket and back again. They would finish at around eleven, deposit their plucking in a bin, and take a leisurely communal lunch break. Not for the first time, Sujata contemplated the lives of these women, how routine their work was, how arduous, and yet how content they seemed. The secret, Sujata concluded, lay in staying close to the soil and believing in the work they did.

"Sujata!"

She stiffened at the familiar voice, at its eagerness. When she turned, she saw Pranab approaching her, a welcoming smile transforming his face. She hadn't expected to run into him quite so soon. Though casually attired, he moved easily along the twisted, rutted pathway, as though he belonged right here in this natural surrounding.

He bade her a casual "Good morning," informed her that he was making his daily rounds to monitor the harvest, and, without waiting for a reply, began to discuss two crop pests, red spiders and green flies, as well as soil erosion problems. Finally he asked her if she had noticed anything in particular during her walk through the field.

She felt flattered at being asked and mentioned that not all the tea workers had gloves on, the gloves they needed for safety's sake. And she added, "I happened to pass by the women workers' break area as I came up here. Their shack has only a bare cement floor. Not even a bench. Shouldn't there be some benches?"

"So you noticed." Before she knew it, an hour had passed and he'd given her a detailed account of the workers' living conditions, as well as his own suggestions for improving their lot. "This is what I think about in my spare time."

So he was dedicated to his charges' welfare. A high regard for him bubbled inside her. Perhaps he was thinking in a similar vein, for when she looked up again, the warmth of his expression indicated that the feeling was mutual and strong. Then her eyes caught his sloping shoulders. His well-defined arms, outlined by thin, clingy cotton sleeves, looked as though they could crush her in an embrace at any moment. A shameful desire tugged at her, its pressure increasingly difficult to ignore. Fretful, she said, "I have to get home. I'm already late."

"When shall I see you again?"

The gentle tone notwithstanding, it was not so much a question as a promise. She turned without answering and fled with as much dignity as her flustered state would allow. Once, she stumbled and barely caught herself. By the time she reached the bungalow, her hips had tightened from the unaccustomed pace and her ankles were crosshatched with scratches from brambles and weeds. She hurried directly to her room, where she flopped on her bed and remained there, eyes closed, head swarming with fantasies. She resolved to tell no one in the family about this chance encounter and she trusted that Pranab would not, either. The consequences would be grave indeed.

The very next day she returned to the field. What harm would there be, she told herself, in meeting someone who was a fiery crusader for the rights of the oppressed, even if he happened to be her sister's fiancé? Their paths crossed. Once again, she experienced a rush of feelings.

For the next two weeks, Sujata maintained the same routine. She would greet Pranab and they would end up in an animated conversation. He was someone she not only agreed with and esteemed, but also wished to help. On the way home one evening, she began silently blaming the attraction that had developed between them on her bizarre actions. How she had changed. All day long she had felt the pangs of a sweet, demanding pain. She realized that nowadays she had no interest in any activity and no appetite except to see Pranab. She skipped meals. She barely spoke to the family members, especially to Aloka. She had noticed changes in him, too. In her company he breathed heavier, his face took on a bright sheen, he laughed with abandon. Often it slipped his mind that he had duties to perform in the field. Worse yet, he acted as though he'd forgotten his engagement with Aloka. He never brought up the subject. Might that be due to Aloka's lack of interest in tea? Her loveliness, her social graces, her generous nature couldn't make up for such a lack. Aloka charmed Pranab in many ways, they played music together, but did she really share his deepest convictions the way Sujata did? Could Aloka ever be his partner in the full sense of the term? No. It was Sujata who had truly succeeded in touching Pranab in his core. A feeling of triumph danced in Sujata's head, superseding her earlier fears.

Today she'd happened to mention to him a news item about a tea workers' strike on an estate in the Dooars area. She thought she was merely passing on some information of interest, but his eyes took on a manic intensity. He paused, as if considering whether to continue, then confided that he, too, was organizing a strike and peaceful protest march. He spoke in a whisper, gazing at her with trusting eyes. Did he realize how difficult it was for her to listen him elaborate a course of action that so clearly went against her father's interest, her family's welfare? Several times she experienced a panicky urge to turn around and flee for the safety of home, but then she gazed up at his standing figure, the intellect and masculinity he projected. He persisted in holding her captive with that manly stature. In the end he convinced her. She trusted his words and wanted to follow his lead, for the greater good of the workforce. When he paused again and peered at her intently, she could only nod in agreement.

Satisfied, he moved to the next item: a written petition that the workers would present to her father following the protest march.

Here was a chance to offer a helping hand. "Let me have a look at the draft," she said. "I know how my father's head works. You have to phrase the demands in such a way that they'll be acceptable to him. He doesn't take orders from anybody, as you know."

"I'll leave the petition in your able hands." He smiled in mischief.

She shivered. She could not back out now even if she wanted to, even if it was in her best interests.

Since the plans for the protest march had finally been completed, Sujata was in a celebratory mood. At home she hummed happily to herself as she packed a large maroon wicker basket with *nimkee* and fruit for their daily rendezvous at the tea garden. A short time later, she and Pranab sat on a rock gazing out over the green expanse of the tea bushes with the basket resting between them. In no time they finished the *nimkees*. Finally she picked a guava from the basket and held it out cushioned on a handkerchief. The jade-green fruit, the finest variety brought as a gift by a relative from Calcutta, was about the size of an apple and so ripe that a finger's touch made an indentation. It was not merely a gourmet treat, but a fantasy.

He examined the fruit. "It's as lush as your lips."

She blushed. She wasn't used to hearing words of flattery or intimacy. With alternating bites, they shared it, the flesh soft as room-temperature butter, except for the tiny, chewy seeds that occasionally got in the way. Then she discovered a black worm nesting at the center of the fruit and discarded a chunk of its flesh on the grass without Pranab noticing.

"I want to thank you for the last few weeks," he said.

"Don't mention. I have done very little. . . ."

"You have much more power than you realize, Sujata. You touch my source, you help bring out a force in me. All parts of me come together. The only other time I feel this way is when I dance."

She sat savoring those words of praise, while inwardly bursting with delight. How intense these last few weeks had been for her, how transforming. In giving him power, she had unearthed her own. It had become clear to her what type of career path she would follow: one similar to his. Yet all through this she had been tormented by apprehension. However much they shared, she had been, as yet, unable to reveal those fears to him.

A cracking sound caused her to look up. The sky, ever changing in this mountainous region, had assumed a blue-black cast. The air had grown still, thick. She could read the signs: A severe storm was brewing, and it would not do to be caught out in it.

"I'd better be going." She started to pick up the basket. "Thakurma will be worrying about me."

He reached out and clasped her free hand briefly, then released it gently.

"I think about you during my dance practice. I want to perform for you sometime."

Her heart rejoiced at his admission. His dancing was her territory, not Aloka's, another manifestation of the great camaraderie that had developed between two people wedded to a common cause.

"Will you meet me by Senchal Lake at four on Thursday?"

He'd asked before and she'd said no. What harm could there be in meeting him this time, even if the location was out of the way? For a moment, the weather was of no concern. Then a strong, gusty breeze whipped up and almost tore the basket from her hand as it blasted through the space between them. Full-blown, punishing raindrops struck their heads. Pranab stood there, staring at her.

"Yes! Yes, I will meet you there, Pranab. Now go, the storm is upon us."

Thursday afternoon, two hours before she was scheduled to meet with Pranab, Sujata busied herself with her wardrobe. Only in the last few weeks had she been drawn to makeup and fine clothing, for whenever she exchanged a glance with Pranab, she saw herself radiantly reflected in his eyes. And nothing about her seemed to escape his attention. Just the other day, seeing her dressed in a black sari embellished with silver embroidery, he had composed a melodious Sanskrit verse, then translated it as, "Your beauty craves a thousand eyes. Alas, I have but two."

Had one of the boys in her college used such flowery language, she would have laughed: What a fool. But coming from Pranab's mouth, those Sanskrit words sounded unique and exquisite.

Now she chose the smart casualness of *salwar-kameez* in purple print. She figured that the color would have a cooling effect on her skin and that the tunic-and-pants set, rather than a sari, would be better suited for negotiating the wooded slopes around the often misty Senchal Lake. The notion of meeting Pranab at such a location late in the day gave her a thrill but also made her edgy. It amounted to an *abhisar*. That one Bengali word implied the journey undertaken by a heroine to meet her beloved and all the emotions that went with it. She slapped some talcum powder on her eyes by mistake and shed a few drops of tears because of that.

Just before four, she struck off on a winding trail that descended toward Senchal Lake, beating pebbles with her feet. The prevailing wind from the southeast had brought moisture in the form of a light mist. Still she could view Pranab, outfitted in tight pants, a body-hugging tunic, and a headdress made of goat hair and cowry shells, waiting for her on the shore. His eyes regarded her with approval as she approached.

"Oh, Sujata, you came after all. You don't know how much that means to me. And you look lovely."

Flooded with excitement, but conquered by shyness, she could only manage, "Would you dance for me?"

"Gladly! Come, sit down." He pointed to a large rock with a smooth top.

She settled herself, scanned the scene over the lake. A breeze flitted across the calm blue surface of the water, ruffling the backs of the swans and teasing the tall foxgloves lining the bank.

When she turned, Pranab began to dance, slowly and stiffly at first. He struggled with an inner reserve, relaxing gradually, his motions becoming more fluid and vigorous. Soon the traditional movements gave way to a more frenzied, personal style. He kicked and bounced and created a ripple in the air in a dizzying demand. All the while his gaze carried an invitation. Bashful, yet unable to rip her eyes away, Sujata watched, bereft of any sense of time. By now the silver mountain light had transformed itself into a deep violet; evening was about to fall. Restlessness puffed up inside her. In what was clearly his final movement, he took a huge leap with his arms flung out and a blue gem ring, *neela*, slid from his finger onto the grass. He halted abruptly and, eyes on the ground, bent down from his waist.

"My good luck piece," he cried out. "Where did it go?"

"I'll find it."

She went down on her hands and knees. Trembling from the soft airy brush of his breath over her neck, yet maintaining the intensity of the search, she eventually chanced upon a glint of color among a clump of weeds. She retrieved the deep blue stone streaked in red. Her neck curved upward as she held the ring out for him.

"What sharp eyes you have!" Gently, almost reverently, he took the ring. "Saved me from a disaster, you know that? I lost the ring once before and immediately came down with a case of flu. You see, it's a *raktamukhi*."

Bloody-mouthed. She recognized with a quiver the legendary gemstone that according to folklore possessed the power to fulfill one's desires, as well as to destroy.

"Why don't you try it on, Sujata?" He pressed the ring on her palm.

Half playfully, half fearfully she slipped the ring onto her finger. The cool shining gold snugly wrapped her flesh. The gemstone gave off a halo. She stared at her finger from many angles.

Like a new bride, but one under a sentence of death.

"Will you take me home?" she implored.

"It's still so early. You know what the ancient poet, Jay Dev, would say? 'Let us go to the bower steeped in darkness.' In darkness, I believe, we find our true selves."

He offered a hand, lifted her up on her feet, and clasping her fingers, led her a few meters away to a grassy area nested by blue-stemmed bamboos. There he arranged a cloth over a bed of grass, drew her down beside him. His tender touch thawed her fear. She breathed audibly. Above her the open sky was flecked with early stars. Crowds of crickets began to trill. She looked into his eyes—dark, bottomless, and steady—examining her. A dampened leaf, from wherever it came, fluttered down and settled on her shoulder. The sudden coolness sent a shudder through her.

"But Pranab—" she murmured.

He reclined next to her, touched her lips gently with a finger. "Forget the past, the future, and other people, Sujata. All that matters is this place, this moment. The stars have decided we're meant for each other."

He let his fingers run gently over her breasts. She closed her eyes, so as to feel his touch with her entire being. For the first time she grasped that he was, above all, a physical creature, not the scholar or the refined *babu* that everyone believed him to be. Then his lips were on hers. The kiss, soft at first, grew urgent, then demanded, and she surrendered.

Much later, she woke. As they lay entwined, breathing in each other's fragrances, Pranab nuzzled her hair, whispering his love for her in four languages—Bengali, Hindi, Sanskrit, and English.

Words that she didn't really hear, only the message of love in that voice.

seven

Thursday evening found Aloka sitting cross-legged on a floor mat with a harmonium, ready to begin her evening music practice. A sweetpea-scented candle flickered on a side table. On this warm summer evening, from her vantage point on the edge of the veranda, she could glimpse the first emerging stars as the alpenglow faded. Off on the eastern horizon a luminous radiance hinted at the imminent rise of the moon.

She was waiting for Pranab to join her. Since they were now engaged, it was his custom to drop by as often as he could, especially on Thursday evenings. He would usually burst through the door like a troubadour, his lips breaking into a mischievous grin and a song, "Aloka! Aloka!" that he'd composed himself. He wasn't a particularly gifted singer, though that hardly mattered. Tonight, besides music, she had some news to share.

What could be delaying him? What could be more important than their music? It was past eight P.M.

The sting of Pranab's absence gave rise to a feeling she'd tried to suppress lately: At times he seemed to be neglecting her. He'd forgotten to return her calls more than once in the last two weeks. Also, in their early courtship days he would bring her presents for no reason at all—a silver mirror, a papier-mâché box, a beaded handbag—but lately these little tokens of his affection had become less frequent. She didn't need these objects, but cherished them as manifestations of his feelings for her. It embarrassed her to think how much she missed the warmth associated with those gifts. As if that wasn't enough, the other day, as he accompanied her home from school, she'd detected a certain weariness in his walk, which she took as an indicator of his unsettled state of mind.

Now she searched for reasons. Might he be having second thoughts about getting married? Had her charm worn off? Then she looked skyward and beheld the luminescent full moon suspended above the horizon. The night brimmed with hope under its lambent glow, and she laughed away her apprehensions: Hesitancy before marriage was normal for a bachelor. That was it. Pranab was just suffering from a last-minute case of "bachelor's nervous belly."

Whoever had said love equated to suffering wasn't wrong. Aloka heaved a sigh and let her fingers sense the vibration of the harmonium as she fingered it tentatively. In doing so, she went back to an early age. Her passion for singing and her unusual aptitude became evident to the family when, as a six-year-old, she could imitate an eminent radio singer like Kanika Bandopadhya. Grandma spared no time hiring a music teacher for her, saying that music was one of the sixty-four classic arts taken seriously in ancient India and its practice ought to be continued. She would cite the name of Vatsyayana, who prepared that list of arts in first century A.D. A more likely explanation of Grandma's generosity might have been that the marriage potential of a girl in the present society improved if she could sing. In any case, Grandma made sure that Aloka, throughout her adolescence, was given extensive training, and it had paid off handsomely. These days, whenever friends and relatives gathered, Aloka was asked to perform. "Oh, Aloka, you must sing. Your voice is so soft. It fills our heart." She liked to see the rapt faces around her as her sonorous voice evoked its magic, even in the farthest corner of the spacious drawing room. At the end of the performance they would applaud. She would find herself feeling cheerful and alert, cleansed inside.

Now she began to play the harmonium in earnest as she hummed a poignant Rabindrasangeet: *Je ratre more duar gooli bhangle jhare.* The night a storm broke through my door. That haunting song, composed by the late Nobel Laureate Rabindranath Tagore, always evoked delicate sentiments of adoration, pathos, fantasy, and patience in her. It represented her accidental meeting with Pranab several years ago and the dramatic alteration of her life that had ensued. Her throat swelled with longing.

She was still relishing the lyrical line when Pranab materialized out of the dusk. Stirred by his presence, she looked up. Her happiest moments came from being near him. Magnificent as always in his white *kurta,* he lowered himself to the jute mat in one smooth motion. What exquisite timing. Had he planned this? Of course he had. Gazing into his eyes, the refined Bengali sounds pleasuring her soul, she moved on to the second line and Pranab mingled his voice with hers: *Jani naiko tumi elee amar ghare.* I did not know you would be visiting me that same night.

She smelled the complex and mysterious aroma about him and also noted that his voice had unusual clarity. Soon the lyrics, the tune, and his presence took her to another realm, where judgment didn't exist. As the final note died away, she smiled at him. "You were late and I was getting worried. But when I heard you sing I let all my worry go."

He lowered his gaze as he tapped the mat with his fingers. "I got distracted with some last-minute details at work and it slipped my mind that it was Thursday. Please don't think too harshly of me, *priyatama.*" He addressed her as his beloved using a poetic expression, and this dislodged her frustration.

"I see it in your eyes, *amaar priya.*" She, too, became poetic. "You're preoccupied, but I'm delighted you finally made it. Something has just come up. I have to be away for six weeks in Kalimpong, and I wanted to see you before I left. Kabita's wedding is set for the end of next month. You do remember my cousin-sister Kabita, don't you? Much as I don't want to leave you or my teaching, it's something I have to do."

She expected a protest at not being consulted on this decision. Instead he accepted the news with little other than a trace of sadness around the eyes. "Will you call me often?" he asked, after a time.

"You can be sure I'll keep the Kalimpong telephone operators fully engaged, my darling. And of course you're invited to the wedding. You'll have a chance to see what a Gupta wedding is like—a preview of our own, though ours will be far more elaborate."

A formal wedding? A large affair? How many guests? He didn't ask any of the expected questions, but rather he appeared thoughtful in a way that disturbed her. She observed his profile, etching it mentally as if it were a treasure, then snuggled up and kissed him, to make their parting memorable, to carry his taste with her, and to leave her scent with him.

His lips felt oddly cold and stiff. But then, he'd been preoccupied all evening. Preoccupied with exactly what, she couldn't be sure.

eight

Nina felt the age in her legs as she strained to drag herself up from the lawn chair beneath the solemn gaze of the Kanchenjunga Range. It took all the strength in her arms pushing on a walnut cane to lift the decrepit body that had spread with age like an overfilled rice sack. Gone was the slim-hipped young woman her husband Bimal had once named Nitya Kumari, the Eternal Nymph. Well, having just attained the age of seventy-three, Nina didn't feel eternal anymore.

She was drifting toward the drawing room when she overheard some conversation from the kitchen. Normally the servants whispered or worked silently. They must have assumed Nina was still out on the lawn.

"Sujata-*di*'s breakfast is still sitting over there," said the cook, speaking to the maidservant. "Maybe you should go wake her up."

The maidservant cackled. "Sujata-*di* needs to sleep. She has a busy day ahead. She'll meet Pranab-*babu* in the afternoon."

"You mean . . . ?"

"My aunt sees them together in the tea field all the time."

Nina could picture the devious glances they were exchanging. She cleared her throat in an exaggerated manner. At the sound, the servants lapsed into silence.

In the drawing room, the implication burning in her, Nina sorted a year's worth of *Monorama* magazines in a basket. For the past several weeks, save for Nina's company, Sujata and Pranab had been left alone. With Nina's consent, Aloka had gone to Kalimpong to assist in Kabita's prewedding preparations. From the turmeric ceremony to the "auspicious night," a traditional Bengali wedding included nearly fifty mandatory rituals that required involvement of relatives for months on end. Aloka, who possessed tremendous organizational skills, could instruct the relatives or the hired help if a single detail was missing. In the two years since her parents' accidental death in an airplane crash, Kabita had drawn close to the Guptas, particularly to Aloka, who was therefore entrusted with the wedding arrangements. Her selfless act of devotion to a relative had separated Aloka from Pranab for the first time.

Nina had believed the two would experience *biraha*. Ancient Indian literature was imbued with the concept of exquisite pining for one's love that made the next encounter that much more passionate and meaningful. Nina had fancied *biraha* might even be good for the young lovers.

Come to think of it, Nina had noticed Pranab's untoward interest in her granddaughter Sujata—last week, as a matter of fact. Nina was passing by a doorway when she got a glimpse of Pranab leaning toward Sujata. Seated in a chair, she was looking up at him, a crystalline light on her face. Did Nina detect a desire in Sujata's eyes? Try as she might, Nina couldn't imagine that Pranab would prefer Sujata to Aloka.

At first Nina pretended they were just friends. She put the matter "in the trunk," preferring not to find out more. She overlooked it when Sujata slipped out of the house that same afternoon, insisting she had an errand to run, only to slink back many hours later. Eyes averted and cheeks febrile, she went straight to her room, where she stayed the remainder of that evening.

Nina shifted her thighs in her drawing room seat in disquietude. Was an affair a possibility? Would Pranab, Aloka's beloved, the very future of this household, take the enormous gamble of an illicit tryst with Sujata, risking the combined wrath of his own family and that of the influential Guptas? What would compel him to walk through that fire?

Nina turned on the table lamp. The click, followed by the flooding of light, triggered further clarification. Although Sujata lacked her sister's beauty and poise, she was endowed with intellect and a concealed inner resilience. Obviously, Pranab, a scholar by nature and training and perceptive as well, had scoped that out sooner than anyone. Sujata, much harder to know than Aloka, had been a challenge. And Pranab craved a challenge. Besides, both Pranab and Sujata had an allegiance to tea, the mystical beverage that inspired deification. Sujata and Pranab bowed at the same altar.

How could Nina determine this for sure? She dreamed up an excuse to ring Pranab. "Now that Aloka is away, what are you doing with yourself?"

"I've been helping set up the music for a stage drama, *Chitrangada*," he replied. "It was staged last night, mostly with the children of the tea workers. You should have seen the pride on their faces when they finished. Would you agree with me, Thakurma, that folk theater should be preserved?"

His voice was ecstatic, too much so for a mere show. Might this be the cozy afterglow of a budding romance?

"Of course I do, Pranab. I just didn't realize that you were so interested in folk theater. But then, you're into so many things. By the way, would you like to come over for dinner tomorrow night? It'll be just Sujata and I. A relative is specially flying in a big cut of *rui* fish from Calcutta for us. Have you had a good *rui* lately?"

"It'd be a pleasure to see you. And *rui* is my big weakness."

The following evening, in a dining room fairly swirling with music and the scent of food, Nina scrutinized Sujata and Pranab with new sharp eyes behind a facade of jovial hospitality. They took seats at opposite ends of the table and except for a perfunctory greeting didn't speak to each other directly, but Nina could tell they were acutely alert to each other's presence. When one shifted slightly in the chair, the other turned in that direction. Pranab began the conversation by describing his ride on the speedy Bajaj scooter he'd borrowed from his cousin for the night, a thrilled expression displaying on his face. Soon he fell grave. Nina asked him about his mother's health and he again talked at length, but gave away little about his own days.

At Nina's signal, the servant laid platters of food before them. Sujata didn't touch her beloved *rumali roti*, but Pranab's appetite seemed unaffected by the discord hanging in the air. "Ah, *rumali roti*," he exclaimed. "Smooth as a silk handkerchief—so appropriately named."

He reached out with his long arm for the delicate flat bread, tore one in half, offered Sujata a piece, and put the other half on his plate. Sharing food in that manner was never done, Nina bore in mind, except among close relations.

In no time, Pranab devoured the whole stack of bread with zest, along with a big piece of *rui* fish, as though he hadn't eaten in days. "*Khub tel,*" he murmured, praising the fish as being oily and, therefore, flavorful.

In colloquial Bengali, *khub tel* also meant an energetic person. Nina now directed her attention to her granddaughter. At the other end of the table, Sujata, perhaps aware of the scrutiny, avoided Nina's eyes, and picked at her food. Nina noticed, too, that both Sujata and Pranab drank endless cups of tea. Their obvious intimacy was centered around tea. But Nina wasn't deceived, not for a minute.

By the time Pranab had taken his leave, Nina had concluded that the situation was already beyond repair. These two reckless children had committed an egregious breach of the social mores that governed behavior in this society, heedless of the price they would inevitably pay. Such was the intensity of the passion that fueled their liaison. Nina well comprehended the frailties of human nature, but that was scant consolation for her grief at the tragedy that was about to befall her granddaughters.

She couldn't fall asleep that night. Lying in bed, she conjured up images of Sujata and Pranab departing hand in hand, their eyes full of ecstasy, while Aloka huddled shrunken in a corner of the house, sobbing. To be sure, Aloka, her once-erect carriage crumpled with grief, her golden voice reduced to a lifeless monotone, would make a show of getting on with her life. Marriage proposals would eventually come and she would probably be persuaded to accept one. But Nina shuddered to think that Aloka would cease being a shining presence; that she might never sing again.

The next afternoon, Sujata disappeared again for hours. When she returned, her eyes danced and her hips swayed. She didn't speak with anyone.

Enough.

Nina realized she must intercede for the sake of the family. As always in times of trouble, she reacted with calm decisiveness. First, she called the maidservant and warned her to keep silent in the Sujata matter or risk losing her position and being driven out of town. Trembling in fear, the maidservant begged for forgiveness and backed out of the room. Then Nina called her son, Bir, at his office and ordered him to come home at once. She devised ways of breaking the news to her son so he wouldn't overreact. She wanted to reach a peaceful solution for all. Within half an hour Bir knocked at Nina's door.

Nina ushered him in and asked him to be seated. An ominous silence reigned as she divulged the Sujata-Pranab liaison and the gossip it had generated.

"And I was so ecstatic to have my youngest daughter back." Bir's face was carved with sorrow. "She doesn't make any sounds when she's in the house. But I can always tell when she's around. Still, she has disappointed me. So, it's true," Bir exclaimed. "There have been whispers about her and Pranab walking together in the fields for some time. The workers are beginning to talk."

"It's more than just whispers. If I'm right, we're on the edge of a catastrophe. Everything is at risk. Aloka's marriage, the family honor, even your ability to run the tea estate, my son."

"I couldn't bring myself to believe that they meet secretly at Senchal Lake for hours at a time. What if the young fool gets pregnant?"

"*Ki lajja!*" What shame. "Why didn't you tell me?" Nina erupted. "That *badmas*. I have never fully trusted him. We must put an end to this at once. We must send Sujata away."

"Yes, immediately."

"But just for a short while," Nina equivocated. "Until Aloka and Pranab get married." Then she recoiled at the expression on her son's face. He was radiating anger and hate through his yellowish red eyes.

"No, Mother. Sujata will leave for good." Bir's voice was controlled but filled with menace. "She has already likely destroyed her sister's marriage prospects. I will not let her destroy our family fortune as well."

Nina grasped what her son was implying: Family reputation and family income were synonymous. When one went, the other vanished, too. The Gupta brand name was prominently displayed on every citreous green box of tea the estate produced. When people purchased Gupta tea, they took home a respected dynasty's tradition, they drank, as it were, an elixir of success.

"I have heard rumors that," Bir said in a voice rising with anger, "the two are conspiring to turn the tea workers against me. Now I must give them credence. How do you think I feel? My own daughter betraying me? You know why she's doing this, don't you?"

Still mystified over the matter, Nina wanted to hear her son's explanation. She looked up.

"She's crazy about him, so crazy that she has completely lost her senses. She's going against her family who brought her up, gave her an education, even invited her back in when she lost her job. I didn't think she was ever capable of such madness."

Bir wiped perspiration from his forehead with a handkerchief. Nina sat frozen. She silently agreed with her son. A tree-creeper tapped the bark of a conifer outside the window. Even that delicate sound alarmed her.

"What will happen if the workers go on strike for any length of time?" Bir continued. "I'll have to shut down the factory. We could lose everything we have." He paused, frowning. "I'm puzzled as to why the rascal is causing this damage. He had a secure future with the estate. And if he marries Aloka, he'll run the entire operation someday. But no! He chose instead to betray Aloka and me. He has lost his head over Sujata. I have to separate them."

"Perhaps," Nina ventured, "Sujata could be sent to Patna for a while. We have relatives there to look after her."

"No!" Bir shot back. "They'll only find a way to meet. We'll send her to Canada. I have contacts in the government. I can easily arrange for her immigration papers. Pranab won't be able to follow her. He'll need lots of money for the passage, which I'm sure he doesn't have—he has to support his folks. And he can't get a passport just like that. He has no connections."

Canada, cold and snowy for so much of the year, sounded like an exile. "Does Sujata have to travel that far?" Nina asked.

"I say so."

Nina turned her face away. Her eyes fell on a black-and-white shot of Aloka on the wall. Seated on the railing of the roof, Aloka had allowed her sari to flow about her like a river. Generally, for a picture-taking session, she preferred a sit-down pose. She could express her innate grace and harmony better that way.

"I'm worried about Aloka," Nina said. "She loves her younger sister. And she loves Pranab. This will be the biggest blow in her life. Somehow we have to shield her from all this."

Bir snorted and his head quivered in disgust. "The rumors are already flying. It's only a matter of time before Aloka finds out. Better she hears it from us."

"Aloka is big-hearted. Perhaps she'll forgive him. And she'll keep the engagement, I'm sure—"

"Better for us to cancel the marriage," Bir said.

"We can't do that." Nina realized that a hint of desperation had crept into her tone. "Aloka would not marry anyone else. Maybe, with Sujata far away, Pranab would come to his senses. And speaking of that, what if Sujata doesn't want to go abroad?"

"Mother, she has no choice. And you should be the one to tell her that. She'll only listen to you. Besides, if I have to do it . . ." A threat was left hanging in the air.

Bir fixed his gaze on Nina, who stared back at him. So! He was leaving the fate of the family in her hands. As the matriarch, the one who'd handled many decisions, she'd expected that. In this case, though, her heart was splintered in two. Fairness for one granddaughter would result in misfortune for the other. Nina, who so keenly believed in family solidarity, now had the task of tearing it apart.

"Very well, then," Nina said after a while. "Much as I care about my granddaughter, you are her only parent. I'll have to accept your decision and act accordingly."

"And I'll take care of Pranab." Without waiting for a reply, Bir sprang up and stalked out of the room.

Nina sat alone for a long time with the frustration of a mother who couldn't control her own son, much less the fate of an entire family. Finally she got up and stood before a portrait of her husband, taken soon after they'd first moved to Darjeeling. In this portrait, as in real life, he appeared young, generous, and full of hope. Just seeing that expression revitalized her. She asked for his guidance and blessing.

"Hold a little kindness in your heart, even when you're at your angriest," he seemed to say, this genial man who was loved by all.

As she bowed away, Nina wondered if a thousand acts of kindness could atone for what she was about to do.

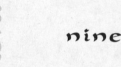 *nine*

An hour later Nina let herself into Sujata's room and quietly closed the door behind her. She wanted to catch Sujata before she left the house, this being precisely the hour when she did so on a regular basis.

Sujata was standing sideways by the window, primping in front of a bamboo-framed hand mirror. For an instant Nina pitied her as the type of woman for whom time spent before a mirror was futile. Then Nina looked closely. In preparation for what must be an important rendezvous, Sujata's customarily unkempt hair was neatly combed. Her cotton-and-silk-blend Jamdani sari was well pressed, its blue undertone softening her dark complexion. Blue, Nina recalled the ancient tale, was the color worn by a maiden tiptoeing out of the house to meet her lover in the blackness of night. And from the way Sujata held herself, her entire physique seemed to be blossoming, like a crocus in spring. Ah, young love, Nina reflected, which erases the words "ugly" or "impossible" or "later" from its vocabulary. She herself was that way once, when only a vague thought of Bimal sent a jolt of electric power through her emotional core. But, Nina reminded herself, this was not the time for romantic nostalgia.

The footsteps must have startled Sujata. Concealing the mirror behind her, she jerked around, her eyes widening in surprise. "Thakurma!"

The high-pitched voice, young and trilling with merriment, momentarily weakened Nina's resolve. She steeled herself. "I want to talk to you."

Sujata pushed a chair over to her, but Nina shook her head in refusal and fired Sujata with a glare. Nina hadn't come to engage in a dialogue. That would imply equality on the part of both participants. She was here to issue an ultimatum. Yes, an ultimatum, even though not of her own choosing. Nina had come to act on the wisdom and insight of many generations, which decreed that for a woman to give her love away except under socially approved conditions was grievously wrong. "Kill the love or kill the woman," the saying went, and Nina had come to destroy.

In the silence Sujata's expression went from bafflement to defiance and, finally, to panic.

"You will stop seeing Pranab immediately."

The sharp-edged words cut the air and their scandalous implication seemed to stain the walls. Hurt and shame contorted Sujata's face. She half turned toward the window, as though seeking light. "I don't know what you're talking about."

"You very well do."

This shameless girl actually needed convincing that she'd done anything wrong? In Nina's time such indiscretion on a woman's part always resulted in her committing *galai dori*, hanging herself by her neck with a rope.

"Listen." Nina's voice lashed the air with a sharp whiplike tone. "Do you really think for a minute Pranab loves you?"

"Yes!" Sujata cried. "He does. He has said so many times."

"Stupid girl."

Sujata trembled. A wisp of hair curled up waiflike at the corner of her eye. Nina wanted to embrace the poor girl, fragile as a kokil bird, lost in a wilderness of human emotions. She experienced a sharp stab of pain along her ribs at the agony in Sujata's eyes.

"Pranab has an eye for beauty," Nina went on coldly, "something you don't have. When he grows bored with you, and he surely will, silly girl, he'll go back to Aloka."

"He wants to call off the engagement." An almost frantic note had crept into Sujata's voice.

"What you might not know is that lately Pranab's parents have been hinting about marriage. Pranab and Aloka have been engaged for over a year now and they adore her. They're terribly flattered at the prospect of having such a lovely and considerate girl in their house. When Pranab's mother was hospitalized last year, Aloka spent days and nights by her bedside. Where were you then? No doubt they also hope that Aloka will one day inherit the tea estate and she'll ask Pranab to manage it. Just like your grandfather and I did."

Sujata seemed to have turned to a stubborn, unthinking, stonelike mass. Though Nina was crying inside, she pressed on. "Not only will you break this off, you will leave this house."

"But Thakurma, you can't throw me out of my own home."

"Yes, dear, I very well can. I will keep this family together—that comes first. You will leave for Patna immediately. I have friends there who'll take care of you until your uncle Kumud in British Columbia can arrange your immigration papers for Canada. When I told him about your banking experience he said that you'd be able to get a job there easily. He's lived there for twenty-five years, so he should know."

Sujata's sobs sounded like mournful little waves lapping up on a beach. She tilted her head up. "Why should I give up Pranab? None of you understand him like I do. He's selfless; he's a revolutionary. He wants to make this a better world for the weak and the oppressed. He needs me to fulfill his dream. And I love him with everything I have."

"Your love is wasted, my dear, and as for his dream, if he's not careful, it'll lead him to an early grave. You'll give him up for everybody's sake, but especially for Aloka."

"Aloka!" Sujata spat the name out as if it were an epithet.

"Lately you two have stopped liking each other. She was the big sister you once looked up to. Do you remember? I might also add that your love for Pranab is but a passing attraction, a sinister and damaging passion, and

I will not allow it to destroy our family. Aloka's love for Pranab is total—body and spirit combined. She has the more legitimate claims to him."

"Thakurma, please. This is the first time I've met somebody who appreciates me. I can't live without him."

"You can and you will. There is no other choice. This is my order. Start packing your bags." Nina turned to leave. "Don't let people call you *nemak haram*—one who takes the salt of the house, then breaks the window."

Nina stomped out. Back in her own room, she shut the door with shaky hands and crawled onto her bed. She felt like killing herself and perhaps she partially succeeded, for in the next few days she existed in a sort of formless limbo, in which her senses were dulled and days were joyless. Her mind couldn't discern any meaning no matter what the endeavor was.

It was Sujata's last day in Darjeeling. It fell to Nina to lead Sujata into the drawing room so she could bid farewell to the extended family, some fifty somber people. In soft, trancelike steps Sujata walked, as though she'd lost all claims to touch the floor. Nina's eyes followed Sujata's as she scanned the faces before her. Aunt Toru, shedding tears and covering her eyes with a crumpled handkerchief. Aloka, who had been called from Kalimpong just for the day on the pretext of a family emergency, had arrived only minutes ago and was huddling with a throng of relatives by the window. She appeared pale, possibly the result of a bouncy ride in a Jeep for several hours. The moment her gaze fell on her sister, she threaded her way through the room. Evidently she was still ignorant of the true circumstances of Sujata's hasty departure.

Grasping and releasing the train of her sari, Aloka implored in all sincerity, "Why do you always have to go away, *bontee*? Be sure to write to us often, will you?"

Sujata's eyes were roaming the room, searching in vain for Pranab. But even in this she was doomed to disillusionment, for, on Bir's orders, he'd been sent to a tea auction in Calcutta. Nor was Bir anywhere to be seen, having left by taxi that morning for Siliguri to meet a tea buyer from Calcutta. Sujata's *bhagya*—her karmic fate—must have conspired against her. She was leaving town without her father's blessings.

Aunt Komola cast sideways glances at Sujata. "It's just as well that the younger one's leaving," she whispered within earshot, observing that Sujata was a loner, a bit outspoken, not good at small talk, clumsy at the table, and "too hard to handle."

Did Komola have to be that cruel?

The driver's hand gesture indicated that the luggage had been stored. Without delay, Nina escorted Sujata outside. A sharp high mountain wind struck Nina full in the chest and numbed her flesh. She watched as Sujata, eyes low, climbed into the backseat. Hardly anyone waved at her. Then, as the car sped away, Sujata seemed to be peering out the car window for one last view of her cherished tea garden. Nina could picture how swirls of drifting mist would conspire with the tears welling up in Sujata's eyes to obscure that vision.

Nina looked up skyward with a prayer to the gods to protect Sujata. Then she turned back with regret. An era had ended for the family.

With Kabita's wedding over and Aloka due home in a matter of days, harmony returned to the household, though not to Nina's heart. She missed her youngest granddaughter. She traipsed into the girl's room often and pictured her. Sujata moving about restlessly, then settling into a chair by the window for the view of the Kanchenjunga she so prized. The windowpane seemed etched with a faint outline of Sujata's face; her unfulfilled wishes agitated the air. Nina told the maidservant not to disturb the room.

Days passed. Nina put on a courageous face, but her health suffered. Her body became anarchy as it were with eyes, knees, liver, and heart abandoning their duties in grief. Overcome with exhaustion, she spent most of her time lying in bed, where she reflected on who had been most at fault, who had paid the heaviest price, and why love had exacted such a heavy ransom.

ten

On Aloka's first day back home after six weeks in Kalimpong, she was looking forward to spending time with her father in the evening and catching up on the family news. In the afternoon, filled with vigor and buoyed by a cheerful mood, she swept into the kitchen and began preparing *balushai*. She worked ghee into the dough, which she formed into balls, then deep-fried them till they were almond-hued. As she worked, she smiled at the image of her father's childlike delight at the sight of the tender rounds, flaky to the touch, with a dimple in the center. Bir could never stop at one or two.

How much Aloka had missed him and the whole family, including Sujata. How disappointing that Sujata had left again. For Canada, this time. But then, she'd always been unpredictable. Aloka planned to dash off a letter to her sister soon.

One by one she dropped the deep-fried pastries into a simmering pot of sugar syrup and waited for them to rise to the surface. The worst part of being away had been her separation from Pranab. What a pity that they'd spoken so few times on the phone and that he'd failed to attend Cousin-Sister Kabita's wedding. Didn't he miss Aloka? Why did he seem a bit reserved on the long-distance conversation? He answered her queries about what kept him busy at work with a minimum of words and didn't venture into any topic of his own. He was to return from Calcutta tomorrow. He was constant in her ruminations, alive and full of power, from when she first awoke in the morning to the time she went to bed, and every waking hour in between. Her feelings for him became woven, in a sense, into whatever she happened to be doing. Hers was a long, constant, deep affection.

With a slotted spoon, Aloka removed the delicately browned *balushais*, now glistening with a coating of the syrup, from the pot and allowed them to cool on a platter. It had given her great satisfaction to witness Kabita getting married. It was a lovely wedding, with a gigantic floral arch, twin-klers, colored lights, boxes of presents, platters of sweets garnished with silver leaf, and Kabita, the delicate bride, presiding over it all. A pendant dangling on her forehead, sandalwood dots painted around her eyebrows, chin upturned in elation, Kabita had exchanged a garland with the man of her choice. He had lifted her iridescent red bridal veil and brought his face closer to hers. With sixty people surrounding them, they gazed long at each other, signifying that they were, from this point on, each other's universe.

Aloka had pictured herself, equally jubilant, in a similar setting with Pranab.

As she arranged the *balushais* on a platter in an artful pattern, she fan-tasized about her own impending wedding, which her friends had dubbed "Darjeeling's most romantic wedding of the decade." Local sweet shop own-ers and flower vendors had already sent her their proposals for catering arrangements. The girls in her school were trying to wheedle an invitation. The Darjeeling Planters' Association had offered their large hall for her wedding reception. If there had been one exception to this enthusiastic re-action, it had come from a longtime school chum who had expressed concern that Pranab might be more interested in snagging a key executive position in the tea estate than in Aloka. This she had dismissed as pettiness on the part of the friend. In the next few days—Aloka now smiled inwardly, opening the gate to treasured sentiments—she'd give Grandma the permission to formally start the wedding preparations.

Aloka carried the snacks and the usual glasses of limewater on a tray and stepped into the drawing room. As always, Bir was lounging on the couch, his eyes fixed at a point on the wall. He appeared somewhat restless, from the way his big toe tapped the floor.

"Father!" Aloka cried happily. She hastened to settle herself in a chair.

"Aloka, my dear."

In the next half hour Aloka furnished details on what had been going on in the extended family: Kabita's husband seeking a job transfer to Darjeeling and how nice it would be to have them closer; Aunt Aparna flying to Singapore for a shopping spree; Uncle Govinda had stopped writing his travelogue again, this time echoing Tagore's words as his excuse: " 'I have wandered far and wide, but haven't spared the time to look out my window and observe a dewdrop on a rice stalk.' "

Aloka couldn't help but notice that Bir barely touched the *balushais* and only sipped occasionally at his limewater.

"Is something bothering you, Father?"

"Yes, as a matter of fact." Bir cleared his throat. "Will you close the door?"

Aloka couldn't remember ever having a private conversation with her father. She struggled to gather her poise, taking extra time to walk back the length of the room. Her feet nearly tripped on the front sari pleats as she returned to her seat.

"There's something I have to tell you, my child." Bir's lips were tightly compressed into a severe line. "It'll not be easy."

"Does it have to do with Sujata?"

Head down, his eyelids veiling his true expression, Bir nodded.

"Is she all right? Could you tell me why she left home so quickly? I'm completely at a loss. She seemed so interested in the tea business and was spending so much time in the fields that I thought this time around she'd stay. I was just starting to get reacquainted with her. We've drifted apart in the last few years. Sorry to be losing my little sister again."

"My dearest child." Bir pressed on the couch handle with his fingers.

"What I have to say is going to be quite painful for you. I know how much you love and respect Pranab."

In a flash Aloka grasped the situation. A vision of Pranab entwined in an ardent embrace with Sujata, writhing in some secluded forest, emerged before her. They taunted and tortured her with the intensity of their shared pleasure as one. They looked up at her imploringly, as if asking her to leave. Now she lifted her eyes to Bir and saw a mortified face, as though he were privy to the same sight. She couldn't think or speak, nor could she get up and run away. The lights in the room dimmed before her. Much like her, they seemed diminished by the magnitude of the betrayal.

Bir spoke, far longer than he usually did at a stretch, painting in detail what had gone on. Several times Aloka touched the slippery surface of her glass bangles to impart in her a sense of what was real. After a while she no longer comprehended his remarks, only the feeling of shame and disappointment they conveyed. When Bir finished, a long empty silence ensued in which her mind echoed the questions: Why, Pranab? Where did I go wrong? Why? Why? Why? Life that had seemed so full minutes ago was looted of its treasures.

When she finally regained her focus, she found Bir leaning toward her. "You don't know how much it hurts to see you upset like this. And you have good reason to be. You've been grievously wronged. I feel your *bedona*." He used the deeply felt, poetic word for sorrow. "I feel it every bit."

She bent forward. "Oh, Father . . ."

"You will break your engagement with Pranab. He is not worthy of you or the family."

"But Father." She cried those words. "I love him. Even now I love him. I can't see a life without him."

"That will soon pass, my child. And remember, there's more at stake than your feelings for Pranab. We have the Gupta reputation to protect, and we must be practical. The other day, your Thakurma reminded me that you are thirty-two years old. It's getting late for marriage, at least in this conservative town. We're behind Calcutta or Mumbai in that respect. Still, I get so many proposals. Mr. Mazumdar brought one the other day. His son is a chemist in Pennsylvania. Nice boy, thirty-four, doctorate in chemistry, good manners—"

"Please, Father. See it from my point of view, for a change. I know Pranab deep down where he dreams. That affair must have been a passing infatuation, with me being gone. I mean, what chances of a marriage does Sujata have other than a completely arranged one? She must have started it. Yes! That had to be it. Pranab loves me. I know he does. At heart he's honorable. Difficult as it might be, I'll forgive him. Once we're together again, we'll be back to where we started. Besides, who better to relieve your burden at the tea estate than Pranab? He has a brilliant future there. You said so yourself, Father."

"I'm not so sure."

"What do you mean?"

"There have been rumors for some time that he's inciting the workers against me. Nothing has happened so far, and I haven't worried too much or investigated. Besides, he's valuable. He has tremendous ability to judge tea and market it. I need him. But now, with the recent strike at a tea estate in Dooars—you might have read about it in the newspaper when you were in Kalimpong—there's reason to worry. The state government has intervened on the workers' behalf and it looks as though the proprietor might lose the estate altogether. The government threatens to take over. I'm keeping my fingers crossed that our workers don't get ideas from that precedent. That could be the end for us."

Aloka trembled. She hadn't been able to confide in her father or anyone else in the family about the secret meeting between Pranab and the tea workers she observed a couple of years ago. How could she? Pranab had begun courting her right after that. They'd vowed their love for each other, spent all their free time together. Now it flashed through her head that she'd been disloyal to her father. She'd not only put him at risk, but the entire family for Pranab's sake. It wounded her deeply to see Bir gazing at her now with a caring expression.

"Will you do me a favor, Aloka? Will you find out if he's indeed agitating the workers? Figure out a way of stopping him. Can you do it as soon as you can?"

"Of course I will. Tomorrow is my music night. Pranab will be coming over. I haven't seen him in so long and we now have many things to clear up, but I'll make it a point to feel him out on this matter. And stop such a terrible thing, if I can do so." A yawn snuck out of her, one of deep fatigue. "Father, I'm so very tired. Could you please excuse me? This has been a long and difficult day."

"Of course, my dear. We can continue this later. I'm just so glad that you're back. This house doesn't shine without you."

Quietly Aloka got up. She returned to her room, where she flopped down on her bed, buried her face in a pillow, and surrendered herself to her *bedona*—her deepest sorrow.

eleven

The next morning soon after tea, Nina began preparing a shopping list for the servant. It was more for Bir and Aloka; she no longer cared much what she ate. Nor did she enjoy fighting the crowd at the market. Bir had to have freshly made curd with his meals; Aloka snacked on shoestring potatoes when she got home from school and she liked to dine on *shukto*. Tonight, on the occasion of Aloka's return, Nina planned a big family meal that would include specially ordered *aahu* rice from another state, and a *dalna*. A few relatives would be invited.

She was halfway through making the list when she heard shouts from outside. At first she assumed it was a march for some political party, but then it occurred to her this was not the season for elections. And in any case, no procession ever came to her quiet neighborhood.

Nina rushed to the window and peered out. A swell of demonstrators, about fifty of them, clogged the street as they marched abreast from the direction of the town's center. They turned to face the house, and now she recognized them. Oh, Ma Sarada. They were workers from her tea estate! The two women in the front row, Gayatri and Priya, their hair confined under rainbow-colored scarves, tea-gathering baskets hanging on their backs, thrust their clenched fists rhythmically in the air. Tenured male employees Jyotin, Bhim, and Nripen hoisted a slogan-emblazoned banner overhead and glared defiantly up at the house with fierce eyes. These were the same workers who'd always greeted her with the utmost respect, calling her "Gupta-*maharani*," "Queen Gupta," or "Owner-*ji*."

Children trailed along behind the marchers, a baby began to scream. A mangy dog, wound up by the commotion, ran about snarling and yipping on the periphery of the mob.

What did they want?

Then a loudspeaker crackled. A portentous chanting assaulted Nina's ears.

"Better pay, better medical care."

Nina gripped the windowsill, feeling a flutter of humiliation, followed by the beginnings of fright. Curious eyes peeked out from neighbors' doors and windows. The entire town would soon gossip. The marchers were lining up along the brick fence, their numbers increasing by the minute. Would they surge through the metal gate, smash the front door, stream inside and attack her?

The slogans had barely died away when Nina heard screams. Khaki-clad police had rushed in from a side street and were throwing themselves on the crowd, wielding their willowy bamboo rods with relish. In the pandemonium that ensued, one woman slipped and fell, the skin on her arm laid open by a well-aimed blow. She must have grabbed a policeman's leg, for he stumbled and slipped, too. Blood splattered on the pavement, a revolting red, a warning. Whose blood? Nina couldn't tell. She felt as though she herself had suffered a blow. The marchers began to scatter at the onslaught. They fled down a winding path toward the tea garden.

Nina pushed herself away from the window, slouched onto a chair, and reached for the phone. Her fingers were too stiff to dial and her chest had the sensation of being squeezed in a vise.

Bir couldn't be reached at his office, so Nina left messages with an orderly, then fell to pacing back and forth in her room, shopping list abandoned. She phoned Toru, a niece who visited her often, for advice. She was disappointed when given the news that Toru had left for Kurseong, the place of white orchids, on a photography outing and wouldn't return till the next day. On reflection Nina realized this was just as well, for Toru, given to emotional outbursts, would be useless during this period of crisis. Nina would just have to handle this one alone.

Two hours later, Bir stomped in. He was possibly taking a break from work. His eyes obscured under a frown, his mouth forming a permanent pout, he inquired, "They didn't do any damage here, did they?"

Nina noticed the pallor of his face, the hunch of his shoulders, how the head led the body, and replied, "No, my son." Then, leading the way, "Let's go to the veranda and get some fresh air."

She grabbed a chair by a wooden planter containing double-petal black tulips. She paused to contemplate their striking color and their nurturing cavelike shape, as a way to compose herself. Bir squeezed himself into a chair opposite her. He thrust his chin out, a habit acquired as a child whenever events went out of his control.

"What was it all about?" Nina finally asked. Her head still throbbed with the marching sounds and the slogans.

"The workers staged a walkout this morning. They're making outrageous claims. I can't say it caught me completely by surprise, so I didn't hesitate to call the police as soon as I found out."

"Nothing like this has ever happened before, Bir." If there existed a hint of complaint in her tone, Nina tried to minimize it.

"It's that Pranab rascal." Bir's words, seething with anger, had a brittle quality. "I know it's him, spurring the workers on, telling them what they want to hear. And all of a sudden they're making huge, unrealistic demands. They're actually asking that I pay their weekly wage even if they don't pluck the minimum quota. Can you believe it?"

"I can. Have you considered that Pranab comes from a poor family himself? His interest in their welfare might be genuine. Why don't you try increasing the workers' rations to defuse the situation, at least temporarily?"

Bir stared vacantly at the tulips. He had never noticed a flower in his life. "It's not that easy," he blurted.

Bir didn't need to remind Nina of the difficulties he faced as the owner-manager of a tea plantation. Two straight years of drought had resulted in a smaller-than-usual crop, and earnings had fallen accordingly. Many of the tea bushes were nearly a hundred years old and needed to be replaced. Though the finest Indian tea was grown here in Darjeeling, the yield was lower than in Assam, so that even in a good year the profit margins were low. To make matters worse, unscrupulous manufacturers were passing off inferior tea as premium-grade Darjeeling, further cutting into Gupta profits.

Still Nina sensed that the tea workers had some legitimate complaints. Their daily wage hadn't increased in years, even as the price for staples like *dahl* and cooking oil had doubled. And paying them a measly fifty paise for every extra kilogram of leaf they plucked over and above the normal quota constituted an insult.

"We have to keep labor happy, my son," she counseled. "Our destinies are bound together."

"I've been in contact with the Darjeeling Planters' Association. They know the labor situation intimately and have dispatched a representative to speak directly with the tea workers. If necessary we'll put a call in to the state labor commissioner in Calcutta. We'll soon have this little uprising under control. But I may have to dip into the family savings in the interim, Mother."

Nina ignored Bir's money woes for now, as another urgent matter had popped into her head: Bir, who was an influential member of the business community here, appeared extremely distraught. In fact, she'd never seen him so maroon-faced, so agitated. Might he be on the verge of losing his self-control? It occurred to her in a flash of insight that things could go badly for Pranab if this protest went on much longer.

"How do you plan to handle Pranab?" she asked.

"I dismissed him today." The blood vessels that tracked diagonally across Bir's temple were pulsing visibly and his huge nostrils were flared. "First he disgraces my family, then he tries to ruin my business," he growled. "He's through around here."

Nina's own tongue felt coated with a distasteful slime. She had suspected as much: Sujata was at the center of this drama. Her departure must have caused Pranab to react in this fashion. The two men were gripped in a struggle for dominance, and that could adversely affect Aloka. It could only worsen Bir's already poor health as well.

"Sujata's gone." Nina maintained a calm demeanor. "But do not forget Aloka's still here and Pranab is her whole life. You need to think this through."

"He's *not* a part of this family," Bir snapped, and thumped the chair handle with a palm for emphasis, like squishing a mosquito. Absently he examined the palm for damage.

"We have to keep him around for Aloka's sake."

"I am calling the marriage off." His voice seemed to catch and he swallowed hard before continuing. "I want that *shuar* thrown out of town."

Bir was calling Pranab a dirty pig. He had never used such profanity in Nina's presence before.

By now Nina was taut in her body and so thoroughly alarmed that she began to fear the worst. "Aloka will go wherever he goes," she countered.

"Not where I'm going to send him."

"What do you have in mind, my son?" Receiving his only answer of a forbidding scowl, she insisted, "Answer your mother."

Head down, Bir sprang up from his chair and trotted inside the house.

What audacity. Just as Nina stood up to follow him, she heard the front door slam with an enormous bang. He was going back to his office, for sure. She almost fell backward over the tulips.

Nina sank back down into her chair, sick at the realization that events were twisting out of control. Bir, the child who had grown inside her a cell at a time, the boy she cherished more than her own life, was about commit an abominable act. She would have to stop him.

Later in the afternoon, Nina found herself hoping that Bir would reach some sort of compromise with Pranab and the tea workers. She left several messages for him. But hours dragged by and no reply came. Nina moved from window to window and checked the telephone to make sure it was functioning. She listened for the door. Anxiety tinged with disgust bloated inside her. For the first time in her life she realized it was possible to love and loathe one's child in equal measure.

At last Nina decided to approach her chief servant, who had been part of the household ever since she could remember. He also served as an orderly for Bir and carried out many of his personal duties. Now that he had reached the age of sixty, this venerable retainer was soon to retire and return to Nepal where his five grown sons lived.

Nina found him sitting on the side lawn, puffing on his hookah. It made a burbling sound that matched the look of gratification on his face. The pungent smell of tobacco smoke turned her stomach, but she stood there, waiting for him to become aware of her presence. It took a few seconds. Eyes widening, he set the hookah down and scrambled to his feet as fast as his aged limbs would allow him to move. "Memsahib!"

She wouldn't allow him to gain his composure. "What does Bir plan to do with Pranab?"

A tremor passed through the servant's body. He dropped his gaze and shuffled to his feet. "It is a most serious situation, Memsahib."

"Indeed. But that doesn't answer my question."

He began to wring his hands. "Please, Memsahib, *barababu* has ordered me not to say a word about this to anyone. If he finds out, he'll be very angry with me. He'll dismiss me and worse."

"*Barababu* is my son. He will do nothing to you without my permission. Remember, also, I paid for your daughter's wedding. When your wife died, I gave you a month off. Wouldn't you like to go back to Nepal safely with pension and a big bonus?"

His head bobbed at the prospect, but his eyes informed her of his anxiety. He pondered; then, in a whisper, "*Barababu* has hired a couple of *goondas.*"

Bir had hired ruffians? Nina's pulse quickened. "What for?"

"Tonight they will break into Pranab-*babu*'s house and take him away."

"To where?"

"I'm afraid," the man whimpered, "he'll not be seen alive again. It is not unusual for a person to fall into the Teesta River, you know."

"We have to stop that immediately."

"That is all very well for you, Memsahib, but I could lose my own life if I go against Manager-Sahib's wishes."

"No, you will not. Both this house and the tea plantation are in my name. I will deal with my son."

Nina draped the train of her sari around her shoulders like a shawl in an imperious gesture of authority. Deep inside, she dreaded her son's wrath almost as much as this servant did. Yet, what choice did she have? She must rescue Pranab—at this point his life was in her hands—and stop a crime from happening. Otherwise Aloka would sustain a destructive blow, one from which she might well never recover.

The man breathed audibly. "I will try, Memsahib, but it will cost you *lakhs,* maybe *crores* of rupees. Those *goondas* will have to leave Darjeeling for good. Otherwise *barababu* will hunt them down."

Nina realized with dismay that the family savings account couldn't produce such a colossal sum. "Let me work on that. I may have to send you to the bank. Meanwhile, you must try to bargain the *goondas* down."

"I'll be back as soon as I can."

By the time Nina returned to her room, she had settled on the only possible solution: to sell her jewelry. In the society she'd grown up, a married woman wore ornaments to indicate her status. Ornaments, a savings of sorts for her, gave her a measure of financial independence. The thirty or so pieces Nina possessed had been bequeathed by her parents, relatives, or by her husband. She had hoped to pass them on to Aloka and Sujata someday, but now there was a more pressing need.

Nina opened the iron safe hidden inside a dresser, extracted a blue velvet box, and snapped it open. In the top tray rested an emerald-studded choker necklace that her mother had worn at her own wedding. One last time Nina fastened the coolly luxurious necklace around her throat and admired herself in the mirror. For an instant, she was again a demure bride with a hopeful gaze and a soft smile. Next, as she pinned a gold-and-amethyst sapphire brooch on her left shoulder over the sari folds, her eyes dampened. The brooch was a gift from a favorite aunt on her deathbed. Then came a pearl-encrusted ring Nina's husband had bought in Chennai on a business trip. Memories of him blazed as she slipped it on her finger. She stared at a thick *hansuli* necklace that Sujata had often eyed. And there was the *haar,* with a sunburst-shaped, *minakari* gold pendant, which Aloka had often borrowed on special occasions, believing it was just the right adornment for her.

Here was a dazzling collection, imbued with memories. But how would Nina ever be able to touch them again if she chose jewelry over Pranab's life? If Aloka was miserable, or worse?

Slowly, Nina took out all the ornaments from the case and even took off those she had on. The tiny gold stud earrings she'd worn since she was fifteen smelled of her own skin. She bundled them together in a rag, shoved it inside a shopping basket, then covered the top with a cloth. Her decision made, she huddled in a chair and waited.

In two hours the servant returned. Though exhausted from his long trek, he had signs of good news bubbling on his face. He'd caught the *goondas* in time and they'd made an offer: a *crore* of rupees in exchange for Pranab's head.

If she trembled inside, Nina didn't let it show. She handed him the basket in an ordinary way.

The old man opened the bundle and gasped in horror. "These are your family heirlooms, Memsahib. You must not sell them." Eyes glistening with tears, he said, "You have even taken off your earrings. It hurts me to look at you. You're making a huge sacrifice. But I'm sorry, this jewelry alone will not do. We're dealing with some real rogues."

Nina had expected as much. She signaled the man to wait, went to her desk, wrote a check, and signed it. In less than a minute the family savings were gone. In the process, she'd started a chain of events that would put the lives of those closest to her in peril. She had always prided herself in doing what was best for the family, but what a terrible cost pride could exact.

With a stern face, she held up the check to the servant. "You've got what you need. Go now, before they change their minds."

The servant scuttled across the room. Then, at the door, "One more thing, Memsahib. Pranab-*babu* must flee tonight. You must make sure he does. It will not be safe for him to stay in this town any longer. There are other *goondas* and *barababu* will be very angry, indeed." And then he was gone, down the hallway and out the door.

Her strength was draining, but Nina pulled herself together and phoned Aloka at school. Normally Aloka taught till four, then counseled students as a volunteer for another couple of hours. This marked the second time Nina had called the girl back from school. The first time was when Aloka was a young girl and her grandfather had suddenly died of a heart attack. How the girl needed consolation that day. *"Dadu, Dadu."* She kept asking for her grandfather and sobbing. She wouldn't take food or go to bed. She wouldn't leave her grandmother. Then, as now, Nina wouldn't have the time and solitude to grieve.

twelve

All day long, between classes and at recess, Aloka had been on tenterhooks about seeing Pranab this evening since learning of his dalliance with Sujata. She recognized she would have to rise above acrimony, look deeply into his eyes, sense the message in the touch of his hands, and hear him out. Only if she listened to the beat that played inside him could they have a chance to regain what he had so foolishly cast aside.

She faced her last class of the day, a lecture on world geography. Clad in navy and white, their hair fastened with red ribbons, the ten-year-old girls arched their necks to stare at a map of the United States extending across the wall. With her left hand Aloka pointed out the city of New York. Though this was a geography lesson, she began reviewing the city's history, for she believed the two were intertwined. She became lost in the story of the Algonquin Indians, the meadows, streams, and hills that had sustained them, and the harsh, glittering metropolis of today.

When she paused, she overheard an earnest-looking girl seated in the second row by the aisle whispering to her seatmate, "That's where I wish to live someday."

Aloka found that curious in one so young. Even at her age, she'd never desired to live anyplace other than Darjeeling. Her loved ones resided here. Her history was written in the hills and the valleys outside the window.

She had just begun speaking again when the headmistress's assistant motioned to her from the doorway. Aloka excused herself from the class and went over to see what he wanted. "What is it, Uday?"

"Your grandmother is on the phone."

It took a moment for the significance of the message to sink in. Grandma would never phone unless something was seriously amiss. Aloka rushed to the headmistress's office. "What is it, Thakurma?"

"Come home, Aloka dear. Come home right away."

"As fast as I can, Thakurma." Aloka was out the door as soon as she hung up.

Just after the wall clock had chimed four times, Nina heard Aloka climbing the stairs to the second floor two at a time, but without any seeming sense of urgency. Even when she hurried, Aloka maintained her usual poise. To keep her inquietude from showing, Nina rearranged the items on a side table: Nivea cream, a letter opener, a bottle of Ayurvedic massage oil, framed photos.

A graceful form in a pale green sari appeared in the doorway. "What's the matter, Thakurma?" Aloka laid a soft palm on Nina's forehead. "You're not feeling well?"

"It has got nothing to do with me. Have a seat and listen carefully to what I have to say."

Briefly and emphatically Nina told her of the death threat on Pranab. Aloka's eyes misted with sorrow and her body shrank in alarm. But, from the way she nodded at the salient points in the story, she seemed to comprehend the situation and accept it. If there was a temptation to judgment, if a momentary impulse to lash out arose from within her, she tightened her face and controlled it with dignity, as a Gupta girl would be expected to do.

"I can't believe what's happening," Aloka said. "Tonight I was going to talk with Pranab to make sure he still loved me and wanted to marry me. But there's no time for that now. His life is more important than my pride. I have to convince him to leave Darjeeling, and the only way that'll work is if I go with him. I have contacts in other cities; he doesn't. We'll leave tonight when everyone's asleep."

"Please reconsider, Aloka. Don't go with him. Not only will you put your life in danger, your father might not let you come back to this house ever again."

"I do understand, Thakurma. Never for a moment have I thought about leaving Darjeeling or my family. But my life is with Pranab—I've made a commitment to him."

Nina's chest fairly burst with pride. Aloka, self-sacrificing, so bold in her love, a veritable goddess from ancient times. But how many goddesses would devote themselves the way Aloka did, especially when love turned into a field of suffering, love for a man enamored of her own sister? The selfless girl had an unlimited capacity for forgiveness. Aloka had proven that over and over again since the time she was a little girl. Once, when her sister broke her doll handmade by Calcutta's famed Kumartuli artists, Aloka had sobbed a little, but didn't make a fuss. Her heart encompassed everyone. When she served food at family festivities, she always ladled herself last and the smallest portion.

Nina jerked up the trailing end of her sari to her eyes. "Be careful, my darling."

Aloka touched Nina's feet. "Please bless us, Thakurma. I'll write to you no matter where we are." And she was off.

Nina stood at the window to get a glimpse of Aloka as she emerged onto the street. Her sari kept slipping off her shoulder in the breeze. She walked, her gentle tread now heavy with responsibility and care.

thirteen

An hour after she'd spoken with Grandma, having made the necessary arrangements, Aloka arrived at Pranab's modest residence. Lack of frequent painting had turned the outside white walls of this old brick building into an ashen shade stricken with black. Her head touched a rapidly growing squash plant, a common vegetable grown around here, stretched out over a trellis arched over the gate. She'd come to this house many times in these past two years to visit her beloved and his family, always with high expectations. She had always marveled at the clean, sparse, and welcoming interior. Today her legs shrank as she let herself in through the front door.

She paused at the door of the music room, which also doubled as the drawing room. Pranab was sitting on the matted floor. Surrounded by bolsters, he was staring at a pair of tablas before him. He had often expressed his belief that in the right hands these simple drums could transport both the musician and the audience to another realm. And indeed, the last time he'd played the tablas for her, the sounds had shimmered and risen through the ceiling, taking her consciousness with them to a space far beyond this room. Now an aura of hopelessness surrounded him as he sat with head bowed and fingers dangling over his knees.

Aloka's inner calm crumbled. Aware of how little time they had, she plunked her purse down, scuttled across to him on her knees, drew his head to her breast, and whispered, "Oh, Pranab! I missed you so."

He pulled away from her. "Aloka! Didn't expect you so early." As Aloka tried to control a choked feeling, he went on. "Do you know I was dismissed from my position this morning by your father? We had a little talk, then he had an orderly escort me out. I was told never to come anywhere near the tea garden again."

Aloka glanced at the bamboo grove beyond the window, sucked in some air. "We have to get out of this town immediately."

His eyes widened as he gradually grasped the words. "I suspected I was being followed this past week, but I didn't take it seriously."

"My father can't bear the thought of losing to you, even though he knows what you mean to me. His nature is to win. It's the way he lives."

"I'm no coward." Pranab's fingers, playful and whimsical for a moment, drummed a defiant beat on the tablas. "I won't leave. I'll fight this out."

"Don't you realize his influence in this town? You won't stand a chance."

"I'll do my best. The workers will support me. Together we will prevail in the end."

"Please, Pranab. The police will only respond with more force. This time they'll come for you as well and they won't be gentle. The commandant is a friend of my father."

There came a rap at the door. Pranab leaned back in an alert posture. An elderly tea worker shuffled in.

"Come in, Jyotin." The frown in Pranab's forehead disappeared. "Have a seat."

But the old man remained standing. "I only slipped out for a few minutes to see you, Pranab-*babu*. The woman who was hurt has been taken to the doctor. Her injury isn't serious. She's been given paid leave for two weeks."

Then, rubbing his hands together, he added, "Everyone has gone back to work."

"Were they bribed or intimidated?"

The man flinched. "Right now a representative from the Darjeeling Planters' Association is discussing our demands."

"That representative should be talking to me."

"Please, Pranab-*babu*, I have a much bigger concern. There are strong rumors that *barababu*—"

"He has sent *goondas* after me?" Pranab tossed the word out lightly, a harsh edge to his voice. "I guess I'll have to be careful about where I go from now on."

"I'm afraid that may not be enough."

"What are you both trying to tell me?"

"You must get out of town quickly. Go fast and far, very far."

Pranab slumped back against the wall as though he'd been slapped in the face. "What crime have I committed?"

Jyotin folded his hands at his chest in a prayerful gesture. "I love you as much as I love my sons. Please consider what I've said." With quick steps he backed out of the room. Aloka rose and followed him out to the sidewalk.

They stood in silence for a moment. Aloka thanked him for taking the risk to come here and convey his message. She asked him to be careful and keep this visit a secret.

"Please do your best to convince him, Aloka-*di*," Jyotin whispered. "He's a good man." He disappeared behind the dark curtain of dusk.

Aloka shut the door and stood motionless a moment, overwhelmed by the shapeless vision of the future that swirled about in her mind. Her utmost concern was Pranab's safety. Wherever they might end up, she would help Pranab find a larger cause, a higher calling in life. And with Sujata out of the way, she'd be able to rebuild their bond. When she returned to the music room, she noticed how pale Pranab's face had become.

He forced a smile. "So, my head is that precious?"

"It's even more precious to me." She checked her wristwatch. "We'll go to Calcutta. I have a family friend there who'll put us up, but we have to hurry."

"How can I leave? Darjeeling is all I know. All I've ever wanted is to live and die here."

"If you stay, you will surely get your wish, and soon. Now go and pack quickly, take only what you can carry."

"But what will I do, wherever it is we're going?"

"You're well educated and respected, you'll find a satisfactory career in whatever field you want. And, more importantly, we'll have each other."

"But it won't be the same, Aloka. Do you understand what the tea estate means to me? I am a plant doctor. I know exactly when the bushes will sprout new leaves, when their roots are beginning to dry out, how much pruning they each need. My favorite time of the day is when I watch the sunrise from the field surrounded by the bushes. I get a holistic sense of what this is all about."

"What good is a tea field at sunrise if you're lying dead in it? Listen, I'm going home to get myself ready. You should do the same. And whatever you do, don't answer the door."

"You must not come with me, Aloka. You'll lose it all—family, students, your friends, a whole way of life."

"But I'll have you, and that's all that really matters. Yes, it's been that way from the day I met you. . . ."

She caught his expression of awe as he looked up at her. "You're so good, Aloka. You're making the highest sacrifice for me. Do I deserve you? How will I ever live up to you?"

"Don't be silly."

She laughed off his attempts to put her above him. They were lovers, equals, and she held him in the highest regard. She knelt on the floor, drew him nearer, and planted a kiss on his lips. This was a kiss of confidence, a kiss to indicate all that he meant to her. His lips remained hard, immovable, and he didn't appear to be fully participating. Was it the stress of the moment, or had something been lost forever? She was no longer able to avoid considering the potential implications of the Sujata affair. Pranab might still be emotionally entangled with her. How long would that last? By now Sujata must already have reached Canada. No one knew her whereabouts or her address, Father had made sure of that. How would Pranab contact her, and vice versa? He was about to leave town, with no forwarding address. Away from the tea garden, their daily meetings curtailed, Pranab would forget Sujata. Surely he would. Over time that name would carry no more significance than a fallen tree on the streets of his memory. This notion, if illusory, gave Aloka the sense of optimism she needed to go on. She sprang up and looked through the window, which by now resembled a black mirror. There was no time to lose.

She collected her purse and told him of a specific place to meet. "We'll have to leave in the middle of the night so no one sees us. I haven't been able to reach Uncle Govinda this afternoon, but Auntie assured me he'd pick us up no later than ten-fifteen."

She studied Pranab. Fear and uncertainty had drawn a curtain over his eyes. His cheeks looked leaner. Perhaps suffering a feeling of danger, he rose, peered at her with a plea to save his life, and stood uncertainly. The enormity of her decision struck her. They were about to wipe out their existence from this beloved land. Pranab had once described Darjeeling as "snowfields, mountain quail, orchids with a honey fragrance, the air with an alpine tang, acres of tea fields, and us sharing it all."

Her voice didn't waver as she said, "Just a few more hours. We'll be together again."

Alone in her room, a fully packed suitcase sitting by the door, Aloka paced back and forth. The cool marble floor tugged at her bare feet. So much life had happened within these four walls, the center of her existence, and now she was forced to leave it all. Her eyes wandered lovingly over the furniture and the artifacts she'd long taken for granted: that half-read novel on the bedside table, the soft pillow that cradled her head at night, the black and yellow decorative vase on the shelf, throw cushions stitched from colorful textiles, and her photo album. In the warmth of this farewell glance, each was etched in her memory.

Then she heard familiar footsteps whose language she understood well. It was Father coming home, fatigued, with his back acting up again. She burst out of her room into the hall, hoping for a chance at reconciliation. Perhaps her presence would soothe him a bit, as it had invariably done in the past. But for the first time she couldn't come up with the right words to greet him as she waited at the doorstep.

He reached the top of the stairs and walked past her without turning, as though she were a phantom. No courtesy. No warmth. Not even a hint of recognition. The exaggerated sound of his shoes receded, leaving in its wake a sense of dark finality.

"Father!" she screamed after him, then stiffened in horror; she'd never done such a thing before.

He hesitated for a moment, stalked into his room, and slammed the door behind him without bothering to look in her direction. The sound shook her to the bone. She retreated into the cocoon of her room with a heaviness settling inside her.

Minutes later, leaning against the railing of her portico and still shivering, she asked herself: Would his suspicions, his feelings of betrayal be allayed if she knocked on his door and demanded to speak to him?

Just then she saw the lights in his window go off.

The instant the clock struck ten, Aloka sprang to her feet, took one last look around the room, hefted her suitcase, and stole through the back entrance. Misty pine-scented air formed a cloak about her as she scurried along the edge of the rear grounds, keeping to the shadows. Rounding the corner, she saw a blurry figure in white standing at a window on the ground floor. It could only be Grandma. Aloka paused, straining to see her face one last time and to receive her silent blessing, but she could make out only an imperfect outline through the misted window.

A light, hesitant rain began to fall. Her forehead and arms stung by icy drops, Aloka stood there and stifled a sob. How could she leave this birthplace, her moorings, and the sacred Himalayas? Then, out of the corner of her eye, she spotted a figure waiting under a juniper, its branches illuminated by the watery light of a street lamp. It was Pranab. Inside she felt the same sweet surge as on the first day they met.

Pranab stepped out toward her, reached for her arm, grasped it, and whispered, "I'm so relieved you got out okay."

"Let's go."

A wind howled at their backs as they half ran, half stumbled down a steep hillside, guided by a small flashlight. When her feet slipped on a rain-slick rock, she managed to pull herself up and keep going. What a relief it was to find Uncle Govinda waiting in his Jeep at the bottom of the hill. He opened the car door, let them in the back, and handed them two shawls.

"Cover yourselves up well," he whispered. His voice, caught up in the tension of the moment, had become hoarse. "I'll have to drive fast. We barely have enough time to make it to the train station."

Aloka was still panting when he revved up the engine. He negotiated the rough, hilly, twisty road, keeping a vigilant eye out for other vehicles. Aloka and Pranab slouched down in the backseat, their torsos and heads bundled in shawls. Each bump on the road gurgled through her; the zigzagging course made her feel nauseous.

After they'd passed the Darjeeling city limits, at Uncle Govinda's insistence Aloka chewed on a potato patty and gulped down a bottle of Limca. This settled her system a bit. She appreciated his kindness, even as she worried that family loyalties had been compromised beyond repair. Uncle Govinda, a kind and sedate man, was her father's first cousin and former classmate. She dropped that thought for now and watched with affection as a preoccupied Pranab stared listlessly out the window into the dense darkness. He was holding onto the edge of the seat with one hand. He seemed resigned to his uncertain future. Oddly enough, now that the waiting was over, she felt quietly confident. In fact, the idea of fleeing with Pranab filled her with anticipation. He was hers now, totally. She could revel in that reality.

Three hours later they reached Siliguri, a rustic town best known for its voracious mosquitoes, and pulled up at the train station. Seated on a bench at the platform, Aloka fought with the winged vermin. For every one she squished, two seemed to get through.

After a short wait they boarded a train for an overnight trip to Calcutta. By now fatigue had set in and she could barely feel her legs as they climbed into a compartment. Standing on the platform, Uncle Govinda dabbed at his eyes with a white handkerchief, then waved at them with it forlornly.

Aloka held Pranab's hand throughout the journey. If any danger awaited him, they would face it together.

The next morning they arrived at Salt Lake, a satellite city of Calcutta, where they took refuge in her friend's home. She was struck by the flatness of the landscape, the crowding, and the sultry air thick with soot.

"We shouldn't stay in the country much longer," she told Pranab after a week. "It's not safe, and in any case, since we need a new start, there's no point in procrastinating."

"Where can we go?"

"How does New York sound to you?"

"You used to teach a class on the States, didn't you?"

Aloka smiled in remembrance. The research for her class had paid off. She told him about New York's art, music, and literary scene, its lively Indian community, and job prospects. "New York has something for everybody, I'm told."

Pranab had some initial reservations, though finally he agreed. "I'm not too optimistic, but we'll give it a try." He reminded her that his nephews, who lived a short train ride away in New Jersey, didn't much care for New York City.

It took many months to complete the immigration formalities. While awaiting the arrival of their immigration papers, they private-tutored school-children in the neighborhood to earn pocket money, Aloka teaching English, and Pranab, Sanskrit. Aloka maintained tenuous contact with Grandma by sending letters secretly through a friend so her father wouldn't know her whereabouts. Grandma answered every letter, mentioning at one point that Father had fallen ill.

To hide her identity, Aloka kept her head veiled whenever she went out. Pranab grew a beard and wore sunglasses. He believed he was followed a few times, but nothing ever came of it and the days passed until their immigration papers finally came through.

On May 1, much to Aloka's relief, they landed in New York to begin what she hoped would be an exciting new time. If the sight of the Statue of Liberty from her plane window brought a few sentimental tears to her eyes, she hid them well from Pranab.

fourteen

1993

Aloka had just slipped into a bra with lacy cups and a full skirt reaching her knees when she heard Pranab murmuring from the other side of the room, "Where are you going, *priyatama?*"

She turned swiftly, reveling in the soft slippery sensation of the skirt's fabric next to her skin. Sprawled on the bed, hugging a pillow, Pranab was watching her with eyes still dark and luminous from their lovemaking. His face, open and defenseless, radiated a masculine vitality, even as the window behind him filled with mauve evening shadows. She brought the past hour back to her mind, saw it as the prolonged time and care that a fruit takes to ripen. Her skin and flesh suffused with blood, her body felt acutely alive. There came over her a sense of weightlessness, of release, as if her being were expanding to encompass a larger reality.

A yearning for closeness and affection and a desire to please seeped into her. She forced herself to finish buttoning the sleeves of her blouse and strutted to the middle of the room, where she flung her arms out and gave him a kiss.

"Where am I going, you ask?" She looked around the shabby, overpriced studio they'd leased in Manhattan. "To my baby-sitting job, *amaar priya.*"

He grimaced and turned over on his back. "Isn't it awful, the kinds of jobs we have to take here?"

"But at least we're safe and happy. And we have each other. What more could we ask?"

He fell silent, a heavy silence she couldn't penetrate.

On the long hike to her baby-sitting job, Aloka had a chance to assess her current situation. They'd been living in New York four months now. Her optimistic outlook about immigrating here had produced results: Once again they were close. They shared the same towels, the same pillow, as well as problems and frustrations with trying to adjust to this new life. In this alien environment they were forced to depend on each other. Most importantly, they were far away from Bir's wrath and the corporeal danger it had threatened. Pranab had grown stress-free and was back to being his old self. Lately he had even been hinting about getting married. Aloka took that as a sign of deep commitment, as well as of his settling down. She wanted to wait, however, until they both had secured permanent positions and could afford a wedding ceremony.

Although Aloka was happy within the four walls of their tiny apartment, she was baffled by the ways of the new world outside. Everyone seemed in a tremendous hurry regardless of the time of day or the nature of the activity. Long used to the elaborate politeness and sedate pace of the Bengali society, she found it difficult to fathom the undercurrent of irritation that seemed to lurk beneath the surface of even the most banal conversation. Thus it had come as a shock when, on her second day in New York, a waitress in a coffee shop snapped at her. "You want hotter coffee? Everybody wants everything right now, just the way they like it, lady!"

Aloka had thrown a few dollar bills on the counter and walked out. She waded into the concrete ocean, through the raucous traffic, the Band-Aid strip of sky above offering faint solace, realizing it would require a combination of a blind faith and a superhuman constitution to survive here.

Soon, however, she was swept up by the city's crazy rhythm. What a mind-expanding and body-loosening experience for someone raised in a provincial town like Darjeeling, to wander out of a Dale Chihuly glass exhibit and munch on a knish, while swaying to the beat of a reggae street band. She came to understand why so many people were drawn to this outwardly brusque, even rude city: If New York made them feel small, insignificant, and unloved, it also offered them a broader, more exalted sense of what was possible.

On her own she would meander for hours. The incongruities mystified her. In the shadow of gleaming skyscrapers, fetid slums with broken sidewalks festered. Many nights she went to bed disturbed, yet awoke to a cool, fresh Manhattan morning, with the aroma of brioche baking somewhere. That beckoned her to make a clean start.

In between part-time jobs as a baby-sitter, henna artist, truck accessories salesperson, and grant writer for New York University, she explored new enclaves: Soho, Washington Square, the United Nations, Little Italy. She discovered a comedy cellar, a transit museum, industrial music, chestnut vendors, and a carriage house converted into a library of books on transportation. On Sundays she would invariably end up in a bazaar set up on outdoor tables and racks along a stretch of Second Avenue, where native-born and immigrants alike gathered to gawk, haggle, gossip, and search for bargains. It overjoyed her that even though Manhattan belonged to the affluent and the glitterati, much of the city moved to the beat of the common man and the less well heeled.

Despite all the excitement and novelty, at times she longed to return to the life she'd left behind. She called this the "immigrant condition": Never to laugh the deepest possible laugh or give oneself over to the possibilities of life in a new land without the niggling awareness of a vague dissatisfaction, doomed to find in every meal a missing course.

Meanwhile, Pranab had retreated into his Sanskrit books, declining invitations to join her on her urban safaris. "The streets all look the same, just pizza signs and 'Going Out of Business' notices, never a hint of anything refined," he would sneer, ignoring her glowing descriptions of art galleries and museums. He didn't even laugh as he attributed it all to Kaliyug, which according to Hindu mythology was the world's fourth, current age, an age of decadence and decline. She grew weary of his negative outlook. In Manhattan, she'd found "home and the world," to borrow a Tagore phrase from her youth, while he seemed to have lost both, along with his sense of humor.

Early in his search for employment, Pranab had typed a lengthy application for a Sanskrit professorship at a local university and waited with high hopes, only to be rejected. He learned later that a Dane—also a Sanskrit scholar—had filled the position. "Never mind. I'll teach Bengali!" he exclaimed. The opportunities turned out to be even scantier there. Only five universities in the entire nation taught Bengali and none had a vacancy.

Pranab would trudge in with the mail and read aloud to her the occasional communiqués from the tea workers. They were satisfied with their pay raise and ecstatic to have running water in their homes. They missed his inspiring talks, they insisted, though it was clear that their militancy had been diminished by management concessions. "*Maharani* takes care of us." They praised Grandma. "She understands what we need to make ends meet."

Pranab would put the dispatch aside and mumble that he needed to find some worthy cause where his talents could be put to use. Aloka made calls on his behalf and came up with a list. Pranab declined most of them as beneath his dignity, but finally agreed to volunteer with the Free Tibet movement. At first it seemed that he'd found his niche. Each evening he would stride out the door and return a few hours later full of enthusiasm for the justness of the Tibetan struggle. But gradually the energy seemed to seep out of him and he would return silent and morose.

"It's just not the same," he bemoaned after a month. "All I do is stuff envelopes and file petition papers like a faceless robot. In Darjeeling, I was a leader."

Five more months passed by. Letters from the tea workers had ceased altogether and Pranab's mood deteriorated further.

Then one snowy evening a phone call from Uncle Umesh brought the news of Father's death, the result of a massive heart attack. The receiver still in her hand, Aloka sank to her knees, sobbing.

"Aloka, you mustn't . . ." came Uncle Umesh's tinny voice.

He reminded her of the ancient Hindu saying—death is not finality, but release from suffering—though Aloka remained inconsolable. She'd deserted her father, this an act beyond forgiveness. Her absence had caused a void in her father's life, one that had left him with little incentive to live. The next day she went to a local Hindu temple, placed an earthen lamp brimming with oil on the altar before the deity, and made circular movements with a burning *dhoop* to honor her father's spirit and purify her mind. It tormented her for weeks that they couldn't afford to fly back for the cremation.

Over time, her grief and anger melting into compassion, Aloka reflected on how much Bir must have suffered, what a price he'd paid. As she would scrub a pot in the kitchen sink or rub the surface of the wooden dining table with furniture polish, she would ask herself, but then why had he been so vengeful toward Pranab and forced her to choose between them? What was it about Pranab that had so enraged him?

The following March, Aloka and Pranab were married in a simple civil ceremony. She had a party in their apartment for close friends, with a seven-course meal beautifully catered by the Taj Dinner Service. Shortly after, they announced the news to their relatives in Darjeeling. Gifts and congratulatory notes came pouring in. It saddened Aloka that Grandma sent a rose *tussar* silk sari embroidered in silver thread and an identical choli instead of the family heirloom, a sunburst-shaped gold pendant, that Aloka had been promised as a young girl.

Finally it was safe to return to Darjeeling. With Grandma running the tea estate once again, albeit with the help of a manager, the threat hanging over Pranab's head was gone. Aloka pined for her family, her large circle of friends, and the succor of those who cared about her. She missed the pupils in her geography class. Even now she could visualize their trusting gazes and hear their adolescent chatter echoing in the halls between classes, their attempts to catch her eyes when she passed by. But most of all she hungered for their childish enthusiasm for life.

What would be the point of returning? Pranab was reluctant to pay even a short visit.

A fallen leader has no place in the territory he has lost.

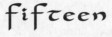

fifteen

Summer 2000

Aloka left her Union Square office at six. As she stepped outside, the remains of a balmy seventy-degree Manhattan day immersed her in a buoyant mood, just as it had seven summers ago when she and Pranab first arrived in New York. Tonight she wasn't taking work home, for a change. Instead she planned to observe May 1 by taking him out to dinner at one of her favorite bistros.

It had not always been this way. The first couple of years in this pricey town, when she had been forced to take several part-time jobs, it'd been necessary to count every dime. But now that she was well established in her position as a reporter for *Manhattan, India*, with a promotion on its way, the pocketbook was less of a concern.

On the street Aloka joined a throng of pedestrians, part of the five million people who poured into and out of Manhattan every day to work. How well she blended in. At five-foot-five, with ivory skin, lustrous black hair sweeping down over her shoulders, high cheekbones, and a Bloomingdale's dress billowing about her ample thighs, she was just one of the countless transplants who called New York home. She found herself sandwiched momentarily between a blowsy woman and an elderly man who was mumbling obscenities to no one in particular. Seven years ago, this would have unsettled her; now she thought nothing of it.

Pranab's situation, on the other hand hadn't improved much. Like her, he was initially forced to accept a series of menial positions out of desperation, first as a tree stump remover, then as a Xerox operator at a copy shop, finally as a clerk with New York Life. Recently he'd found full-time employment as a telephone repairman. He was devastated when his mother, on hearing the news, wrote to him, "So, now you get a decent wage and have security, but what about all those years of studying Sanskrit? Every now and then, when I get your school medals out of the trunk and look at them, I just shake my head and think 'all that work.' "

Still, if anyone were to ask, Aloka would say that they'd been reasonably happy together the first six years here. She recalled their last wedding anniversary, when they'd taken a stroll together down a tree-lined street in Manhattan. Over the faint crunching of dry leaves underfoot, he'd hummed a Sanskrit verse in a soothing voice: " 'I can only offer you a crown of velvet leaves, you, the lovely maiden.' "

Aloka arrived now at the subway entrance. On the artificially lit platform, surrounded by strangers, she reflected on Pranab and the changes he had undergone. The once-loquacious man had grown silent. His mobile face had become an expressionless mask. The boisterous laugh that used to ripple through the entire upper half of his body had subsided into an occasional sneering chuckle. His sullen presence rendered their once-cheerful home a claustrophobic prison. Head down, face frozen in a grimace, he would alternately pace back and forth or flop down on a couch where he'd sit motionless for hours. He took to clearing his throat before he spoke; he began to wear darker colors. Lately he had even stopped drinking tea. He smoked an occasional cigarette. But worst of all was his inability to accept her devotion and belief in his potential. She had continued to cook his much-loved

Bengali dinners of *kumro bhate* and *maach bhaja*, tidy his study, buy books suited to his taste, and lend him a concerned ear whenever he needed it— all out of genuine love. Yet the issue of respect, so important in the tradition they both had grown up in, hung in the air like summer smog. For a whole year she'd sensed his growing fear that she no longer respected him. She had never lost respect. "I love you, I respect you," she'd reassured him time and again.

Just the night before, she'd waited for him to come home. He walked in silently, a scowl on his face, eyes ablaze with helpless anger. "You know," he began, "I was standing on a traffic island on Park Avenue, waiting for the light to change, when this old hag stuck a leaflet in my face. She nearly cut my cheek. As if I gave a damn about palm reading. The police should arrest people like her."

Two nights before that, he'd told her a similar story. A waiter had brought him pizza for lunch instead of the salad he'd ordered and hadn't even bothered to apologize, much less take it back. And surely he would never have disembarked at the wrong subway station if the signs had not been defaced by a gang of young hooligans.

Worst of all, he'd complained, he barely received a nod from his customers in his new job as a telephone repairman. No longer was he at the center of his social and political universe. Though they'd befriended Dr. and Mrs. Chopra, engineer Partho Banerjee and his teacher wife Suparna, and architect Sushil Nayak and his actress wife, Manka, it greatly annoyed him that his acquaintances weren't interested in discussing India's defense budget, the severity of its urban pollution, the threats to its press, or the caste and communal strains. Indeed, they preferred to talk about the New York club scene, budget vacation packages to Bermuda, the stock market, or the Yankees.

The whole environment reeked of commerce and vulgarity, he criticized, and the city was sterile—nothing but steel, concrete, chrome, and glass, a greedy mouth in constant need of feeding. The maple and the pear trees on the sidewalk were withering, and was it any wonder that the people were so unfeeling and aloof? "They don't even give me the propriety of a glance, Aloka," he spoke of crowds in general. "I'm invisible."

His gloomy outlook hung like a faded garland around his neck. She admitted now, as she got into a subway train, that his endless litany of injustices, real or perceived, was growing increasingly monotonous. She could confront him and tell him to come out of his funk—but then, could she? In India she'd been taught to cater to a man's wishes, not challenge him. Modern woman that she had been, she still couldn't quite shake herself out of traditional ways. She offered him larger servings at dinner, let him sleep on the window side of the bed, even made sure he got first chance at the front section of the *New York Times* in the morning. Right now she glanced up at the conch shell bracelets, conventionally worn by married Bengali women, that clung to her arms as she held on to a handrail in the subway car to keep from falling.

Difficult as it had been, she still cared about him and wanted to hold their marriage together at all cost. Once more she blamed herself. Would all this have come to pass if they'd stayed in India? Would Pranab have been a different person, happier and more successful there?

A man standing a few feet away and bouncing from the ride gave her a casual look. This reminded her: Pranab no longer gazed deep into her eyes.

And he'd taken to staying out late night after night. They were living like two birds placed in separate cages. Friends had hinted that he was having an affair with a colleague. Aloka had brushed off the suggestion, though it had gnawed at her. Now that a seat was empty, Aloka sat down.

She believed it was still possible to bring the thrill back to their marriage. Tonight at a leisurely dinner she'd suggest ways. She'd phoned him earlier and asked him to come home on time. Candlelight, soft music, linen table-cloth, flowers, grand cuisine, and her feminine wiles ought to set the right atmosphere.

The subway train had just reached her station. Aloka eased out of her seat and glided through the length of the platform, passing some funky odor on the way. As she approached the turnstile, a buzzing drew her attention to a half-extinguished fluorescent tube with an intermittent blue glare. She hastened her walk.

The apartment was dark when Aloka let herself in, and she felt her limbs stiffening. Absence of light conveyed an absence of welcome. Might Pranab be working late? But then, he'd promised to join her for dinner. Even before taking her coat off, she hurried across the living room and peeked into the bedroom. Sure enough, there he was, sitting on the bed, half hidden in the late afternoon shadows, head bowed, shoulders hunched, hands stiff on his thighs, his black T-shirt rumpled and stretched across his back. He didn't look up as she stood in the doorway and peeled her coat off.

She was about to turn the light switch on, then, on second thought, decided against it. She approached him, murmuring soft words, one hand extended to caress his cheek.

At her touch he brushed her hand away and lurched up from the bed. In a low voice, he muttered, "I've been waiting for you, Aloka. Listen, I don't want to go out to dinner, we need to talk."

His coldness hit her like a swift punch to the belly. Short of breath, she propped her coat on the floor, which was totally out of character, and pulled a chair over. The screeching sound provided just the distraction she needed to partially regain her poise. He sat down at the edge of the bed, not opposite her but at an angle, and a little too far away.

"I've been doing a lot of thinking." He brushed his hair back with his fingers, a habit he displayed when he was unsure of himself. She noticed the hesitant fingers curling up. "I don't think it's working out between us, Aloka. Much as it hurts me, I'm moving out."

"Moving out? But why?" The words came out thin and tinged with panic. She hadn't faced such an enormous question in years, nor a more excruciating rejection. And this situation had sneaked up without advance notice. "True, we've had some rough times, as every couple does, but we're finally settled here and we're getting along fine." She tried gamely to end the sentence on a cheery note.

"You might think so, but that's certainly not true for me." The grim pause that followed underlined his remark. "I haven't found a new niche ever since I left Darjeeling. Here I merely exist, floating from activity to activity, but I keep most of me suppressed. It's like I've lost my compass. I must find it and get my direction back. And I can only do that on my own."

She recalled a bit of advice Uncle Umesh had given her early on about the long narrow winding streets of her hilly hometown: If the direction you're pursuing is the wrong one, then simply turn back and attempt a different route, but never lose sight of the ultimate destination. Growing up, she'd taken that as a guiding principle in life. But did Pranab really need such a philosophical answer? Was a lack of direction really the reason?

Now the question that had been bothering her a long time popped out of her mouth unbidden. "Is there someone else?" His silence was eloquent and slapped at her already agitated cheeks. She fought the urge to jump up and run out of the room; instead she pressed on. "I'm at a loss. Where did I fail, will you tell me?"

"It's not really your fault," he replied at length in a dispassionate tone. "Yes, as a matter of fact, there have been others on occasion, but they're only a symptom. Our problems are deeper than that."

She suppressed the rage that had displaced her initial feeling of shock and panic. "Do you have any idea how humiliating it is to hear you admit that? Would you at least give me the courtesy of explaining just exactly what those deeper reasons are?"

"I'm not the man you fell in love with, Aloka. Maybe I never was that man. Oh, yes, you saw some qualities in me that you liked, formed those into an idealized image, then worshiped that image. But you never had any idea how unhappy the real me was. My life has been reduced to a monotonous ticking of the heart, nothing more." He swallowed hard and went on. "Sorry, but marrying you hasn't given me the blissful life I'd hoped for. I don't sleep well at night—I carry such a full load of sadness in me. The pain is even more unbearable in the daytime. But how can I expect you to understand that? You're such a success."

She swallowed the insult dripping from those words. He still hadn't gotten around to the real reason. As she watched him slip his feet into his shoes and start tying the shoelaces, she realized she had little time left. "We've gone through worse together and this is the first time you're being open about it. It's a good start. Maybe we can talk more and resolve the issues between us. There's nothing we can't resolve if we put our heads together, I really believe that. Shall we give it a try? I care so deeply about you, *amaar priya*. I've given you my all. Please don't throw it away like this."

"You've been wasting your love." He raised his head from his shoes. "I don't care to live with you anymore. The worst loneliness is when you're with the wrong person, when you don't care to speak."

Wrong person. The words injured her worse than the blow of a newly sharpened ax, and brought with it a new suspicion. "I'm not the right woman, but Sujata is? What is it about her that—"

"You're beyond reasoning. Please, get on with your life, Aloka, and let me get on with mine."

Before her disbelieving eyes, he pivoted and started to stride out of the room. "Oh, please, Pranab! Don't do this!" she stood up and implored him.

No turning, not even a mumble of a good-bye. The emptiness swirling around her offered the curtest reply. Now, even more inflamed, she wanted to shriek equally damaging words at his disappearing back: He wouldn't be alive without her; he'd lived off her for years; how dare he call her the "wrong person" when in reality he hadn't fulfilled his responsibilities as a husband at all. But the sounds remained trapped in her vocal cords, a swarm of frustrated bees buzzing in a confined area. She pressed her lips tight. She'd never stood up to him; that was not the way of a Hindu woman, and this one last time would be no different. However difficult, she would give him respect and honor his wish. The loss had so paralyzed her that suddenly it all seemed meaningless anyway. Standing there, hands clenching and unclenching, she watched the darkening sky weave a charcoal web on the window.

sixteen

Autumn 2000

As usual, this morning Suzy (these days she thought of herself as Sujata only in relation to her family in Darjeeling) looked out through her living room window at the jagged blue-gray pinnacles that rose above a bank of fog across the Juan de Fuca Strait. How small the Olympic Mountains seemed compared to the soaring drama of Kanchenjunga, the third highest peak in the world, the "roof that grazed heaven." She hadn't experienced a sunrise over that heavenly roof, the uplifting sight of red-orange grandeur spread over the eternity of blue, in far too many years now.

She went over to the desk of her home office. Sorting through yesterday's mail, she came across a flimsy blue envelope with a Darjeeling address. Feeling a knot in her throat, she set it down. All of Grandma's kind correspondence in these eight years couldn't erase the fact that she'd sent Suzy to an exile in Victoria, British Columbia. Yet as she stared at the shaky script, she gradually began to feel the way she did as a five-year-old. In those days she had clutched the *aanchal* of Grandma's sari and trailed along behind her, the demigoddess in whose exalted presence she felt safe and pampered.

Lifting the letter now, Suzy sensed this wasn't one of Grandma's little periodical notes, but rather that it was an announcement of some sort. What could it be? With a flick of a letter opener, she slit the envelope. She skimmed the pleasantries, then chuckled at Grandma's comment on how Indian nursery rhymes were finally being changed: Mary and her little lamb had become Meera and her little cat. She scanned quickly until she found the pulse of the letter.

> *Whatever else I might forget, and I have forgotten plenty during the long days we've been apart, I will never misplace your sweet face in my heart. With your little hands in mine, I taught you how to walk.*

Suzy smiled in relief. At least it wasn't a funeral.

> *Throughout these past eight forlorn years, your touch has been with me. Might I now ask you to put your hand in mine one more time? Would you come home to celebrate my birthday on November 16? Come at least a week early so we can spend some time together before other guests arrive.*

Suzy fell back in her chair limply. How could she return to Darjeeling?

She'd have to face Aloka, kneel before her father's ashes, revisit a turbulent period of her life, and be cast back into the agony of her tragic affair with Pranab. He came dancing to her consciousness now, taller and larger than anyone she'd ever known, and never lacking in surprises. Her breasts still ached for the touch of his fingers. It made her ecstatic even now to remember how he had needed her with the desperation of a madman, a drunk, a drowning swimmer.

Her ecstasy was cut short by the realization that he was living with Aloka, apparently happily, while she was still single at thirty-six.

How shameful that must be for the Guptas. Grandma had been married at nineteen, Mother at twenty-two, and Aloka at thirty-three. How would

Suzy return to the family-centered town without a mate? Aloka and Pranab, an amorous married couple, all starlight and sitar, would receive cordial glances of approval. Suzy, on the other hand, would get narrow, speculative looks from her kinsmen for being lone, separate, and unworthy.

Her mind raced through the excuses she would have to use to avoid the discomfort that awaited her there: illness, professional obligations, her apartment being broken into, even fear of earthquake in India.

None would appease Grandma.

The air in the room felt tyrannical. Suzy went over to the window, opened it wide, and savored the tangy breeze coming from the ocean across the avenue. The beagle from the next house barked. Fond memories of Darjeeling flashed before her: hillsides splashed with rhododendrons in brilliant purple and crimson; the three-note calls of the blue-throated barbets; mingled snippets of Hindi, Tibetan, Nepalese, and a dozen tribal dialects in the bazaar; fragrant wood smoke; the delicate tinkle of evening bells in the temple; tiny tea shops with their offer of scented mementos. She recalled one of the commonly uttered blessings in that hilly region: "May you climb from peak to peak." Yet the very notion of seeing those peaks filled her with apprehension.

Should she call Aloka? Ties between them had the fragility of spun sugar and none of its sweetness. And what if Pranab answered? Suzy sighed. Perhaps later.

The telephone rang. Suzy deliberated a moment, then picked up the receiver and was relieved when it turned out to be her assistant at her wholesale tea business. The young Janaki, who was also her niece, went by the name Jane.

"Good morning, Auntie," Jane said. "It's not been very busy. Only one new order has come." She proceeded to give Suzy a roster of calls to return, then asked for instructions on how to set up the display room.

"It's going to be an important demonstration," Suzy told her. "We need to perk up sales. Use our best china and silverware. Make sure they're spotlessly clean, but don't match everything."

"My sentiments exactly. It looks *so* institutional when everything matches," Jane replied archly before hanging up.

Even though it was comforting to know that Jane was learning the business well, Suzy felt a whiff of guilt. How could she take time off for an extended period and thereby burden her young niece with extra responsibilities?

The wall clock read eleven-thirty. With a two P.M. tea demonstration looming, Suzy decided to wait until later to sort through the implications of Grandma's summons. She returned the phone calls, lunched on freshly cooked rice and leftover *labra*. The spicy seven-vegetable stew redolent with anise seeds had sustained her since childhood. It was one of the few dishes she had mastered—she wasn't much of a cook otherwise. Following lunch, she wrapped herself in a subtle lilac-blue silk sari. In this flowing garment she slowed down, floated through space, exhibited a softer side of herself.

On the way out, Suzy checked her reflection in the hall mirror. Rich black waves of long hair tied in the back framed the confident outline of her face. At thirty-six, Suzy could finally discern a presentable woman in the image she projected.

The beagle from the next house barked again and possibly danced around in jolly anticipation, as it always did when Suzy pulled out of the garage. On the weekend she would take the dog out for a romp on the beach. Now she drove toward downtown Victoria. Her preferred route included James Bay Inn, several mom-and-pop grocery stores, and the National Museum. A Royal Blue Line motor coach approached from the opposite direction, taking sightseers on an excursion through the greenery and scenery of the greater Victoria area. Eight years ago, she had been such a tourist herself when, at Grandma's behest, she had emigrated here and begun a new life. Uncle Kumud and his wife, who lived in the Fraser Valley, had provided financial and emotional assistance and treated her as their own daughter, thereby alleviating much of the initial loneliness. She had never felt more accepted and welcomed, or more determined to succeed. And living in this quaint island capital had helped. Neat and compact as a rosebud, Victoria exuded grace and gentility that suited her taste. Like Darjeeling, another popular resort, Victoria had learned to survive the annual hordes of summer tourists. The similarities made the exile bearable, even satisfying.

Suzy cruised by a branch of Scotia Bank. Soon after her arrival, her college degrees and previous banking experience had landed her a position here. For five years she kept her head down at her desk and accrued several pay increases and a promotion, all the while tolerating the stiff suits, pointless paperwork, measured conversations, and cubicles that confined her vision.

She arrived at 200 Bastion Square, a vintage brick building smothered by ivy. She parked in a parking space reserved for her and glanced up at the "Anytime Is Teatime" signboard above the entrance. Under the name was etched her trademark of a pair of tea leaves and a single bud. As soon as she'd become financially able, she'd struck out on her own. Over the last three years, she'd established a small wholesale business selling imported tea. Anyone searching under "Tea" in the Victoria Yellow Pages would have no trouble locating her; with her typical Gupta flair, she had taken out an eye-catching half-page advertisement for Anytime Is Teatime. In this city, fine tea expressed nuances of silk gloves, elaborate necklaces, ornate parlors, and discreet whispers. Suzy hoped to overcome that reputation and insinuate the beverage into the consciousness of the young and the hip as well as the staid segment of the society to whom coarser tea had long been a practice. Everyone should indulge in the pleasures of a light, lively, and health-giving cup of quality tea, Suzy often argued. Still, it hadn't been easy. Most consumers didn't want to pay an exorbitant amount for fine tea, as they would for fine food.

Upon entering the office, Suzy took an immediate left to the display room, distinguished by a high ceiling and the soft sheen of its polished maple floor. This was where she held seminars for retailers and the public, as well as special events for the press, in her attempts to educate people in tea. Group tastings had proved to be popular. Floor-to-ceiling windows admitted plenty of natural light, though no direct sun, and allowed no shadows. In tea tasting, often called the "art of reading tea," ample, uniform lighting was essential; perception of color played a significant role.

Suzy eyed the setup. All five tables were laid with crisp white linen, Limoges teacups, gold-plated spoons, strainers, crystal sugar bowls, and a product list. A sideboard set against the east wall held colorful canisters of her company's premium offerings.

At two, prospective clients, mostly men, began to wander in. The first to arrive were chefs and buyers from several restaurants, most of whom she had already met. One of her consulting efforts involved pairing various dishes with the right blends of tea. Next came four managers from the

Country Grocer chain. Suzy shook hands with a controlled exuberance, always maintaining eye contact. If she felt shy as a single woman among a group of mostly married men, she didn't reveal so.

She looked over to the door just as dark-haired, dark-eyed Ashraf Hamid, owner of Celeste Restaurant, sauntered in. Suzy had yet to try that restaurant, whose name had been popping up lately in newspaper food columns. He reminded her of someone, this man, who was smiling broadly through a set of sparkling teeth. The collar tabs of his navy shirt formed parentheses around his salt-and-pepper beard. Shaking her hand, he asked, "Is Suzy your real name?"

"No, my folks call me Sujata." Suzy removed her hand from his grip. Practicality and the fact her clients might be put off by a foreign name had prompted her to adopt a Western diminutive. Over time, she had begun to like the short, brisk sound of the new designation. "Suzy's the Canadian version."

The manager of an Italian bakery, a six-foot-six giant with red hair and beard, lumbered up and extended a huge paw. "I have to admit I'm a confirmed coffee drinker, signora. Tea tastes weak to me. It's more a lady's drink, I suppose."

"Perhaps you're using inferior leaves," Suzy replied. "Or perhaps you're not preparing it properly."

Before Red Beard could retort, Suzy asked everyone to take a seat. While chairs creaked against the floor and expectancy rose, she tucked the loose end of her sari around her waist with a businesslike promptness. Standing poised, she issued a formal welcome to all. She explained how she'd been reared on the family-owned tea estate in Darjeeling and how the beverage had become her life's passion at an early age. Her family didn't merely produce tea, they offered a way of life. As a teenager she had mastered tea preparation, the first consideration being the water. And so she began her presentation with an emphasis on this important ingredient: water. "Poor water amounts to poor tea."

"Is that all tea is?" Red Beard said. "Good water?"

"No! Just as important is the freshness and age of the leaves." Suzy directed everyone's attention to the sideboard, where representative samples of a dozen bulk teas stood in canisters. The precious leaves—crisp, twisted, and uniformly black, many with golden tips—had been imported from various tea-growing regions of Asia and selected for their unique taste, color, bouquet, and strength. "The younger the leaf, the better the quality."

Red Beard stroked the wiry hair that jutted from his chin. "You mean I can't use tea bags?"

"Only if you're in such a hurry that you can't help it." Suzy couldn't resist boasting that she didn't sell tea bags. Derogatively referred to by connoisseurs as floor dustings and labeled low grade by manufacturers, the tea found in tea bags yielded a fraction of the flavor of the whole leaves.

The plug-in electric pot whistled. Suzy moved to the sideboard, poured water, and listened to the trickling sound as she brewed six different specialty black teas in as many porcelain pots. A giddy aroma curled up in the air and a hopeful hum spread among the tables. "Steep three to five minutes max. Don't stew it. And voilà, it's ready!"

She outlined the tasting procedure: Take a small sip and swish the tea liquor around in your mouth. Note the flavor, the strength, and the briskness. Check for color, "nose," and smoothness. Soon her enthusiastic pupils were expressing their opinions in professional terms such as, "malty," "bright," "bracing," and "clean."

A tea-tasting episode with Pranab came dashing to her mind. How he said it all in one breath: "This is superfine, tippy, golden, flowery, first-flush Darjeeling." Then, after tasting several more blends, he would say, "The first tea has a green, immature taste. This second one is more balanced. This third one is very female." And he would give her an affectionate look.

Seeing Ashraf pucker his mouth after swallowing a pungent Ceylon blend, Suzy slid a steaming pitcher of scalded milk toward him.

He pushed the pitcher aside and raised a disdainful chin. "In my country," he said, "we drink tea straight. Only children are given tea with milk."

Irritation percolated through Suzy's body. Grandma always added milk to even the finest Darjeeling harvest, which is conventionally savored for its lightness, bouquet, and apricot-yellow color. Grandma's stomach could no longer tolerate the acidity due to her advancing age. She insisted that milk toned down the "bite" of tea.

"Milk is optional," now Suzy replied, "but I highly recommend it. It gives the tea a fuller taste and masks the bitterness of the tannic acid."

"What's wrong with tannic acid?" Ashraf countered. "My grandfather, who lived to be seventy-six, drank black tea even on his deathbed."

"My grandmother adds milk to her tea. She's eighty-one and still alive."

Ashraf clamped his jaw shut, as though suppressing a smile, finally offering weakly, "But you lose the beautiful color."

Red Beard grabbed the milk pitcher, splashed some milk into his cup, watched the color transformation, and observed, "Personally, I'd rather live to be eighty-one."

Ashraf lowered his eyes in defeat. Again an image of Pranab rippled before Suzy, how he once provoked interest in her about a natural plant compound, polyphenol, that gave tea its astringency.

As the assemblage happily sniffed, imbibed, and rated the mélange of brews, Suzy began to feel alone and separate. What bond did she have with anybody here? She was merely performing a function. Grandma's invitation rolled before her mind's eye. Grandma, who emphasized the "emotional" value of tea: affection and reliability.

Suzy stepped over to the window with a cup of her favorite Darjeeling and traced the curvature of the handle with her fingers. Immediately she linked with the long-gone years. The delicate china reminded her of the fragility of the leaves, fragility of human existence. As taught by her family long ago, she inhaled the rising aroma, or the "breath of tea," to savor the fruity bouquet and cleanse her system. Finally, she took a sip. A smooth, complex taste, reminiscent of fresh peaches, spread across her palate. The tea nourished her soul, the way even the scantiest rainwater nourishes the roots of a tree.

The tasting over, Jane circulated among the tables, taking the few bulk orders for tea that came in. Suzy hovered in the background, listening to the muted tinkling of spoons and murmurs of conversation, hoping for more sales.

"I didn't mean any disrespect, sister." Ashraf signed an order for several boxes of golden-tipped tea. "In Morocco, we argue for fun."

Suzy relaxed her frown and smiled at him in concurrence. "In India we do the same." She reminisced how at home she argued with Grandma about the merits of a Ritwik Ghatak film, why India was the world's largest buyer of gold, or why the country had one of the highest savings rates in the world.

The topic was inconsequential; it was the loving openness and good-natured repartee that mattered. Voices rose due to interest and absorption in the subject matter rather than animosity. How Suzy missed that convivial atmosphere. What would life be like if she never saw Grandma again?

Singly, then in twos and threes, the guests rose and took their leave. Ashraf hung back after the others had left, "sistering" her some more. Just before slipping out the door, he gushed, "You must come to my restaurant sometime for dinner. You'll be my honored guest."

Suzy mumbled a vague promise, belatedly realizing this extrovert merely wanted to strike up good relations and that this was his playful, if clumsy, approach. It grated on her that she had become bureaucratic and restrained to the point where she had forgotten the old, nonlinear social ways.

Going home that evening, Suzy took a longer route. Somehow she seemed to think well when she was on the move. She drove through the Heritage District, with its rows of remodeled homes, then circled Beacon Hill Park, slowing down to catch a look at the arbutus grove and the ducks floating on the limpid surface of a pond. At the ever-mobbed ice-cream stand a grandmother tried in vain to keep a toddler from painting his cheeks with an ice-cream cone. It all seemed scenic, even idyllic, but distant as a picture postcard in a bulletin board. She didn't feel intimate with this environment. Even the biggest festivals here didn't arouse sensation in her the way a simple song of wrens in her family farm did.

She arrived at her apartment building and, after parking her car in the garage, took the elevator to the third floor and let herself into her apartment. Her feelings of vacillation had evaporated. Impatiently she hung her coat on a hanger by the door. Yes, she *would* attend Grandma's birthday festivities. She rushed to the computer and selected a sheet of her company's letterhead stationery in a cream color. It bothered her a little to use the computer for such a personal correspondence, but her handwriting was notoriously illegible. She sat for a few minutes, organizing her thoughts, then began keying in a quick note; composing long letters simply didn't suit her. After the salutation and elaborate ritual pleasantries, the body of the letter seemed almost a postscript:

I'll be there by the 28th. It has been far too long.

Your loving granddaughter,
Sujata

She enclosed a recent clipping from the *Victoria Times Colonist* about her enterprise (with a picture of her standing in the display room behind a tower of tea boxes) and sealed the envelope.

What a fabulous opportunity to show them all. The nonconformist girl, nobody's darling, emigrates to the West and becomes an entrepreneur in the best Gupta tradition. She returns to her home transformed—poised, charming, witty, and sophisticated.

They would see that she was Aloka's equal—at last.

seventeen

Perched on a straight-backed chair in the drawing room, Nina took her morning tea. Her mood leisurely, she envisioned the social gatherings to take place on the occasion of her eighty-first birthday in just over a month. A profusion of red roses, often called blood roses, interspersed with violet orchids in a mass design, would grace every nook. Nina was once poor and hadn't been able to afford high-priced flowers, so now she indulged in them on the slightest pretext. Relatives and acquaintances would troop into the house, their fine saris rustling; and yes, pants and miniskirts, too (however much Nina disapproved of them). Gold, silver, and precious stones would flash, as would glass and cheap metal trinkets, these being the modern times. Spiked heels would clack on the floors, their heights causing Nina to grimace with distaste. Laughter, murmurings, and cigarette smoke (hopefully not mingled with that of another weed favored by the younger set) would pervade the air. Servants would ferry platters of *nonta* and *mishti,* savory and sweet tidbits, to the dining room table, the aromas teasing the senses and inviting intimacy. Friends would abandon their cares in the excitement of a festive occasion and the chance to meet with the lucky "America-returned" people.

Just as Nina tried to picture Aloka, Sujata, and Pranab in the room, all smiling brightly, the maidservant announced the arrival of her friend Tami. Nina had barely collected herself when, adjusting her sari over a mountain of a body, Tami swept in.

"Oh, Tami! So early!" Her morning peacefulness had vanished, but Nina swallowed this small inconvenience out of consideration for their friendship. "Come join me for tea."

Tami dropped her bulk in a chair, glanced at the tea table, and whispered, "Tea, another time. I have two pieces of news to give you, then I'll be off."

A double dose of gossip? Nina, eager to collect the latest tidbits, turned her complete attention to Tami. She gushed about a relative's arrival from the States for vacation. Such news was always welcome to the residents of this mountain town, who felt isolated from the rest of the state. This relative, it appeared, had brought the usual gifts of cameras and camcorders, and a heap of old *Playboy* magazines that had proved more popular with the men.

"What's your other news?"

Tami's face darkened, she shrank into the chair, her legs did a swinging movement under her sari. "It hurts me to relate this to you. Goddess Kali will never forgive me in this life or the next—"

"What is it?"

Tami squeaked, "Aloka and Pranab have divorced."

"*Ki bolcho?*" Nina exclaimed. Are you out of your mind?

"Pranab's nephew had called from New York yesterday." Tami bobbed her head up and down for emphasis. "Apparently Pranab's parents have known for some time that they'd separated. The divorce just became final."

Nina leaned heavily on her cane as she made an attempt to rise, then flopped back down again. Her mind had pieced together the scintilla of evidence, from Pranab's silence, to Aloka's avoidance of any mention of her husband in her recent posts, to her increasingly shorter notes. Still, the verification of her worst misgiving rattled Nina to the bone. She knew what a divorce would do to Aloka. She loosened her grip involuntarily and her cane tumbled onto the ground. She bent unsteadily to retrieve it, stalling for a few moments to compose herself.

"I know how you must feel, Nina."

Nina inhaled, though she couldn't absorb much oxygen. "Mostly I feel sorrow for both of them."

"Sorrow? After all you went through for those two?"

"Ever since their birth, I have been more involved with my two grand-daughters than their parents." Nina stared at the gold-rimmed cup, a Gupta heirloom. She would not be able to finish this cup of tea. "I realize now that a family is not just an investment, but also a checking account. You just have to hope that whatever you put into it today will grow enough to cover what will surely be spent tomorrow. But you know, Tami, I still love them as much as I ever did. I'm anxiously waiting for them to come back. I'll try to get them back together again."

"You will?" Tami rose. "Who's ever heard of a divorced couple getting back together?"

Nina stood up on her own, wished her friend good day. She was glad that Tami had more "gossip errands" to run.

Several hours later, Nina lazed on her lawn chair, her sandals dampened by the wet grass from the morning's sprinkles. Letters from both her grand-daughters had arrived, but hadn't cheered her as much as she'd hoped. She looked down at the elegant note embossed with Aloka's monogram on the side table. Normally the girl, with her inherent beauty and grace, came alive in her long letters. She chose the brightest words, strung them together in style, using ellipses so that the reader could take a moment to consider the meaning. Aloka wrote about what she was doing, thinking, hoping, and feeling. She included news, humor, sentiment, and always a little of herself. She would draw a flower in the margin, or a Big Apple street scene. Reading such a letter, Nina felt as though she were walking hand in hand with her beloved granddaughter to explore the byways of New York. This time, Aloka had filled the sleek ivory paper with her exquisite penmanship and had color-coordinated the stamps, but the message was brief, almost like a telegram. It was devoid of any mention of Pranab, and now Nina understood the painful reason why.

She watched the branches of a magnolia tree tremble in the light breeze. Her eyes darted to Sujata's note, short, plain, functional, computer-printed, but more optimistic.

A dreadful thought hiccupped through Nina. Had she hurled a lit match at a tank of petrol by inviting all three back for her birthday? What sorts of damaging liaisons would ensue this time? How could she have been that obtuse? *"Petni,"* she muttered a curse word to herself. Ugly ghost.

Then again, she observed, after all these years, wouldn't her granddaughters, presumably more worldly now from having lived abroad, be wiser as well? Time, the sternest teacher. Old grievances might have faded under life's many tribulations, like pebbles smoothed by a mountain stream.

Her slipper slid off one foot and fell. Nina lurched and steadied herself with the cane, even as she tried to reach for it.

Reenu, the young maidservant, clad in a faded woodblock-print sari, fluttered up the gravelly path on bare feet. She protested sweetly in Bengali, "Please wait, Thakurma."

Thakurma. Appropriately so. The girl was even younger than her granddaughters. And now Reenu, slender and resilient as a newly sprouted bamboo stalk, leaned forward with a mingling of concern and reverence in her eyes. "Please let me help you."

In this cosmopolitan town where one heard English, Hindi, and at least ten other tongues, this sweet ingenue spoke only in Bengali. How Nina adored the melodious language: soft, rounded vowels coalescing with powerful consonants to form words, which then made loving liaisons to form lyrical sentences. The sounds, never harsh or vulgar, floated in the air like offerings to the gods. How appropriately here beneath the Himalayas, where those gods made their abode.

"I can manage." Nina gestured toward the envelope in her hand. "Look, I got a note from Aloka today."

"Aloka-*di* is coming?"

Nina nodded. Reenu, who had never met the grandchildren, was already referring to Aloka as her older sister by attaching the honorific of *di*. Though

Nina employed three other servants in this household—a cook, a driver, and a gardener—she had a special fondness for this artless maid. Reenu's father had been a trusted worker at the tea estate for several decades until his death two years earlier. Her mother had been occasionally employed as a cook's helper in this house until arthritis prevented her from working. Reenu's mother was famous for her cabbage *ghanto*. She knew just how much five spice, or *phoron*, to sprinkle on that dish and had enough brains to add tomatoes for a hint of tartness. Thus far, Reenu had proved to be as loyal and dedicated as her father and as fine a cook as her mother. She never missed a day of work, performed all her duties with unusual care and attention, and offered many extras, such as providing Nina with company. As was the custom, Reenu didn't share meals with the family members or join in any family functions, but she'd adopted forms of address reserved for relatives without appearing presumptuous. She accepted occasional gifts of saris and toiletries from Nina with gratitude.

Reenu was asking, "Where will Aloka-*di* be staying?"

"Her old room upstairs, the best bedroom. She is the older of the two daughters of my late son Bir and in our family the oldest child always receives special treatment. Aloka had such a good disposition. Everyone loved her when she was a baby. What a smile. Then, when she started to walk, she brightened up the house with her gentle footsteps. I still remember her grabbing the handrails—her pink fingertips against the chestnut-brown wood—as she came down the stairs. She always kept her back straight, like a princess. We tried to make sense of the few precious words she mumbled. When she had her 'first rice,' we invited two hundred people. That day, with everyone applauding and blessing, we named the house after her—Aloka Kutir."

Nina watched Reenu glance about with surprise. And she should be surprised that this yellow-washed, ten-room dwelling, with its extensive lawn and flower and vegetable gardens, could be called a *kutir*, or cottage.

"Sujata always resented the fuss we made over her sister, so we named that tree after her." Nina gestured to the magnolia tree. A mere sapling over a quarter century ago, it had reached its splendid height and was still producing new branches. A brass plaque nailed on its trunk at eye level proclaimed, "Sujata *gaach*," or Sujata's tree.

"So Sujata-*di* is coming, too?"

"Just as I hoped for. We'll have plenty to talk about. She's in the tea business."

Nina's mind had already formed a scheme: She would seek Sujata's help with the nearly bankrupt family-owned tea estate. After her son's death, Nina had hired a manager and ordered him to give the workers a wage increase, paid medical care, and running water, all at a substantial cost to the family's income. The quiet and unassuming manager hadn't always performed well in his duties. Under his care the production had become sluggish. Last month, the tea pluckers had received their pay several days late. And all he had had to say was, "Just a slipup."

Nina would never forget how, eight years ago, tea pluckers had rebelled against just such cavalier treatment by management. That had strained Gupta family ties and contributed to Bir's untimely death. Nina shuddered to think that the experience could be repeated. Sujata, now an astute career woman, could handle those grievances before they reached the point of revolt.

Nina's mouth moistened at the relish of another thought. "It's time Sujata got married."

"A wedding!" Reenu chirped her excitement. "That's exactly what this big house needs to come alive."

"But first I'll have to introduce her to the man. What else is an old woman like me good for? Mreenal Bose is the son of a prominent Calcutta doctor. He's coming here on holiday. His great-aunt, Tami, who's a friend of mine, dropped by this morning. She lives only four kilometers away. Mreenal went to a boarding school here for a year. He even met Sujata briefly. She was about twelve then, he, a few years older."

"Would Mreenal-*babu* and Sujata-*di* still remember each other?"

"I doubt that—even though they were about that age when children start noticing the opposite sex. Mreenal was brilliant. He graduated from Calcutta University, first in his class, then went to the States to study at Stanford. He now lives in Seattle, which I'm told is a couple of hours by boat from Victoria. He works for a software enterprise, an electronic plantation, you might say. From all I've heard, he's a decent boy with no bad habits. Oh, he goes out for a hamburger every now and then—but who can blame him for eating fast food over there? We don't teach our boys how to cook."

"If he lives so close to Sujata-*di*, why can't they meet over there?"

Nina pondered. Most employers assigned little importance to a servant's words, but not Nina. Reenu possessed common sense.

"Perhaps I could get them together sooner," Nina answered. "That might make my job easier, and it won't seem like an arranged marriage. You never know about young people these days. They can be foolishly romantic one moment, cynical the next. They think of arranged marriage either as a savior or as a curse. Still I have high hopes for Sujata. She'll know what's right for her. Better get the downstairs bedroom ready for her. That had always been her room."

"Isn't it a little small?"

"So? It's closer to mine and the view is great." Nina loved the granddaughters equally, or so she told herself. "I have asked Sujata to come earlier. She'll have a couple of weeks to relax with me and have a chance to spend time with Mreenal before Aloka and Pranab get here."

"I can set up tea for Sujata-*di* and Mreenal-*babu* on this lawn." Reenu seemed caught up in the scheme. "I'll help you in any way I can, Thakurma."

Now it occurred to Nina that Reenu would be useful for spying on the young singles. And goddess Durga would forgive Nina for that. She had much to accomplish in a short time.

"I'll take you up on it." With that cordial end to the conversation, Nina hobbled unsteadily up to the house with Reenu in tow. Once settled in her room, she asked, "Before you go home today, would you get the big trunk out? You know, the one with the family photos?"

Her niece, Toru, who lived nearby, was a superb photographer. At family functions Toru quietly snapped everyone's pictures. The only problem was Nina seldom bothered to arrange the prints in albums. Hundreds of pictures from over the years were lying loose in the trunk.

"I will, Thakurma."

"Maybe I'll find a snapshot of Sujata and Mreenal together. Wouldn't that be something?"

eighteen

"Aloka?" Pranab sounded as though he didn't recognize her voice.

So soon? It had been only a week since their divorce. But the more important question in Aloka's mind was, why was he calling at seven-thirty in the morning, just as she was leaving for the office? She held the receiver in one hand, strapped her pumps on with the other. "Aloka speaking," she offered again. If her voice quavered, it had to do with the dream she'd had of him last night in which they traversed a narrow trail in Darjeeling, so narrow that they could only pass it single file.

Now she listened for clues.

"Meant to ring you last night, Aloka, but I was up to my ass in work."

She suppressed a smile. This was the first time the high-minded Sanskrit scholar had uttered the A-word, at least in her presence. In the past, differences between them had often resulted from his inability to adapt to rough, brusque metropolitan life. Alone now, perhaps he was finally being forced to adjust. She checked a loose brass button of her double-breasted suit to make sure it would stay in place the rest of the day.

"Did you take your Sunday walk?" he asked casually. "It was such a lovely day. My apartment in Brooklyn isn't far from a park. I've been spending a lot of time there in the evenings and on Sundays."

She slipped on her trench coat, taking note of the eagerness in his delivery. He was avoiding the real issue, which was not unusual for him.

"Of course, there's litter on the paths. Why can't the city municipality put a waste bin next to each park bench?" Finally, in a guarded tone, "I left my warmest sweater—you know, the cable knit one—in your place, and a few incidentals."

She swallowed as she recalled seeing the sweater hanging in her bedroom closet. His last connection with his former life and with her was about to be taken away. Not a cozy way to begin the day.

She picked up her purse, checked her keys. "Look, Pranab, I really have to scoot now, otherwise I'll be late for work. I'll have a messenger deliver your belongings to you. Okay?"

"No, no, Aloka. A messenger is too much of a bother, not to mention expense. I'll come get it."

"I can put the stuff in a plastic bag and leave it just outside my door. My neighbors will ring you in."

"I don't want to inconvenience them. Besides, it might get stolen. I'll come over."

She clutched the receiver tighter. It wasn't exactly that she didn't trust him enough to let him in. During the last six months of their separation, he would frequently escape the tiny room he'd rented from a friend and come over here to catch up on reading or to write letters. Her muscles twitched another warning. "Where did you leave the sweater?"

"In a dresser drawer. If it doesn't bother you too much, Aloka, I'll stop by this evening, say around eight? It won't take but a few minutes. I'll try not to get in the way of your Thursday music practice. I'll just grab the stuff and be gone."

He had the habit of hiding objects in the oddest places, then forgetting all about them. This, he'd once explained, came from his childhood when his large family lived in a two-room house and he had to conceal his personal items away from the prying eyes of his siblings. Once he hid a cluster of fresh, plump grapes in a shoe box, intending to consume them at a later time when no one was about. Days later, he opened the shoe box and discovered some withered, bad-smelling "raisins."

She said, "I don't see why not."

She hung up with a bit of regret. In happier times, she had believed in his words and never doubted that he trusted her. Now, a week after their divorce, he didn't want her to even look for an old sweater.

An instinct told her he might be searching for something else. What could it be?

She glanced at her wristwatch, threw her coat, purse, and keys on a chair, and raced to the bedroom. The small room, outfitted with a dresser, double bed, and end table, was no longer cluttered. Pranab had always been the messy one. But the room, alas, also felt less intimate. She pulled the dresser drawers open one by one and combed through layers of saris, blouses, petticoats, scarves, and stoles. She went to the closet where her suits, dresses, and jeans hung neatly, well spaced out to fill the area where Pranab's clothes had hung. Sure enough, his sweater hung there, its long sleeves splayed like a suitor about to hug. She fingered the wavy knit and held it against her breast and cheeks, then let it droop there as before. Turning, she kept looking around the entire room and its shadowy corners for more of Pranab's belongings.

She walked over to the bed. Devoid of male presence these many months, it seemed shrunken in size. She smoothed the down cover. On a hunch, she knelt and peered beneath the bed. Steeped as she still was in the family folklore, she did so with a strange anticipation. Back home, the bed was more than a platform for sleeping, especially a high Indian *khaat* thrust up above the ground by posts. According to tales told by Grandma, the empty space underneath was where clandestine lovers hid, children tinkered with their broken toys, and a newly married Grandpa had once shoved a week's worth of laundry while his homesick bride was visiting her mother. Though this Western-style bed was too low to conceal a clandestine lover, there was definitely enough room to hide a small package.

And so it was.

Directly under the center of the bed, barely visible in the gloom, lay a buff-colored envelope. She snaked her hand forward, retrieved the envelope, and sat down cross-legged on the floor. She placed her find on her lap, brushed the dust from its top surface. The envelope, embossed with a faint outline of a swan, was addressed in Pranab's careful hand in indigo ink. She had never known Pranab to indulge in such choice stationery or such fine ink. Then the mailing address caught her eye. Oh, goddess Durga. The letter was waiting to be mailed to Sujata in Victoria. Aloka sprang up and unfolded the dainty paper with shaky fingers: Dated a year ago and obviously never mailed, the letter had probably slipped out of a manila folder that normally housed all of Pranab's letters.

Sujata, manorama,

Sujata, mind's delight. Dizzied by the endearing form of address, Aloka tore her eyes from the sheet. Should she read it? The Guptas believed that a letter was a messenger of the gods and must not be intercepted by a third party. Forget about the Gupta code of privacy, she told herself. She would pursue her heart's dictate on this matter. After all, she'd already discarded family tradition in so many ways. She'd gotten a divorce and shed the sari; she lived alone.

She steadied herself against the dresser and finished reading the damning letter. The contents didn't register word for word. Only the yearning expressed in it floated before her eyes like a bad dream. She became convinced that Pranab had been meaning to get in touch with Sujata for a long time. What Aloka had believed to be long-forgotten lurid history was actually a current affair. Although Pranab had never given her the true reason why he'd left her, she'd always harbored a suspicion that it had something to do with Sujata. The contents of the letter transformed that suspicion into a rage. With a shaky hand she refolded the sheet and put it back inside the envelope.

She wiped the beads of perspiration on her forehead with a hand. Though she couldn't see her own image, she could feel that her mascara was running, her lipstick smudging, and the curls of her hair going limp. With rigid fingers, she slid the envelope back into its hiding place beneath the bed.

nineteen

Nina gazed up at the sky from the large window by her writing desk. At this elevation the light was uncommonly pure, direct, and generous. The sun god with his seven horses had descended in his kindness to give the mortals their day, as Hindu scriptures would suggest. Despite her failing eyesight, Nina could see well in this benevolent light and she thanked the sun god for it. She was leafing through snapshots scattered on the desktop before her—miniature life portraits frozen in eternal moments—when she discovered one she'd been searching for. In discordant contrast to the bittersweet quaver of *shehnai* droning on the stereo, she blurted out an exclamation of joy and surprise and turned toward Reenu, who was on her knees wiping the floor with a wet rag.

"Look, this is Mreenal when he was about twelve."

Nina brought the photo closer to the light and studied it, nodding approvingly at Mreenal's even features, his direct gaze, his smoothly brushed hair, and his respectful demeanor. "Doesn't he look like a fine, well-mannered boy?"

Her shell bracelets jingling as she bounced up, Reenu peered intently over her mistress's shoulder. Curious and animated, she smelled of the talcum powder that Nina had given her during the recent Durga Puja celebration. "Very nice." Reenu nodded also.

"Sujata will soon get a surprise phone call from this very nice young man," Nina murmured.

"You haven't told Sujata-*di* yet?"

"Should I ask my grandchildren to approve what I do?"

As if to press her point, Nina settled herself firmly in the chair and drew her gaze back to the snapshots. This was not her usual way of spending time. Photographs and reminiscences often absorbed her elderly acquaintances, but Nina had always been more engaged with what lay ahead, especially now that she was nearing her eighty-first birthday. In her youth, the future had been a road extending to infinity; now it loomed ahead as a high wall. She still had much to accomplish before she hit it.

A black-and-white shot caught Nina's eyes. "Here's Pranab, ten years ago." Staring back was an earnest young man, wedged between waist-high tea bushes, a white work apron hugging his slim midsection. His eyes still had dream, a vision of the future.

Then came the sight of a photo of Aloka, who was then about thirty years old. Perched regally in a peacock chair, she was grinning into the lens, her skin dewy, her eyes glowing. She must have been holding a whimsical thought about Pranab, whom she'd just met.

"Doesn't Aloka look gorgeous in that mauve brocade?" Nina said to Reenu. "I'd bought that sari for her because the color went so well with her skin tone. What you'd call *dudhe aalta*. Ivory pink."

"And here are Kabita's wedding pictures. You haven't met Kabita yet. She's Aloka's cousin-sister and they were close friends." With misty eyes and gnarled fingers, Nina traced the photo of the glowing bride peering shyly at the camera. Now, years later, that same woman, mother of three children, had the body of a guitar and skin of a blemished guava. Nina blew out a sigh.

Reenu pointed her finger at the next group photo. "And who's that?"

"Sujata, at a house party." Something in that image had caught the maid-servant's attention, causing Nina to examine it more closely. Her youngest granddaughter and Pranab were standing against a wall, away from the pack of guests, unmindful of the camera's presence. Their eyes were plainly re-served for each other; their shoulders were touching, a kiss hanging in the air between them. Now, even Reenu had caught it.

The print slipped from Nina's hand and fluttered to the damp floor, barely missing the maidservant's green plastic bucket of water.

There lay the story of an aborted relationship.

Would Sujata ever be able to forgive her?

With a queasy sensation in the pit of her stomach, Nina bent down and strained to reach the photo, but her hand stopped short.

Reenu stooped to retrieve the photo. "You're shivering. Let me get you a shawl."

"Yes, a shawl, that'd be nice."

Nina was still shivering when Reenu's strong lean hands tucked the fleecy heat of a pashmina shawl around her shoulders. To mask her disconsolate sigh, Nina pretended to sniff the lingering scent of neem leaves that had protected the wrap through months of storage. She must somehow get Su-jata and Mreenal to meet and perhaps marry. By doing so, Nina might be able to put things right.

Her silence must have disconcerted Reenu, for she said, "Are you sure you're not sick, Thakurma? Should I call the doctor?"

"Quite sure." Nina drew her gaze up, then away quickly, for fear of be-traying her distressed mental state to the maidservant. "It's just that I've made decisions that I will always regret."

"I don't know much of anything, Thakurma, I went to school only up to class four. I didn't like going to school."

"We're like rivers, Reenu. We tumble toward the ocean, our destiny, until the obstacle of a powerful desire tries to change our course. Then we flood to regain our direction and finally pour ourselves into our great master."

"Very wise. I can learn a lot from you."

"How old are you, Reenu?"

"I am eighteen, maybe nineteen, I don't know for sure. My mother can't remember what year I was born. She had eight children. And in those days, a birth certificate wasn't required."

"Is your mother going to find you a husband?"

"I have found a man myself."

"Who's he?"

"He's a bus boy at Hasty Tasty. I don't see him much during the week, but on Sundays he takes me to Rink Cinema. I put on my best cotton sari and all my glass bangles. At intermission I eat a *paan* and he smokes a *bidi*. He explains to me what I don't understand in the story."

"For my birthday, I'll buy you a silk sari, Reenu. What color do you prefer?"

"A silk sari? Oh, Thakurma, I've never worn silk. I have only touched it. You're so very kind. I like bluish green, if that's not too much trouble."

Ah, aqua. Nina reflected that she, too, liked colors that fused into each other. "You must invite your man for my birthday celebration and introduce him to me."

"But Thakurma . . . what will people say? We're not of your class."

"Don't worry about people. I want to see at least two cheerful faces that evening."

twenty

Aloka rode the elevator to her sixth-floor office. In an instant the uniform cubicles beneath the sterile, vanilla-shade walls, the clacking keyboards, and the jangling telephones obliterated her distress over the love letter. Cheerfully she threw herself into today's assignment of writing a thousand-word piece on India's booming information technology, the so-called IT industry. She had just begun laying out the position of India's domestic computer makers who sought an easing of government regulations when she was startled by the thud of an object falling. Her assistant had dropped a bulky packet of mail in her in-tray. Usually she glanced at the mail with curiosity and eagerness. Not today; the sight of any letter tormented her.

Once again the Sujata-Pranab liaison loomed large in her consciousness, giving rise to an ongoing inner dialogue with herself:

How long had Pranab been writing to Sujata? How much did Sujata still mean to him? It all boiled down to one existential question: Was Sujata the real cause of the breakup of their marriage?

If so, and if Sujata and Pranab were to reunite, would they become lovers again, now that both were free?

As she turned the questions over in her mind, Aloka summoned up a few sentences from an article she'd recently written: "Inherent in any migration is a loss of certainty about the self, a hardening of the spirit, the walling off of a section of the heart. Immigrants pine for a way of life forever lost, but they also forget. They do so to survive."

Now that Sujata and Pranab lived in a cold, unfeeling new world geared to speed and efficiency, their old love would likely be hopelessly dated and adolescent. But then, Aloka hadn't explored another possibility in her article. What happens when immigrants return to their homeland? Do they regain their lost self? In other words, could the magic of Darjeeling possibly rekindle the passion between Pranab and Sujata?

The letter would have the answers. Except that Aloka couldn't remember a single complete sentence now. However painful that might be, she needed to read the letter again.

The next few hours agonized her, even as putting "The End" at the conclusion of the article gave her a sense of satisfaction. She even managed to finish answering all her phone calls by the end of the day. She sprang up, donned her trench coat, picked up her purse, and vowed to read—no, dissect—that cursed letter as soon as she returned home.

On the way home, convinced that she would need all her strength for the upcoming ordeal, she got off the subway and headed for her favorite bakery on Fifty-fourth Street and Third Avenue. There she purchased a dozen freshly baked Pleasure Dome cookies.

Her next stop was at the delicatessen on Fifty-third and Second Avenue. The cramped store bustled with evening shoppers. Entering, she bumped into an Indian man of medium height and unremarkable features who was busy inspecting a ripe yellow papaya. He seemed vaguely familiar, though she couldn't recall where she'd seen him before. As he regarded her, his eyes seemed to broaden in recognition mingled with a frank appraisal. Aloka felt blood flowing to her cheeks. Back home, as a young unmarried woman, she had worn her beauty—which she believed was nothing more than inner serenity—easily, as unconsciously as if it were her prerogative. She'd believed that somehow she'd lost her looks, her serene expression, when Pranab left her. That might not have been the case.

She muttered an apology, a few seconds later than was appropriate, and retreated to the salad bar, where she hastily scooped out some *kasha varnishkas* into a plastic bowl. She needed something substantial to fill her suddenly growling stomach. Moments later she hastened out the door, a plastic bag dangling from her hand, relieved by the dark anonymity of New York.

She walked past a Japanese-run beauty salon and an English-as-a-second-language school, finally arriving at the entrance to her apartment building. Abruptly, she halted. Pranab was sitting at the top of the concrete stoop, engrossed in a paperback.

He must have sensed her presence, for he now sprang up. "Aloka! I thought I'd come early."

Just this once why couldn't he have been late? She mumbled something about this being perfectly okay, then unlocked the door, realizing she was falling back into her old habit of deferring to him. Aloka, ever the understanding one, the one who absorbed life's little shocks so Pranab could go about his day unruffled.

Now, with no further attempt at social amenities, he slipped past her and headed for the bedroom. Trailing in his wake, she watched the hurried steps of his chestnut loafers. He paused at the dresser, while she folded her arms and leaned against the doorjamb. Bending, he rummaged through the drawers with focused eyes. How could he do this? He hadn't used those drawers in the last six months and they held her personal articles. Anger swelled inside her, but with a struggle she froze her face into a mask of tranquillity.

He glanced at her over his shoulder and mumbled, "Not there."

Her eyes caught a blemish on his chin, perhaps a cut from shaving this morning. "Where could you have put what's not there?"

He opened the closet door and grabbed his sweater. The wooden hanger made a somber noise, even as it slid over the rod. He made a further show of peering hard into the closet's shadows. Then, acting as though a revelation had occurred to him, exclaimed, "Oh, I know." With that he lowered himself to the floor next to the bed, reached under, and pulled out the envelope.

She shifted her gaze. That wretched letter beneath their marriage bed. He briskly stood up, then exhaled with, "I have no idea how it got there."

She spun around and flew out of the bedroom, feigning calmness, though a tension was claiming her back. Pranab trailed after her.

At the apartment door he asked innocently, even amiably, "Have you heard from home lately?"

He had the gall to ask about her family? Still she spoke with a quiet gentleness. "I got an invitation. Grandma's eighty-first birthday is coming up in November and she wants me to be present at the festivity. Of course I'm going. By the way, she mentioned you twice in her letter."

He adjusted his glasses and ran his fingers over the front plume of his hair, a telltale sign that he was pondering the matter with some concern. "Did she invite your whole family?"

She stared at the tarnished brass-coated doorknob. "If Grandma has her way, she'll get Sujata to attend, too."

She watched Pranab's reaction minutely. He was hugging the sweater to his chest, taking some pleasure doing so. "How nice, two sisters together again! Well, my cousin Babli is getting married in November. She'd love to see me there. I have to check with my boss, but the timing seems right." Then, animatedly, "I'll make every attempt to attend Babli's wedding and Thakurma's birthday."

His enthusiastic response crushed her. The Guptas were still unaware of their divorce. How would they take it when she and Pranab arrive in Darjeeling separately? They would have to come up with a coordinated strategy to disclose the news. Before she could broach the subject, he slipped out through the door with a furtive glance at her and a mumbled good-bye. In quick motions he retreated down the steps, his loafers slapping the stairs, while she stood there dazed, her sensibilities too bruised to carry on.

After a while she went back to her evening chores—ironing a suit, watering the geraniums, paying the bills. She did these routine tasks with half her mind, though in the end they stabilized her. Finally, as she practiced singing—several Rabindrasangeets—and, giving voice to her emotions, she saw the path ahead more clearly. With Pranab also returning to Darjeeling, there was hope of reconciliation. She could easily visualize taking a stroll with him through Darjeeling's vibrant streets: curio shops displaying turquoise amulets, a purveyor pushing a cartload of lychee ice cream, flute music breaking the pure high-altitude air, and Pranab gazing deeply into her eyes and repeating what he'd said shortly after they first met. "You're a country, Aloka. I see a beautiful, mysterious landscape in your face, full lips, and velvet hair." He would smile like the sun mounting over the Kanchenjunga. And they would return to their once-pure relationship.

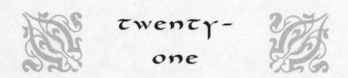

twenty-
one

The top of the flip chart read: "How many cups of tea do North Americans drink per year?" Just below it on the graph paper, Suzy inscribed a rising curve, then jotted the answer: "Over 50 billion cups annually. More than 90% is black tea."

Her assistant Jane appeared and motioned her aside. "A Mr. Mreenal Bose is on the phone. He says it's personal."

Bose, a Bengali name, grabbed Suzy's interest. Like other Indian expatriates, she could make a pretty good guess as to an Indian's ethnic origin and mother tongue from a surname. Mreenal Bose most likely spoke Bengali. Also, there was a Bose family in Darjeeling, she now recalled.

"Please ask him to call back."

"He says he's in town just for the day."

"Ask him to try back this afternoon, then."

Suzy turned her attention back to her clients. In trying to make up for the lagging sales of last quarter, she emphasized that she had added new tea varieties, such as black tea bound up with the essence of jasmine, blackberry, or rose petals, as well as an assortment of herbals, which combined herbs, roots, bark, and seeds. The clients pored over the numbers and asked questions about her tea's caffeine content. Suzy reassured them that a cup of black tea contained only about fifty milligrams of caffeine, compared with the average hundred in a cup of coffee. That drew a rebuttal from a retailer, a purist who owned Fruit Juice Forever, and in whose opinion fifty milligrams measured a lot. Suzy didn't mind responding with facts about other benefits of black tea—its antioxidant and automutagenic properties. She fought the battle against coffee and other beverages one client at a time. In another hour, the meeting was over.

She plowed through the rest of the day, contacting a distributor, planning for the next Tea Council Conference, and checking inventory. After lunch she finalized the design of a new package, hoping that would spur sales. She chose a puncture-resistant box with an ersatz wood-grain finish and a new marketing phrase: "The taste only quality can bring." The lettering would be done in red, green, and yellow, the colors associated with tea. At the end of the day, it dawned on her that Mreenal Bose still hadn't called back. Who was he anyway?

On the way home, she stopped at Far and Away, a travel agency that she had looked at wistfully for years. It took two exhausting hours to finalize her trip, at the end of which she got into her car with a round-trip ticket to India and a mood of elation and started toward her apartment.

It was nearly eight P.M. when she parked at the garage of her apartment building on Beach Drive. A blast of salty ocean air and the consistent splash of waves dissipated her fatigue. She shuffled to the mailbox and emptied its contents on her way to the third floor.

Once inside her apartment, she threw the mail on the coffee table: gas bill, a free latte coupon, a Damart catalog, and a personal letter. She picked up the letter, glanced at the return address, and . . . oh, Bhagowan . . . her fingers went limp.

Why would Pranab write?

And from Brooklyn?

Had they moved?

In a previous correspondence, Aloka had described Manhattan as "the best and the worst of man; marvelous." Reading that, Suzy had believed Aloka would never leave that island.

Holding the prized possession, Suzy slouched in an old leather armchair. Her fingers fumbled at the sealed edges of the crisp envelope. Nearly eight years later, she was touching Pranab again.

Sujata, manorama,

I am hiding behind a siris tree and watching you skip along a narrow path in the tea field. You move so nimbly and your smile is so radiant. Is it from being near the tea bushes or are you thinking of me? You seem not to have a single care. Your beauty tempts me to cry out in ecstasy, but I won't announce my presence until I've drunk in your face, body, your every movement, until I am so full that I am ready to burst.

These are the memories that make the chill of New York bearable for me. Though we have been apart for a very long time, I haven't forgotten our times together for a single day. Still I hesitate to write to you, and may never mail this letter, but my sentiments will be there for you forever.

I think of you with all the tenderness in my being. I know your family forced you to break up with me. If only I had the courage to follow you then.

She paused for a while, peered out the window at the heart-shaped leaves of a sprawling Judas tree illuminated by the streetlight, and absorbed the meaning. Goose bumps rippled down her arms as she read the next two paragraphs—about his divorce and his plan to visit Darjeeling. She paused again, then turned to the rest:

Our Darjeeling. Nimkee, Senchal Lake, bamboo bushes, and the nightingales. As preparation, I have been practicing Bhangra dance. You remember?

The Sanskrit proverb, "Delay not that which is good," rings in my ears constantly. I feel an urgency to be with you. Do you still love me, Sujata?

Did you ever? Could you in the future? Reply only if your heart prompts you. And take as much time as you need. I'll be waiting.

Yours always,

Pranab

Suzy refolded the letter. The bees were buzzing again.

twenty-two

Triple taps at the door brought Suzy back to the room. Clutching Pranab's letter in hand—how many times had she read it? five? ten?—she sprang up and opened the door. "Oh, Eva! I didn't expect you. Come in."

Her neighbor slipped in. Eva Pavlova, née Yee Hong, sported a bright red and gold vest that blazed and overwhelmed the muted maroon color scheme of Suzy's living room. An excited glow made Eva's olive face seem rounder. She took a seat in the leather recliner, while Suzy lowered herself to the futon with rosewood arms. Between them rested a black-framed glass coffee table.

Eva glanced at Suzy's hand. "Am I interrupting anything?"

"Not at all." Suzy tucked the letter back in its envelope and set it on the coffee table. She wouldn't elaborate, not quite yet.

Though they'd known each other for a number of years, it still took Suzy a little time to be frank with Eva, especially when the issue was something as affecting as this letter. They'd met six years ago when Suzy had moved into this apartment complex, with its choice oceanfront location. Out of curiosity, Suzy had checked the names on the mailboxes. Reading the name "Eva Pavlova" on box 411, Suzy had conjured up a squat Russian matron in a faux fur coat, a schoolteacher, with the baggy eyes and thick speech of someone afflicted with a chronic case of the sniffles. What a surprise when Eva turned out to be this trim woman, as neat and precise as the dress patterns she worked with all day. And she wore fur only rarely. She possessed the smoothest skin this side of the Pacific. Tofu was Eva's dietary secret, Suzy learned later.

In the years that followed, they became allies, Suzy believed, in the Asian way, close and trusting, yet maintaining a personal reserve, each safekeeping a few secrets, and neither one unduly inquisitive. ("You don't have to talk about last night's disastrous date with that magician guy.") Both had been raised not to inflict their problems on others. Still, life in North America had drained their habitual reserve. They chatted more freely and openly now and occasionally offered advice on intimate personal matters that was accepted without offense. ("The alchemist who made that special perfume for you is a fraud. It doesn't smell like you.") Each saw that the other had her best interest at heart. ("You look awful. You need to take a couple of days off from work and just play.") At the first hint of distress, one would show up for the other. They suffered neither jealousy nor guilt, always side by side, at ease in each other's company and looking forward to their next rendezvous, serving as mirrors for each other's soul. If Suzy was careless or misbehaved, Eva would be sure to point it out. ("Hey, you were pretty rough on that waiter.") Eva wasn't a laid-back observer. She was center stage in Suzy's life, playing a supporting role.

As to her name: Eva had explained that she'd come from China via Europe and at the port of entry had been asked to adopt a Western name. To register it would cost a sizable sum, so she'd decided on the designation "Eva," which, she later confided with a facetious grin, was cheaper than the longer, more pretentious "Natalie" or "Olivia." The "Pavlova" part was never explained and Suzy had never asked.

"Today was crazy at work," Suzy said. "Then I came home and found this letter waiting for me. . . ."

Eva cocked an eyebrow inquisitively.

Suzy could feel her face flush, the red shade spreading to her ears. Her emotion was a hodgepodge of shame and embarrassment and fierce pride that comes from having truly loved, even in vain. She dropped her eyes and rearranged her feet on the floor, ever conscious that her friend's eyes were on her. No use trying to fool Eva.

Eva made a gesture of rising from her chair. "I didn't mean to pry, Suze."

"No, don't go, Eva. I need to talk to somebody. It's been so long, and still I can't let go of the memories."

Eva settled down in her chair again and turned a sincere, eager face toward Suzy. Slowly, haltingly, Suzy filled her friend in on events of eight years ago. "All these years," Suzy poured out in conclusion, "I'd convinced myself I didn't care, that he was my sister's husband. I certainly never expected to hear from him. Then this letter came. It was like being together all over again."

"But remember, you aren't the same person you were then," Eva said. "I react differently to my older sister now. When we were growing up, we didn't get along. My younger brother and I used to gang up on her. But now we can really talk. It's better that we didn't have a perfect start. Our sisterhood is more meaningful now."

"I wish I could say the same. Aloka and I used to be so close—we shared everything. Then, as we grew up, somehow a third person always seemed to come between us, whether it was Grandma, Father, or Pranab. I can only imagine how horribly she must be suffering because of her divorce. I'd like to help her if she'd let me, but this letter complicates things once again."

"You should hold off writing to him. I would. Letters can be misleading. You can say things in a letter that might not hold true in reality."

"I'll see him when I go home. The moment our eyes meet, we'll know how we really feel about each other."

"Don't be in any hurry to reveal your true feelings, even if they are ambivalent." Eva tugged at the lapel of her vest. "You look worried, Suze. Worry is part of the travel package, I guess. When I get ready to visit my mother in Shanghai, I keep asking myself: Did I get the right presents? Have I gained weight? Will my mother like my shorter hairdo? Once I'm there, those considerations seem unimportant. My family reminds me who I really am at my core. I become my best self in their presence."

"I'm not sure what I'll become. I'm just glad to finally get my itinerary firmed up."

"So that's why you came home late tonight?"

"How did you know?"

The South Sea pearls on Eva's ears shone. "I got home around six and saw a man dropping something into your mailbox. He looked Indian. When I turned around, he asked me courteously if I knew you. He said his name was Mreenal Bose."

"Mreenal Bose? Damn him." Suzy got up, fished through her mail, and located a card. Then, reclaiming her seat, she noted, "He's from Seattle. I wonder what he wants. Is he a weirdo?"

"No. I assumed you were old friends, or he was your cousin."

"What did you tell him?"

"Just that usually you came home around six-thirty."

Suzy stomped a foot on the floor. "You didn't really give out that information to a stranger, did you?"

Eva's smooth appearance belied a loose tongue. Still, Suzy knew that was simply Eva.

"Look, Suze, I meet people all day. I can tell who's up to what."

"You size them up in a glance?"

"It was a tad more than a glance. We chatted for a few minutes. I'd have invited him over to my place until you got back, but my living room is such a mess with fabrics and patterns spread all over. I suspect he's the kind of guy who'd overlook all that. In any case, he must have read my mind, 'cause he said he couldn't wait."

Her clenched teeth relaxed, Suzy held eye contact with Eva and willed her to furnish more details.

"He's a neat guy. I can't imagine him being evil."

"Might he be looking for a donation for some cause?"

"His cause might be you." Eva winked. "He seemed disappointed that you weren't here. You never know—he might take you out."

"I'm through dating another stranger from India. I haven't told you the story yet. A client of mine, a nice married Irish woman, set up a blind date for me with a friend of hers. The man is originally from Bihar. He took me to McMorran's. It turned out that he was very proud of his alma mater and his degrees and couldn't stop talking about them. He was also very proud of his father's and his brother's degrees. He went on and on. When I got a chance, I brought up a topic of current interest—the spraying of the gypsy moth and how it could harm pets and older people. That was the biggest local news of the week and just happened to be on my mind, but he didn't seem interested. He ordered the salmon, I ordered a vegetable platter. The food was delicious, but I couldn't eat more than three bites and I really didn't see the point of ever seeing him again. A week later, I showed up at McMorran's with another colleague, and there he was, sitting alone at the next table, with the same salmon dish before him. Imagine my discomfort! Later, it was hard to explain to my Irish client that I didn't click with her friend. She thought, because we both came from the same country, we would automatically find each other interesting."

"This is a little different, Suze. You'll know when you meet him. Oh, I just remembered Mreenal Bose saying something about catching the Clipper tonight to Seattle. Seems like you won't be able to meet him this time."

Suzy laughed. "Will you stop talking about Mreenal Bose?"

"I promise, I will. It's just that I'm not involved with anyone right now. I'm sort of going through a dry period, you might say, and really I don't want to turn into a desert. I'm living my romantic life through you." With an eye to her wristwatch, Eva got off the recliner. "My, it's almost ten. I'd better go and let you get some sleep."

Suzy smiled a good-bye and watched her friend disappear down the hallway. Now it all fell in place as to why Eva had stopped by so late in the evening. She had come bearing a spark of hope that she would be able to experience the thrill and magic of connecting with someone, if only vicariously. And she could quite conceivably be interested in Mreenal herself.

Suzy closed the door. Loneliness was a prison from which she and Eva were both trying to escape. No amount of business success, no measure of easy living in this lovely city could make up for that nagging void in their lives. In that they were equal, simpatico.

As Suzy shrugged her shoulders to chase the stiffness out, an image of

Pranab showed up before her: Pranab, strong and powerful and complete as a galaxy; Pranab, with his forceful gaze and lively wit, the masculine vitality that swept away all her inhibitions.

At one A.M. Suzy awoke on the futon. In her dazed state she couldn't remember when she had drifted off. As she got up to retire to the bedroom, she noticed a calling card lying on the carpet. She bent to pick it up.

Mreenal Bose's card.

She tossed it into the wastebasket.

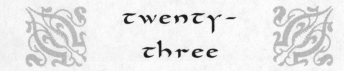

twenty-three

Nina reached out and grabbed the phone at its first twitter. Older people deemed the machine intrusive, but for her it provided a welcome reprieve from loneliness and boredom. She eagerly spouted a hello into the receiver.

"Tami speaking," came the animated reply. "I'll be right over. I have news about Mreenal."

Nina's heart began to beat so fast that she had to draw in a deep breath. Her doctor would have been horrified, but this telephone nudge had sent a surge of adrenaline coursing through her system, making her doubly alert. That it also aggravated her hypertension mattered not in the least to her.

Soon she and Tami were seated on the lawn. Tami gave a few enthusiastic details about her day: how she'd visited the Tibetan Self-Help Center and bought a beaded necklace for her granddaughter and didn't have to bargain for it. Nina found herself disinterested in Tami's adventure. Containing her curiosity, Nina casually asked, "So, have you spoken with Mreenal?"

"Several times. Needless to say, he remembered you from his high school days. The prominent Guptas of Darjeeling."

"Never mind me. Does he remember Sujata?"

"Oh, of course. He told me what a pleasure it'd be to sit down and chitchat with her in Bengali over a cup of real Darjeeling tea. With the right people, he's pretty social."

"My Sujata is the quiet sort, you know, like a lot of Bengali girls. But just get her talking about tea and—"

"Better that she's quiet. Mreenal's last girlfriend, a Portuguese business-woman, was too talkative. Whenever she got angry, she harangued him in Portuguese. He didn't understand a word, of course, which was probably just as well."

"How long were they together?"

"Two years."

"Two years and he didn't marry her?"

"No. Even though our boys act modern, they're actually tradition-bound at heart. A Portuguese girl just wouldn't have done for Mreenal. And his mother would have had a fit. I have a hunch he wants to marry a Bengali girl and raise lots of children. He once told me he spoke computerese all day at work. When he got home he'd like nothing better than to relax to the beautiful sounds of Bengali. The boy has so many talents. He's picked up a new hobby recently—photography. He has sent me pictures of the Rainier. They're quite good. He likes to photograph nature."

"Sujata likes to trek the tea garden trails."

"The boy is definitely lonely in Seattle. It's a big city and he's not used to approaching girls the way American men do. The good news is his company plans to open a branch in Bangalore, which will be their Asian head-quarters. He's very excited about the prospect of transferring there."

"Do you think he actually might move back?"

"Let's say it's quite possible. His parents are all for the idea. They have five children and Mreenal's the only one who lives abroad. He also happens to be the one most devoted to his parents. He has made it big in the States, but he misses our Indian ways. He gave me the list once—festivals, food, conversation in Bengali, respect for elders, and last but not the least, cricket matches. Every December he flies home for a month, but this time I've talked to him about coming earlier. At first he said he couldn't, then it turned out he either had to use up all the overtime he'd accumulated or lose it. So, he'll be here in a week."

"Oh, my, the house isn't ready."

"Take your time, Nina. Mreenal will fly to Calcutta first to visit his parents. He won't get here until the twenty-fourth."

"That's four days before Sujata gets here. I'll have a chance to meet Mreenal first, then. It seems we share affection for the Bengali language. Bring him over for tea as soon as he arrives, will you? And give me a list of his favorite dishes. My maidservant Reenu is a superb Bengali cook. She's very young, but she can make *bhaja, pora, ghanto, chochchori,* and all the tea snacks you can name."

"I'll call Mreenal's closest cousin right away and get the list—his mother isn't a good cook. Then we'll both have to get busy."

"How exciting it will be if I can pull it off." Nina sighed. "In spite of the fact that I get calls from my ancestors more and more frequently these days that I'll soon have to answer, I hang on to this fragile, precious life for opportunities like this."

twenty-four

Inspired by the sun, the crisp morning air, and the cup of tea before her, Nina drew a box of stationery close to her on the desk. She felt tired already—she hadn't slept well last night. Just before bedtime, she'd overheard banter and laughter coming from the back lawn. Must be the servants, at the end of their workday. She had gone to the open window and craned her neck, and sure enough.

On that moonlit night, at the far corner of the lawn, the servants, some five of them, sat in a circle, smoke of *bidi* rising. Their faces were barely visible from this angle, but Nina could identify most of them from their voices and manners of speaking: Reenu, the cook, the wispy gardener, and a few tea factory workers who'd dropped by. The servants and their guests were chatting freely. They did so despite differences in age and religious and cultural affiliations. Their occupation united them. And since little news of the outside world reached them, they usually talked mostly about personal matters.

"What I meant to say is—don't you know there's a ghost in this house?" It was Jyotin, a former tea worker, and a lazy old troublemaker to boot, with his characteristic speech pattern. He was teasing Reenu. "Aren't you afraid to work for Mrs. Gupta?"

Nina, who had been raised on ghost stories, was amused by the tea worker's comment and craved to hear the rest. She flicked off the light switch and edged closer to the window. For an instant she only heard the murmur of the night insects.

"Afraid? Why, no. She's most kind." Reenu had laughed a shaky, fearful laugh. "Whose ghost?"

"Manager-sahib's. What I meant to say is, his soul isn't at rest. He tried to kill Pranab-*babu*, who was our leader at the time. What kind of a creature would try to kill a good man? The very low kind, I guess."

How dare that lunatic speak disrespectfully of her dead son? In her mind's eye Nina could see her only child, the adorable baby boy, the naughty youngster, a dedicated tea merchant, a protective father, an overworked man who worried constantly and who often flew into rage. She could visualize the resignation on that face on his deathbed. A wealth of tears, from wherever they lurked, flooded Nina's eyes. She slipped away from the window, crossed the cube of disturbing darkness, and tumbled onto the bed. Shutting her eyes tight, she hoped for peace to emerge, but it never did.

Since the morning was still bright, Nina decided that composing a letter might help erase the residue of weariness. She was renowned in her circle as a natural correspondent, one who could summon stories and gossips at a moment's notice. She inscribed her letters painstakingly either on airmail flimsies or on light blue sheets. Her loopy handwriting wove connections, especially with her granddaughters.

This letter would be addressed to Sujata and tea would be the link. Nina sipped from her cup. The pungent taste loosened the grip of anxiety and once again gave her morning a direction. Mentally she reviewed a brochure recently released by the Darjeeling Planters' Association. It had emphasized that antioxidants were the big concept in North America these days and that a gentle cup of tea contained plenty of them. The brochure had sug-

gested another reason for the beverage's popularity—an element called flu-
oride. Nina had instinctively known tea's nutritional values for a long time.
Hadn't she repeated to her adolescent granddaughters the old folkloric advice about not reaching for a glass of water immediately after taking tea?

Nina squinted at the tall trunk of the poplar tree beyond the window and
hovered over the letter pad:

*So, now that our national drink is the trend in the world, the business at our
estate needs to keep pace. We still believe in selling only pure organically grown
tea, avoiding cheap blends that detract from the Gupta reputation for
excellence. Unfortunately, both yield and sales have been stagnant for some
time. The management team is eager to explore with you ways to stimulate
business growth.*

Nina moved her hand away from the pad. Was that enough of a hint to
Sujata to get her to consider coming back here permanently for everyone's
sake? Tea was synonymous with life in this region. Elderly workers still
measured distance in terms of tea breaks. The town of Ghoom, for example,
where many went for religious services on Sunday, was "two tea breaks
away." Both young and seasoned workers still set considerable store in the
saying, "Sell the tea, bring home the gold," even though the yield hadn't
brought much gold home lately. These workers would heartily welcome
Sujata at the estate. Word of her successful company in Victoria had generated considerable excitement. Sujata, the girl they'd known since she was
a baby in the crib, had taken a commodity so close to everyone's heart and
was helping make it the rage in Victoria. She had "conquered Canada with
her tea," they proclaimed.

A small noise caused Nina to swivel her chair around. In the opposite
corner of the room, Reenu was folding and arranging saris in a wardrobe.
Usually the girl darted through her duties, but at the moment her nimble
fingers erased an imaginary wrinkle on a sari over and over, while she stared
out the window, dreaming.

What could be on Reenu's mind? The workers' conversation from last
night reverberated in Nina's ears. She caught Reenu's startled expression and

spotted the hand that clenched reflexively over the delicate fabric. *Ghosts.* Nina felt her stomach gurgle.

Hastily Reenu hung the last piece of clothing and made for the door, where she hesitated a moment. "I'll shop for groceries now, Thakurma. Is there anything I can get you before I leave?"

"Yes, the calendar."

Nina watched the vanishing figure of Reenu, counted the number of days before Sujata arrived, then turned and poised her Parker pen over the stationery again, but words refused to flow. Sujata hadn't been informed of her father's shameful act. Upon her return, she would mingle with the relatives and the major players at the tea estate and the secret, embellished by opinions, judgments, and the passage of time, would roll out. It was unavoidable, as there had been little turnover among the employees. And they had long memories.

"Tell me, Thakurma," Sujata would demand, impatience pushing her body forward in the chair. "Is it true? How could Father do such a thing?"

Nina dropped her Parker pen. Would Sujata respect her father's memory when she came to know the truth? Would she respect Nina?

How badly we disappoint our progeny, Nina lamented to herself. Worshipful, they look up to their elders with the romanticism of youth. But the elders, mere creatures of muscle, blood, and bones, tumble to the ground like a straw hut at the approach of a cyclone. A long life can mean a thousand deceits, a thousand funeral pyres.

twenty-five

The crisp, bracing chill of autumn air stimulating her senses, Aloka started toward home after work. Ahead, a setting sun pierced the slate-gray clouds lying low in the sky in bars of yellow-gold light. Vehicles honked and screeched and people flitted in and out of the darkening shadows, all symbols of energy and aliveness. She would call Pranab tonight. Planning their trip home would give her the excuse she needed. The initial shock of divorce had subsided, but she missed him and their life together. How his presence brightened the color of her day. How solitary she found it was to perform little acts like reading the newspaper or preparing the monthly budget. How hard it was to close the day without exchanging loving words. Yes, a call to Pranab. Quickening her pace, she made for the grocery store-cum-delicatessen on Fifty-third and Second.

Chain grocery stores abounded at every corner of this neighborhood, but she patronized this individually owned Korean-run shop, named Sunrise Market, that carried hard-to-find Asian produce. As she stepped inside, she was haunted by a slight musky, fruity smell that she couldn't place.

"They have fresh jackfruit today," announced a voice above the ringing of the cash register.

The Indian accent, the clear and distinct pronunciation, the eagerness of the speech all belonged to a dusky-skinned man in a Madras plaid shirt. She made eye contact and noticed a pair of jet-black eyes and eyebrows and a ripe smile. He looked familiar. Yes, she'd glimpsed him before at community functions—the India Day Parade, the Diwali gala, and the Navaratri festival. She often reported on such events in *Manhattan, India.* This man took an active part by sweeping the floor, arranging chairs, greeting people, and serving *prasad.* Now he was leaning over a pile of the oblong, spiky, greenish fruit she had favored from childhood, and occasionally lifting his head, giving her a glance. It hit her that although he was seemingly absorbed in assessing the fruit's quality, he was assessing her qualities as well. That made her blush. Obviously he was not a native New Yorker. He needed to relate to someone he'd met in passing, even if it was simply to discuss the merit of a fruit.

Belatedly she realized that a question mark was nestled in his statement about jackfruit: Did she know the fruit, and if so, did she fancy it? She nodded politely to answer yes and, at the same time, signify the end of the encounter. If she were to meet him again at another community event, she would not hesitate to chat with him about jackfruit, or whatever. In times like this, in a public place, she followed the motto of New York women: "When not comfortable, split."

She slipped past him to a central island of steamer trays. She paused in front of the *orzo* and wild rice salad, a medley in yellow and black, and inhaled the mild woodsy aroma. She scooped a large portion into a plastic container. Since Pranab's departure six months ago, she hadn't prepared many meals at home. Carry-outs had sustained her, though now her digestive system cried out for real food. How fresh was this salad? After a moment's reflection, she moved on to the next item: a glistening stir-fry of rice noodles.

"We must be neighbors." The voice again.

She blinked when she saw that he was at her elbow, this obviously lonely man. Playing for time, she let her eyes rove the shop. The young Korean owner was hand-spraying a pyramid of shiny red and green chilis. An elderly Indian-American woman patron, bent over a bread display, was taking the pulse of each loaf.

Her tone impersonal, even philosophical, Aloka replied, "In a way I suppose we're all neighbors."

"Yes, indeed we are," he came back, emboldened. "I see you shopping here—all the time. And I've seen you at Diwali and Republic Day celebrations. I'm on the committee for both."

She gave him a glance of extolment. It occurred to her now that in keeping with his tradition, he hadn't introduced himself. Indians often procrastinated in this matter. The conclusion: He belonged to the category of "Indian Indians." A man, half a life away from the motherland, who still couldn't shed his accent, mannerisms, habits, or perception of the world.

"I live across the street." He indicated a brownstone whose ordinariness made it seem like part of the scenery. "Mrs. Chatterjee over there lives on my floor. I help carry her groceries. You must live close by, too."

So he was helping an elderly woman shop. She considered that a sign of decency, but still wondered if she should continue this conversation, when he blurted, "My friend Holly and I would like to invite you over for dinner."

Holly? "Thanks," Aloka managed, "but I really have to go now."

"I can tell you have many important things to do. But please, I'm making a good Indian meal—*sukhe aloo, gughni,* and *pullao* rice. It'd be an honor if you joined us. I'd very much like to talk with you."

She could taste the thickly sauced potatoes, stewed spicy chickpeas, and fragrant rice. But . . . Her gaze fastened on the current copy of *Manhattan, India* under his armpit. She hadn't looked at this week's headline yet. Flood, refinery fire, border dispute, or nuke, she couldn't tell. Her "Ask Seva" column was inside the fold. Did he read her column?

"We're from the same country, ma'am, perhaps even the same age. We belong to the same community here. It might ease your quite reasonable concern to know that I'm a vegetarian and a pacifist. What's your name?"

"Parveen," Aloka said cheerfully, in a goofy sort of a way, tickled at her own invention.

"What a pretty name."

Nodding in silent agreement, she appreciated the music, the fluidity, and the appeal of a new manifestation. From whence it stemmed, she didn't know.

"I am Jahar, born and raised in Ahmedabad. Where in India are you from?"

"Oh, from everywhere." Now hungrier, she sneaked a look at the tangle of rice noodles, cuddled in a reddish brown bean sauce, before her. "I was a railway brat. We lived all over India. Since my father's retirement, my parents have made their home in Bombay. I still have trouble calling it Mumbai. Old habit." She flashed him what she believed was a convincing smile.

"You seem to live an interesting life. What are you doing here?"

Her eyes skimmed a brochure rack on the rough, plastered wall. She extemporized, "I'm a real estate broker."

"I'm a night watchman at the AGC Building." Jahar gave a laugh. "My boss doesn't believe I'm Indian. He says Indians are doctors, engineers, high-tech gurus, or writers."

"How does a vegetarian pacifist fight off prowlers?"

"I sit on a stool by the entrance and read the Bhagavad-Gita aloud all night. Perhaps the strange sounds of the Hindu scripture frighten the prowlers." With a twinkle in his eyes, he added, "Or maybe they think I'm crazy."

Aloka felt a smile blossom on her lips. His way of carrying himself, as well as his professed vocation, confirmed that he had a humble upbringing. Despite his modest situation, he was bursting with the gladness of being alive.

"Why don't you put that bowl away and come with me, Parveen? I promise to leave my apartment door open. Anytime you don't feel at ease, you can leave. Besides, Mrs. Chatterjee is right next door." Jahar's chin rose in anticipation of an answer. When it became apparent that none was forthcoming, he said with as serious an expression as she had seen him make, "I have a large photograph of my parents on the living room wall. I'd do no evil in front of them, you can be sure of that, Parveen."

How beautifully he sang her new name. As Parveen, she would wear the reddest lipstick, strut on three-inch pumps, chat with a newly met man, and laugh without inhibition. Parveen was big-hearted. She accepted impromptu dinner invitations and didn't fret over trifles like Aloka did.

Her gaze followed his to the jackfruits. It had been so long since she had tasted one. According to Grandma, the gigantic fruit was meant for sharing. Grandma would wrap the train of her sari around her chest, then take out the sections—scores of pulpy, creamy yellow morsels, each concealing a glistening chestnut-brown pit. She would serve the sweet, fragrant meat to the eager family members, who consumed them in an appreciative silence. Yes, Aloka mutely agreed with Grandma now, it was a sensuous fruit, not to be enjoyed alone.

She restacked the bowl. "Suppose I buy a jackfruit?"

A hailstorm of a smile spread across his face, lending a debonair cast to his features. "Excellent. I like the fruit so much my friends refer to me as Jack."

His earnestness was amusing. And how naturally he claimed his share of happiness from the simplest of things. Parveen could learn from him. Yes, she could learn from him by osmosis.

She groped through the pile to select the heaviest fruit, which tipped the scale at nearly twelve pounds. To the bemused shoppers behind them in line, Jahar proudly proclaimed this jackfruit to be the largest fruit in the world. A smile pulled Mrs. Chatterjee's lips wide like an automatic sliding door opening.

Jahar cradled the fruit in his left arm like a precious infant and balanced Mrs. Chatterjee's groceries on his right. The threesome crossed the street, entered the nondescript brownstone, and rode a creaky cage to the third floor. They swept up a long hallway whose walls, lights, and ceiling shaded into a monotone of ocher, permeated by a smell evocative of the rusty, the ancient, and the overused. The dullness didn't sap Jahar's spirit, however. He walked just ahead of them with eager, bouncy steps until he reached Mrs. Chatterjee's door, number 303, and lugged her grocery bags inside. The senior thanked him and waved a good-bye to Aloka.

"Three-oh-five is my apartment number." Jahar announced this as he stopped in front of apartment 304 and knocked twice, informing Aloka with a guileless smile, "I want you to meet my friend Holly."

The door opened to reveal a statuesque woman in purple spandex with a barbell in one hand. Nearly six feet tall, this temple of muscle filled the doorway.

"Oh, hi, Jahar." The expression was no-nonsense, the carriage erect, the voice wispy. Staring down at his arm, she exclaimed, "Ha! Another jack-fruit?"

"Well, you know how it is. I can't leave them alone." He glanced at her with admiration. "The reason I knocked is to introduce you to my new friend, Parveen. She is from my country. I've invited her over for dinner, but she isn't sure."

"Oh, he's okay." Holly winked. "And wait till you smell his cooking. It drives me crazy."

"Why don't you join us, Holly? You could lift this jackfruit instead of that dumb barbell. That is, until dessert time."

"Thanks, but I'll have to pass. I still have several hours of working out and I couldn't do it on a full stomach. Would you like to come in for a few minutes?"

"Maybe later. Right now I have to work out in the kitchen."

"I might come over later and help you with the jackfruit. You'll never be able to finish it by yourself, Jahar. Nice meeting you, Parveen." Holly winked again and closed the door behind her.

They turned to 305 and Jahar put his key in the door. "Holly seems to have some friendly bones in her body," Aloka said, "or should I say muscles?"

That called a grin to Jahar's lips. "But you wouldn't want to meet her in a dark alley. I guess it's not surprising that she works as a bodyguard. The first time I placed my eyes on those abs, glutes, and biceps, I was so intimidated that I decided I'd better make friends with her."

Jahar whirled around, unlocked the door, pocketed the keys, and showed Aloka into the living room. Following his lead, she kicked off her shoes and deposited them by the door. His large feet were encased in old, dark brown socks. She found it pleasing that he had preserved the Indian custom of not letting the dirt and germs of the street tarnish the sacredness of his living space. Her feet in nylons sinking into a grayish-blue rug with a diamond design, she stepped into the modestly furnished sitting area. Her eyes moved from a large parental portrait that hung high on one wall to a stack of *Manhattan, India* issues on the occasional table, to a large tree branch suspended horizontally from the ceiling, before finally coming to rest on the open kitchen. A once-fashionable avocado-hued refrigerator wore mustard-yellow spice smudges on its door. A pair of shiny green cucumbers waited on the kitchen counter.

Jahar gestured to the couch. "Please sit down, Parveen." He put a Hindi film sound track on the CD system and glanced over at her. Swaying rhythmically to the beat of the music, he slipped into the kitchen and switched on the graying fluorescent light overhead. "Just like Ahmedabad sunshine."

He began peeling potatoes with the long, slow strokes of a peeler. As he had promised, the front door remained discreetly ajar. While she admired the esthetic effect of the tree branch overhead with a votive cleverly hung from it to create an average wage-earner's chandelier, she grew concerned about her safety. Out in the glum corridor, anyone might approach unnoticed: weirdos, ruffians, drug pushers, or psychopaths. Finally, unable to contain her disquiet any longer, she ventured, "It doesn't bother you to leave the door open?"

He put the peeler down and swung around. "Not with Holly around."

Smiling, she walked to the chest-high partition dividing the living room from the kitchen. Folding her arms on top of it, she leaned forward to watch him at work. She noticed the hooked nose, the black mole on his right jaw, the nimble fingers, and the concentration in his deep-set eyes. She heard the sound of his footsteps as he moved about the kitchen.

"On weekends I invite people over." He paused to sprinkle spices on the now-bubbling oil he had poured into the pan a few minutes earlier. A fragrant mist curled over their heads, then settled there like a cloud cover. "Friends and relatives, about twenty of them, come over. Somehow, I manage to fit them all in this room. When you're having a good time, you don't need a lot of space to spread out. My two oldest uncles take the couches. The others sit on the floor. Too much furniture just separates people, you know. This is a newer chair; that one is more comfy, we think, but on the floor we're all the same. We talk, sing, play cards, and eat till two in the morning. You know, just like in India."

She gave an emphatic nod to convey agreement. In happier times she'd spent entire evenings just talking with Pranab, about nothing in particular, munching on a packet of tropical mix and lazing on the sofa, the television turned off, reveling in that ideal state of mutual understanding. A longing for Pranab, a desire to retreat to those days blew through her. She quickly suppressed it.

"Why such a long face, Parveen?" He looked up from his stirring. "My mother says if you let the bird of sadness rest on your heart, it'll soon build a nest."

She had slipped back into Aloka's skin. She shrugged it off, stood straighter, and became Parveen again, that ethereal creature, one who lived in the present moment, one who moved about as capriciously as tempestuous clouds. Looking up at him, she replied, "I was just missing that whole way of life back home. New York's so busy and so empty for me right now. The worst loneliness is where there's a lot going on, but you aren't a part of any of it, where the noise level is high, but you can't identify any of the sounds."

"One real friend can make all the difference."

Their eyes met and locked for an instant, then moved off in different directions.

"How long have you lived here, Jahar?"

"Twelve years."

She heard Parveen say, "Have you ever been involved with a woman?"

"You're asking if I've ever been disappointed in love? Yes, I have. Some people are in the business of causing others pain."

"Have you ever been married?"

"Kind of."

"Kind of?"

"She was pretty and vivacious and spoke little English, which made her doubly charming." He slid a handful of onion slices into the pot, where they sizzled furiously, exuding a pungent note. "She had the kind of life energy that made even the furniture in the room dance. We got married soon after we met. A month after that, I went home alone to break the news to my family that I'd married a Bulgarian. To my surprise, my mother accepted it. She begged me to bring my wife with me the next time I came to visit. 'So she's not a *desi*,' my mother said. 'No matter. Now she's part of the family.' I was so relieved and so grateful. When I got back after three weeks with a big box of presents for her from my family"—his lips twitched in agitation and his words were garbled a bit—"the apartment was empty. I was frantic and called the police. They had already found her body in a wooded area in New Jersey. They couldn't come up with any motive for murder. Neither could I, but then, I didn't know much about her past."

A deep sigh caused a vein in his throat to stand out. He drew himself erect and went back to stirring. From the CD player behind them, a vocalist chanted an open-throated tune tinged with pining, and Jahar sang along, lips twisted, his foot tapping on the floor. There was pain in his taut fingers as he scattered chopped fresh chilis over the potatoes.

A heavy sensation inhabited Aloka's chest, but Parveen refused to give in to it. "In New York, you have to make your eyes sharper and your *dil*, your heart, harder."

He grabbed the handles on either side of the pot and shook it vigorously. "I guess my *dil* is still a bit soft."

"What's that spice you're adding?"

"Fenugreek. It smells somewhat like maple syrup, but tastes a little on the bitter side. My older sister turned me on to it. 'You must take a measure of bitterness along with the sweetness, Jahar.' I didn't believe her until I found out how good this dish tastes when you add fenugreek. I can give you her recipe if you like."

"Thanks, but I don't cook anymore."

She looked down at her arms folded on top of the half-wall partition, arms that had developed well-defined cords of muscle from kneading dough for the *luchis* Pranab demanded. Several days a week she had packed a meal in his lunch box, a real Bengali one: puffed bread and batter-fried eggplant accompanied by fresh tomato chutney, for he liked to finish his lunch on a sweet and sour note. She still remembered all the little things that lightened his frame of mind.

Jahar flipped a long fat cucumber in the air and caught it. "Let me tell you a secret. Every man has a fantasy, which women usually misinterpret. They think all we want is . . ." He shrugged. "Well, I won't deny it crosses our minds now and then." His hands became a blur as he chop-chop-chopped the cucumber into even rounds with a long sharp knife. "My secret dream has been to cook for you. Just like this, with you standing there and watching, your hair catching the light. I am hearing your musical voice, drinking in the sound of your laugh. Under the glow of your loveliness, these mundane food preparations become extraordinary. This is a moment of great happiness for me."

Imagine falling in love over a plate of cucumber under the fluorescent light of a cramped New York kitchen. In their early courtship days, Pranab had once composed an impromptu "Ode to Aloka," glorifying her as the "essence of a lily." They'd been sitting beside a pond graced with delicate white water lilies, in a tranquil forest glade beneath the third highest mountain in the world. How extraordinarily different, yet somehow alike.

With brisk movements Jahar removed the newspapers and covered the coffee table with a colorful cloth. She watched as he ladled the food, a conspiracy of colors, shapes, and sizes, onto serving platters. She examined the large gentle hairy hands threaded with prominent veins, as they fetched the platters and arranged them with care on the coffee table: the freshly prepared *sukhe aloo* and *pullao* rice, leftover *chana*, and, of course, the sliced cucumbers. He gave it all one final careful glance and, satisfied with the effect, he motioned her to the couch.

She nibbled at a piece of *sukhe aloo*, followed by a bite of the cooling cucumber, savoring the contrast. Belatedly she realized that she'd been hiding an intense hunger for far too long. She was catapulted back in touch with her inner self. Parveen had returned to a simpler time when connections were made quickly and every encounter had an innocent quality. "When I left home I changed in many ways," she said, "but when it comes to food I'm still that little kid."

One caring glance at her and her nearly empty plate and he whooshed a sigh of relief. "A man is never completely sure when he cooks for a woman. It is my belief that women understand food more instinctively. They have a more natural feel for it. We men can only hope that our efforts are pleasing to women."

He charmed her, this unpretentious man, and brought out the animated side in her. Indeed, she hadn't felt this way since her early days with Pranab. She accepted a second helping of the *sukhe aloo*, which for her was an indication of being at ease.

His fully loaded obedient fork moved in a rhythmic arc between his plate and his mouth. "Hunger is a good sign, Parveen. It means you're alive and healthy and keeping on. Cherish it."

"A good cook is both healer and magician."

Beaming at her accolade, he cleared the table and stacked the empty dishes into the sink. He gestured at her to remain seated. "Wait right there. Dessert is coming."

She looked on in amazement as he whirled jackfruit sections, yogurt, a pinch of sugar, and ice in a blender and returned with two tall glasses brimming with a frothy yellow elixir. "May I offer you a jackfruit *lassi*?"

She sniffed the musky smell appreciatively. "A *jassi*, you mean?"

He laughed boisterously. "A *lassi* made with jackfruit become a *jassi*. How witty you are, Parveen."

She took a long slow sip. Immediately she was transported from the humbleness of her surroundings to a landscape of lavender and honeysuckle, where her clothes flapped against her body as lightly as a breeze.

Jahar exhaled, "Ahhhh!" as he took another healthy swallow from his glass. Eyes on a copy of *Manhattan, India* that was lying on the floor, he said, "Perhaps I should send this *jassi* recipe to the 'Ask Seva' column. That Seva woman is okay."

"You read her column regularly?"

"Oh, of course."

She drained the last drops from her tumbler, consulted her wristwatch. "Well, it's getting late. I should probably be going. I'm planning a trip to India soon. I have to make a list of presents to buy."

His barely audible "Oh" didn't conceal his disillusionment. Yet he rose with her and graciously helped her collect her jacket, footwear, and purse. At the door he asked gently, "May I walk you home?"

"Thanks, Jahar. That's really not necessary."

She lingered a moment longer to express her gratitude and, feeling words inadequate, lightly kissed him on the lips. She pivoted and strode down the corridor, aware of his dazed stare until she rounded the corner. As the elevator droned its way down, it dawned on her that he hadn't asked for her phone number. But then, she hadn't accorded him much of an opportunity.

She laughed in relief, for Parveen had just arrived in the big city. She did not yet have a telephone.

twenty-six

The fog outside Suzy's kitchen window, a delicate shield, cut out the late October sun. She was making *chai*. The tempo of this Saturday morning ritual was much to her liking. She measured milk and water into a large pot, followed by the greenish black leaves of exquisite black tea, one level teaspoon per cup, then sprinkled in whole spices, cardamom, cinnamon, and cloves. For added lift on this cool morning, she incorporated slivers of ginger root. Adding the rhizome to *chai* was a trick she'd learned at home; it was a folk remedy that kept winter colds at bay.

She placed the pot on the stove and allowed it to simmer. Ashraf and tonight's dinner plans rose in her consciousness, and along with that a question. He'd sounded so eager and pleased that she'd be dining at his restaurant. Did he harbor a romantic interest toward her? For business reasons—he was a major client—she couldn't refuse, even though such an invitation intersected business and social life and made for a delicate situation. She would have to tread this one carefully.

Suzy turned up the heat and stirred the pot with a well-worn wooden spoon. Within minutes, the milk coagulated, and the shrunken tea leaves surrendered their essence and formed a dark green lace on the white surface. The resulting brew blushed a pink radiance. The *chai* was ready.

Enveloped by the cozy heat of the stove and the aromatic mist from the pot, Suzy poured the steaming brew into a delicate English bone-china cup. She listened to the fullness of the trickle and took pleasure in regarding the richness flowing over. As she held the gold-bordered lime-green cup filled with the amber liquid and indulged in a sip, she fretted once again about Ashraf's invitation. Did she need this complication in her life? She'd be going home soon and seeing Pranab again.

The telephone sang. Suzy picked up the receiver and dropped onto a stool, and from the other end came Grandma's fragile voice with Darjeeling sun dappling it.

Why would Grandma be calling? Although international long-distance dialing had become more affordable, there was a time difference of half a day. Usually the grand old woman's call brought major news: births, weddings, graduations, anniversaries, nuclear testing, and deaths. To mask her worry, Suzy replied lightly, "Thakurma, what a surprise."

"I hear you didn't receive Mreenal Bose."

The note of disappointment in Grandma's voice didn't escape Suzy's attention. "So you sent him! Well, I wasn't home. Sorry if I put you in an awkward position—"

"I expected you'd be out today, too, an active young lady like yourself."

"Not much is happening, at least not until this evening." Suzy went on to list her chores for the day: laundry, vacuuming, shopping, and finally dinner with her friend Eva at a well-regarded local restaurant.

"You do your own housecleaning? You never liked that sort of work."

"I still don't." Suzy controlled a chuckle. Grandma considered Europe and North America to be enchanted lands where exciting, beautiful things materialized with little effort. She took a minute to explain how routine the days here could be, how lacking in sunlight; how people lived mostly inside themselves in a closet of solitude. In contrast, Grandma, despite her age, received a constant stream of cronies and relatives, Suzy was sure of that. "Company twenty-four hours," was how Grandma had once described her days in a letter.

"You're not dating?"

"This place isn't as ideal for dating as you might think. Or maybe I don't have luck on my side." Suzy wondered again about the reason for this call.

"Talk about luck—Cousin Bakul's daughter got married in Houston two weeks ago." And Grandma was off on a roll, listing the bridegroom's credentials—salary, degrees, caste and clan designation, profession, even height.

"Mind you, it was an arranged meeting in Houston," Grandma added. "The boy lives in Dallas. They hit it off right away and decided to go ahead. If someone had suggested an old-fashioned arranged marriage, they'd have said no. I saw the wedding pictures. The groom came in on a horse, like it used to be in the olden days. Funny how overseas Indians follow customs we've forgotten here. Their parents' plan worked well in this case, wouldn't you agree, my dear?"

Suzy placed her elbows on the kitchen counter. Another "happy match" call. At this point in her life, health and marriage were Grandma's top priorities. Suzy would have to fight off these matchmaking attempts. She expressed her happiness for the bride, then added, "I'm drinking *chai*, Thakurma, the whole bit with spices, like you taught me."

"*Cha?*" Her voice brighter, Grandma pronounced the word for tea in the Bengali fashion as she always did. "Not coffee? Very good. I hear Mreenal also likes *cha. Mone prane Bangalee.*"

Suzy smiled inwardly at Grandma's description of Mreenal. The mind and soul of a Bengali, eh? Perhaps she had dismissed him too lightly.

Suzy asked about Grandma's health and listened as Grandma heaved a sigh.

"My spirit is still here. After a certain age you know your body for what it is, a fragile vessel to house your soul. I'll feel much better when I see you again, dear girl. According to my calculation, you'll be coming home in two weeks and ten hours. It's a pity your grandpa won't be here to greet you." A poignant pause followed. "Today would have been our sixty-third wedding anniversary. Bimal would always buy me a piece of jewelry for this occasion. Once I said to him, 'The days you have given me are more brilliant than any jewels you can buy in the market.' And I really meant it. You should have seen his smile."

"How fortunate you were in love, Thakurma. I still remember the story you told us about how you met Grandpa."

"Do you really? He's still with me. He always will be. Well, dear, I really must go now. *Koyek dinee dekha hobe.*"

That sad yet triumphant note ringing in her ears, Suzy hung up. She couldn't let go of the rhythm of Grandma's speech, the voice that was so heartening during the childhood years. She picked up her cup and found herself in Grandma's room many years ago.

Sujata was eight years old then, and Aloka twelve. On that early afternoon Mother had sent them downstairs to spend time with Grandma. They dashed past Grandma's Usha sewing machine to where she was sitting on the wall side of the high bed, pillows cushioning her back. The sun flirted through the curtained window and a light breeze rustled the stationery on the writing table. Yarn hooked over her index finger, her eyebrows furrowing, Grandma was knitting a sweater in green wool splashed with cream in a filigree pattern. Knitting was a pastime of women in Darjeeling. Sujata had watched women spinning woolen threads even as they strolled the streets. And Grandma was one of the town's expert knitters. Many neighbors came to her for advice on knitting. The big yarn ball that lay on Grandma's side unraveled now at the command of her fingertips like a tamed cobra. She made sweaters for the whole family that the frigid Darjeeling winters made necessary. "Ready-made sweaters won't do for Gupta girls," she was in the habit of saying. Sujata liked the hand-knits because Grandma would often sew in a pocket as an extra.

That afternoon the children erupted on either side of Grandma, Aloka on her right, Sujata on her left, took their seats, and looked up expectantly. Though Grandma let her knitting drop on her lap with ostentatious reluctance and assumed an appearance of mock irritation, it was clear she didn't mind the interruption. She took pleasure in telling stories, of gods and goddesses or family exploits, stories as lavish and textured as her sweaters.

"Today would have been our thirty-fifth wedding anniversary," Grandma began with an elaborate sigh. She had never spoken about her wedding, so

Sujata drew closer in anticipation. Grandma added, "It still seems only yesterday that I met Bimal."

"Tell us how you met him," Aloka chimed in.

"I was eighteen, well, nearly nineteen then, a suitable marriageable age in those days—"

"I won't marry till I'm the age of Gayatri-*masi*," Sujata said proudly, looking sideways at Aloka, and reminding her of the aunt who had waited till she finished her medical studies to plunge into matrimony.

That drew an immediate retort from Aloka. "Only because it'll take you that long to find someone, skinny. I'll be married a lot sooner."

"By taking my time, I'll marry a better man."

Grandma put her arms around both of them. "You don't know whom you'll marry, or when," she said in that veteran manner of hers. "I never expected to marry your grandpa. He was rich and handsome. I was poor and plain."

"Did you use magic, Thakurma?"

"Oh, no, nothing of that sort, Aloka. In those days women were said to belong to the respected tribe of mothers, but when a baby girl was born, it was treated as bad luck. We didn't wish for something and expect it to happen. Making a direct request was out of the question. We only tried to change the atmosphere around us and hoped that men would notice."

"So, how did Grandpa know you had fallen in love with him at first sight?" Another romantic question from Aloka.

"He read the signs of love in my wide eyes and shaky lips. You might say I was acting like a heroine in Bankim Chandra's novel. You see, I was going to college in Calcutta, where I stayed with an uncle and aunt who paid for my tuition and living expenses and hardly ever asked me to do any chores. I had plenty of time to read novels. I was enrolled in an honors program in English. It was my summer vacation and I'd returned home to Malipore."

"Where's Malipore?" Sujata's practical self wanted to be cognizant of the nuts and bolts of things.

"Oh, it's an isolated village in East Bengal, what is now known as Bangladesh. Even in those days, it was backward by most people's standards, though, thinking back, the village did have a certain rustic charm. It took two days from Calcutta by train, steamer, and taxi to reach there, and we thought that was swift. When I was a little girl, your age, Sujata, it used to take five days to get there. It was a friendly place. The villagers shared everything, their joys and heartbreaks, and also a fancy teapot if someone from the city came to visit. Our households were so closely woven it seemed we lived many lives at once."

Sujata asked, "Can we go there sometime?"

"It's still a difficult journey. Maybe, when you're both a little older, we can take a trip down there." Grandma's eyes grew hazy with sorrow. "I'm sad to say that our home has been sold. Some other family lives there now."

For a minute Sujata lost herself in a vision of the hamlet: palm-thatched mud houses ringed by a sugarcane grove, a mustard field ripened to a greenish gold color and reaching up to her knees. She heard plaintive strains of live *kirtan* music, deeply felt and devotional, and brushed past a window from which wafted out the smoky smell of *dhoop*. A much younger Grandma and a clutch of her friends milled around the village tube well, showing off their newest glass bangles and swapping gossip: Whose mother was pregnant again? Which boy winked at whom? Which family could afford the finest rice?

"You didn't even have a radio, Thakurma?" Wasn't it just like Aloka to ask such a silly question?

"Or electricity, for that matter. But we had other ways to amuse ourselves. Our trees bore so many jackfruits that we fed our cows on them. And we enjoyed the littlest things, like making a flute out of a fruit pit, a trumpet out of palm leaves, or simply taking a dip in the pond on hot days. 'Happiness is more important than money,' our elders taught us. That year I'd come home to relax the entire summer and catch up with friends. That is, I thought so until one afternoon when my mother announced that a family was coming to see me." Grandma's face took on a glow, yet a shade of concern deepened the corners of her mouth. "I understood very well what 'seeing' meant."

"An inspection."

"Right you are, Aloka." Grandma elaborated that a marriage broker had approached her parents with a proposal and the prospective bridegroom and his family would come for a visit. She gathered that they would make her walk, question her about her studies and whether she could cook and sew, and ask her to sing. They would check her out as if she were a prize buffalo. "I was frightened, but terribly curious," Grandma said. "Through gossip I'd heard the interested family was well off and highly respected. I'd also found out that their oldest son, Bimal, was not only intelligent and handsome, but also kindhearted. People adored him. He was special. That meant many prominent families would want their daughters to marry him, so, of course, I didn't stand a chance. I told myself to relax and enjoy the show, to practice 'being seen' for future use." Grandma strained to catch a shallow uneven breath and smoothed her front hair, perhaps experiencing anew the uncertainty of that young age.

"Tell us how that went." It seemed Aloka could barely contain her curiosity.

"It started with a long bath. I scrubbed my skin with green gram flour so it would glow. After drying myself, I outlined my feet with brilliant red *aalta*, then I put on a peacock-blue silk sari. It was my best sari and showed my dark skin to advantage. I wrapped the *aanchal* around my shoulders in a show of modesty. A scene from *Ramayana* was woven into the *aanchal* and the sari border—followers waiting for the god Ram's return. Finally, I combed my hair."

"Was your hair very long?" Sujata had figured out from experience that Grandma often needed prodding to supply missing details.

"It reached all the way to my calves. In those days, Bengali women didn't cut their hair. Even so, mine was the longest hair in the village, undoubtedly my best feature. It was thick and soft and reflected the sunlight. My father called it Brahmaputra, after the long river known for its ferocious currents."

Sujata looked up. Gray curls, scented with Keo Karpin oil, framed Grandma's wrinkled brows. Since becoming a widow, she had cropped her hair to just below her ears. Secretly Sujata wanted to stroke Grandma's hair, but that would be disrespectful. Instead she simply asked, "How did you wear your hair that day, Thakurma?"

"My mother piled my hair up in a coil at the back of my head. That was the custom. If you were over the age of twelve, you had to keep your hair braided, knotted, or covered, anything but down. Even very young girls plaited their hair. And under no condition should you let your hair hang down or show it to men outside your immediate family. They might get 'ideas.' Only bold and wanton women would do such a thing. Our village society considered it shameless. The situation was different for wealthy women living in big cities. They could wear their hair bobbed, shoulder length, and loose."

"But you went to college in Calcutta," Sujata said.

"I came from a poor family. I had to look conservative and act submissive."

"So, Grandpa and his family came to see you. Did you feed them?" Aloka's thoughts never strayed far from food, it seemed.

"Oh, yes. My mother spent the whole day in the kitchen, preparing a seven-course meal we could hardly afford: *luchi, aloor dam, begun bhaja, cholar dahl, payesh,* and two kinds of *sandesh*—all for an afternoon tea. At four o'clock, when we were ready and quite exhausted, Bimal, his parents, and four of their relatives arrived. I still remember the day. It was hot, damp, and very still. The rooms were stuffy, so the guests were escorted to our clean courtyard. We had no fancy flower beds, fountain, or sculpture. There was just a tall bel tree and a tiny holy basil plant, tulsi, in a raised planter."

Sujata remembered how Grandma had often emphasized the sacred quality of the bel fruit. "Touch a bel; wash your sins." Once every Hindu household planted such a tree in the courtyard so children would grow up in its divine shadow.

"The guests sat under the bel tree in a semicircle, facing the tulsi plant," Grandma picked up her tale. "I stayed inside the living quarters, just far enough back from the doorway to watch the proceedings without being seen."

"Do you remember what Grandpa was like then?" Sujata asked.

"I remember him as though it were yesterday. He was dressed simply in a white shirt and *dhoti,* but there was an air of dignity about him and just the right amount of deference on his face. He greeted my parents sincerely and remained standing until both sets of parents took their seats. Then my father beckoned me to join them. I said a mute prayer to the bel and tulsi and, with my gaze lowered to the ground, as any proper girl would, stepped into the courtyard. The crowd, who had been waiting for this moment with eager anticipation, fell silent. I shivered. The judging had begun. Knowing

I wasn't pretty, I positioned myself under the bel tree, so the sun filtering through the leaves would highlight my hair. Then I remembered my mother's words. My teeth were as dainty as pomegranate seeds and my smile was my second best feature. I parted my lips slightly. As I raised my eyes, I found Bimal, his mouth half open, staring at me. Like I was a goddess with a halo who had just descended from heaven in a chariot. I wondered how he saw beyond my exterior into my soul so quickly. Our eyes locked for a split second, and I, too, was smitten. I'd never seen so much vitality and intelligence in a man, or playfulness evident in the twinkle in his eyes. He was like Krishna, our fearless god, sitting on a raised pavilion and playing his flute—silly stuff I'd seen in a movie. Before I knew it, I pictured myself as barefoot Radha, made totally helpless by his call, responding, swaying, looming toward him. Bimal's father broke the trance by saying, 'Please be seated, Nina.'

"Just as I had folded my sari-clad self into a chair, Bimal's mother parted her veil. Her features were perfect, like an artist's work. Her skin had a pinkish radiance, as though she regularly bathed in a pool awhirl with rose petals, like ancient Mogul princesses did. She must have been quite a beauty in her youth. She swung her nose ring and asked in a small, whiny voice, 'Bring me a glass of water, Nina. And one for Bimal.'

"It was an order. I shuffled inside, quite excited to be doing something for Bimal. Brass tumblers in either hand, I returned, again with baby steps, as I'd been taught, not spilling a drop. I was convinced I had passed the walking test. Bimal accepted a glass from me, grimaced as he swallowed, then caught himself and mumbled, 'How refreshing.' He sloshed the water and painfully took another tiny sip.

"His mother snatched the other tumbler from my hand, then immediately set it down firmly on the ground. 'But this water is boiling hot,' she sputtered indignantly.

" 'Please, please,' my mother cried, 'I'll get chilled water in an instant.' And she rushed inside.

"*Ma* Durga! I prayed to my protecting goddess. In my excitement and haste I'd forgotten to pour chilled well water from the earthen pitcher that was kept in one corner of our kitchen. I'd gone straight to the tap. On this scorching day, the pipes were nearly melting." Grandma roared with laughter. "Such was the spell we had cast on each other that I hadn't felt the heat from the brass tumblers, and neither had Bimal, or so he pretended. By then totally humbled and embarrassed, I bowed to his mother with folded palms. From everyone's silence I could tell the inspection was over. I stood there with a failing grade in my hand, only sorry that nobody understood the humor in the situation. Didn't our scriptures say that humor and laughter, *hasya rasa*, were second only to the emotion of love? The guests sat for another few minutes, then Bimal's mother muttered an excuse to leave. She shot up from her chair and so did her family. Bimal and I exchanged one last longing glance as he hurried after his mother. My father stood there with folded palms, looking pathetic and worn and old, his eyes glazed, and begged them in vain not to leave. After they'd disappeared around the corner, my mother lowered her head on the tulsi planter and sobbed. To my relief, they didn't chastise me, in fact they said nothing at all, but I could tell what a letdown it was for them. I wanted to die."

"But Grandpa loved you in spite of it all." Aloka, always the one dreaming of a prince. "I'm sure he didn't mind the hot water. He drank it, didn't he?"

"Yes, despite this little mishap, Bimal wanted to marry me. His mother said she'd go on a hunger strike if he did. I think she had a whole stable of candidates who were nothing but bundles of jewelry. In the meantime, Bimal and I began meeting by the village tube well without our parents' knowledge. My fearless god confessed he couldn't live without me and I told him he was the only one I wanted. I realized that he'd treat me as his other half, *ardhangini*, as our scriptures had dictated. He was still respectful of his mother. It took him four months, but eventually he wore her down and she agreed to our marriage. I hadn't expected her consent, so when the news came, I was delirious with happiness. I promised myself I'd win her over."

Aloka asked, "What was your new mother-in-law like?"

"Horrible and disgusting," Sujata replied condescendingly. "You have to ask?"

"Do you know what she did to me?"

Sujata slid closer and, in an instinctive gesture of protection, held Grandma's hand. "What, Thakurma?"

"It was only two weeks after our wedding. We were living with his parents, of course. That day Bimal and his father had to go to the next town,

Shaktipore, on business and weren't expected back till late. In the afternoon, his relatives were coming for a visit, so his mother made me slave in the kitchen all day. I prepared a ten-course meal for twenty-some guests. She had given the servants the day off, her way of punishing me, since I didn't bring any dowry. Besides, her son was too much in love with me, which meant loss of control for her. Late in the afternoon, when I was nearly fainting from exhaustion, she asked me to go freshen myself. When I'd changed and come out of my room, she ordered me to veil my hair and face and to follow her. I couldn't see the ground under my feet. Like I was barely human, allowed only to walk shamefully. The guests were seated in the family's beautiful courtyard lined with plum and bel trees, a tulsi plant and rosebushes, laughing and joking. When I heard their laughter and breathed in the fresh smell of roses, I felt more at ease. Then my mother-in-law presented me to the guests in a voice sweet as *malai*."

At the mention of rich, thick cream, Aloka licked her upper lip.

"How did they greet you?"

"The usual, Sujata. 'What a lovely bride'; 'Oh, she's so modest'; 'See how beautifully she walks.' They kept heaping praises on me until my mother-in-law interrupted, saying, 'Wait till you hear this.' "

"That was very rude."

"More than that, Sujata. She began mouthing the hot water incident. What a clumsy, stupid girl I was. How my poor, uncultured parents didn't teach me any manners. How I didn't deserve her golden boy Bimal. Everyone was roaring. An aunt said that such a bride should be locked up in the maid's room. A cousin blurted, 'Her face is as interesting as the underside of a lorry.' Again, I think it was all due to the lack of dowry. So there I sat, head down in total humiliation, praying to the tulsi plant. My eyes stung with tears. My scalp began to feel like it had been trampled on. I sprang up faster than a tigress leaps at her prey, threw off the veil, and took the pins out of my hair, allowing my tresses to cascade down my back and over my face. Mouths fell open. They'd never seen such long, shiny locks, and certainly no one expected a young married woman to assert herself in this fashion. *"Choop karo,"* I said. Shut up. My mother-in-law nearly fainted, her old cousin breathed terribly hard, and the rest looked up at me in shocked silence. I felt glorious—in a couple of words I had changed the atmosphere around me. I twirled once, so they could see me from all angles, smiled like thousand stars twinkling, then, with a raised chin, walked back to my room with sure, regal steps."

"Bravo." Sujata and Aloka both applauded gleefully.

"I became the talk of the village. My mother-in-law respected me a trifle more after that, though she never accepted me fully. I was neither rich nor beautiful. Bimal fought for me. When nothing worked, he came up with an excuse to move us to Darjeeling. The area was known for its jute, wool, cardamom, and, most of all, tea. We were to take care of his family tea estate.

"And so this mountain valley became my home. Legend has it that when the god Indra came down from heaven on a thunderbolt, or *dorje*, he landed at the peak of a mountain that later became the site of Darjeeling. His chosen beverage was tea, which is why it grew here so well. That incident in Malipore had affected me like a thunderbolt and burned my inhibitions. I became an equal partner with your grandfather in the management of the tea estate. Little did I know about fine tea then, having been raised on strong, coarse tea poor people could afford. However, a fact I'd studied in a college text had stayed with me. That in earlier times people spoke of tea, silk, and porcelain in the same breath.

"Then Bimal served me a cup of second-flush Darjeeling. I'd never tasted anything like that in my life. Silk and porcelain would pale before such tea. 'It's truly fit for the god Indra,' I told Bimal. I was pleased that we'd relocated in this cosmopolitan town. The limited Bengali society here was quite modern, educated, and Anglicized. We joined the Darjeeling Planters' Association, which threw a supper party every Wednesday night. The local term for a tea plantation owner was a 'planter.' I soon learned to fit in with the other planters and their wives."

"I'm so glad we live here, Thakurma, and not in that silly village with your mother-in-law. Did you ever go back?"

"I made a point to, Sujata, fifteen years ago." Grandma laughed delightedly. "I found that my name had been forgotten, but the tale had grown. Once upon a time, the village folks raved, there lived a brave bride who defied her evil mother-in-law. Her weapons were her long hair, a brilliant smile, and two words. In her support, the sparrows circled overhead, the bel tree swayed, the tulsi plant shed its leaves, the temple bells rang. The sky wept, though not a single drop of rain fell on her."

Sujata said, "You're a legend, Thakurma."

"I was also told that 'To drink boiling water on a scorching day' had become a household expression. Even your grandpa used that expression to indicate an unbearable situation."

"What happened to Great-Grandma?" Aloka again.

"She died," Sujata answered firmly.

"Yes, within a year," Grandma said, "from a heart condition. Her relatives suggested that the humiliation from the incident killed her, but I tell you I had nothing to do with it. I was expecting my first child by then. Your father was born shortly after the second anniversary of our marriage. Your grandpa got over his grief when his eyes fell on the sweet baby face of your father."

Even at that age Sujata had heard many sad tales of marriages gone sour. What joy to know Grandma's was blessed. With regret Sujata said, "I never did meet Grandpa."

"I did," Aloka said.

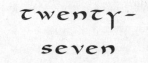

Twenty-seven

An hour after her phone conversation with Grandma, Suzy found a place to park her car on a commercial block of Fort Street. She joined a throng of antique collectors dawdling along and reached number 1018, alerting a pair of red robins pecking away at a branch above her on a mountain ash tree. She glanced at the water drops gleaming like silver beads on a purple cabbage plant outside the store window. The signboard just above proclaimed in big black letters: "Eva's Custom Tailoring." Etched below was Eva's trademark logo of a spool of thread. Suzy slipped in through the door.

She became aware of the smell of machinery and cloth that swirled about her. She passed a heavy old Singer sewing machine standing in one nook and, next to it, bobbins of thread in myriad colors. The foot-pedal model, ancient and blackened with age, would not be out of place in one of the neighboring antique shops, and it added personality to the space. A rack of clothes, consisting of finished men's suits, women's dresses, and pants— new, shining, fashionable—stood waiting in the middle of the room. She heard a snatch of conversation, something about "pure cashmere and tweed," as a clerk helped a customer choose from bolts of fabrics stacked on a tall shelf.

Eva emerged from her office, impeccable in a tailored turquoise suit. Gladness broke through her professional restraint and spread across her face.

"I'm sorry I'm late," Suzy said.

"We managed to keep busy." Then, with an eye to Suzy's blouse, "That's a fine lavender shade. It'll go nicely with your new pants."

Eva stepped to the rack, scrutinized a label, and handed the garment to Suzy. The plum-colored gabardine pants shone under the fluorescent light. Eva steered her to a fitting room in the back, where she changed into her new pants before a full-length three-way mirror. She brushed her fingers over the supple fabric. From outside the closed door, Eva chattered about the benefits of a drawstring waist.

"It's nonirritating," she insisted.

"And easy to adjust after a big meal," Suzy said.

She studied her body image, admitting to herself that the drawstring waist snuggled her midsection and the pencil legs seemed to boost her height an extra inch. What a pleasure to be able to order custom-made clothes! She opened the door and struck a pose.

Eva, who was waiting with a tape measure, a tailor's chalk, and a see-through ruler in hand, cast a keen, professional eye at Suzy. "You have just the figure for these slim-legged pants. Wait." Eva drew near, examined the seams, then stepped back and tilted her head. "The hem needs to be taken up. The work will be done by Tuesday and I'll deliver them to your door."

No use arguing with Eva, the meticulous seamstress. "Okay," Suzy murmured as she stepped into the fitting room. She changed back into her original clothes and came out.

With Eva muttering, "Let's have coffee," they stepped into a tiny office. A large desk in the center of the room was cluttered with lace, zippers, buttons, scissors, ribbons, and a papier-mâché dress form. While Eva cleared the desktop, Suzy eased down on a chair and dropped her purse to the floor.

Her eyes caught an artist sketchbook on a side table. On the open page Eva had sketched an apron and made some notations.

"I got an order from Brandywine Delicatessen." Eva poured coffee from a Braun machine into two gilt-edged white mugs. "Two hundred aprons for their caterers."

"Fantastic." Suzy placed her hand over Eva's wrist. "A real break for you."

"I'll have to hire extra stitchers," she said excitedly, then held up a fabric sample and reviewed the design she had been visualizing. Then, as though embarrassed to be so enthusiastic, she put the fabric aside and asked brusquely, "How do you like the coffee?"

"You make a wonderful cup. What kind of a blend is this?"

"It's Peruvian. Nothing like your ginger *chai*, though."

"Oh, that! That's my grandmother's recipe. She called this morning, you know. After she'd hung up, I kept thinking about the stories she used to tell Aloka and me, and somehow I got lost in those years."

"You'll be seeing your sister soon, won't you?"

Suzy nodded, then looked away, her eyes settling on an aggregation of invoices on the shelf.

"Why not give her a jingle? You have a good excuse now, after your grandmother's call."

Eva's comment, quiet and natural, came as a complete surprise and dampened Suzy's falling spirits even further. Call Aloka? Whatever for? She pulled her eyes up to a life-sized woman's dress pattern, serving as a decoration on the wall.

"You're trying to avoid her," Eva said. "I know how your mind works. Don't be foolish! I waited too long to call my aunt after our big argument. By the time I did, she was in intensive care and we never did have that talk."

"I never told you, did I, Eva, that Aloka is perfect?"

"You're stalling, you know." Eva surged to her feet.

Suzy stood up, too. This was vintage Eva: Drop a hint, create an atmosphere, then leave the conversational thread dangling, only to pick it up at a later time after both parties had had an opportunity to go over what had been said. Still, Suzy had to admit to herself that Eva perfectly grasped the crux of the matter. "See you this afternoon," Suzy said.

She departed from Eva's shop and wandered out. With the sun warming her back, she strolled down the street, stopping at B&E Food Market for milk and paper towels, neither of which she needed badly, before finding her way back to her car. An image of Aloka circled her mind as she drove.

Looking back, Suzy realized she hadn't been a loving sister to Aloka. She was the one to blame for a rupture in their closeness. But then, how could you be close to someone who was so perfect in her looks and manners and so talented? Suzy derived an almost perverse pleasure knowing that Pranab had turned away from perfection.

How betrayed Aloka must have felt. How that must have bled her a drop at a time.

And yet, Suzy believed that Aloka would eventually forgive her. Aloka had that quality of magnanimity, a nobility of spirit that made her believe in the ultimate goodness in people. She would extend her long, marble-smooth limbs to hug Suzy and mean it when she would say, "I've never stopped thinking about you." Aloka never forgot anybody.

Perhaps it was not yet too late, perhaps they could reconstruct a caring attachment. It could even start with the fulfillment of their childhood fantasy of visiting Grandma's birthplace, the village of Malipore, with its constant mild breeze, bowing guava trees, and simple people who went barefoot as they tended the rice paddies. Arranging such a trip would unify the sisters in a common goal. A joyous feeling of expectation tempered with anxiety waved through Suzy.

Back at her apartment, she forced herself to walk up to the phone table. The older sister should call first, that was the Bengali custom. This time, Suzy needed to initiate the contact, and she should do so before her newly born courage deserted her. She ran her fingers down her waist-length hair, an act that usually imbued her with a flutter of power but right now merely made her aware of how panicky she was.

It would be midafternoon in New York. Suzy had no idea how Aloka spent her weekends, since they called each other only on special occasions. On the last New Year's Day, they had heaped wishes of health, prosperity, and longevity on each other, but never went beyond that. Today, however, Suzy would convey to her sister how regretful she was for not staying at-tuned, how much she looked forward to their getting together in Darjeeling and catching up on the events in their lives, while sharing a pot of ginger *chai.* Suzy wouldn't talk about Pranab's letter, even though the beige envelope was peeking out from a side table.

Heart thudding, her throat dry as a desert on midday, Suzy looked up Aloka's number in her address book and, after a final moment of hesitation, punched the buttons. The phone kept buzzing at the other end in a forlorn, insistent monotone, while Suzy impatiently twisted the cord around her finger. After six rings she heard Aloka's musical voice on the line and cheerily put in, "Hi, Aloka, it's me, *bontee.*"

She had hoped for an enthusiastic greeting in return. Hadn't Aloka always treated the telephone line as a friendly messenger? Instead there ensued a long, prickly pause, then Aloka began to make the usual polite inquiries about Suzy's health and the state of her business. Was her tea company making a bigger profit this year than the last? Suzy detected the hint of a sneer, or perhaps she imagined it, and shifted the topic.

"Do you know Grandma called me this morning? She sounded as chipper as ever. Her call got me to wondering. Do you think we could go to Malipore together? Just for a couple of days. We always talked about it, but never did visit the place."

"Go where? What are you talking about?"

Now, even more subdued, Suzy asked, "How's Pranab?" Instantly she regretted the words.

"Why don't you tell me? You know better than I do."

Suzy felt the weight of a hatchet on her chest. So, Pranab was the cause of Aloka's frostiness. Aloka, still acting possessive after her divorce, still wanting Pranab back. Oh, no, not again. It should be Suzy's turn now. Suzy was equally entitled to love him. So, Aloka, wouldn't you kindly step aside?

The receiver still in her hand, Suzy leaned against the wall. She had managed to ruin this opportunity. She had failed to appease Aloka. Furthermore, with Pranab between them once again, there remained little hope for reconciliation once they both reached home. After a quiet period, Suzy made some feeble excuses—"Must go food shopping, it's Saturday"—and terminated the conversation. She didn't sound convincing even to herself.

There was only a sharp click at the other end.

twenty-
eight

On this Saturday afternoon, Aloka vacuumed underneath the bed—the first time since discovering that accursed letter—and, as her ears became attuned to the grumbling roar of the machine, she brooded about Sujata's phone call. *Bhoot,* stupid ghost, she had once shouted in childhood anger when Sujata accidentally knocked over her favorite clay elephant, breaking it into pieces. That had been the worst expression in Aloka's vocabulary then.

The same fury stirred up inside Aloka again. What really was the purpose behind *bhoot*'s call this morning? Had Pranab mailed that letter after all? He must have. *Bhoot*'s telephone call certainly had all the earmarks of a triumphant declaration.

Aloka dusted the bedroom furniture ferociously, admitting at last that Pranab had cheated her. What a hellish laugh those two must have had at her blindness. Come to think, Sujata was ready to play the same game again.

Sujata, her very own sister. But then, Aloka hadn't been blessed with genuine sibling affection in a long time. There had always been sticky dark issues between them, not the clarity that emanates from a close bond. Aloka believed she was lovable, everyone said so—everyone, that is, except her own sister. Detached, unfathomable, and sulky, Sujata resembled a mountain range that appeared close, protective, and kindly, when in reality it was chilly, harsh, and miles away.

This morning, despite Sujata's mysterious presence all around her, Aloka kept up with the cleaning, fluffing every pillow and giving the oven a once-over. In two hours she finished her chores. Even the brass tray stationed on the coffee table gleamed and the plumeria spilling out of a vase gave off a fresh scent. By now her quadriceps had cramped, her fingernails were lined with soot, she perspired profusely, and she'd managed to put *bhoot* aside in her mind.

The mail came. The sight of a blue aerogram, a missive of news and affection from Grandma, exhilarated Aloka. Only two more weeks before leaving for home, and still Grandma had taken the trouble to drop a note, and this despite the fact that the woman didn't see too well these days. Aloka took the stack of mail up the staircase to her living room, perched on a chair, shoved the bills aside, and opened Grandma's letter with cheery expectation.

Cousin Murty called to say that my old village now has a special booth for video e-mail. Imagine having such new technology in a place where just a short time ago there wasn't any electricity and people went barefoot. It costs only a few rupees to get an e-mail address. All the more useful, as only a small number of Indian villages have long distance phone service and a good connection is nearly impossible. The first person to attempt e-mailing in my village was a young woman who had never before seen a computer. As the woman walked inside the booth and seated herself in front of the Hindi keyboard, an operator showed her how to punch the keys. At first the woman tried holding on to her veil with one hand so she could see enough and keep her face covered at the same time. But soon she pulled the veil away from her face entirely. She punched a message to her brother in Calcutta, urging him to come home for Durga Puja (this year it fell on October 4) and pressed the "Send" key. The moment "Your message has been sent" flashed on the screen, the people queuing outside applauded her, "Shabash, shabash."

Usual social commentary by Grandma. Engaging, uplifting, and invariably leading up to something. Aloka went to the next section of the aerogram.

Computers intimidate me. Or else I'd have gotten one to figure out what the neighborhood children are saying when they gush about their favorite website Rediff.com, and, what's more important, to keep in contact with you and Pranab on a more regular basis.

You see, my dear, I am very worried. In the last six months I haven't sensed Pranab's presence in your letters. Before you always mentioned how he had just teased you, tousled your hair, or was waiting to take you out. This time he simply didn't exist.

Will he be coming with you to Darjeeling? It could all be my imagination, still, please have him phone me right away to let me know that he is well. At my age, I don't believe in letters, fax, or e-mail. I only believe it when I hear a human voice.

Aloka's stomach twisted. She hadn't spoken with him since Pranab's brief visit to retrieve his misplaced love letter to her sister. Prior to that, at least once a week one or the other had called. This time it was her turn to stay in touch, and though she dwelled on him often, she had put it off. However, with this request from Grandma banging at her door, it was imperative that she contacted Pranab.

She rose and picked up her leather-bound address book from her desk, then, after a moment's reflection, put it down. It would be best to have a face-to-face contact with him. That was what Parveen would do—startle a man by her unexpected appearance and her outrageous attire; win him over by her generous smile.

Aloka went to her dressing table, where she dusted powder on her face, lined her eyes with charcoal eyeliner, and drew a persimmon-shade lipstick across her lips. Then she peeked into her closet and selected a showy gold-

trimmed purple wool dress with a ruffled hemline, a dress that had lan-
guished at the back of her closet for years. She complemented the attire with
a purple scarf whose sensuous folds fell in waves over her chest. With luxurious strokes, she combed her black hair with its curly ends until it gave
off a smooth, natural shine. She sensed the faint stirrings of anticipation
inside her as she peered into the mirror: Parveen was ready.

Aloka traipsed down the stairs and emerged onto the street. Her destination—Brooklyn—was a short subway ride away, just across the Brooklyn
Bridge. As she drifted toward the subway station, she became overjoyed at
the prospect of exploring a new area. Come to think of it, she'd spent long
weekends in the Bahamas and Puerto Rico, but had yet to venture into New
York's most populous borough right next door to Manhattan. Brooklyn had
been receiving much press lately for its parks, restaurants, museums, and
promenades, as well as for the joys of bird-watching. Also, Aloka admitted
her great curiosity about where Pranab made his new home.

She got off the subway and strolled a few blocks, squinting up at street
names and house numbers, then figuring out that Pranab resided just beyond
the park that now stretched before her. She sailed into the park, a spread of
grass with veins of pathways and sprawling trees standing like open um-
brellas. An old man bent stiffly to pick up a newspaper from the ground. A
Chi Gung practitioner gracefully raised his hands above his head, as though
attempting to draw force from heaven. Under an immense tree a man danced
alone to the accompaniment of a tape deck, his legs flying, his arm making
a circle overhead with an imaginary stick. Aloka instantly recognized the
leap, the vigor, and the staccato tabla beat as hailing from India's folk tradition in commemoration of a new season. She was about to move on when
he spun around in her direction. She froze midstep.

Pranab. Dancing.

Aloka gasped in shock. To be sure, Pranab had always had well-muscled
legs—she still remembered their weighty touch vividly—and an innate sense
of rhythm; still, it was hard to imagine the cerebral man expressing his heart's
lyrics through his limbs. The Pranab she had been married to lived through
his vocal cords and his intellect.

She stood behind a waist-high bush and watched his movements flow out of him; she felt the vibrations in her own body. His eyes met hers at one point, but they displayed no sign of recognition. Then, as the drumbeats tapered off, he stopped abruptly and grabbed a tree branch for support. His glasses fell off as he lurched to a halt.

"Aloka!" Chest heaving from the exertion, he called out, "What are you doing here?"

She approached him, the ruffled golden hem of her skirt rippling. She stooped and picked up his glasses, then pressed them into his hand, masking her surprise with a tone of compliment. "I came to see you perform."

He put the glasses on, smoothed his shirt, turned off the music, and examined her face closely, as if searching for any hint of mockery. There was a new openness in him as he leaned toward her. The dance must have drawn long-buried emotions from his interior. His voice seemed to drop an octave and thicken when he finally spoke. "You look so new, so alive. I see a special brightness in your eyes."

She felt quite triumphant as she recalled that a long time ago, on the trails of Darjeeling, a discussion about light had gotten them started. Perhaps those carefree days could be re-created. "Glad I ran into you—I finally got to see you dance." Leavening her voice with seriousness, she added, "I just got a letter from Thakurma. She's worried because I haven't written much about you lately. As you know, she's very perceptive. She wants to hear from you."

"So, you haven't told your family yet?"

"I want to tell them face-to-face, it'll be too much of a shock otherwise. Do your parents know already?"

He nodded solemnly. "The news travels fast in India. They've already called me; they're very sorry, you know." Beneath the gigantic tree, in the twilight that was creeping in, Pranab cut a lonely figure, lessened by his uncertainties. A gust of wind batted a stray lock of graying hair across his forehead. "It seems they've been sorry ever since I got here," he observed.

Aloka was aware that Pranab's family had been concerned about his lack-luster performance in America, not to mention his cynicism about his adopted country. When children go abroad, especially to America, family expectations run high. Parents wait for the sons and daughters to return with degrees, honors, dollars, and loads of presents. And yet, Pranab shouldn't be made to feel ashamed.

She mumbled, "It's never too late."

"I remember you saying that we came here to get a fresh start. And you did get yours. You have a loving and courageous heart. You'll do well anywhere."

Only moments ago he was dancing beneath a transparent sky and the luxurious expanse of trees, leaping into the air and trusting the earth. "I enjoyed your dance, Pranab. It's the last thing I thought you'd do."

"This park has saved me. Actually it's the dance that has saved me."

She began to get a glimpse of why he danced—it wasn't just entertainment. He was seeking a source of inspiration, a source that would reawaken his potential. The joyous energy expressed through dancing reflected his considerable inner power. Here in Brooklyn, it was his dance, and only his dance, that involved him completely. Too late she was discovering that there was more to the man than she'd believed.

At the same time she grew more hopeful. Yes, she could help heal his attitude. He could succeed in life. They could return to their earlier days of bliss.

He picked up the tape deck. "This music is old, from when I first started dancing."

"But," she said hesitantly, "you never told me."

"There would have been no point. I stopped even before I left Darjeeling."

Why had he given up a hobby he held so dear and at which he was obviously talented? Did it have to do with Sujata? An impenetrable, secretive look on Pranab's face confirmed Aloka's suspicion. When Sujata left Darjeeling, she took his dancing with her. At that instant Aloka had a revelation. Late at night, in deep sleep, when one is immersed in one's truth, she would curl up against Pranab and hear the uneven thump of his chest, as though a deep longing from within him wanted to manifest itself. That longing, Aloka could see plainly now, was for Sujata. The longing that had caused so much suffering for so many and ultimately destroyed a marriage.

And then the pain returned—the pain she thought she had long ago moved beyond. She told herself that she wasn't giving him up yet. Sujata would have to fight hard, but that almost didn't matter, for in due course Aloka would win. "Please be sure to call Thakurma tonight. A short call to say you're well is probably all she needs to hear." With that she turned to go.

"She's such a dear," Pranab called after her. "Yes, of course I'll call her. Wait just a second and I'll walk you to the gate."

They started walking. In the lull she took in his new Adidas and how his chest heaved as he sighed. "Now that it's getting close to going home," he said, "I'm beginning to wonder. What will I find there, what is still left?"

"Remember what we used to say. The mountains will always be there. They're our oldest relatives."

He grew silent, and when he replied it was in a tone of wistful admiration. "You managed to bring the mountains' blessings with you, rather than seek refuge in their memory. You opened up and gave yourself to this place. You've adjusted so well here. My years here, on the other hand, have been a waste. I never could let go of the old ways. I remained what I was instead of being what I could be, and for that I've paid a heavy price. . . ."

They'd arrived at the park entrance. She stepped to one side to let a woman with a baby stroller pass through. Pranab continued to repeat the same tired refrain: He'd sold his time in New York for paychecks, he'd lost his spark, he was diminished.

She suppressed a spark of irritation and instead replied, not unsympathetically, "But don't we all pay a price when we uproot?"

"I used to think so, but it always seemed so easy for you, as if the old ways didn't really matter."

The irritation returned, this time stronger, but she merely smiled indulgently. She refused to allow him to turn this encounter into an argument. "I've flown out of my nest, that's true, but Darjeeling is still there, deep inside me. It's in my heartbeat. How can you be so sure I've forsaken the old ways? Let's continue this discussion after we get there."

He stood there. Lost in introspection so deep that it seemed to cloud his eyeglasses, he didn't respond or look at her. Out of the corner of her eye, she glimpsed the Chi Gung practitioner as he folded his palms toward the already shadowing sky, drawing the last rays of light to him.

She said her farewell, but Pranab just waved at her. She strode toward the subway station with a distinctly unsettled feeling.

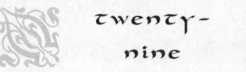

twenty-
nine

"Shopping must be your calling," Suzy said to Eva as they left Eaton Centre, one of Victoria's largest shopping malls. "Do you realize I've bought all the presents in one afternoon? Had I come alone, I'd have needed two more days."

A pink windbreaker, puffy as a parachute, augmented Eva's beaming face.

Then it occurred to Suzy that she'd forgotten to buy a present for Pranab. When they were lovers, she knew Pranab's tastes. He preferred gifts that were intensely personal, like the fine cotton handkerchief she'd embroidered herself and given to him secretly. He'd carried it in his breast pocket everywhere. He'd developed the habit of touching his breast pocket often.

As Suzy carefully stowed four full shopping bags in the trunk of her car, a primrose-yellow fabric shone through a rip in the paper. A dress for Aloka. In spite of all that had come between them, including this morning's wretched phone call, Suzy still needed her sister's approval. This dress would surely please Aloka. Suzy imagined the gift-giving session: Aloka rushing to a full-length mirror and pressing the silver-belted dress against her body as she did in her teen days. A bit of wistfulness would fleck her eyes, even as she delighted in her own exquisite image.

Now Eva asked, "Doesn't your sister wear saris anymore?"

"According to Grandma, no. Aloka says, 'It just isn't New York.' At home in Darjeeling she wore nothing but saris, even though *salwar-kameez* was very much in fashion."

As she transferred the dress to another shopping bag, Suzy got a whiff of chocolate from the russet box of Victoria Creams. Only the best for Grandma, this hand-wrapped Roger's chocolate, the city's finest. Even though the woman was missing a few teeth, she had managed to hang on to her sweet tooth. Her trembling fingers would hesitate at the gold ribbons. She would open the box, take a bite of a chocolate, and utter, *"Bhalo."* Good. She would impart much meaning to that one word.

Suzy had selected gifts for other relatives just as carefully. The Polaroid camera was for Aunt Toru, who at any gathering preferred to be behind the lens capturing the antics of others. Then there were T-shirts, watches, clocks, and fountain pens for uncles and aunts and their offspring, and a giant floor puzzle for a young cousin who had been a drooling one-year-old when she left Darjeeling. He'd be nine now. Would he hug her? Or would he feel shy and fly away? She would know soon.

She drove toward Sooke Road. When Celeste Restaurant's neon sign came into view, she pushed aside her conjectures and eased the car into a side parking lot. Suzy and Eva walked through the restaurant door and a familiar voice greeted Suzy exuberantly.

"Welcome, sister!"

Ashraf, the Moroccan owner and milk-free tea drinker, stood there. He was nattily attired in charcoal slacks and a crisp white shirt. A confident smile creased his neatly trimmed bearded face. "I've been waiting for you all day."

Suzy made the necessary introductions. As Eva and Ashraf discussed the boon of the recent pleasant weather, Suzy found herself at the threshold of an elegant beige dining area trimmed in gleaming metal and offset by plush blue carpeting with a moon-and-stars motif. It was contemporary, rather than conventional Moroccan decor. Yes, her tea belonged here, in this pleasant ambiance.

A faint bouquet of hazelnut oil, basil, and some unknown ingredients hung in the air as they settled at their reserved table. Suzy's hand brushed the velvet trim of the tablecloth. It was smooth as a bird's plumage. She peered up at the starry pattern cast on the ceiling by the chandelier, then back to the room. The subdued lighting, the wealth of space between tables, and quiet music were conducive to intimate conversation.

The waiter leaned over them and handed out outsized menus, elaborately bound in leather and edged with gold embroidery.

"This is really an elegant celebration before you go home," Eva said. "If there's anything I can do while you're away . . ."

"Your support means a lot, Eva. Who else could I have talked to about Pranab?"

"How long since you've seen him?"

"Eight years."

"Almost like my story. Ten years ago, I divorced my husband. He was a stereotypical Russian: drunk, long-faced, irresistible. . . . Now, listen to my foolishness. There was always this wild attraction between us, even though he'd been unfaithful to me more than once while we were married. In the last ten years, we've tried to get back together three times, but it has never worked. Time and absence warp all bonds. At any rate, I'm finally over it, I think. Old lovers are clothes that no longer fit."

"Believe it or not, my clothing size hasn't changed in eight years."

Suzy believed that this time things would work with Pranab and, despite Aloka's interference, the same spark would return between them. Pranab's neat script, his choice of stationery, and his words of yearning were the proof that he still loved Suzy. It must have been *his* choice to get a divorce. What would it be like to meet him again? She mapped it out now: She'd sit on a boulder by Senchal Lake and wait for him, listening to the birds, her hair heated by the concentrated rays, watching the hilltops try on a new veil of light. Pranab would sprint down the hill and approach her. Two pairs of thirsty eyes, an anticipation disturbing the air, eventually broken by a whisper or a cry, a key moment dissolving into a deep realization.

Suzy looked up to see Ashraf hovering attentively. "The menu is just for browsing," he announced. "Your dinner is being specially prepared by my chef. He has read about you in *Coffee and Tea Journal* and is very excited to have you pay us a visit. My customers can't seem to get enough of your tea, especially your Darjeeling blend. It's our good fortune that you're in this town, teaching us proper tea customs. I'll be back in a moment."

Eva dipped a thin round of lentil cake into the green cilantro sauce. "Did you call Mreenal Bose?"

"Not yet. Grandma sent him here to see me, so I'm in no hurry."

"I called him." Eva's lips curled into a smile. The pungent sauce? The subject? "I was just checking him out for you."

"Are you interested in him, Eva?"

"His answering machine said he wouldn't be back in Seattle till January first."

"Oh, well. I'll call him next year, then. Plenty of time."

"Just remember, Suze, ripe persimmons don't hang on a tree forever. I can really say that because I've botched up something recently myself."

"You, Eva, botched up something? You surprise me."

"It was an encounter of the losing kind. It still hurts a little, but I can finally talk about it. A couple of weeks ago I was invited to a party hosted by a friend, who's a dressmaker. I didn't want to go, because I'd had a long day, but you know me. Do the right thing, keep up the appearances, et cetera. When I walked into the party, I saw a man standing in one corner smoking a cigarette—a Russian. With my experience, I can spot Russians a kilometer away. He turned and our eyes locked. Just then the hostess came over and introduced me to him. Mikhail. He bowed as he shook my hand. I liked the way he carried himself. He turned out to be a furrier."

"Is that why you were staring at a fur coat in a shop window this afternoon?"

"I love fur, but own only a pair of fur gloves that you've seen me wear. Mikhail told me an interesting story about how he got interested in furs. He used to wait in a long line in Moscow to get his turn to take a shower. People passed books and magazines back and forth. One day he got a book on the Russian fur trade. He read the whole book standing there and missed his shower, but he was hooked." Eva took a breath, then continued with,

"Mikhail seemed so genuine, so interesting, that pretty soon I was laughing and joking with him and had forgotten everyone else at the party. We talked for over an hour. Then I started to get that old, familiar feeling and I froze up. Eva, this is dumb, I told myself. You have to get out of here. And so I did. But I sure regretted it when I got home. I wanted to be with him so bad. The next day, much to my surprise, he showed up at my shop. He put down my fur gloves on the counter and said that after I left he'd found 'a pair of gloves unattended.' "

"Oh, how poetic. Did you get that feeling again? Did you go out with him?"

"I was petrified, not because of anything he did. I was just afraid of getting hurt again. We chatted for a while, then he gave me his phone number and asked me to give him a buzz when I was free, and went away. The same day the hostess called. She asked me what I thought of Mikhail. 'Oh, I suppose he's okay,' I said. She laughed. 'I knew you two would find each other interesting.' Still I hesitated to call Mikhail. It's so hard to trust again. Then my ex-husband flew in from Toronto on business. We met for lunch in Chinatown and spent three hours together. How he can talk and turn on the charm, even now. I forgot that he had cheated on me. He distracted me so much that even after he left I put off calling Mikhail for another couple of days. On the afternoon I was going to call him, I spotted him near the Parliament building. He was holding hands with a petite blonde."

"You missed an opportunity," Suzy said after a while. "Cheer up. There'll be plenty more."

"What bugs me is I didn't act soon enough. I was divorced at thirty-four. At my age—I'm going to be forty-four—I don't meet very many men who excite me. The Chinese way is to be married and have children early in life. My relatives still use the word 'spinster.' I feel so odd these days. It's like I've crossed a bridge and left the land of courtship behind. When I look back, the desire is there, the heart is ready to spring, but my mind is like a stalled commuter car. It blurts out excuses, and it won't budge."

Aloka's face flashed before Suzy. Aloka, at forty, was in the same age group as Eva; Aloka, who had been in love with Pranab for ten years, would have difficulty getting over him this late in life. Might Aloka hesitate with a new, exciting man and walk away from him, only to regret it later?

"Enough of my woes. Tell me what your grandma is up to." Eva reached for the platter of sautéed snow peas.

"Grandma is remarkably modern and normally wouldn't force anyone on me," Suzy said. "But at her age, she might think that she doesn't have much time left. The last thing I want is to hurt her feelings. Make that the next-to-the-last thing. The *last* thing I want is to end up in an arranged marriage to some traditional guy who expects his wife to cook his meals, bow to his every wish, and produce babies."

She paused as Ashraf reappeared. He must have overheard the last part of her conversation.

"Sit down with us," Eva said to Ashraf lightly. "You might have some advice for Suzy."

It was clear that Ashraf had been waiting for the invitation, for he pulled up a chair and nodded in wise man fashion. Then, turning to Suzy, he said, "I'm sure your family is looking very hard to find a suitable match for you."

Suzy sipped from her tall, frosted glass of Evian; it tasted appropriately chilly. "I can find my own husband."

A mischievous smile flickered on Ashraf's lips. "Parents have their ways."

"That sounds like the voice of experience," Eva said.

"Let me tell you my story," Ashraf said. "I went home after thirteen years. The first couple of days were splendid. My father and I bantered back and forth, and as usual, he didn't miss a thing about me. He saw streaks of gray in my beard and no gray hair on my head and said, 'My dear boy, you talk too much and think too little.' While my father showed me around, my mother got busy cooking. Then, one evening when I got home, I noticed that the living room was full of young women. At first I wondered where all these pretty things came from. Had my district changed all that much? Little did I know they had been gathered from all over the city."

"Doesn't seem like you objected too much." Eva apparently was trying to get him to the point.

"The beauties fawned over me. 'Oh, Ashraf, you're so smart. You speak English so perfectly. Your beard has so much character.' All except one, a tiny thing with a thunderbolt of energy, who was walking in and out of the room constantly. I ignored her and noticed her at the same time. At one point, when the other stars were stuffing their plates with appetizers, she slid next to me on the couch and whispered, 'You know, Ashraf, I'm not interested in you. I came here only out of curiosity to meet someone who lived in Canada. Now that I've watched you for a couple of hours, I don't think you're any different from the men here. I'm going home.' She got up with great dignity and walked to the door."

"Smart, that one was," Eva said.

"At first I was deflated." Ashraf slouched, as though reliving the rejection. "Then I burst out laughing. Finally I stopped laughing and rushed to catch up with her. 'What's the hurry?' I asked her. 'The lamb hasn't been served yet.'

"She returned and sat down with me again, looking like an empress before her subject with a petition, while the other women whispered among themselves about us. I didn't care. I grabbed every bit of charm I had in my system and told her stories of my travels through Canada. When that did nothing to perk her up, I sang the Canadian national anthem, which was silly on my part because I couldn't hold a tune. Then I realized my father was right. I was trying to talk my way into this instead of thinking and planning my next action. I had to be much more clever. So I got up. 'Look,' I told her, 'I'll show you a dance they do in Canada.' And I started to tap-dance. 'All around Victoria in the evening, they don't walk the sidewalks, they tap.' To be sure, it was a bit of an exaggeration, but fortunately I was a tap master. When she rose, I took her hand and demonstrated the steps. She picked them up rather quickly. From there we went on to do a folk dance we both had learned as children. Our hands clapping, we walked forward and backward. When at last both our feet clicked on the floor in unison, I said to her, 'I hope I haven't bored you too much.' Her eyes became brighter than pearl dust. 'Oh, no, Ashraf, I'm exhausted, but this is so much fun.' That was a most memorable night and a learning experience for me, as well. I learned the secret to a woman's heart. Get her exhausted. That, by the way, is also the secret to a man's heart."

"What happened to her?" Eva asked.

"We got married. The marriage lasted only a year."

Was this a true story, a man's fantasy? Why did it matter? Ashraf was trying to steer Suzy away from prearranged matrimony.

"The stage was set for you, Ashraf," Eva said. "You walked in and became a hero."

"That's the eternal tug between men and women," Ashraf said. "Who gets to be the lead on the stage. I always get a kick out of it."

"I don't," Eva said. "I tend to lose."

"As for me," Suzy said, "I'm not one for 'arranged meetings.' "

"E-mail us, Suze, with the details, will you?"

"We'll be sure to e-mail you back right away," Ashraf said. "Won't we, Eva?"

"Thanks, guys." Suzy pushed her plate away. "You two love experts have given me a lot to think about. And I'll need you both before this is over with."

An interlude like this was proving to be just the thing to fortify her for the journey ahead. This dinner had opened up a more candid way of relating with her friends, and though she would be leaving them soon and was experiencing a twinge of pain at the prospect, she derived some security from their nurturing.

The meal over, Suzy stepped outside and looked up at the velvet sky. The crescent moon radiated a faint soothing light and the billion stars glittering in the inky blackness wrote an unreadable script. The droning of an airplane prompted her to envision what it would be like to fly home. All at once emotions of joy, pain, and uncertainty swelled deep in her interior and she struggled to get hold of herself. Then, as she made her way to the parking lot with Eva, she saw the trip as an assessment of her years abroad: Where she had been, what she'd become, where she was destined to go.

The Bengali word *pratikkha* surfaced in her mind. Waiting that was long and painful, but mixed with hope and devotion. Her *pratikkha* for Pranab had finally come to an end.

thirty

Nina sat at the lawn table with Mreenal. She was becoming rather fond of the fellow, so recently returned from America, and had to keep reminding herself that he was actually a man of forty. *Namro*—that Bengali word described him well: gentle, unruffled, and restrained. His mien and build weren't particularly striking, but his eyes sparkled and his dark skin still had a youthful glow. Most importantly, he seemed to accept his own appearance without judgment. Today he was clad simply in a blue-checked shirt and khaki slacks, though he surely could afford to dress better considering the salary he received at Comsys, the company in Seattle where he worked. In respect for her old age, he was keeping his feet tucked well beneath the table, unlike most foreign-borns, who usually stuck their feet out and, as if that weren't enough impertinence, fluttered their toes. Even after all those years in the West, Mreenal had retained his reverence for the elderly, which, Nina bemoaned to herself, was a trait fast fading from Indian society. Mreenal didn't seem to mind taking tea with an old lady, and in fact he appeared to thoroughly enjoy Nina's company.

He'd arrived several days ago to visit his great-aunt Tami and unwind in this mountain town. During their first encounter, Nina had discussed Darjeeling and its history. Mreenal had been particularly interested in Nina's firsthand account of the emergence of the Gorkha separatist movement decades ago, the curfews, the *bandh*, the disruption to daily life, and the eventual settlement with the state government, lamenting that he could get almost no details about it in Seattle. During his second visit, Nina had showed him family photos and talked about entrepreneurial Sujata. Nina had noticed how his eyes lingered on Sujata's images in the family album. At one point Mreenal had even admitted, in his characteristically understated manner, that he'd like to meet this Gupta girl.

This marked his third visit to Nina's house. Today, however, he sat hunched in his chair, and even with the back glow of the sun a shadow played on his face. Was he simply waiting for her to spark the conversation? Nina wouldn't mind that. She had plenty to find out about the man: When would he settle down, and where? Did he prefer dashing out as a pair on a date to spending time in a group? Did the frenetic pace of modern America suit him, or did he long for a slower, more conventional life with time for loved ones, family, neighbors, and rituals?

So now, her expression neutral, Nina leaned forward. "What do you want?" She asked what she believed was a serious question. Then, noting the bewildered expression on his face, she added, "In life."

He surveyed his empty plate, bereft of even a single crumb, and privileged her with a disarming smile. "What do I want? More *patishaptas*, of course."

"Of course." Nina felt exhilarated. A man who relished home-cooked food was likely to make a good husband. And though he hadn't answered her question, she prized the cleverness of his reply. She was about to call Reenu when the maidservant appeared, an aroma of freshly grated coconut and thickened milk drifting up from the platter in her hand. Reenu placed a mound of stuffed rice-flour crepes on Mreenal's plate as gently as though she were putting an infant in its cradle. Though Nina had long since given up afternoon snacking, she could still revive the taste of these crispy sweet lacy-thin delicacies on her palate. She sipped her tea in silence as Mreenal rolled up a crepe and popped it into his mouth.

A blissful look stealing over his face, he swallowed and looked up at Reenu. "Ah, you put *gur* in it."

Reenu beamed. "You got it, Mreenal-*babu*. The first of the season."

Mreenal's eyes brightened, then seemed to sink deep into reverie. Once again Nina was impressed. The man who had spent years in the West and whose days were crammed with all manner of technical wizardry, whose taste had been tempered by hot dogs and burgers, and the gods only knew what other animal flesh, could still detect the presence of unprocessed palm sugar in a dish. He hadn't lost his Bengali soul.

At length Mreenal sat up with a start and turned to Nina. "I think I understand what you're really asking, Thakurma."

How affectionately he addressed her. "Forgive me, please," Nina said, "for asking such a personal question—"

"Not at all. Actually, I'm a bit flattered." Mreenal paused, his attention apparently caught by a mynah, which had launched itself from a nearby tree in pursuit of an unfortunate insect. "Lately I've been thinking a lot about what I want to do with my life."

Out of the corner of her eye Nina caught a glimpse of the bird. Keen powers of observation, she told herself, another good trait in a bachelor. "I hope marriage is in your plans."

"Marriage is easy; finding a mate, that's hard. So far I haven't found a suitable mate on my own, although I've come close a couple of times."

"It must be lonely, so far away from home. How can you cut a limb out of a tree and expect it to form roots overnight?"

"Lonely, yes, at times, especially since most of my friends in Seattle are married. A few years back, when everyone was single, we used to throw great parties on weekends or go skiing as a group. Now my friends all have kids. They're short on cash and have no free time, not to mention their houses are a mess. They envy my freedom and tell me, 'If I could have even one day like yours, Mreenal . . .' But to tell you the truth, I'm getting tired of my 'wonderful' days. I tell myself I'd gladly exchange my affluence and freedom for their comfort and security, even with its responsibilities. But then, would I?"

"Ah, yes, a good question."

Mreenal glanced at his empty plate. "My mother doesn't make *patishaptas*. What a special skill it is to transform ground rice into such delicate crepes."

Nina smiled to herself. What a perfect afternoon this was turning out to be: Nina giving Mreenal an introduction to the Guptas, their style of living, their way of welcoming guests, even before Sujata arrived.

"The world can be cruel to singles," Mreenal continued, "but I run into kindness, too. When I caught the flu bug a month ago, my landlady brought me a steaming bowl of soup. I don't much care for soups, yet I sipped at her minestrone until I had finished it all. I imagined the care and generosity that had gone into it and I brimmed with the same feelings for her. Perhaps because of it, I got better quickly. For my landlady's birthday, I bought her a pet rabbit. Now we chat all the time in the hallway about that rabbit. So, in a way, living alone has helped me grow."

"My Sujata lives alone and she's also changed a lot. I talked to her a few minutes the other day. Too bad you didn't get to meet Sujata when you were in Victoria recently."

A gentle afternoon breeze teased Mreenal's hair and he brushed a few wisps off his forehead. "She's quite elusive, that granddaughter of yours."

"She'll be arriving tomorrow. You shouldn't have any trouble finding her here. Then you two can compare notes on the blessings of a single life . . . over more *patishaptas,* of course!"

"Wish I could, Thakurma, I very much wish that." Mreenal rubbed his chin. "But I have to return to Calcutta tomorrow. My mother called this afternoon. She wants me back right away on an urgent matter."

Nina fussed with her sari hem. The afternoon abruptly turned gray, dull, and soundless. All her planning had come to naught. What a wonderful opportunity the headstrong Sujata had missed.

"Will you be able to attend my birthday celebration?"

"I plan to fly back."

Nina heard a greeting and the slap of *chappals* on the pathway; she looked toward the house just in time to see Tami waddling into the yard. The train of her stiff sari, like a ship's sail, created such a bustle that the happily fed mynah, now perched on a shrub, began to whistle and squawk.

Sighting his great-aunt, Mreenal rose and expressed his gratitude to Nina for the hospitality. Then, with a sorrowful expression, he said, "I have to go now, Thakurma." He made his greetings to Tami and started toward the exit.

Tami waited until Mreenal was out of sight. She craned her neck toward Nina and whispered hoarsely, "I have some news." She dropped into a chair and adjusted the veil of her sari. "I'm so sorry, Nina. It seems lately I only bring you bad news. Mreenal's mother has found a match for him and she's terribly excited. No one else knows it yet except Mreenal and myself."

"But I was under the impression that his mother knows Mreenal spends a lot of time here."

"I suppose she does. She also knows that I tried to get Mreenal and Sujata to meet in Victoria, and that it didn't come off."

"Call her back, tell her how much I enjoy Mreenal. What a fine young man he is."

"Isn't it a little late, Nina?"

"No. Mreenal and Sujata will meet tomorrow afternoon."

Tami leaned forward in puzzlement. "But how? Mreenal's leaving early in the morning."

"No, he won't. Just leave that to me, Tami. Just leave that to me."

thirty-
one

Aloka had just thrown on her overcoat when she heard Jahar murmuring from the other side of the room, "Why do you have to go?" The full, sensuous lips that had so tenderly murmured against the dimple of her cheeks only minutes ago parted as if to beckon her back. He extended a sturdy, well-proportioned hand toward her. "It's not even six."

"Tomorrow's Monday and there's work I absolutely must finish."

"I'm making *sukhe aloo* for dinner," he said in that hopeful manner of his.

She made a detour to the bed, where she bent and took his face in her hand, then kissed his lips to wipe out the pain of parting. "Save some for *sukhe aloo* for me, will you?"

Heading for the door, she sidestepped the Hindi comics and picture books on the floor for which Jahar had a decided fondness. She passed the shelf on the left where a silver-framed photograph of Jahar's guru stood.

Pausing, she admired the fragrance of the fresh marigold garland placed on an arc around the picture of Baba Muktananda. She respected his belief, though she wouldn't adopt the same. On the right was the closet, littered with boxes, where Jahar was now searching for his clothes.

He wrapped the sash of a dingy bathrobe around his waist. "Why don't I come to your place tomorrow?"

She switched on a demure smile. "My windows face north. You told me you like to see me in the light of the sunset."

Only Parveen could come up with an excuse this charming, but she was running out of them fast.

"I don't care about windows and sunsets," Jahar pressed on. "I just want to see you walking from room to room, humming a song, your hair catching the overhead light. My mother says a woman is most beautiful when she's surrounded by her own things."

Aloka managed a weak smile. How much longer would she be able to conceal her identity from Jahar?

She couldn't invite him over when her old Aloka self resided there, and Pranab did, too. Like the smell of the cigarettes he had started to smoke occasionally, traces of Pranab persisted there. The bed they'd shared, the furniture they'd shopped for together, even the books they'd selected for the study bore Pranab's emblem. Until this evening, Jahar had displayed only mild curiosity about her place.

She waved from the door in a cautious but grateful gesture.

He smoothed his tousled hair with his fingers and gazed after her. Softly he said, "Until tomorrow."

She carried an imprint of that loving expression with her as she exited the building and crossed Second Avenue. In front of her stood the delicatessen where they'd first met. A pigeon cooed a welcome from near the entrance. She checked the snipped flowers—roses, carnations, lilies, and daisies—wrapped in cellophane and arranged against the front wall, like a corsage for this dowager of a building. Golden melon cubes peeked out from plastic containers nestled attractively in a tub of crushed ice. She and Jahar had often shopped here together for fruit and flowers. Barely a fortnight had passed since that first encounter, yet, in thinking back, their time together seemed as full and complete as an entire season. She couldn't remember precisely at what point their lives had converged, but it hadn't taken long and this delicatessen had helped.

The truth remained, however, that she hadn't given herself to him as fully as she had to Pranab.

Entering her apartment, Aloka bumped her hip on the edge of the table placed in the hallway. Oh, not again! she told herself in a flash of irritation. For some time now she had felt a vague dissatisfaction with the angular layout of this apartment, its narrow dark corridors, not to mention the high rent.

Lately, contemplating a move, she had checked out a few real estate ads and scouted for a rental unit in an enclave called Gramercy Park South. Such a move would cut down her commute time to her office. Or was she rationalizing an attempt to distance herself from Jahar? Was she afraid that Jahar would drop by unannounced and discover her real identity?

How would he react if he found out that she was a serious newspaper reporter undergoing a painful divorce, one who wanted her husband back? That would shatter his fantasy of the frivolous Parveen who dabbled in real estate to pay her bills. Aloka wasn't Parveen, the whimsical woman of his dreams, certainly not twenty-four hours a day.

She dropped her purse to its designated place near the entrance, took off her shoes and jacket, snapped the barrette off her ponytail, and sagged into a chair in the living room. Jahar's face flashed in her mind, that splendid profile etched with experience, the rough skin belying his inner friendliness. He was loving, courteous, generous, and protective. In the midst of the brutal chaos of the city, he'd created a small oasis and carved a nook for her in it. But what would her friends say about a man who didn't attend City Arts and Lectures or hang out in the Theater District or at Spierman Gallery, one who couldn't comment on Paul Taylor dances? Would Jahar find himself in a discomfiting situation if a colleague of hers asked his opinion about India's balance of payment? Would her family approve of a man who hadn't graduated from college?

He had fidgeted when she had taken him to the casually elegant Beacon on his birthday. The five-course dinner served by an exquisitely formal waiter in a white uniform had overwhelmed him. "Too many forks and spoons," he had grumbled later. He seemed more at ease in the corner coffee shop where linoleum floors and careless servers were the norm, where the waitress sloshed coffee on his lap as she set the grotesque mug down on the table. That amused him. And now that she dwelt upon it, she hadn't been to a gallery opening or attended an author's reading since she met him. His cronies were taxi drivers, gas station attendants, and construction workers, who worked hard and preferred entertainment of a different sort at the end of the day.

"Got any beer?" they would demand as they settled into his living room for an all-night game of cards. She would curl up in a chair and watch them until finally, overcome by clouds of cigarette smoke, she would return home, coughing and repelled. In the long term would she be able to meet his needs and adapt to the simplicity of his existence?

Most important of all, she still believed she and Pranab would get back together once they returned to Darjeeling.

When Aloka next studied the clock on the wall, it said seven P.M. She pushed aside her thoughts of Jahar, rose slowly, went to her desk, and picked up a fat manila folder. This week her readers had sent quite a few cards and letters. She began to run through them, choking on the smell of sautéing onions and ignoring the sounds of a shouting match that drifted up through her open window from the restaurant bar at the corner. Soon her consciousness merged with that of her readers and she entered a state where she could reply to them not only as a friend but also someone who had toured miles in their *chappals*. The first letter was neatly typed.

> *I speak English fluently, you know, like most* asli desis, *our compatriots, but no one seems to understand what I say. I repeat myself three, four, five times and more, and still I find people staring at me. The other day a colleague joked that I carry pebbles in my mouth. (Believe me, I don't even chew gum.) And a sales clerk at the candy shop told me flat out, "Speak American, or I won't wait on you."*
>
> *Pronunciation challenged*

And on to the next.

> *Vegetarianism sucks in New York. My family in India hasn't touched meat in the last hundred years and I am trying to continue the tradition, but I have*

had it with limp Caesar salad (like chewing on water), bean soup (the color
of mud and the same consistency), and cheese-melt (the texture of glue). Still,
merely entertaining the idea of eating meat makes me want to throw up.

Starving in Manhattan

Such routine letters.

Aloka found herself wishing to delve into a deeper problem, something
that would reawaken her troubleshooting skills. Her eyes were nearly closing
when she came across a handwritten note on lined, straw-colored paper. The
script was uneven and awkward, with letters that veered off the line. Oddly,
it reminded her of a clay doll from childhood, made by an amateur artisan
in which the body proportions were comically wrong and laughably so, one
arm twice as long as the other, one thigh considerably fatter. She had held
the doll dear, until one day when her father made fun of it. *"Bichchiri,"* he
had said, ugly, very ugly, whereupon she had hurled the toy against the wall,
shattering it into pieces, then bursting into tears.

She returned her attention to the letters.

I met a terrific woman at a delicatessen right across from my building.

Delicatessens replacing singles bars and dance halls? Aloka chuckled. She
could relate.

She is higher than me in class and education, but she is kind. A mere glance
at her beautiful face fills me with tenderness. I don't understand her too well,
average man that I am, but I love her completely. I have never felt this way
about any woman.

Lately I am beginning to fear that she'll leave me. Our worlds could never
merge. She prefers high-end restaurants, theater, and art events, which are
above my taste. I have given her all I have, happiness at home and my steady
company, but that doesn't seem enough for her.

If I lose her, how will I pass my days? What will my future be then?

The letter was signed "J."

The sheet of paper slipped out of Aloka's hand, floated in the air for an instant, and fluttered to the floor. So, it was as she had suspected all along: Jahar was capable of making a deep commitment, but true to his Indian nature, he was holding the sentiments inside, preferring to give them expression through gestures and actions. What she *hadn't* realized was that he saw the chasm between them so clearly. In his own honorable way he was preparing himself for the day when she would give him the last kiss and tiptoe away.

Aloka's eyes begin to sting. She gazed at the plaza fountain across from her window, striving to hear its soothing splash down the wall, though the sound didn't reach her ears. At this late hour the fountain was shut off.

Always she would look back wistfully at their time together, the care with which he sliced the cucumbers and served her *sukhe aloo,* how he'd freed her from the tyranny of divorce and led her toward brightness.

"Dear J," she keyed in with fingers that didn't cooperate very well.

If it's time for her to go, let it be. Sometimes there's no future in love, only the moment.

She pushed herself away from the keyboard and rose to stand at the window. Before her stretched the city, with its weary lights. Its smells, sounds, and features were gradually being stolen by the prowler of the night.

thirty-
two

It had been a steep, winding four-hour ride from the Bagdogra Airport. The driver turned for an instant and reminded Suzy that the locals jokingly called this ride a "full-body massage." The mountains were at first an indistinct wavy line in the horizon. Now, as Suzy gazed out the car window, Mount Kanchenjunga, shimmering above a sea of clouds like a massive temple carved out of ice, loomed ahead. Nestled below on a subsidiary ridge was Darjeeling, a jumble of red and black roofs interspersed with a dense stand of cedar, silver fir, cypress, and chestnut. Beyond the town she could discern the storied seven hills stretching to the horizon, their flanks webbed with tea plantations, some ninety of them in all. Somewhere on that emerald canvas was the hallowed Gupta tea estate and, down the hill from it, her home. She found herself leaning forward eagerly, trying to spot the house.

The family servant driving her was a new hire. Maintaining the deferential silence he'd retained throughout the trip, he pulled into the driveway of the sprawling bungalow where she had been raised. It was just as she remembered: the high brick fence, yellow-washed exterior, sunlit portico, a nightingale's melodic chatter from the rooftop, even the damp smell of the mature sycamore's leaves. The frame of the house seemed less stately, more aged, though just as endearing as it had been throughout her childhood. Some rain had fallen earlier and everything glistened under the afternoon sun. Her heart thumped as she reached for the car door.

The driver protested. "Please, let me help you, *didi*."

But Suzy had already scrambled out the door. Aware that the driver had silently disappeared into the house with her valise, she hurried up the crushed-rock pathway bordered with lovingly tended flower beds on either side. The late-season marigolds, some as tall as four feet, splashed a yellow-orange shade on the luxuriant green plants. She bent down and touched the rich red earth that produced such wondrous bounty. The smooth, comforting sensation was not unlike caressing a lover's skin.

She rose slowly. Her eyes fell on the entrance to the house.

It was empty.

Why no bustle on the porch with Grandma and a procession of relatives chanting, *"Esho, esho,"* welcome, welcome? Suzy had expected one of the woman kinfolk to blow a conch shell to commemorate her return, another to sprinkle sacred water on her head to cleanse the spirit after such an extended journey, a third with the traditional platter of fruit and sweet offerings. Belatedly Suzy realized that her expectation had been unrealistic.

A neatly dressed man, exuding an air of calm assurance, appeared in the doorway. "Please come in, Miss Gupta," he greeted her. Keeping the door ajar with a hand that formed a dark contrast to the wood's beige surface, he gestured her inside with the other.

Suzy was taken aback. Who was he? Definitely not a Gupta. That much was certain.

A hint of a smile flickered across his genial face. "I am Mreenal Bose."

A jolt shot through Suzy. Might this be part of Grandma's plan to bind her in wedlock? Already?

"So we finally meet," she said as she slipped past him into the shadowed hall. She nearly knocked over a brass umbrella stand, but became careful as she brushed past a wooden planter from which the luxuriant vines of an ivy plant tumbled out. At the foot of the staircase she paused, viewing the drawing room on the right and a string of bedrooms with curtains strung across the doorways on the left. She smelled a turmeric fragrance wafting out of the kitchen at the far end of the hall and heard the customary rhythmic thump of stone on stone—the cook grinding fresh turmeric root for the evening meal. Nothing much had changed. Yet Suzy waited there like a voyager without a map.

"Thakurma!" she cried.

"Please." Mreenal spoke in a hushed tone from behind. "Your grandma isn't feeling well. Your aunt and my great-aunt are both attending her. Wait just a minute. I'll fetch your aunt."

With that he was gone, leaving Suzy bewildered. Grandma taken ill? Had Suzy waited too long to return? And why was this outsider acting as if he were in charge of the house?

Suddenly Aunt Toru, a swirl of white, flew out of a room on the left. She lived nearby and often came for a visit. She appeared more compact than before. Face creased, black eyes widened in warmth and expectation, she threw her arms out and embraced Suzy tightly. "My little girl." The words came softly and in starts. "How are you? It has been so long . . ."

"I'm okay." Suzy swiped at her own tears with the back of a hand to prevent them from wetting her aunt's shoulder. "And you?"

"What does my life mean? I'm all right, but your grandmother has a fever."

"Can I see her?"

"A little later. She's sleeping now and she needs the rest."

"But Thakurma knows I'm coming today. Hasn't she asked for me yet?"

"Of course, she talks only about you, but—"

"Sujata?" queried a wispy voice, barely audible but definitely Grandma's, from one of the rooms.

Suzy raced to the room, only to pause at the threshold. Grandma was resting on a plush bed covered with a jacquard comforter. She looked ancient, *boyoshko*, as Bengalis would say. Age had happened to her. Her skin, lips, scalp, and hair had turned into the same ashen color. But the eyes held the same compassion as before.

At the sight of Suzy, Grandma's gaze flared with recognition. She made an attempt to rise. Suzy swallowed around the lump in her throat and rushed to help Grandma sit up.

"Look at you," Grandma murmured, touching Suzy's chin. "What a lovely face. Did you have a good trip?"

"Oh, Thakurma," Suzy half wailed. "What's the matter?"

"Hush, child, I'm not so terribly sick. Just a touch of a cold," Grandma barked with a trace of her old imperiousness. She grimaced as she pointed to a bottle on the side table. "Oh, that bitter medicine I have to take. The doctor has ordered bed rest for me, but how can I rest when you're here?"

It struck Suzy that Grandma wasn't wearing any jewelry, not even the few discreet pieces she customarily wore, not even the earrings, but she didn't dare ask about that. Once you leave home, you lose the privilege of asking personal questions. "You must stay in bed today, Thakurma. We'll talk tomorrow."

An elderly woman charged in. Grandma introduced the new arrival as Mreenal's great-aunt, Tami. Now Suzy gleaned the reason behind Mreenal's visit. He and his great-aunt were good neighbors, helping out in a time of need. Suzy expressed her gratitude to Tami, who gushed, "Oh, Sujata, you look just like your pictures. And you still wear a sari. Most unusual."

"You must be exhausted," Aunt Toru said, intervening, "after the long trip from Canada and that terrible car trip from Bagdogra Airport. I'll help you get settled."

And suddenly Suzy was back in her tidy old quarters. She stepped to the window and parted the sheer georgette panels to take in the blue-purple shape of the mountains, the one constant she remembered from her childhood. She watched the ever-capricious clouds moving in and cloaking the peaks. Then she swung back to the room. At first glance the room was just the way she'd left it. The intermittent afternoon sun cast an intricate dappled pattern across her bed. The honey-gold bedspread, thick and heavy, promised skin-hugging comfort. The east wall was lined with black-and-white mountain pictures Aunt Toru had once shot. Pushed to one corner of the same wall was an old black trunk full of keepsakes. When she was eleven, Suzy had embroidered a pansy pattern on its lacy white cloth cover. She smiled at the childishly crooked design, done in ribbon stitch and French knots. She had never been proficient at needlepoint like Grandma was.

A large gilt-framed photograph on the nightstand attracted Suzy's attention. Grandma, her coif still dark, her son and grandchildren fanning out before her, glowed with pride. A glance at that vibrant face and Suzy felt the pressure of tears behind her eyes. Was Grandma really ill? She couldn't be sure.

After a hot bath, Suzy wrapped herself in an orange-printed crepe sari, braided her hair, and, after deciding at the last minute against applying any makeup, made her way to the living room. She fought her sense of uncertainty by focusing on a set of abstract terra-cotta murals on the wall above the staircase and listening to the cook's heavy thumping in the kitchen. She would have to reacquaint herself with the goings-on in this house.

She heard the voice even before she recognized him. Mreenal was standing there, his back to her. She noticed the neatly trimmed hair blending into a distinct neckline that disappeared under his shirt. He was speaking to a young maidservant, who was dusting the books on the shelf with a feathery broom, updating her on the doctor's visit this morning. "Dr. Malaviya specializes in heart disease," he was saying. "That's the most common ailment in this town." He seemed more at home in this household than she was at the moment, not an encouraging notion. She cleared her throat to gain their attention and they both turned in surprise.

"Ah, we thought you were taking a nap." Mreenal's eyes radiated a mischievous sparkle. "This is Reenu. She works for your grandmother."

"Sujata-*di*! Very good to meet you." The girl's lively gaze glistened with an amalgam of curiosity and respect. She smiled excitedly, then bowed her head and pressed her palms together in a *namaskar*, in what seemed like a genuine welcome. As a young girl, Suzy used to greet the arrival of a relative from another town with some of the same ebullience, but also more shyness.

"Would you like some tea?" Reenu turned toward Mreenal.

"Perhaps later."

"But Sujata-*di* hasn't eaten in several hours. Thakurma asked me to make *puli-pithas* especially for her, and they're ready."

Suzy smiled in bemusement. An older servant, more constrained by custom, would have taken Mreenal's demurral in silence, or with the utterance, "As you wish, *huzur*," but this young maid was practically dictating. Yet her spunky nature was endearing. Then, too, the mention of the canoe-shaped autumnal treat sweetened with *khejur gur* brought saliva unbidden to Suzy's mouth. Swallowing, she gave her assent to Mreenal with a nod.

"Perhaps now," Mreenal corrected himself.

"Please." Reenu gestured toward the back lawn, then led the way.

On the veranda Suzy's eyes fell on her favorite swing, moving gently to and fro in the breeze, where she'd spent many a carefree afternoon. Sloping gently downhill from the veranda was the neatly mowed lawn beneath a spreading magnolia tree with a weathered plaque nailed to its trunk. Just as Suzy deciphered her name on the plaque, a fairy bluebird began to warble from a low-hanging branch. The foliage had grown so dense that the bird was invisible until it hopped to change position. Come spring, the tree would burst into a profusion of velvety pinkish white blossoms. Suzy's eyes roved over the valley beyond the fence where she used to romp amid lush grass and glades splashed with yellow, white, and red wildflowers. She heard crickets and spotted a grasshopper as it launched itself in a long arc, its wings clattering. Her eyes sweeping the horizon, she took in the splendor of the yellow light on the ramparts of Kanchenjunga.

When she turned back, Reenu had finished rearranging the chairs. Suzy sat down across from Mreenal. The small oval tea table between them had been laid with a homey blue-and-white-checked tablecloth with hand-sewn hems, a setup that invited relaxed conversation. "The view is stunning, just as I remember," she remarked casually.

"Wish I had my camera with me," Mreenal answered. "The backlighting is good."

"So you're a photographer."

"I don't know if I can call myself a photographer. I picked up the hobby when I was vacationing in Portugal a few years back. I didn't speak the language, but I discovered that by shooting pictures I connected with the local scene better. People forgive you if you're carrying a camera. They talk to you, they let you go ahead of them. I like connecting with people."

"I'm sorry if I was rude to you earlier."

"No need to be sorry. I realize you're close to your grandmother. Her sudden illness must have been quite a shock. I know it was for me. I've become very fond of her over the last several days."

"I'm not a naive nineteen-year-old anymore and I don't need match-making, however well-intentioned."

"I don't understand. . . ."

"I might as well be blunt. I'm wondering if Thakurma is really ill or if she is feigning a fever. I mean, she's been trying to get us together, hasn't she?"

Mreenal exploded into a merry laugh. "Clever woman! If that was indeed her intent, she has succeeded famously. Actually, I was supposed to have flown to Calcutta this morning, but I postponed the trip when I heard she'd suddenly fallen ill. Now I can't get a flight back for several days."

"I should make it clear—I'm not interested in an arranged marriage. It's a matter of principle."

"Well, I'll certainly respect your wishes. How do you think we should handle the situation?"

"We'll have to be coconspirators in this and act like we're getting along really well—as long as you're in town."

"Just a few more days. Now that we have this sorted out, we can relax, can't we? You see, dating is not instinctive for me, or most Indians, for that matter, I think. I tend to act shy or silly on a date. An arranged meeting is even more inhibiting. But you seem so westernized."

"I hate that word, 'westernized,' " Suzy retorted hotly. "When applied to a woman, it means she is career-hungry or has loose morals. When applied to a man, it means he's smart and well-adjusted."

"I'm sorry if I have offended you. I simply meant that you seem so free and independent. You seem to know your way around. Can I call you Sujata?"

Suzy nodded as she collected herself.

"Here's tea." Reenu had reappeared, hoisting a large tray with a teapot surrounded by platters of richly browned oval *puli-pithas* and glistening white rounds of coconut *naroos*. As she set the platters on the table, a rich aroma of ghee, thickened milk, and freshly grated coconut pervaded the atmosphere. Mreenal helped himself to a *naroo*. The tension dissolved as Suzy attacked a *puli-pitha* in all its crumbly, syrupy goodness.

Reenu, who was hovering at a distance, drew closer to Mreenal. In a low voice, she let out, "I just got the good news from my mother's cousin who works for your sister-in-law in Calcutta. So when will you be bringing your new wife here?"

A chunk of *puli-pitha* still impaled on her fork, Suzy stopped eating. So, Mreenal Bose had found himself a bride. This confounded her. She felt terribly foolish and humiliated.

"It's all up in the air. I haven't consented to the marriage yet." Mreenal sat quietly for a moment, then, perhaps feeling as perturbed as she was, folded his napkin into a perfect rectangle, eased back from the table, and stood up. "I really must be on my way." Turning to Reenu, he said, "The tea was exquisite. By the way, is there anything you might need for Thakurma?"

Before Reenu could reply, Suzy broke in, "Now that I'm back, I can take care of what's necessary."

"I'm sure you can manage things, but please realize that in the long-term view Thakurma's health isn't good. I want to make sure—"

"Perhaps I'll speak to her doctor privately."

"Dr. Malaviya went to medical school with my father. If you like I can take you to his office tomorrow or whenever I can get on his calendar. He's extremely busy, but I'm sure he'll allow me a few minutes."

"That's kind of you—I'll take you up on your offer," Suzy relented, somewhat mollified by his suggestion.

"I'll ring you tomorrow." He turned and strode across the lawn to the gate and was soon lost from sight.

Still thrown a bit off balance by this unusual man, Suzy returned to her *puli-pithas*. She let her hunger rule her for the next few minutes. She felt lonely. She hadn't expected to feel lonely at home.

"Oh, my, Mreenal-*babu* barely touched the *naroos*," Reenu exclaimed as she picked up the plates. "And I made them just for him." She stalked back toward the house in a huff.

The setting sun limned the mountain ridges with molten gold, even as the air took on an edge of chill. Soon the clouds would turn heavy and leaden. Suzy rose from her chair and returned to her room, where she kicked off her slippers and unpacked her laptop, then took a seat by the window. Time to dash off an e-mail to Eva, so far away in Victoria, yet at the moment just about the only person Suzy could relate to. Soon her fingers were tapping a staccato beat on the keyboard:

Dear Eva,

I'm watching an incredible golden sunset from my room, but my spirit is a sodden gray. After an absence of eight years, India seems slow and heavy, and a place to emote. I feel something or other every second I'm here. I am not as hard or callous to my family or my homeland as I thought I would be.

She went on to give Eva the news about the family and Mreenal, and signed off with:

The mountains steady me.

Lovingly, Suzy

thirty-three

At dawn, even as the last vestige of sleep enveloped her in a cozy cocoon, Nina sensed that Sujata was in the room. The girl didn't make much noise, never had; yet Nina could feel her presence far more strongly than in the past.

She evoked the tempestuous afternoon when she'd broken up Sujata's budding love affair with Pranab and sent her far away. In all the letters she and Sujata had exchanged since, neither Pranab nor the incident had ever been alluded to, but the skeletal remains of the issue were lying between them. Now, in response to the hushed, faint padding of bare feet audible from across the room, Nina opened her eyes wide.

Sujata was plunking some wildflowers and spiky leaves, a melee of grays, yellows, and evergreen, in a vase on the occasional table by the window. In the dim light filtering through the window shades, the usual topaz ring flashed on her finger. A dot of *kumkum* gleamed between her brows, drawing attention to eyes that were shaped like a pair of bamboo leaves. The sari that draped her lithe body was green with flashes of blue, her two most commonly worn childhood colors. One assertive braid was suspended stylishly over her right shoulder. How handsome Sujata had turned out to be.

"Thakurma! You're awake."

The girlish voice had been replaced by the pleasantly throaty feminine tone of a mature woman. Nina pushed aside the blanket, propped herself up, and stuffed a pillow behind her back. To think they would have a little time alone before the servants came in and friends and relatives bustled about. They had important matters to thrash out. She reached for Sujata's yielding hand. "My golden girl. You're up so early."

With lightness and grace, Sujata switched on a table lamp and remained standing. "Thought I'd surprise you with some flowers, but I should have known you'd be up early, too."

Sujata's tone was upbeat and musical, her attentive face radiated goodwill, and their exchanges, so far, had been cordial. Still Nina wondered if she'd been forgiven.

"For someone my age, just waking up is a miracle," Nina began. "A new day pops out of the sky and I'm grateful to be able to dip into its treasury of hours, minutes, and seconds. Don't worry about me; I'll be just fine. Dr. Malaviya sends a junior doctor here to check my progress every morning. Toru and Reenu have been making sure I take my medicine, and now you're here. What more could an old girl ask? So, my dear, how does it feel to be back home?"

Sujata pulled a chair up to the bed and for the next hour poured out the details of her life in Victoria. Impressive story, Nina mused, as she listened and watched. Sujata's allure was that of a rare bloom in the desert, sprouting despite harsh conditions and many times more striking because of it. Classic beauty was an ornament Sujata didn't need. Her dynamism gave her a sort of beauty. But she hadn't mentioned Pranab at all. Nina wanted to wait, but her ill health carried with it a flag of urgency and she must speak her heart.

"You know, Sujata, I do have a regret concerning you, perhaps the biggest in my entire life; certainly it's been the one that has hurt me the most."

"What is it, Thakurma?" A little frown creased Sujata's smooth forehead.

"It was a mistake on my part to ask you to break up with Pranab."

"Mistake?"

"In retrospect, you were a better match for Pranab than Aloka. Why did I have to get in between you two? Pranab saw so much in you that he risked it all—his engagement to Aloka, his position at the tea estate, his family's reputation, not to mention our approval. When a man risks his all, it's true love. Why didn't I recognize it at the time?"

Sujata's body went rigid. She stared off into the distance, visibly struggling to maintain her composure. "Don't you think it's a bit cruel to speak about it now, Thakurma? I paid for your mistake dearly."

Nina could tell that there had been many a tear, many solitary evenings and sleepless nights over that weighty decision, and though Sujata had wisely walked away from her remembrance, she had had a difficult time letting go of her resentment toward her grandmother.

"I have paid for it, too, Sujata. Much of my enjoyment of my life has been leached away as a result. I haven't forgiven myself. I blamed you for breaking up the family, but it was I who did it."

Nina paused as a welter of emotion raged behind her eyes. In the silence she heard a faint voice chanting "Hare Gouranga." It was the cook singing exaltation to a deity in the kitchen, as was his practice every morning before starting work, so his dishes would turn out pure and nourishing. He never failed in his duties, but she had failed in hers.

A strained silence descended. Nina watched as Sujata turned her attention back to the room and shrugged. So typical of Gupta women, who were trained to consider others.

"Please don't cry, Thakurma. It's not good for your health. You did what you believed was the best at the time. You had to get me out of the way so Aloka could marry Pranab, and to protect our family name. "Once I got settled in Canada," Sujata launched forth, "it was like I had a rebirth. And my life has been full ever since. Actually, in some ways, I'm grateful to you for giving me a chance to start over. It's because of you my life is what it is today."

Nina looked at the glaring light that was now flooding through the window, banishing the gloom to the far corners of the wall. "Have you heard from Pranab?"

"Yes, he has written to me."

"I got word from his mother that he arrived last night. She said he'd call this morning. But remember, Sujata, time can't be reversed."

"I'm the one to decide that, Thakurma."

Though Sujata asserted this, doubt flickered across her face, and in that moment Nina grasped the situation: A lost love, now in tattered clothing, had found its way back. Sujata, who still idealized the memory, was having difficulty recognizing it.

"I'm sure," Nina said, "Aloka wants to get back together with Pranab again."

"So that's what you're after." Sujata's words came out sharp and loud. She stood up. "Would you stop messing around with our lives?"

Without warning, a sharp pain shot through Nina's chest, lasted a second, and disappeared. She blanched, then recovered and rubbed her chest discreetly underneath the covers; then, feeling her heart palpitating, she slid down gingerly beneath the covers. "Time for my nap."

Sujata tucked the comforter around Nina and gazed at her. "I'm so sorry. I shouldn't have kept you up so long. And I shouldn't be yelling. We'll pick this up later, okay?"

Reenu tiptoed in, looked around, and, after ascertaining that she wasn't interrupting, announced in a cheery voice, "Mreenal-*babu* just called." Then, addressing Sujata, "He asked me to tell you that he'll be here tomorrow at nine."

At the sound of Mreenal's name, Sujata uplifted her chin slightly. She indicated her assent to Reenu with the barest nod and the maidservant backed out of the room quickly.

Even in her plight, Nina couldn't help but react. She nestled her cheek on the pillow and observed coyly, "So, Mreenal's coming tomorrow."

Sujata fussed with the tassel of her sari. If she appeared a bit irritated at this comment, Nina ignored that and went on. "I do like that boy. I'm sorry again, Sujata. Can't I do anything right? I wanted to introduce you informally to a nice man. Then I find out that a marriage proposal is waiting for him in Calcutta. Who knows what'll come of that? My guess is he's caught between his duty toward his parents and his own wishes."

"It doesn't matter, Thakurma. Pranab's back."

"Sujata! I'm warning you!"

"This time I'm not going to listen."

Nina watched as Sujata slipped out the door with angry, purposeful steps.

thirty-four

Sitting at her office desk, Aloka sorted through the mail. Only one week remained before her departure for Darjeeling. Her last two columns were due by the end of the day. She flipped rapidly through the cards first, encountering the usual assortment of announcements and notifications. It pleased her to receive these invitations each week from her readers, but however generous they were, as Seva she couldn't attend any function. She tried to imagine who sent her the birth announcement, and came up with an overextended young mother who skipped breakfast but somehow stole a few minutes from her eventful day to scan the "Ask Seva" column.

She opened a gift box from a fan, discovering a gilded bookmark and some chocolate nuggets. Remembering the extra pounds she was still working to shed, she pushed the box to the farthest corner of her desk. Then she picked up a letter. The well-formed, even stylish script in blue ink became progressively more cramped and downward slanting as it neared the end of the page. She could sense the frustration lurking in the writer.

I went home after ten years and no one could recognize me. At first I assumed it had to do with my putting on twenty pounds and losing my hair.

To hide my embarrassment I switched from Hindi to English, thinking my family would praise me for getting rid of my accent. Also, since I had been taking acting lessons, my gestures were smoother, more controlled, and I thought they would surely notice that, too.

Instead my aunt asked, "Is this really our Biju?"

Everyone around was too polite to comment that I had changed physically, but my aunt added, "You used to pronounce the word 'nothing' the way we do, kind of tongue-heavy. Now you seem to speak from the top of your head and don't gesture with your hands."

"Did you have a 'rebirth'?" my sister whispered. She'd read about such things in an American magazine.

I sat there, cringing. They were reacting to my new self, even as they searched for the young adult they remembered.

Yes, this is a new me: Actor Biju. The changes are, however, external. I am the same person, and I want to be accepted by my family just like before. I wonder if that's even possible.

Disappointed in Delhi

Aloka put the letter down, pushed her chair back from the computer monitor, rolled her shoulders, and considered the roles she herself played, flipping back and forth between being Seva to her readers, Parveen to Jahar, and Aloka to others. The realization came to her that with each assumed identity, she had welcomed strangers into her boundaries and possibly made strangers out of some she was already acquainted with.

Resolving to address this issue of multiple role-playing in one of her two last columns, she began to peck at the keyboard. In the lead paragraph she gave a highlight of this week's happenings: a chess competition, the screening of a new Telegu box-office hit in Queens, the launching of a new E-zine for Indian music lovers. She followed that with a personal note:

A letter from one of you has got me thinking: how, when living away from home, we take on new identities. This we do to fulfill a job requirement, to be accepted at a workplace, or simply to stretch our selves. As immigrants we have tremendous freedom to do so. When we land here, few people know us or notice us, and the family doesn't hover in the background. We can be who we want to be, not only during the daytime, but also during our spare hours.

There you are, Ayesha, dropping your salwar *suit and* dupatta *and putting on a skirt because you've always wanted to. You, Kumar, crooning a country-western song at the top of your lungs rather than* kirtan. *You, Vineet, Kripal, Ajay, and Resham, setting your briefcases aside in the evening and dashing out the door. You want to be a storyteller, do origami, go climb a mountain, or volunteer for the Sierra Club.*

This new you is your creation. You must care for it. Be aware (as the reader's letter points out) that the family you left behind safekeeps only the old you in their memory bank. Your new self may seem fraudulent to them.

This is a risk we take when we leave home. You may never again be fully recognizable to those you love the most. For an immigrant, renewal is the constant state of being.

Aloka got up from the desk, stretched up her arms, downed a large glass of water, then proceeded to wade into the rest of the mail. Most didn't require an answer; her readers simply wanted to express what was on their minds. She paused over the one that began:

I am a street musician by trade.

Immediately a street singer came to Aloka's mind. She had heard about an Indian-American man who sang equally well in Hindi, Bengali and Marathi on street corners in Manhattan. Just two weeks ago on a Saturday, on the way to run an errand, she had been stopped by snatches of a well-known Bengali beat, "Dakbo Na, Dakbo Na." I Will Not Call You Anymore.

A Bengali love song in the center of Manhattan? Her curiosity heightened, she turned to see a sizable assembly of mostly Indian-Americans standing three-deep around a musician. She wiggled her way through the tightly packed bodies to get a closer view. The singer, who appeared to be in his forties, seemed content as he crooned the conventional lyric of unrequited love. Halfway through the final refrain, Aloka spotted a familiar face, equally enraptured.

It was Pranab, nearly unrecognizable in a ski cap pulled down low on his forehead. He was moving his lips silently, in sync with the singer's, his face smooth and handsome, a change from the past few years. Aloka stared at him, expecting to cut through his trance and perhaps to receive an acknowledging glance in return—after all, they used to sing the very same song as a duet—but he seemed oblivious to her presence. As the music ended and the crowd thinned, Aloka purposefully looked up at Pranab again. He dropped a few dollars in the musician's hat and walked away.

Why didn't he recognize her? Had she changed so much? Does an altered destiny make one over?

Aloka puzzled over that issue once again as she picked up the street musician's letter:

You're probably wondering how this humble man makes a living and why any respectable Indian would work as a mere street artist. Or, perhaps, like my sister, you feel pity for me. "If not a doctor, a scientist, or a Silicon Valley mogul," she advises her children, "at least be a Wall Street broker." I am achingly aware of how our community boasts of producing the most professionals of any immigrant group.

But mine is not a bad life. As I play my flute, sing a Hindi film hit, and draw a group of passersby close around me, I feel as though I'm back in Calcutta, Delhi, or Jaipur. The streets are the same everywhere. True, you'll find no paan juice splattered on Manhattan sidewalks, but you'll notice people rushing about, making contacts, and searching for meaning. Some are jerks, others civil, most simply surviving, just like folks in India. Even here the streets belong to the common people.

As I finish my song, I watch pedestrians drop a few coins in my hat, then stoop to pick up a copy of Manhattan, India *from the corner newspaper box. I'll bet they can't wait to get home and dig into your column. You see, dear Seva, like you I understand the habits of humanity.*

Do stop by when you have a chance.

From the corner of Fifty-sixth and Third

Aloka made a decision: She would devote an entire article in the future to the wide variety of occupations taken up by her readers.

Now it was time to compose her last column. Unbidden, a subject came to mind and her fingers flew over the keyboard. She announced to her readers her forthcoming trip to India and gave the exact dates of her absence. She concluded with:

We immigrants live to return home. Our savings of a dollar here and a dollar there go toward that sweetest of goals. We think of our families in India when we pick up the newspaper, when we bump into a desi *in the subway, even as we engage in the mundane task of whirling lentil batter in the blender. We live in a "here and there" mode, instinctively comparing all our experiences in the States with the previous ones at home. "Milk tastes better in India," a man once told me, although, I found out later, he had never taken dairy there.*

If we're putting in extra hours at work, it is often as much to prove ourselves to those we have left behind as to impress our bosses here. There exists no happier phrase in our vocabulary than "I'm going back to India." You're never more envied in the community. "Eat some rosmadhuri *for me," your best friend whispers in your ear; "Bring me back a jar of Ganga water," an elderly neighbor implores; "I wish I could leave this mess behind and go with you," a colleague mutters.*

We don't care so much about what will be new there but what is still as we remember it. Auntie with her toothless smile, the shoeshine boy who bugged us every time we passed him on the sidewalk, the three-deep jostling mob at the bus stop, and the triumph of securing a seat in the 2B bus. All will be there, we hope.

I confess to having my apprehensions about going back. How will my family react to me? How well will I fit in? Yet, right this minute, much as I know I'll miss you all, I am seized with a delicious anticipation and a tremendous jubilance.

I'll look forward to chatting with you again upon my return.

Love,

Seva

thirty-five

As Suzy hopped out of the car, the late-day sun bathed her in soft golden light. Four o'clock, that enigmatic afternoon hour, had always been Pranab's favorite time for a rendezvous at the secluded lake hidden in the jungled valley below, where he loved to picnic, and especially to dance. She instructed the driver to come back a couple of hours later and pick her up. He reminded her disapprovingly that they needed to leave promptly at five, since Grandma was visiting some relatives this evening and would need transportation.

In her eagerness Suzy chose to ignore his insolence and headed for the trail without replying. Her heart beat faster as she descended the hill and neared the shore. At first glance the place hadn't changed. A small fish shattered the limpid surface of the lake in a glistening spray to seize an unwary water bug, just as it would have done years ago. She wandered along the gently lapping edge of the water, searching for the man whom she had once seen as the sole reason for her being, occasionally casting her gaze to the sliver of road high above. Slowly she began to notice subtle changes. Vehicles cruised the road, amassing clouds of reddish dust in the air, far more often than she remembered. Three young boys scampered about at the far end of the lake. Eight years ago hardly anyone came here.

Now she spotted the driver. Instead of taking off for an hour, he was waiting under a tree at some distance. He was obviously keeping an eye on her—on Grandma's order. Still Suzy found herself grateful for the brief solitude. A chattering bird hopped excitedly from branch to branch of a once-tiny poinsettia that had flourished into a tree in her absence.

Hearing the crunching of footsteps on pebbles, she twisted around and caught sight of a man working his way down the trail. Silently she willed him to hurry.

The figure, draped in *khadi kurta-churidar*, was slightly heavier than it had been eight winters ago. As Pranab approached, his feet rolled unsteadily over a loose rock that seemed to shiver him to the bones. The forehead was lined and the eyes seemed drowned in their sockets. The broad white smile still dazzled, but the lips disclosed a tremor of hesitancy.

Eyes brimming with pleasure, he cried out, "Sujata," and reached out to take her hand. "You look wonderful."

In that moment of stunned happiness she wanted to reply, but her words had dissolved into a choke. Pranab broke the silence and her embarrassment with a burst of forced cheer. "Hard to believe I'm seeing you again after all this time. It felt like a century."

She gestured toward a bench, where they took their seats under partial shade, close but not touching. Once she resumed control of her voice, she chanted, "I knew we'd meet again."

"Hope kept me going. Sujata, please tell me everything from the day you left Darjeeling."

"I want to know all about you, too. What little I got from Aloka's letters didn't give me much to go on."

Suzy began recounting her life during the past eight years. At first she spoke haltingly, as she relived the shame of her departure; but once she was past that initial traumatic episode, it became easier for her to begin talking about settling in Canada. She grew animated as she spoke of her tea enterprise. He listened with a light in his eyes, as though he were discovering her anew. Soon the conversation shifted to that infinite topic of the triumphs and difficulties of adjusting to a new land. Pranab's expression changed; his lips curled in bitterness. Purposefully she lightened the mood with a humorous anecdote: Her first encounter with a hamburger and how it reminded her of the spicier version, *shami kebob*, back at home. How in the past week she had been eating and eating, three full meals a day, including *shami kebob*, and still not feeling satiated. Pranab laughed, though not the same bright laugh she remembered, which used to go on and on, carrying the full force of his personality. This time it was a short, weak laugh, following which he collected himself and became solemn. He began narrating his own experience of waiting for the subway in a dingy station in New York at night. How, to make the wait bearable, he'd imagined the luxurious beauty of the tea garden and her meandering along ahead of him in a purple *salwar-kameez*, only to be rudely elbowed back to the present by a passing hoodlum, who called him a "stupid foreigner" for being absentminded. As he finished telling the anecdote, he lowered his head, overcome by frustration. She hadn't expected him to be so affected by a dark, urban incident that could happen to anybody.

Two birds fluttered and dove in a frenzied ritual of courtship at the far end of the lake. She considered it a blessing that they hadn't tried to verbalize their tenderness for each other quite yet. Those feelings required a gentler place to flourish, and more nurturing. Also, with the driver clearly in view and with the recent arrival of a swell of sightseers within speaking range, such confessions wouldn't be appropriate.

"Did you get my letter?" he finally inquired.

"Yes, it was a big joy and a huge surprise." She wrapped the end of her sari train around her index finger. "I found it hard to believe you and Aloka are divorced. It'll be quite a shock for everybody. Is there no chance of a reconciliation?"

"None. It's time to move on with my life. I had to come back here to get my bearings, to get away from the chaos of New York. Aloka loves the bustle of that city. She sees energy and progress. I'm hopelessly un–New York."

"Is that the whole reason you split?"

"No. You were in my mind all the time, Sujata. On cold nights I'd get your photo out and look at the star of my life. I'd recall what your skin felt like to touch, the fragrance of your hair, how you moved. I'd imagine I was dancing for you. I'd feel the rush of blood in my legs. You see, losing you did it to me. Then, too, I made another mistake. I'd believed that once I married Aloka I'd forget you, settle down to a new life in a new country, and be happy. But I was wrong, utterly wrong. I led a tortured existence. I called myself a coward a thousand times a day for not standing up to your family, for not eloping with you. Looking back, Aloka and I should never have gotten married. Poor Aloka, she loved me so much, she gave me all she had. In return I only hurt her." He turned half away with a sigh and ran his fingers through his hair, as if to wipe away the shame of the memory.

"I thought in all these years you'd been with her . . . you loved her."

"Had I never met you, I'd have said Aloka was the ultimate prize for a man. She has beauty, grace, manners, and kindness. She lets a man into her life so generously. But you're the woman who helped me see my possibilities. When I danced for you, it was like my body and mind and spirit and other dimensions joined together. You took me to the inside of a dance."

His admission of her effect on him astonished her. Had she actually been that powerful, at such a young age, when she had considered herself shy and insignificant? A speck of fright mixed in with the joy of that realization.

The driver signaled impatiently from the road above. That grated on Suzy. Once again they were being interrupted when they had barely gotten started. And yet a sense of family duty compelled her to rise. "It's time for me to go," she said apologetically.

He rose, too. "As it turns out, I have to go visit a relative. Shall we meet again tomorrow?"

He stared with a hungry eagerness as she promised to return the next day at the same time. She sighed as she walked up the trail. The atmosphere, like an old portrait, had taken on a sepia tint. The leaves at her feet were dried, crunchy.

thirty-six

Suzy stepped out of Dr. Malaviya's office onto the sidewalk, with Mreenal just behind her. On this morning the sky wore witch's colors of dismal gray-black. A sudden wind whipped down the street and cut through her sweater and cotton slacks.

As they walked slowly down the street, the doctor's words still echoed in her mind. What was wrong with Grandma? Age and high blood pressure, coupled with an obstinate refusal to take her medicine and the walks that had been prescribed, were all contributing factors to her generally poor health. Her current cold wasn't much of a problem.

"You're worrying too much." Mreenal reached out, squeezed her hand fleetingly, then let it go.

At the next intersection he seemed to hesitate. Her house and that of Mreenal's great-aunt lay in opposite directions on this cross street, whereas the way ahead would lead to a high ridge looking out toward a range of hills.

"Do you have to go back right away?" he asked. "Perhaps we could take a stroll?"

Suzy hesitated. She wasn't quite ready to show her reddened, moist eyes to Grandma. There were still several hours before she was to meet Pranab. She stole a glance at this solid man, who had accompanied her to consult with the doctor, then listened quietly as she aired her concerns. Only when he was sure she was finished had he asked his own questions, addressing points she'd missed. Belatedly she realized that despite their rocky beginning, his imminent wedding to a Calcutta woman, and her impending tryst with another man later in the day, she considered him something of an ally. And the sun was peeking through the clouds. "Why, yes, a stroll would be nice," she said.

She glanced up at the white feathers of a bird swooping over the trail's steep incline, then, struck by an inspiration, suggested, "How about a hike up that hill? It's pretty bare. It's called the 'Fallen Tree' hill. There's a great view of a misty lake in a valley with Kanchenjunga as the backdrop."

He gazed doubtfully at the steep trail. "I'd love to."

They started up the path dotted with poplar, oak, spruce, and fir, with friendly ferns lacing it all together. Soon the road angled up steeply. Her breathing was becoming labored and he had slowed his steps. A sudden harsh clattering startled her. She looked up and glimpsed a man rolling his fruit-laden cart down the slope.

"Tangerines," Suzy cried above the roar of a lorry somewhere below. "Darjeeling grows the sweetest tangerines."

"Shall we try some?" Mreenal stopped before the man, bought a pair of tangerines, and handed her one. Standing by the trail, she peeled the fruit, separated the sections, and bit through the thin membrane to savor the explosion of its delicate juice.

"Exquisite." Mreenal wiped his lips with a handkerchief. "This is the most time I've spent in Darjeeling since high school, and I must say I'm enjoying myself. I only wish I could tackle these hills as easily as you do, you the mountain girl."

They passed several shacks made of tin and wood, with brightly hued doors, and paused before a decrepit shop that she remembered from childhood. A gaunt old man in a black turban crouched on a mat on the floor, shelling smaller-than-a-fingernail-sized green cardamom pods. Serenely, he exposed a cluster of tiny black seeds, which he then dropped into a container. Suzy paused and let the fragrance run through her. "There's a saying here that we have three kinds of land—rice land, maize and wheat land, and tea and cardamom land. I still remember how Aloka and I used to shell cardamom at harvest time from the nearest cardamom land. We'd have a competition to see who could shell the most."

"My great-aunt always called cardamom the spice of kings," Mreenal offered. "I'm not much of a cook, but I put in a few cardamom pods when I brew my morning coffee for a great flavor. Speaking of that, would you show me your tea garden sometime? I've never seen how tea is grown."

Suzy's eyes fell on the wide-mouthed blossoms of a foxglove plant that was growing out of a hollow in a rock. She started to hike again. "I'll see if I can arrange for someone to take you to the estate."

"I understand." Mreenal caught up with her. "I'm staying a few extra days, by the way. Thakurma has asked me to."

Suzy frowned. Grandma and her constant interference irked her. Then, as she looked ahead at the summit and treacherous loose rocks leading to it, she realized it was time to concentrate, or she would slip and hurt herself. She flexed her knees and, with one foot firmly planted first, took one bold step after another, finally reaching the hilltop. It was a moment of utter exhilaration. She wiped the perspiration off her forehead and turned back. Mreenal, struggling over the same rocky terrain, grabbed hold of the branches of a bush for support and before long managed to plant himself next to her.

He held up both arms in triumph. As his breathing came back to normal, he said, "We've met the challenge, it seems."

Suzy shared the jubilation. Together they peered down at the deep valley below. Sunlight filtered through the conifers in lambent green beams. A small lake shimmered aqua through the rising mist. The atmosphere was so still that it invited closeness and silence at the same time. A faint breeze, fresh and cool, tickled her face.

She turned to Mreenal. "They have a saying around here that views don't repeat themselves. If you spit, show up a second later, or don't pay attention, you've forever missed a special sight."

"Looks like our timing was just right," he replied.

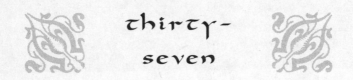

thirty-
seven

It was about four o'clock the same afternoon when Suzy returned to the shore of Senchal Lake, where the blue water rippled under the caress of a whimsical breeze. She perched herself on a rock by a clump of elegant broom grass. She suffered a twinge of sadness at the thought that such a splendid plant could be transformed into the crude broom used by maidservants to sweep the floor.

Since seeing Pranab here yesterday, she had analyzed their relationship many times, though no matter how she approached it she came away feeling as if she had scraped an open wound. Finally she had realized it would be futile to reestablish their bond. The pain he had inflicted eight long years ago had callused her feelings and left her wary of permitting him into her life again. And quite naturally her perspective on what it means to love and be loved had changed. Yesterday Pranab inferred that he needed her to feel complete. Suzy had long since learned that need didn't equate to love.

Within minutes he arrived and joined her. He greeted her warmly and took her hand in his, seemingly blind to the barrier time and distance had put between them. His touch didn't reassure her or form an attachment. She attempted a smile, but, feeling slightly restive, avoided his searching eyes and gazed off at the lake.

He talked nostalgically about playing a little tabla music last night with his cousins. How rusty his fingers had felt on the drums, how off his beats were. Then he leaned toward her, as though picking up where he had left off yesterday. "Did you miss me in Canada?"

"Yes, at first. For a long time I didn't think I'd make it."

"But you did. I hear you've done very well."

"Yes, all those years I threw my life into my work. A small business is a constant struggle, but it also gives you a lot of satisfaction. This morning when I called my assistant, she asked me when I was coming back. She made me feel good deep down inside."

"I wrote many letters to you, Sujata. I just didn't mail them."

"It's just as well you didn't. We both needed to put the past behind us. I thought about you on many occasions. I'd look back and wonder if I was a complete fool."

"But now you know the truth."

The silence between them rang with the hard edge of that truth. She stared as he squinted up at the sky. Once his expression would have reflected the vibrancy of the Darjeeling sun. Today his wrinkled forehead only betrayed pain and frustration.

"You're a career success," he said abruptly, "but you don't know your heart."

How presumptuous of him to say he knew her heart and she didn't. At this juncture in life she was closer to understanding herself than she'd ever been.

"My friend Eva says, 'Truth, like software, has new releases.' Jokes aside, Pranab, options, new truths come to you. You follow them and you're changed."

"Oh, no, Sujata, you haven't changed." He forced a laugh, which ended up as a cough. "I know you inside and out. You're the same girl you've always been, and I'm the same man who's always loved you. Don't worry. I'll be patient. I have a few weeks here. We'll see each other as often as we can."

It was as though he were dancing alone in a room long after the guests had left and the music had stopped playing. "But, Pranab, it's not a question of seeing each other more often. We can never get back what we lost."

"Lost? The only thing we've lost is a little time. Look, the next couple of days I'll be busy helping with my cousin's wedding. Her father is ill and there's much preparation left to be done, but I'll be sure to stop by your house when I can. Just wait and see. In no time all things will be just like they used to be."

Eyes glittering, he stood up and clutched her hand. She felt her palm becoming clammy, rigid under the insistent grip. Her desire had gone cold. Like digging into an old excavation. Like touching tarnished gold.

She stood with him. "It's not going to work, Pranab."

He gave her a warm look. "You'll change your mind."

Before Suzy could protest, he had turned and walked away, his silhouette little more than a few dark strokes in space.

thirty-
eight

Aloka felt a rush of apprehension as the car pulled up in the driveway and saw a small congregation of people pouring out of the pastel-yellow house, her childhood home. Steeling herself, she climbed out of the car. There was a commotion at her presence. Her favorite aunt, Toru, came rushing out with a conch shell and blew at it. Three successive booms heralded Aloka's initiation back home. Cousin-sister Kabita garlanded her with a marigold *maala*, a giggly young cousin-brother lowered his head to her feet, and a great-aunt gently pushed a tiny rectangular *sandesh* into her mouth, saying, "This is to sweeten your homecoming. Oh, Aloka! We've missed you so terribly." The same great-aunt mentioned last night's downpour and what a blessing it was for the crops, concluding with surety that it had something to do with Aloka's arrival.

Eight long years of absence and yet Aloka could trek so easily back into the family sphere. India was reassuringly there. Then, realizing this high-spirited welcome had to do with her status as the oldest child in the family, she was frozen with anxiety.

Grandma stepped forth and greeted Aloka with an outstretched arm. She ushered Aloka into the house. They talked for a few minutes, at the conclusion of which Grandma whispered, "By the way, Pranab's back. He called me the other day."

"So . . . you know?"

"Yes, my dear, I have known it for a while. I was saddened by the news, but then I'm too old to let it get me down. I only want what's best for you. I know you married Pranab for love and, when you divorced, it must have been for reasons of the heart as well."

"Your understanding makes it a lot easier. Where's Sujata?"

Grandma mumbled, "Sujata had some errands to run. She'll be back soon."

Had Sujata forgotten the old customs? To be present at this occasion would have been the best gift she could bring.

In the living room, Aloka found herself surrounded by more aunts, uncles, and cousins. "How well you look." One uncle looked over to Aloka's denim pants and fancy red satin jacket. "A little New Yorkish, if you don't mind my saying."

A cousin pinched Aloka's cheek and complimented her on the extra couple of pounds she'd put on. "No matter how much progress we've made, our women don't have to be quite as thin as women in the West. Isn't that nice?"

The maidservant brought a tray of soft drinks, and the relatives drifted to one side of the room. Aunt Toru motioned Aloka to the window. She seemed to have some private words for Aloka.

"India is changing, as you'll surely find," Aunt Toru said. "We have cows pulling the lawn mower, but our young women are now attending 'software finishing schools.' Our door-to-door vegetable seller calls every family in the apartment building from his cell phone and collects orders before we even go down. He no longer gives you chilis and coriander sprigs free of charge with your purchase."

Just as Aloka began to laugh, Aunt Toru said, "But let me warn you that some relatives might snub you because you're divorced. You'll notice many signs of progress in India, but not in this matter. Whenever there's a divorce, they blame it on the woman."

"So I see. Is that why Aunt Dipti and her family aren't here?"

Aunt Toru stared into the space and said no more. Suddenly Aloka ebbed into the fatigue of traveling. She excused herself, but couldn't go very far, as lunch was being served in the dining room.

After a lovely lunch of *begun pora, cholar dabl,* and steamed rice, Grandma sent Aloka to her room, telling everyone, "The girl needs to rest after her long trip." But less than an hour later, Aloka, restless and unable to sleep due to the change in time zones and tidbits of conversation that had clung to her mind, wandered back to the now-deserted drawing room. Except for the mutterings of the domestic help in the kitchen, the house was silent. She strolled along the walls, adorned with framed photographs of generations of Guptas. Eventually she stopped to peer at a portrait of her grandfather on his wedding day, elegant in the classic cone-shaped crown of a groom, then at the black-and-white shot of Mother, taken a year before her death. The resemblance to Sujata was unmistakable. Aloka slid to the next picture, a group photo of a high school class, with Sujata crouching in the back row. Only her eyes and the front wave of her hair were visible.

Aloka heard the front porch creak and turned toward the door just as Sujata sauntered in, slender as ever, her cheeks rosy from the brisk mountain wind. The sari train was tied neatly around Sujata's waist. The birch-bark print complemented her whimsical orange lipstick perfectly. Aloka couldn't remember when Sujata had looked so well put together. As if to complete the picture, a handsome man followed her into the room.

Aloka felt a wave of warmth inside her. She cried out, "Sujata!"

Sujata stretched out her arms and gave Aloka a quick embrace. "I meant to come back a lot sooner, Aloka," she chirped, "but the car broke down."

No shyness. How unlike Sujata. She appeared transformed, this vivacious woman, full of gusto, informal in her manners, able to look her elder sister directly in the eye as an equal.

"The driver couldn't get help in time," Sujata went on. "Fortunately Mreenal was with me, so we walked back together. It took two hours." She sighed a bit histrionically and her bracelets clinked in seeming accordance.

The man smiled and nodded, as though the car problem hadn't bothered him the least bit. "Two hours? Was it that long?"

"Oh, Aloka, this is Mreenal." Then, as greetings were exchanged, Sujata added, "How about some tea?"

How odd that Sujata was acting as the hostess.

Just as they entered the drawing room, Reenu slipped in. "Sujata-*di*, you're back! You got so many phone calls." The maidservant reeled off a series of names, handed Sujata a stack of telephone messages, and proceeded to consult with her about prospective meal menus. Sujata ordered a big pot of stewlike *khichuri* for the evening meal and a side dish of *begun bhaja,* just the right pairing. She spoke to the maidservant with authority and kindness.

Aloka pulled up a chair opposite Mreenal. "How did you two meet?" she asked, all the while keeping a discreet eye on Sujata. She still couldn't believe the changes in her sister.

When Mreenal answered, it was obvious that most of his alertness was focused on Sujata. His eyes wandered in her direction frequently as he recounted the circumstances of their first meeting. Aloka recognized that Sujata and Mreenal were in that early, feverish phase of courtship when every moment spent together was euphoric. This town, with its lush natural surroundings, was conducive in that regard. Aloka called to mind her first encounter with Pranab nearly a decade ago in the hills of Darjeeling. That day had a special brilliance. Perhaps she and Pranab still might be able to slip away from the house together and retrace that hilly route. Now, with Mreenal around, Sujata would be less of an obstacle.

"How does *chire bhaja* sound to go with the tea?" Sujata inquired.

"Perfect," Aloka answered. The freshly roasted rice flakes sautéed in ghee, so ethereal on the palate, were a rarity outside India. "Haven't had it since I left."

Over tea, with the perfume of ghee thick in the air, Aloka listened as Sujata chattered enthusiastically about her hikes and sightseeing adventures with Mreenal. Their faces radiated a special fondness for each other. Often they finished each other's sentences and they agreed more often than not. It was obvious they inhabited their own private universe. Aloka had ventured into it without the proper documents.

Aloka had barely begun to nibble at her *chire bhaja* when Sujata polished off her plate. Since when did Sujata appreciate food so much? She used to be such a finicky eater.

Presently Sujata turned her gaze to the clock on the wall. "Mreenal's cousin is acting in a school play. We're going to a four o'clock rehearsal. Would you care to join us?"

"It's nearly three A.M. in New York. My eyes won't stay open much longer. I should take a nap before dinner. But thanks anyway. I'll see you both this evening."

Just as Aloka eased up from the couch, Reenu reappeared. "Pranab-*babu* is here!"

Aloka observed the sudden shock that rippled across Sujata's face. Did she dread his visit? Before she had time to consider the situation, Pranab strode into the room, fresh in a printed *kurta* and loose pants, appearing casually confident, perhaps even a bit cocky. Without his trademark tortoiseshell spectacles, he seemed to have regressed to an earlier era, to a younger, more carefree self. She wondered if his attire had been selected to achieve that effect.

Aloka, her throat suddenly lumpy, dropped back onto her seat. She had waited for this moment for so long—to be alone with Pranab in this cozy ambience, to have their voices mingle in small talk, to feel the radiance of their love once again. She hadn't even remotely pictured a foursome, and least of all one that included Sujata.

Pranab noticed Aloka first and walked straight over to her. He seemed to struggle to come up with an appropriate phrase of welcome. "Aloka, how good to see you. Did you just arrive?"

She nodded, as she caught the touch of melancholy in his voice. For a moment they stared at each other in silence. A swelling of emotion stopped her from speaking. Perhaps this room, where they'd spent much time together, evoked memories in him, too.

He queried her about the long journey from New York: Were both the flights on time? Were they full? How had she passed the long, dreary hours? As they chatted, she couldn't help but detect remorse in his heavy-lidded eyes, in the way he clasped and unclasped his hands.

After a polite interval, Pranab turned and seemed to spot Sujata for the first time. His face broke into an enchanting smile as he gazed at her wistfully, pouring all his warmth and attention into that one act. "Sujata, I decided to drop by and surprise you."

Sujata appeared surprised, even a trifle embarrassed. Aloka sat back stiffly in the overstuffed couch. Her earlobes ached from the heavy gold earrings she was wearing; in fact, her whole body ached. As she looked on, Sujata introduced Pranab and Mreenal to each other, by names only, no relationships suggested. Though the two men exchanged cordial greetings, the glances that passed between them were guarded and uncertain.

Pranab planted himself in a chair between Aloka and Sujata. In an earnest tone he asked Sujata how she'd spent the last few days. His entire upper body leaned in her direction as he talked. Mentally Aloka tried to assay if this was a sign of intimacy, if any of the old passion had been ignited again. Suddenly that horrible morning in Manhattan unfolded before her, the morning when she had discovered Pranab's love letter to Sujata, and all the suffering that had ensued. Now Aloka, her face burning, wanted to lash out at her sister, *bhoot*, who was smiling so coquettishly at both men. How would Aloka survive the next couple of weeks in the same house with this miserable creature?

Something in Pranab's behavior must have alerted Mreenal. Though he pretended to browse an issue of *Outlook* magazine, he stole an occasional glance at Pranab, then at Sujata, possibly waiting for just the right opening to assert his presence. Aloka felt a sudden affinity toward Mreenal and with it a diminution of loneliness. She shook her arms to alleviate the tension.

"Just on my way here," Pranab was saying, "I was approached by a sleek-looking guy, obviously on the take. I figured he wanted a donation and handed him some coins. Do you know what he said? 'Only five rupees, brother? Why, that won't even buy me *dahl* and rice! Surely a man of your class can spare a fifty.' "

Sujata gave a perfunctory smile. "Beggars have gone upscale. They're keeping up with the economy. They have a right to." Not a bad answer from Sujata.

"You're lucky, Pranab," Mreenal quipped. "He didn't lift your passport."

Pranab ignored both comments. "Why are there so few flights from Calcutta to Darjeeling when the route is so popular, do you know, Sujata? And why does the airline try to serve a full meal on a forty-five-minute flight? Such a lack of planning."

Mreenal set the *Outlook* aside and cut in. "Will you take a day trip to Sikkim this weekend, Sujata? We can hike up to Tsangu Lake. For you it'll be a piece of cake, or should I say a plate of *chire bhaja*?"

Sujata laughed, a merry laugh, and both men gazed at her. They seemed fascinated by her naturalness. How things had changed. Sujata was now the spotlight in the family drawing room, Aloka merely the observer.

"Think before you go, Sujata." Pranab cleared his throat and touched his breast pocket. "All those switchbacks and hairpin corners. So many accidents on that route."

Sujata seemed amused by the undercurrent of rivalry for her attention, but didn't respond, no doubt a tribute to her newly acquired social skills. Aloka was cognizant of the bone-rattling drive on a narrow mountain road, which cut its way along precipitous gorges high above the River Teesta. Molten silver water and green banks, colossal mountain pinnacles ever-present in the background, and a sense of serenity she had yet to experience anywhere else.

Quietly Aloka got up. "Excuse me, I'm going to my room now." She was aware of the silence that had descended on the room. Just before slipping out the door, she swung around. "The drive to Sikkim is awesome, Sujata. I hope you don't forgo the chance. There's danger in any choice you make. Just as there's danger in not choosing."

At this Sujata became pensive, as though the words had elicited new reflections in her.

Aloka did not wait to see Pranab's reaction.

thirty-
nine

When Sujata suggested going to Tiger Hill for the sunrise, Nina had readily consented. At almost twenty-six hundred meters, Tiger Hill stood out as the highest point in the greater Darjeeling area. When the sun peeked over the horizon, Nina had marveled at the spectacle of magnificent Kanchenjunga and its lesser sibling Kabru glowing like burnished bronze, as though a flaming torch had licked them in succession. Even after so many years, the view uplifted her spirit and gave her added energy. After sharing a breakfast of tea and buttered toast with Sujata, Nina sank into one of the chairs the driver had set out for them on the ground below the observation pavilion. Her eyelids began to droop and soon she dozed off in the warmth of the morning sun.

Some time later, Nina woke with a start and a sneeze to find herself showered in a velvety light that felt pleasantly warm on her cheeks and forehead. She drew herself up and cast her eyes to the fiery eastern sky. The sun, a giant tangerine, had crept up above the rim of the mountains, splashing its golden elixir across a canvas of fluffy clouds. As she watched, Nina nibbled on a chocolate nugget that Sujata had brought for her, a treat hard to her decaying teeth, intensely pleasurable on the palate.

She looked off to the left where Sujata was standing near the edge of a precarious ledge, the train of her sari flapping in the wind, seemingly lost in the panorama of the cloud-swept valley below. To Nina's surprise, Pranab had joined her there. Had he just happened to come for the sunrise, or had he known she would be here? Most likely he had found out from the servants at home. In any case, he had timed his arrival perfectly. Most of the spectators who had swarmed the area for the six A.M. sunrise had long since departed. Now only a few hardy, shawl-covered souls wandered about, and that meant he had ample opportunity for a private conversation with Sujata. Nina could not make a guess as to how long they'd been having this tête-à-tête, but from the sound of the fragments floating up to her, the conversation was becoming increasingly heated.

"It's over, Pranab. We can't go back to where we were. You must understand."

Though the words sounded dreadfully final, Sujata's tone carried a poignant quality, as though she knew this would devastate Pranab, and yet had to follow inner directions.

Pranab sounded incredulous. "Is it because of Mreenal? You just met him! How can you let him ruin what we had? It was so precious."

To Nina it became obvious that Pranab, not ready to relinquish his position, was grasping at whatever he could. Once he'd succeeded in changing her mind, it would only be a matter of time before he seduced her again.

Sujata: "It's not because of Mreenal. I've changed and moved on. Without that, there'd be no Mreenal."

Nina didn't care to listen anymore. Before her eyes Pranab gestured at Sujata with a sweep of a hand, the way a persistent hawker tries to lure a customer back, and pleaded. Sujata appeared to terminate the exchange and take off by herself to another ledge, possibly for a different view. Pranab stood alone for a while. He must have sensed that Nina had awakened, for he spun around, smiled wistfully, and started walking toward her. A mobile phone stuck out stupidly from the side pocket of his dark woolen overcoat. He looked shabbier. A squirrel scampering across the ground barely avoided his heavy tread. At last, a chance for Nina to speak with Pranab in private. She certainly had a few things to get off her chest.

Pranab greeted Nina with a well-modulated tone of respect and commented on the great view, both with almost comic grandiloquence, as he lowered himself into a chair next to her.

"I never forgot what you once wrote to us about Tiger Hill, Thakurma. How you'd come here to make a wish and say a prayer for us. The breeze would blow your prayer toward the tallest mountains in the world, then up to the heavens, where the gods would receive it. I promised myself then that I'd visit this place again the first chance I got and make a few wishes myself."

"I write too much."

"Your letters were lifesavers for me and Aloka in New York. Every day, I'd go through my daily chores as efficiently as a machine, and with about as much feeling. Then the postman would bring an envelope or an aerogram from you or from my parents, and that'd change everything. All of a sudden I'd breathe more deeply and hum a Rabindrasangeet, and even the traffic noise wouldn't seem so mind-numbing."

"You're not planning to move back here, are you, Pranab?"

He looked away abruptly and hesitated. If in the past Pranab had appeared arrogant to Nina, he didn't do so now. The lines of his face were humbler. His voice carried less conviction.

"As a matter of fact, Thakurma, I'm looking for a new start and thought I might go knocking at some doors hereabouts. Ah, I see you are skeptical."

"I don't have good news for you in that regard."

"Would you care to explain?"

"I'm afraid, Pranab, no tea estate here will ever hire you. My son made sure of that before he died. His influence still remains strong. And what else is there for you in Darjeeling besides tea?"

"But I hear the Gupta tea estate hasn't turned a profit in years." A trace of a sneer had crept into Pranab's voice. "How long can you go on like that?"

"Things are going to get turned around soon." Nina experienced the pleasure of the last speck of the bonbon that had just coated her throat with a flowing sweetness.

"Will that be easy? The tea bushes haven't been pruned properly for a long time now. And even if you were to rectify that, their yield will not improve much for several years."

"The plantation is going to good hands."

"Well, in any case, I wanted to express my gratitude to you in person, Thakurma, for saving my head."

Nina watched an elderly worker lop off an overgrown branch of bamboo, wielding a scythe with an emaciated but powerful hand. She felt equally energetic. She looked straight at Pranab's face. Her clouded eyes, she could feel, were flashing with pent-up bitterness. "You should have thanked Aloka for that long ago, but you never did. She risked her life for you and gave you all she had. You took something precious and defiled it."

A tattered wicker basket of marigold garlands on his head, a roving vendor, who had been making rounds, threw a glance at them, then turned away.

"I've made mistakes," Pranab said. "I won't deny that. But I've made Aloka happy. She wouldn't have stayed that many years with me otherwise."

"We'd raised her in the ancient tradition of Indian women who don't question their husbands. We thought she'd be a fine wife and mother, but that didn't work out, thanks to you. Still, I'm proud of what she has accomplished in her life." With enormous difficulty, Nina suppressed the accusation that burned in her heart. Pranab had maneuvered her granddaughters for his own selfish gratification. He had tried to appropriate their property and use their innate strength of character to compensate for his own weakness. However wounded by love, however exploited, the two girls had risen above the obstacles fate had placed in their path, whereas Pranab had crumbled in the face of adversity due to his inflexibility, his failure to control his appetites.

"I had it in mind," Nina said in conclusion, "to get you and Aloka back together again. But the more I see it, the more I think that wouldn't be such a good idea."

A wisp of graying hair falling on Pranab's cheek accented the sad eyes. He seemed unable to respond, except to ask, "Where is Aloka, by the way?"

Nina suddenly sensed an opportunity to give Aloka a chance to vent her bridled frustrations to Pranab in private. "Aloka likes to sleep late, then goes to Glenary Bakery for coffee on most days." She said this casually, while gazing at the chestnut-brown plumage of a robinlike bird as it hopped from a tree.

Pranab chitchatted for a few more minutes: How the coffee was abysmal in most restaurants. How the prices had gone up. How difficult he found walking on the almost vertical streets. Without announcing it, he scrambled to his feet. "If you'll excuse me, Thakurma, I must be going."

He looked around one last time for Sujata, but she was nowhere to be seen. Shoulders slumping, he walked away toward the road.

Nina watched fragile clouds scudding past the peaks, as though exemplifying the need to move on. She didn't expect to see Pranab ever again. Their lives had taken different turns. A sudden windblown sprinkle of rain wetted her cheeks.

"It's beginning to pour, Memsahib," Nina heard the driver's voice. "Perhaps I should take you both home?"

Sujata was fast approaching, her face florid from the exertion of the high-altitude hike. "I got lost, Thakurma. Looks like I found my way back just in time."

Nina collected her walking stick. "Yes, home," she said to the driver, glancing at Sujata.

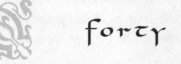

forty

Nina adhered to the notion that a part of her remained in each place where she set foot, and that by revisiting a place she would be able to recapture the essence of her lost self. Today she strolled Darjeeling's Botanical Garden with Sujata. Located only minutes from the town's bustling market named the Chowk Bazaar and an equally busy bus terminus, this tranquil garden with its scarcity of visitors set her body and thoughts free.

It seemed only yesterday that Sujata, then a winsome five-year-old missing several front teeth, had accompanied Nina to the market. The congested area reminded Nina of a swarm of flies stuck on a syrupy *gel-abi*. Here it was impossible to claim enough space so as not to sneeze directly on someone's shoulder. But Nina, a young fifty-year-old then, couldn't leave the critical task of food shopping to a servant's discretion. So she came down here, preferring to do the shopping herself. Her eyes wouldn't overlook the freshest chilis, the reddest onions, and the juiciest ginger roots spread out on the mats. She could give one glance at the open vats and locate raisins from Kabul, cashews from Midnapore, and apples from Kashmir. When she finished, she would direct the servant to load the purchases into the car and wait for her. Then she and Sujata would turn away from the market.

Nina would hold Sujata's delicate, almost boneless baby hand as they would meander through the narrow streets and finally descend a set of steep winding steps. From the very last step they would view the huge expanse of the Botanical Garden, actually a park with flower beds, an orchid house, and tree-canopied trails, and would listen to muted birdsongs. As soon as they reached the garden gate, Sujata would twist out of Nina's grip and bound off after a fluttering insect, or a crow that waddled onto the grass, or a button-sized wildflower that only her child's eye could spot. Her tiny feet tinkled with the melodious sound of the anklets she wore. She amused herself with that sound and all she beheld. Nina would find herself hurrying up after her.

Today, Nina was taking much slower steps down a long, gently rolling path shaded by plum and cherry trees and bordered by flowers. She took the time to stare at the oversized blue bloom of a hydrangea plant. She stooped to give an approving eye at the vivid red impatiens that hugged the ground at her feet. They seemed grayed at the edges, or was it her failing eyesight?

Sujata pointed ahead to the gazebolike shelter furnished with benches. "Shall we go sit for a while?"

Nina nodded. She settled herself carefully on the wooden bench, making sure the long overcoat she was wearing over her sari didn't catch a protruding nail. She gazed idly at a young couple with two children photographing each other in front of a stand of dahlias. The husband, clearly enamored with the camera's high-tech features, fussed with it, displaying a smile of manly confidence on his face. His young wife pretended that she didn't want her picture taken. "Oh, it's such a bother," she seemed to be saying, while keeping a coy smile afloat. Their boy kept shuffling his feet, while the girl played with the border of her mother's sari. How mundane these gestures seemed to an onlooker, yet how imbued with meaning to the family.

The ideal nature of the scene also gave Nina a reminder. She turned to Sujata.

"There's something I want to talk to you about, my dear Sujata. The time has come—it's my will."

"Your will? But Thakurma, you have many good years ahead of you."

"Nevertheless, I'm leaving the plantation to you. You'll be the sole owner when I'm gone."

Sujata opened her mouth to speak, but no words came out. It was as though her thoughts had flown ahead and her lips were rushing to catch up. "Me?" she finally asked.

"Yes, you. Who's better suited? You have a soul connection with tea."

Nina studied the doubt and indecision etched on that face as Sujata said, "You should sell the plantation."

"Sell it? Out of the question. I couldn't bear to see some national or, worse yet, large agribusiness company, taking over. They'll sit in their offices somewhere in Delhi or Mumbai and pay attention only to the balance sheet, not the quality of tea or the health of the land as we do. The plantation has been our fortune for generations. Your great-grandfather owned many other businesses, but in his final days he concentrated on this one alone. He believed it was the family's good-luck charm. Most of my own life has been dedicated to it. Many moons ago, when I would tell my husband that I wanted more children, he would reply, 'Tea plants are our babies. Every kilo of leaves they produce comes from our blood, sweat, nerves, and touch. We pour our love on them.' "

Nina controlled a deep sigh as Sujata drew closer and took her hand. They sat still for a while, with Nina's palm warmly enfolded in Sujata's hands. Nina guessed the queries running through Sujata's head: Thakurma, had you really wanted more children? A girl, perhaps?

"My tea company in Victoria needs constant care," Sujata replied. "I can't leave it. There's so much competition."

"Can't Janaki run that operation? She can be the sole distributor of Gupta Golden Tip in Canada. This is where you belong, here in Darjeeling."

"Is that so? You used to talk about how it was a man's world at the Darjeeling Planters' Association. The men played billiards in the front room and talked shop over drinks, while the women and children lounged in a small room at the back with tea and pastries. How, as a woman, would I break into their clubby society?"

"Oh, no, there are a few women proprietors now, maybe one percent of the total, certainly not as many as men, but they're making their presence known. The men will soon discover that you're very capable. You have the technical knowledge about the soil, the topography, the pests, and the machines. You'll be able to deal with political and government party leaders effectively. And you'll take better care of the women tea pluckers. They're very productive and do the most critical job of all, but traditionally haven't been paid as well as the men who operate the machines or even those who merely weigh the harvest. It's time someone like you came along and treated the women fairly."

Sujata adjusted her seating position to avoid being struck in the eyes by the sun's whimsical rays. "My life is in Canada now."

"You love tea."

"I'm still in a state of shock, Thakurma."

"It's not a sudden decision, Sujata. You know, I've been dreaming of this ever since you were five." And Nina glimpsed herself as she was then, a middle-aged woman tireless in the pursuit of her many aspirations, and felt a flush of that long-ago bounce. "It was right here in this Botanical Garden one day when watching you flop down on the grass that I made up my mind you should inherit the tea garden. That's why I wanted to come back here with you."

"What was it that made you decide?"

"Aloka always preferred to spend time with her friends and cousins, she was social even then, and she was learning to sing. She went to all the musical events. But you were a loner; you came here with me and played by yourself. You loved the trees, birds, and flowers. It was as if you sang their song. As you grew, you developed a keen sense of what quality tea was. That can't be taught, you know. As time went on, you also grasped the ins and outs of the tea trade. I saw all this as preparation for owning the tea plantation someday. It takes a special person with a great deal of dedication to stick to the job day after day." Nina took a deep breath and waited for the oxygen to revitalize her. "I must tell you that we've had drought for many years and our productivity has gone down. Although some rain has fallen this year, it's not nearly as much as we need. In any case, the rain is out of your hands. The major issues you'll have to deal with are how to work with tough labor unions such as the Uttar Banga Anchalik Committee, and how to better market tea to North America."

"What about Aloka? Wouldn't she contest your will? The tea estate was supposed to have been hers."

"Let me tell you about the rest of my will. Aloka will own the house."

Sujata let out a controlled laugh. "The house? Would she ever live in it? Don't you think we've lost her to America?"

"I'm certain she'll miss the peacefulness of this place and come back from time to time."

"Does that mean I couldn't live in that house?"

"No. There's a clause in my will that says you will have the right to occupy it for as long as you live. Tell me, dear, will you be happy taking over the estate? In the end, it's your choice. I can't force you."

"I need time to think. It's eleven-thirty already. Do you want to grab a bite?"

"I'd love that, but Aloka is taking me out to Windemere for lunch."

"Oh, the Windemere! Aloka's classier than I am, always has been."

"Would you care to join us?"

"I have to run to the store for a few things."

Nina squeezed Sujata's hand affectionately and found the particular softness still there. "When you were both little, I'd buy you both the exact same dolls, but you'd put them side by side and measure their heights to see who got the bigger one and which one had more gold on its clothes. Are you still holding on to the old jealousies?"

"I admit I'm still a little jealous of Aloka. I think I always will be, though now I see myself as her equal. Maybe it's the struggles I've gone through, maybe it's doing work I really like, but I've finally lost my feelings of inferiority. But that's not the reason for my bowing out. You two should have some time together. You and Aloka aren't as close as you used to be."

forty-one

The food before her at the Windemere Hotel tantalized Nina with its color, aroma, shape, variety, and, in the case of the cute carrot chrysanthemums, its attempt to entertain. Her appetite had all but disappeared in recent months and so she merely sniffed at the aromatic yellow rice, rolled a dab of gingery sauce on her tongue, nibbled at a sliver of caramelized onion, and sipped at her water. Then, with Aloka in tow, Nina moved over to the privacy of a small lounge, where they settled back in oversized chairs. Outside the window, an expanse of smooth green gave way to a view of scarlet blossoms. In due time a waitress in a black uniform, a white frilly apron, and matching cap turned up.

Aloka ordered two glasses of limewater, then began recounting the details of her years in New York. It was clear that a full measure of joys and struggles were tightly woven into her existence, like the pearl rope coiling around her neck. And if a hint of sadness occasionally crept into her words, she dismissed it with a gesture, a carefree laugh, a glance out the window. Only when she mentioned Pranab was there a note of melancholy in her voice, a flickering pain in her eyes that lingered after the conversation had moved on.

"It must be hard for you, *sonamoni*." Precious jewels, was how Nina addressed Aloka. "Pranab still haunts you in a thousand different ways. But in my opinion, there's nothing like a new love to vanquish the ghosts of the past."

"Your attitudes are remarkably modern, Thakurma. Indeed, I have met a new man."

"Tell me about him."

"His name is Jahar. When I met him, I realized that I have been typecast for a long time—dutiful daughter, suffering wife, faithful friend, reliable relative. The fun-loving Aloka I'd kept suppressed came out. I dropped my seriousness and lived in the joy and the truth of the moment. Now I miss him and that side of me."

Nina watched her with wonderment. Aloka, self-sufficient from being in touch with her deeper self, could attract a man now and enjoy his company without needing him around her for twenty-four hours. It was clear that a traditional marriage was no longer her only option in life.

"Sujata had a very different set of problems with men." Then, noting the instantaneous change in Aloka's expression, Nina said, "You still resent her, don't you?"

"Yes, a little. I'm still trying to get over the betrayal. I'd like to put it behind us, but she hasn't made it very easy. Ever since I got back here she's basically ignored me. When she's not out running around with Mreenal, she seems bent on taking over the house. I mean, the way she orders the servants around, you'd think she owns the place. And then there's Pranab always hanging around trying to get her attention. How would you feel in my place, Thakurma?"

Nina smiled sadly, nostalgically. "Do you realize that was exactly how she felt about you in the old days? You had a boyfriend and many admirers, and the whole household revolved around you. Sujata must have felt miserable sitting alone in her room. I'm sure she developed a real inferiority complex."

She watched as Aloka sat frozen in shock as the revelation sank in, oblivious to the waitress who had returned with a pitcher and the rattling sound of their glasses being refilled. Another hotel employee dashed in with a pile of firewood, stashed it in a container in one corner, and leapt out, leaving behind him the smell of fresh-cut cedar.

"You still have a chance to reconcile with your sister before you go back to America. It's important to me. You two are our family's future."

"So that's why you called us both here. It wasn't just your birthday celebration, was it?"

Nina tried to contain a smile, then plunged ahead. "Sujata seems so determined, so much in control, though inside she's still a little girl craving affection. She needs her older sister."

Aloka glanced at the fireplace, her narrowing eyes losing their almond contour. "I don't know if it's still possible. We let it go for so long. I know I'm supposed to love my sister. But how can I? There's something holding us back, something in her eyes. She still hates me."

"Occasionally I think about my own brothers and sisters," Nina replied. "The four of us were very close. Once, when I was five, my youngest brother tripped and scraped his knee. I cried just as hard as he did. My mother said it was because we shared the same blood. You and Sujata have the same blood bond."

Aloka laced her fingers around the tall glass and took a long slow swallow. "This limewater is so refreshing. I know it's your favorite. We're going to serve some for your birthday party. I'll make it, just the way you taught me— sparkling water, a shot of ginger juice, sugar syrup, and essence of lime."

"What I'd really like is a taste of your *channer payesh*."

"I can make that, too."

"It'd be even more special if you and Sujata made the *payesh* together."

Aloka started to protest, but Nina persisted. "Please. It'd mean a lot to an old lady."

"I guess we could. You've already talked to her about cooking together, haven't you? You've planned it all so well, Thakurma."

Nina brought a sweet smile to her lips and held up her hand, as if to forestall any further protest. "There's more to tell you. I want Sujata to take over the tea plantation when I'm gone. Her heart is here and tea is in her veins."

Aloka sat back. "Are you sure Sujata will be willing to handle the responsibility?"

"She hasn't said yes, but I'm optimistic. I hope I haven't disappointed you too much, have I?"

"Only a little. I've always assumed the tea estate would belong to me. But then, I've never really been that interested in tea. In a way, it's a relief."

"I'm glad that you understand, *sonamoni*. Just as Sujata understands why I'm giving you the house."

"Oh, Thakurma, that house holds so many memories of my growing up. It's the most sacred place for me. You're being very generous, but shouldn't the house really go to Sujata as well if she's going to live here?"

"No, it's yours. Your grandpa and I had you in mind when we built that house. Your sister will merely be serving as your caretaker, but whenever you come back, which I trust will be often, Aloka Kutir will welcome you as the mistress of the house."

"You'd do all this in spite of the fact that I've moved so far from my roots?"

Nina nodded, checking back a smile. In the next few minutes Aloka confessed how in these past several days she'd been visiting family and friends and making excursions to all her old haunts—Birch Hill, Observatory Hill, the zoo—with the hope that she would settle back into the familiar surroundings. But no matter where she went or whom she met, she was aware that something vital had been lost forever. People sensed the difference and treated her with a certain reserve. She was still miffed over an incident in which a store clerk inquired where she was from, even though she'd asked for Chandrika Soap in perfect Bengali. How different from the days when this town had been her playground and everyone an ally or next of kin, when she was *Gupta barir meye*, the girl from the beloved Gupta house. She couldn't discuss this dilemma with relatives, for they envied her flight to New York, her "better life," as they phrased it.

"Oddly enough," Aloka continued, "it's only after I came back and had been here a week did I realize how much I'd changed. The roles I'd held on to so long in New York were no longer valid for me. In fact, they'd become destructive. I'd submitted to Pranab far too much. I didn't see him as he really was, I persisted in viewing him through those 'ideal woman's' glasses."

"Does that mean you're finally going to let go of him?"

Aloka sighed and for an instant her eyes seemed mesmerized by the pulsating flames in the fireplace. "I'm coming to that conclusion gradually, Thakurma. Even though there's still a longing in my heart every so often for him, I've found a new life and its call is strong. I'll leave for New York right after your birthday. It'd be time for me to go. Thanks for your offer. I'm honored to accept it."

With that Aloka made a motion to rise. As they walked leisurely through the vast lawn toward the exit, Nina mused about the irony of the situation. "You see, Aloka, somehow I have the feeling that if you chose to stay, you wouldn't be a stranger to the old ways very long. Even when you're far away, your roots are here. On the other hand, Sujata, I fear, would not have an easy time sliding back into the life in this town. That girl is still a bit of a rebel."

forty-two

Densely planted rows of neatly pruned tea bushes clung to the steep slopes, imparting an odd formal garden accent to the wild mountain scenery. Clad in blue jeans and hiking boots and followed by Mreenal, Suzy climbed up a worn footpath that wound through the luxuriant foliage. As far as eyes could see, steep ridges covered with tea bushes snaked away to merge with snow-decorated peaks to the north. Suzy imagined herself a part of the naturally growing forest, the rough mountains, the grand open space, and the fertile earth. Thousands of feet below, the raging River Teesta, or "river of three currents," was barely visible as a thin, twisted silver ribbon.

Suzy's spine absorbed the sunlight filtering through the fanlike branches of the tall neem trees, which had been carefully interspersed with the low-growing tea bushes to protect the tender shoots from the sun's glare and help control pests. A passing greenfinch chirruped as it winged by just above her head. Suzy turned to Mreenal who was lost in the splendor before him, seemingly unmindful of the engaging wisp of hair teased by the wind on his brow.

"I appreciate your showing me the tea plantation," he said. "It's your first time back. How special this must be to you. It's magnificent. Now I see why it's called a tea 'garden.' "

"A forest is what it really is." She pointed to a greenbelt of laurel, bamboo, sal, and chestnut trees along the top ridges. "We've allowed the original jungle to stay mostly intact. All sorts of animals make their home there. Cobras, panthers, and monkeys abound, and every now and then a tiger will come to look around. We've always believed as long as the animals live in balance and get enough food, they won't bother us. And they never have."

"From the way you hike," Mreenal said, as they continued along the trail, "you must have practically grown up here."

"Our bungalow is down below. You can see the red rooftop through the trees—just to the left. My mother used to bring me here when I was no taller than these plants. I learned about photosynthesis while I was learning to walk."

"I envy you. I was brought up in the heart of Calcutta. I learned about trams, buses, processions, and street flooding. Here you feel the natural pulse of life beneath your feet and above your head, there you hear traffic noise and smell petrol. Do you miss this life, Sujata?"

She stood still for a second. "I more than miss it. When I stand on this ground, I feel one strong link to my ancestors and another to my own self. This is where I can really be myself. Look at the dewdrop on that leaf. How it glistens in the sun! The slightest breeze and it will slide of, but I have witnessed its beauty. For me every moment spent here is potentially full."

As they kept walking, a pastel-hued modern three-story factory carved into the slope loomed before them. A flock of workers standing by the iron-grill gate caught Suzy's eye. The moment they recognized her, they pushed the gate open—it took the strength of two men to do so—and rushed out with exclamations. "Sujata-*didi*, Sujata-*didi*, please come in!" She queried the workers about various family members and they inundated her with questions.

"What's the exchange rate in Canada?"

"How much does it cost to buy a buffalo there?"

Along came a lamentation. "Our industry is in a slump—the Russians have switched to the cheapest Assamese tea. Who would have believed?" Then a hopeful word. "We're eating more soybean, like you'd suggested, Sujata-*didi*."

It was as if she had never left.

Suzy introduced Mreenal, who was standing shyly off to one side. He was soon mingling with the workers and questioning them about their work and life.

"You've got to love this place, Mreenal-*babu*." And elderly man stepped forward. "We call the soil 'red diamond'—it is our only wealth." As Mreenal asked him more about his job, he replied, "Our days are long and difficult. Our only social life is with fellow workers and their families because the plantations are isolated from one another and from the town. We live with our jobs, as the saying goes, and we treat the plants like our babies. That is why the Darjeeling tea you drink is so special."

In a few minutes Suzy led Mreenal up a well-worn teak staircase to a well-ventilated loft lined with long rectangular wooden trays and permeated with a fragrant leafy aroma. "Let me show you the operation here," she said as she ran her fingers through the plump, freshly picked, still-damp leaves spread in a thin layer on one of the trays. Though she hadn't been inside a tea factory for years, the explanation came easily: The first step in making tea is known as withering. It took about fourteen hours to reduce the moisture in the leaves by about two-thirds, making them soft and pliable. In the adjoining room a rolling machine kneaded the withered leaves to break the cell walls and bring the aromatic oils to the surface. They returned to the ground floor and entered a warm, humid room where the kneaded tea leaves were allowed to ferment in low rectangular boxes for several hours to develop their flavor before being placed in a giant oven for drying. Finally the leaves were sorted into various grades for packing.

"Looks just like the tea I drink at home." Mreenal crushed a few twisted dry leaves with his fingers. "What a great education for an urbanite like me. It takes commitment to produce tea of this quality. I saw that in your workers today. Do I see it in you, as well, Sujata?"

If there was a stirring inside her, she suppressed it for now. They walked through the long courtyard in silence. As they passed through the gate, Mreenal turned and gave one last, longing look back at the factory enclave.

"Let me walk you home," he said, as he started back down the trail by which they had come. "I'll miss all this in Calcutta. I have to leave tomorrow morning."

"So soon?"

Then she came to her senses: Of course he would. His intended was waiting for him in Calcutta. She gazed up at the vastness of the hills, where streaks of sunlight backlit the vegetation with a flickering border of orange, and realized that neither despair nor envy was worthy of her when surrounded by such splendor.

He halted and gazed at a grove of cryptomeria set back from the path. "Would you mind if we sat down for a minute?"

"Not at all. I could use a break myself."

He led her to a large flat slab of granite situated at the base of a particularly magnificent specimen, pulled a handkerchief from his pocket, and dusted off the block. She lowered herself down at one end. He left a discreet space between them as he sat down at the other end. In the soft silence and sunlight-dappled shade, she became keenly aware of everything around her: how a woman carrying a huge bundle of straw on her back appeared to merge with the hill as she worked her way steadily up the slope in spite of her heavy load. How Mreenal rolled up his shirtsleeves in neat, quick motions. How his shoe dislodged a pebble, which then made a tiny but distinct *ting* sound as it rolled down the slope.

"I didn't sleep well last night." He paused. "I was thinking about you."

"Thinking about me?"

"Yes, you."

"But you're going away. . . ."

"I'll be coming back soon. I need to straighten some things out in Calcutta. Fortunately, Thakurma has already done much of the work for me."

He pronounced the word "Thakurma" with particular affection. Once again Suzy was reminded that Grandma had spun a wide web indeed. "What work?" she asked.

"For quite some time I've been questioning my mother's desire to arrange a marriage for me. Having lived in Canada, I'm sure you understand that."

He leaned forward and clasped his hands around his knees. His college ring sparkled on one finger. She pushed down an urge to rub the gem at its center. "My mother's heart is in the right place," he said, "but she doesn't know my heart."

"You're not getting married, then?"

His eyes momentarily fixed on the purple-shadowed hills that she so loved. "How can I? I simply can't marry that girl, not now, not since I met you." Tenderly he asked, "Do you feel the same way about me, Sujata?"

"Yes," she whispered, then smiled in delight and drew closer. He leaned slightly toward her and took her hand with great care. She interlaced her fingers with his. The sun blazed brighter and the atmosphere around her, even the brittle leaves scattered on the ground at her feet, vibrated in the light. "I have to give credit to Thakurma," she added. "She had things figured out even before we met. She was way ahead of me on this one."

He said teasingly, "Even so, you resisted me at first."

"There was a reason. I need to explain something. . . ."

"No explanation is necessary." He turned to her a gentle, accepting way. "Let this be our moment together. Nothing could be more important than us and how we feel about each other. I'll know of things in due time."

She shifted her thighs to position herself more cozily on the rock, then leaned her head onto his shoulder, that bulwark of stability and assurance. What could be better? She could abandon her past now and allow her mind to weave a new pattern for the future.

Minutes later, hands clasped, they resumed ambling down the hill. Her eyes roved over to the far left, to a cluster of dwellings fashioned of wood, with corrugated tin roofs. She pointed out to Mreenal that they were the residences of the tea workers. She noticed some changes: The doors had been newly painted, though, as before, they were kept low as a sign of humility. Outside the homes, clothes dried on clotheslines stretched between trees, more pants and dresses now and fewer saris. A radio played a fast musical beat, an *adhunik* number that she recognized, a modern song rather than a traditional *geet*. Still, the scenery connected her to an earlier time.

Mreenal seemed a bit distracted. Soon he began to talk about his upcoming visit to Calcutta, the subway system he found so convenient, old college friends at the far end of the town whom he planned to visit. "I'll have a talk, probably several talks, with my mother," he concluded. "In the end I'll be honest with her and refuse the marriage proposal, but it won't be easy."

"If Thakurma arranged a meeting between us, why didn't she go one step further and contact your mother?"

His shoulders slumped a bit. "Actually, she did—but Mother rejected the overture even though it was pretty indirect."

"Rejected? Why?"

"Mother had already heard the news about your sister's divorce."

"But—these days a divorce in a family isn't that unusual."

"My mother is of another generation. And she thinks Indian women living alone in the West are a wild bunch anyway. She'd rather that I married someone from here. Actually, I lived with a woman for a year in Seattle, but my mother never found out about that. I'm sure she suspected something— we're quite close. Still, there are some things I could never discuss with her, and that happened to be one of them. On the other hand, I'm not totally free of my upbringing. I have enormous respect for my parents and have no wish to cause them anguish. But . . . something different is happening to me now."

She understood his dilemma and how the ripening of their relationship had brought it about. Silently, joyfully, she acknowledged the changes inside her. In such a short time they'd become so close, it almost frightened her.

As they reached the gate of the family bungalow, he flipped his arm up to bare his watch from under his shirtsleeve. "I have to go home and pack. By the way, Thakurma once mentioned how much she liked scented candles. I'd like to bring her some from Calcutta for her birthday."

"That'd be lovely. She loves the rose-scented candles the best."

"I have another surprise. With the help of Tami-*didimoni,* I have located three feisty old college friends of Thakurma's in Calcutta. I have made arrangements to fly them up here for her birthday and stay in a hotel. Tami-*didimoni* will give you all the details."

"Oh, Mreenal. That's most kind of you. Thakurma will bless you a thousand times."

"I want to see the surprise on her face when they show up." His tone turned softer. "It's hard for me to leave you, Sujata, even to go visit my family. Wait for me, will you? I'll be back as fast as I can."

She gave him a happy nod. As she bade him farewell, gently turned, and entered the house, she felt a void. The imprint of his hand, like a tentative note on a piano, lingered in her mind. She'd begun to miss him already.

forty-three

This late morning interlude in Darjeeling's Glenary Bakery wasn't all that different from a coffee break Aloka might have taken at her job back in New York. A maroon-coated, expressionless waiter came by, filled her coffee cup for the second time, and served her a wedge of freshly baked apple pie, fragrant with the lush scent of cinnamon. This happened to be one of the few eateries in town that specialized in the Western-style baked goods that Aloka had grown to love, and it served a genuine cup of coffee. Usually in this tea-drinking town, coffee was a noxious brew made from a domestic version of Nescafé, but this establishment actually took the trouble to prepare it properly using freshly ground beans. Munching on a mouthful of the crust, then washing it down with a leisurely sip of the hot liquid, Aloka looked up from her pen and postcards to contemplate the snow-cloaked spectacle of Mount Kanchenjunga visible through the window. The sight both uplifted her and helped her come up with short personal messages to each recipient more elegantly.

With an inward sigh of relief, she scribbled a final line on the last postcard, this one to her boss, informing him she would return in a few days, and stacked it along with the rest on the left side of the table. Her eyes fell on the framed silk embroidery resting next to the stack, depicting the face of a Tibetan man in traditional headdress. She had made this impulsive purchase only minutes ago from a local artist who hawked his work from table to table. A fitting memento it would be. She examined the finely worked colorful stitching, contemplating where this artwork would fit best in her rental in New York. Her conclusion: the creamy east wall of the living room. The flaming reds and yellows would show well there. In any case, the western wall was already well occupied with a vintage black-and-white street photograph of New York, of soldiers returning in 1941. In her mind's eye she could picture it so clearly. It was as if she were standing in the room.

She gazed out through the window. An onrushing mass of purplish gray clouds rapidly obscured all but the tips of the mountains. Snapped out of her reverie by the changing light level, she concluded that she had better return home before the rain started. The weather gods in this mountainous region tended to be whimsical. Torrential rain followed by landslides often cut off the roads. As she bent down to grasp the chain of her purse, a familiar male voice jolted her.

"May I join you?"

It was Pranab. In a flash she took in the charcoal wool vest, dull black scarf draped around his neck, and receding hairline, noting dispassionately that his sunken eyes seemed oddly intense, his smile a trifle self-conscious. Her own lack of emotion at her observation amazed her.

"What a surprise," she replied with a cheeriness she did not feel, and gestured to the chair opposite her. An accidental meeting? Not likely.

"I remembered our once-a-week tradition of 'Breakfast at Glen's' and decided to come back once more for old times' sake. Then, too, I want to get some postcards written." With a glance at her artwork, he took the proffered chair. "You're alone?"

Aloka placed her hand over the batch of postcards as she nodded. "Sujata is taking Mreenal to the tea estate this morning for the first time."

He turned his face away, though not in time to cover up the hurt in his eyes that betrayed a longing for Sujata. Aloka glanced at the top picture on her stack, a charming view of the Himalayan Mountaineering Institute, and declared, "I've just signed my last postcard."

She expected him to take out pen and cards from his pocket, but instead he launched into, "These days you'll find Darjeeling 'the beautiful queen of the hills' in picture postcards only. Do you know how long it took me to get here from Chowrasta, fighting crowds of rude, smelly hill people and Western hippies? And vendors have taken over this narrow street. How can they allow that? The sidewalks used to be so clean, but now you step on orange peels and cigarette butts all the time. My brother spells out the three *p*'s of India's problems—pollution, population, and poverty. And they can be found right here in abundance, no doubt about that!"

His voice was biting. In their early New York days, she'd taken his sharp opinions as astute observations and worldliness. Not anymore.

Her attention was drawn to the blare of a trumpet outside on the street. A wedding procession? Pranab, apparently mistaking her silence for acceptance of his presence, began recounting the details of his cousin-sister's impending marriage. "Babli met the fellow at the racecourse. Women betting on horses, can you believe that?" he sniffed. She began to tire of the hammering of the words when, finally, with an air of exaggerated casualness, he asked, "So, what do you think of this Mreenal guy?"

Mreenal fit in so well with the family that he didn't arouse questions or concerns in Aloka's mind. "I'm glad that Sujata has met someone she likes."

She said this simply, as a comment, but the change of subject hadn't escaped her notice. She pointedly consulted her wristwatch, then checked a middle-aged couple as they entered through the door, whispering to each other in shoulder-nudging closeness. When she turned back, Pranab was gazing soulfully at her. This outpouring of emotion on his part was simply unbearable. She gathered up her postcards and stuffed them into her purse.

"Aloka." Something in his voice made her hesitate. "I'd like to apologize."

"What for?"

"I've done you a terrible wrong."

At this belated admission of remorse, she looked out the window to the smoke rising out of a chimney and being dissipated by the wind. She'd already accepted the past and moved on to the future with a clean conscience.

"I accept your apology." She paused to give the words their due weight, then started to rise. "It's about to rain. I should be going."

"Please don't leave, Aloka. I want to talk with you." He extended a pleading hand toward her. "The new you. You've changed a lot since I last saw you. It's as if you've started a different life. You're unpredictable and lively, almost as if you're ready to kick up your heels and dance."

Sitting on the edge of her chair, Aloka twisted the corner of the crisp white tablecloth. Just when she supposed she'd buried her past, he managed to reopen an aching wound. At the sound of the patter of rain, she glanced out the window. A dense curtain of water descended, striking the earth in a drumming beat. Why she was sitting here with him in such dismal weather?

She asked, "What's your point?"

"Would you like anything, sir?" Menu in his extended hand, the neutral-faced waiter stood by the table, while keeping an eye on the door.

Pranab took the menu and began perusing it. She studied the imperfections of the face she'd once loved: age blemishes, yellowing eyes, wrinkles of regrets, moles of guilt.

The waiter was about to retreat when Pranab looked up. "Coffee and a scone for me. Would you like a refill?"

Aloka shook her head decisively. The waiter hurried off. For a moment neither spoke.

"I see that Sujata spends a lot of time with Mreenal," Pranab began. "He's too calm for her, one might even say dull and conservative. From what I hear, he has to get his mother's approval for all major decisions."

"Sujata's past the age when one looks for a tempestuous love affair. She can depend on Mreenal. They've become good friends. They go everywhere together. How many men do you think would go sweater-hunting with a woman?"

"It's all a ruse, don't you understand, to win her over. A woman like Sujata needs a romantic someone who's not afraid to reveal his true self and persist. Not someone to take her sweater-shopping." He pinched off a piece of his scone and gobbled it down, no longer bothering to conceal his disdain for Mreenal. "I personally don't have time for such games."

Aha! So, this was where she came in! Pranab was desperate to stop Sujata from seeing Mreenal and this was nothing but a thinly disguised attempt to enlist her support. What a joke! Sujata was no longer the twenty-eight-year-old naïf who had fallen under his spell so long ago. How smartly she conducted herself these days. And how her face shone whenever Mreenal came by.

"It's Sujata's life." It shocked Aloka that her tone of voice brooked no argument. She'd never spoken with him that way before. "She'll choose whomever she wants. As if you, of all people, have any right to complain. You had your chance when she was young and hopeful and ripe for a romantic experience, and look where it led. You sensed her vulnerability and exploited it. Never mind you already had me, I might add, the eldest daughter of the town's most influential man. But that wasn't enough, was it? You just had to have us both. Now I understand Father's distress. Tell me, did he ever confront you?"

Pranab's face flushed; his eyes flickered uneasily. "Ah, yes . . . as a matter of fact, we did have a little conversation shortly after the tea workers' protest march."

"Conversation? What could *you* have had to say? How could you possibly have defended yourself?"

"He called me to his office. His face was red and puffy and he didn't mince his words, although his voice was perfectly normal. He told me he loved you and Sujata more than life itself and that he'd protect you from me, whatever the cost. I could see the veins in his temple pulsing. I tried to calm him down a bit. I told him that I loved you and intended to marry you, but he was beyond listening. He accused me of rabble-rousing, destroying his business, and sullying you and Sujata, as well as the Gupta honor. At one point he jumped up from his desk. I was sure he was on the verge of attacking me. Just at that moment an assistant manager happened to walk in through the door and that probably saved me. Oh yes, we had a conversation, and your father didn't hold anything back."

"He certainly concealed it well. When I saw him that evening before we left, he seemed a little distracted, but now that you mention it, he did seem out of sorts. He walked past me like I wasn't there. How it must have broken him to see me leave with you. If only I'd known all this."

"Would you have changed your decision to go, Aloka?"

She tore her gaze away and looked out the window. Rain, contorted by the wind, was creating bubbly dancing figures on the sidewalk. She realized she couldn't rewrite the past; she could only hope that, with time, the memory would lose its accusing glare. She mumbled, "Let's just say that I have a few regrets."

She noticed how Pranab, hazy-eyed, was stirring his coffee unnecessarily around the rim of the cup, as though his thoughts were traveling in a circle. Sujata. The wretch was dreaming about Sujata.

"It's a pity that you have learned nothing from these last eight years, Pranab. You have no pride, no shame. What have you been reduced to?"

"Are you saying all this because you're angry at me, because I pay more attention to Sujata?"

"Quite the contrary. I have come to consider myself fortunate that you loved Sujata more. I only wish I'd figured things out sooner. All that time I held on to you, playing the dutiful Hindu wife, cost me years of my life. But now, fortunately, I've outgrown all that. Had we remained married, you'd have dragged me down even more."

"But you kept wanting me back—"

"Yes, as I said, it took me a while to figure things out. I had to overcome my upbringing and that's not easy. And, I must say, you were a very attractive man, even as recently as that time in Brooklyn when I saw you dancing. I saw then how powerful you still could be, and I told myself it wasn't that you lacked talent, energy, or intellect. It was just your self-pitying attitude, and if that could be corrected, I was sure you could make a go of it in New York. Then you'd hold no bitterness toward me or feel threatened by my strength and adaptability. I told myself we still had a chance. I was wrong."

Pranab sat frozen in his chair, one arm dangling by his side, the other clasping the sugar bowl, a pathetic figure etched in sadness. Finally her message had gotten through.

"Look, Pranab, there's still time. Think back to when you were young. Ask yourself what you really wanted to do in life. You can get yourself together again, I truly believe you can, if you are willing to make the effort. You have many full years ahead of you."

In the cry that was pushing against her throat, she grasped her own situation clearly. She was finally ready to relinquish Pranab to her sister. This despite the fact that she still had a few unresolved issues with Sujata. Over the years, loving Pranab had become deeply embedded in her psyche, but now she had at last freed herself of that incapacitating habit. Henceforth she would not let him prowl her dreams or put any obstacles in her path to a new way of being. And at that moment, a decade's worth of conflicting feelings melted away, replaced by a feeling of inner serenity. An image from childhood, floating candles and lotus blossoms on a pond's tranquil surface, rose in her mind's eye.

Picking up her purse and the artwork, she rose from her chair. She planted her feet firmly, resolutely, on the floor. She let her gaze take in this oasis of a bakery, with its paneled walls, picture windows, and cozy atmosphere. She would remember it always as the site of her last meeting with Pranab, and her own rebirth.

As she slid past the table, she looked down at him sadly. "Sorry, Pranab, it looks like we won't have that dance together, after all."

forty-
four

Suzy turned on her laptop, checked her e-mail, and opened a note from Eva.

Dear Suze,

It's late, but I had to reply to you right away.

What are you thinking, girl? Get yourself back here.

How would you be able to adjust to the social life there, now that you're used to going about your own way? Does Darjeeling have half as much to offer as Victoria? You fit in so well here. Also, won't you have to spend most of your time managing the tea estate? Will it be worth it?

My eyes are closing, so I'll stop now.

Eva

Grandma's birthday was only three days away. After weeks of elaborate preparation, there was an undercurrent of excitement now that the long-awaited gala was finally going to take place. Though Suzy still had many items to check off on her task list, she had put them aside and hurried out the door when she received Mreenal's cryptic phone message saying, "Meet me at Chowrasta at four P.M." He must have just returned from Calcutta.

Now it was just past four and she was standing at the railing that marked Chowrasta's periphery. Literally named "The Crossroads," the lively pedestrian plaza was perched just below Observatory Hill, the highest point in the city, and commanded a sweeping vista of the Himalayas. Mellow sunlight tinted the area in shades of soft yellow. A haze of charcoal smoke wafted from one of the nearby hotel restaurants. Suzy looked off to the east, beyond the bluish green wavy outline of the foothills to where the eastern flank of the Himalayas rose from the Bhutanese lowlands. A mantle of clouds cloaked the mountains' silver wings. Serenity was always within easy reach in Darjeeling, except in her current state of mind.

Ever since Grandma had offered her control of the tea estate, she had been agonizing over what to do about it. During her past few years in Canada she'd been known as quick and decisive in business matters, but now she was stumped. She stood at what she realized would be a defining crossroad in her life, with the map of the two paths whirling dizzily in her mind: personal vs. the family. Which to choose?

On top of that, a feeling of unease had crept into her consciousness ever since she'd received Mreenal's message. Why had Mreenal chosen this most public of places instead of just coming over to her house? Could it be that his mother had intervened in their relationship? Had rumors of her affair with Pranab finally reached Calcutta? Or was Suzy merely not pretty enough? Last Sunday, browsing through the matrimonial ads in the newspaper, she had confronted the fact that many parents were still asking for a *prakrita sundari* bride, a truly beautiful daughter-in-law. Whatever the reason, Suzy told herself, she would convince Mreenal that though one's own mother is a formidable force, together they could win her over.

He must not have arrived yet, for he surely would have stood out in this particular crowd of people: merchants, laborers, tourists. From her elevated location, she looked out over the jumbled maze that was the town of Darjeeling, sprawling down the steep hillside below: a taxi stand, tiny terraced gardens sprouting green rice stalks, streets that wound up and down in a series of irregular switchbacks, even a flight of stairs carved into the hillside for those hardy souls whose legs had the requisite stamina. On the rooftop of a four-story building under construction, a young boy rinsed his face in a puddle of rainwater that had collected in a blue plastic tarpaulin stretched over a hole.

At the sound of a pair of stout Tibetan ponies clattering across the plaza, Suzy looked around and saw a woman and a child riding up to the Observatory Hill, surely to visit the Kali temple. She smiled at the memory of that same bouncy ride taken so many times as a child. If she stayed, the ride would again become a part of her life.

She turned her head in time to spot Mreenal in the distance. Cradling a package, he cut diagonally across the plaza, his compact form striding toward her. With joy and a frost of disquiet, she realized that she had become accustomed to seeing him on a regular basis. She strained forward as he approached. His head and shoulders were lined briefly by a beam of golden light streaming through a gap between buildings. As he drew closer, she could see that his face wore a tense expression. The trip must have been exhausting, what with a full agenda of family visits and the rough journey to and from Calcutta by plane and long taxi rides.

He greeted her briskly and gestured to the left. "There's an empty bench over there. Shall we grab it?"

As they settled down, she reassured herself that now they would be able to talk things through. Curiously enough, this busy spot offered a measure of privacy. But before she knew it, an old woman and a little girl claimed a part of her end of the bench. In one ungenerous moment she wished they would go away; in the next she chided herself and edged closer to Mreenal. When she inquired about his trip, he replied that his time in Calcutta had gone by quickly, but there were still some loose ends to be tidied up. He had had a few enjoyable breaks, too, such as the celebration of a lesser-known deity, Vishwakarma. Only Calcuttans turned that day into a holiday.

Did she know who Vishwakarma was? He added, "He's the god of all crafts-men—potters, weavers, carpenters."

"And now software professionals," she quipped.

He finally smiled and gazed up at her with a soft, adoring look. "I came back as soon as I could. I told my mother to cancel the marriage. That resulted in a big argument. At one point she broke into tears. 'How could I have held such a son in my belly for nine months?' She just couldn't understand what a rare person you are and how much I want to be with you."

"Oh, Mreenal, did you manage to convince her before you left?"

He seemed to need a few moments to gather his thoughts. She noticed out of the corner of her eye that the little girl had moved around to the right of the old woman. Might even a child's psyche pick up on the gravity of the topic?

"Unfortunately, no," Mreenal came back. "Toward the end of our very last conversation, Mother said I'd failed her. I'd failed her in the situation that tested my loyalty to her the most. I drifted out of the room at that point. Accusations of failure are very tough to swallow, especially when they come from your own mother. It was difficult for me to remain there after that. I was so completely drained. I started packing. But then some impor-tant news came."

"What news?"

"Sujata, we have a chance to live in Bangalore! My company has offered me a good post there. They're going to make it their Asian headquarters."

"Bangalore!"

"They call it an 'air-conditioned city,' the most urban place in South India, our Silicon Valley, and its just a few hours by air from here. We could come here just about anytime you want. You wouldn't mind moving there, would you?"

Suzy's hopes sank, a kite dipping in a pool, then slowly disappearing from view, as she realized the import of his words. "I'd love to, Mreenal, but it'll be very difficult. You see, some important things have happened to me as well. Thakurma has made her will known. She's leaving me the tea plan-tation."

Mreenal recoiled from her in astonishment. "Now, that's quite the bit of news, isn't it?"

"Oh, yes! It was totally unexpected. I'm still in a state of shock."

"That's a significant amount of property. Good fortune for you, no doubt."

"Yes, but it means I'll have to move back here and look after the entire operation." She paused as her voice was drowned by the squeal of a passing cart. Drawn by a saffron-robed priest, the cart carried a hibiscus-strewn temple likeness of the deity Ganesh. A passerby, trailing along behind the mobile temple, shook a holy bell once, twice, three times, as if skeptical of Ganesh's hearing ability.

"Do you intend to manage the estate full-time?" Mreenal asked.

"It'll be more than a full-time job, especially in the beginning. The estate hasn't been well cared for since my father's death. Thakurma believes it's time to infuse some youthful energy into the operation or risk losing it to some multinational company. I haven't accepted her offer yet. I told her I needed time to think it over."

Mreenal's expression became sunny. "So, you have some reservations?"

"I sure do. It'd turn my life upside down. I'll have to leave my business and my friends in Victoria, a whole way of life I've grown to love." She spied the tightness in his jaw, but pushed on. "Would it change anything if I were to accept Grandma's offer?"

She longed to hear that he loved her and that the power of their love would make it possible to work out an arrangement that suited them both. She would make a commitment right here in the town's hub. She would clasp his hand tight. She would utter a promise of never letting him go.

His eyes flickered. "Could you really be a tea planter? Darjeeling is a nice town to visit and for escaping the summer heat of Bangalore, but to settle here . . ."

She winced and gritted her teeth as a boisterous little boy scampered by chasing a ball and stepped on her toes. Compounded with that pain was the inner ache of having reached a decision that, however right, was going to have excruciating consequences.

"I know it must seem a bit strange," she began, "but you have to understand I grew up with tea. It's a religion in our household. Even though I've been away, it's still who I am and what I do."

He sat in silence for a time, sighed painfully. "We seem to have different plans for our respective lives. You want to stay here and run the tea plantation—I can understand that. I really can. But . . ."

A shoeshine boy was setting up his craft on the sidewalk, dragging chairs, and sprinkling water on the ground to suppress the dust. "*Aashun, boshun,*" he called out to bystanders in a shrill, youthful voice. Welcome, have a seat.

"I don't think a man should wait around the house for his wife." Mreenal's voice dipped into the palette of sorrow. "I'm forty years old. I have seen it all, done it all. Yes, I'm a bit of a homebody, and I won't apologize for that. I don't mind a home-cooked meal and clean laundry. As a plantation owner, you'll leave the house early in the morning and get home late. You'll move in a circle of businessmen, entrepreneurs, and wealthy investors. Tea planters, I'm told, are the kings and queens in this town. You'll be invited to dinners and cocktail parties, and treated royally. That'll be quite exciting for you, no doubt. But what would *I* do in Darjeeling?"

"Do you really think Darjeeling is all that backward?"

"I'm a city boy, Sujata. I can experience all that Darjeeling has to offer in three days. Then what? What would I do for a career? I'm a software guy and Darjeeling isn't exactly Silicon Valley or Bangalore. And I've lived alone for too long. I want my wife to greet me when I get home and have dinner on the table for me. And, of course, I want children. If you're willing to sell your business in Canada and move with me to Bangalore and work part-time, if at all, I'm sure our relationship will flourish."

"You mean much to me. When I wake up in the morning, I want to hear your voice. In the evening I want to sit by you. I can't even imagine what it'd be like to go visiting places in Darjeeling without you. But I can't just walk away from my family. They've given me life. You see, I've never taken any real responsibility toward them. I've always stayed a little apart. This is my chance to show how much I do care. I'm the only one who can save the ancestral line of work and our family's reputation. That has to be my mission now."

"Does Pranab figure into this?" Frustration had seeped into Mreenal's words. "Is he, by any chance, going to work for you in the tea estate?"

"No, I have no intention of hiring him. What gave you that idea?"

He stared away, though Suzy caught the anguish in his eyes. He said, "My mother had heard some rumors. . . ."

"So, she has reservations about a woman who—"

"As I've said before, my mother is old-fashioned. And you have to admit that something like that happening in a family can cause concern in this society." He turned to offer her a penetrating, almost accusatory stare. "Is it just a rumor, Sujata?"

"It's a mistake I made and for which I've paid a price. Do I have to go on paying a price for the rest of my life? Will this society ever forgive me? I've become a different person. Doesn't that matter at all?"

"I'm not judging you, by any means, Sujata, I'm just shocked. But then, I should have known. You're pretty westernized."

"Cut out the 'westernized' bit, will you? I think the real problem, Mreenal, is you don't want to be overshadowed by a woman who would, at least locally, be more prominent than you." Suzy flipped her plaited hair back over her right shoulder in a gesture of defiance. "Your mother has chosen the right woman for you, after all. She can give you that tidy little house, children, and the feeling of importance that you crave so much."

Her mournful tone must have affected the little girl, who suddenly started crying. The old woman—calloused, perhaps—ignored the tearful face and the moaning sounds and sat staring into the space. However sympathetic Suzy felt, she couldn't stay and console the girl. It was time for her to be on her way. She rose quietly and was turning to leave when she heard the rustle of paper behind her.

Mreenal thrust a gift-wrapped package toward her. "Please give Thakurma my apologies for not being able to attend her party." His words were edged with genuine regret. "Sujata, I'll always remember you."

Her composure unruffled, Suzy took the package wordlessly and strode away without a backward look. The boisterous plaza seemed drained of life. The neon lights along a row of hotels twinkled through her damp eyes and the din of traffic seemed faint and far away. She walked aimlessly, unmindful of the warning whistles of the traffic constable and the curses of annoyed drivers, barely knowing where she was going, and caring even less.

forty-five

In the early morning hours, when dreams are fragmented like scattered pieces of a broken tile, Aloka heard the sound of soft rain and an exuberant laugh—Jahar's laugh. Later, after breakfasting on *suji halwa* and tea, and visiting with Grandma, all the while thinking of that dream, she picked up the *Hindusthan Standard* and burrowed in on an exposé on the suffering of the underclass in a village in Uttar Pradesh. "We want to be served tea in a cup like everybody else, not in a coconut shell," a villager is reported to have said. "We want to be able to live without being constantly humiliated by our rich neighbors."

Aloka put the newspaper away and wandered from room to room, though she found nothing to put her mind at ease. Once again she pondered the meaning of that dream and found herself wishing to bring it to reality. Eventually, she sidled over to the phone. Given the time difference, she guessed Jahar would be in the kitchen, tending a fragrant pot on the stove and peeling a cucumber, a Hindi film song wailing in the background as his accompaniment.

She picked up the receiver and punched the numbers from memory. A clear and wistful hello from another corner of the globe came through so clearly that Aloka silently thanked modern technology for it. But then she found herself unable to speak. She heard another hello, low and guarded, and managed to blurt out, "It's Parveen."

"Parveen?" Jahar pronounced the name with gentleness. Like he was protecting a lit match with the cup of his hand. Then a stronger, "Where are you?"

"In Darjeeling. I'll be back right after we celebrate my grandmother's birthday."

"Please give her my best. Grandmothers are most precious. So, is that the reason why I haven't heard from you? Why you went away? Did I do something to offend you?"

"No, no, nothing like that. I didn't call you before because I felt foolish . . . and ashamed."

"I was very angry with you," he admitted. "And I told myself I'd never speak with you again. But the funny thing is, as soon as I heard your voice I forgot all that. The anger melted into water, as my mother would say."

Aloka's reserve melted, too. "I have some explaining to do. . . . I'm not a real estate broker and I invented that Parveen name. My real name is Aloka and I work for a newspaper."

Jahar chuckled, then began to laugh, the same carefree laugh she had heard in her dream. "And my dear whatever-your-name is, did you go to all that trouble because you didn't trust me?"

"I'm sorry, Jahar, there's more to it than that. I enjoyed being with you. You brought out a new me. I could be livelier and more spontaneous . . . and look at the world differently." She hesitated. "I just wasn't ready."

Jahar's voice grew thick with exasperation. "Do you realize I practically went crazy? I even wrote to Seva twice. That's how desperate I was. You said you work for a newspaper. What do you do?"

"I write an advice column under a pseudonym."

"What advice column?"

" 'Ask Seva,' " she mumbled, and waited.

"You're Seva, too. How many names do you have?" Jahar laughed again. A small scraping sound indicated that he had pulled up the stool he kept by the telephone and was taking a seat. "Oh, my heavens, you're Seva. Then you've read my letter. You must have, because you answered it."

"I was scared, Jahar. Your letter forced me to examine my feelings."

"Now I understand. I rushed things. I mean to apologize for having been so emotional . . . and falling in love so hastily—I just couldn't help it, especially with someone as special as you. I found it so hard to hold back."

"Oh, Jahar, I missed you terribly. I thought about calling you, but . . . I wasn't afraid, exactly. It wasn't that—not with you. And I still want to see you again."

"But there's too much hurt. I don't open up like I used to anymore, Parveen. New York isn't the same as my village. This city isn't about feelings. I have shrunk the size of my *dil*, I don't speak to strangers anymore."

"Sometime I'll have to tell you about my whole life. Right now I'll just mention that I'm finally over a marriage. I'd tried to forget him, but I couldn't. I tried to go back to him, and that didn't work. Only by rebuilding myself as Parveen have I survived."

"When I was a child I used to throw a coin in the air and if it landed on my palm, I felt richer. Every time I talk to you, I feel the same way. I feel rich. When you're absolutely sure you're over that man, call me. We'll try again."

Now Jahar proceeded to fill her in on what had been going on in his life. How he had bought some weights and taken up lifting; would Parveen care to give the practice a try? How luscious the newly arrived black grapes were at their favorite delicatessen; wouldn't it be nice if they lasted until she returned? How a freak storm had cracked his window; wouldn't it be perfect if the repairman replaced the glass before she returned?

As she listened, she pictured herself next to him and surrendered to a new kind of emotion; not what she had once felt for Pranab—gigantic, overwhelming, and dizzying love—but rather a gentle and deep caring, interwoven with life's everyday details. She looked around the room and noticed how the ordinary furniture and knickknacks had sprung to life and become one-of-a-kind. It wasn't as if the world had been suddenly set right, for the world never is, only that a streak of sunshine had managed to find its way through her window. She remained enchanted until she heard him saying that they should say good-bye for now to avoid horrendous telephone charges, and then she murmured, "Only four more days," and hung up.

forty-
six

With Grandma's birthday only two days away, Aloka had given the family cook the afternoon off, so she could prepare the birthday dessert she had promised. Now, alone in the kitchen, she stared at the white mound of fresh cheese still steaming in its bowl on the counter, filling the room with a pleasant lemony aroma. The cheese, just drained of its whey, was the main ingredient of *channer payesh*, Grandma's favorite finale to a meal. It was still terribly important to serve sweets of the highest quality at any Bengali gathering. The motto "Eat sweetmeat and you'll speak sweet words" was uttered often.

Channer payesh, a classic sweetmeat, was time-consuming to prepare and required much care and commitment on the part of the cook—enough so that the corner sweet shop no longer bothered serving it. Older Bengalis still considered *channer payesh* a welcoming symbol for special guests. Grandma had often lamented that it was becoming a lost art, disappearing along with many other aspects of the traditional Bengali way of life, so gradually that most people failed to notice its absence in the menu at home or in restaurants.

Aloka had perfected her techniques years ago, enough so that whenever Grandma would take a taste of Aloka's *channer payesh*, she would blissfully close her eyes and declare it an *amrit*. Coming from her lips, this reference to ambrosia didn't sound like an exaggeration. "No one, not even the best *mithaiwala* in town, could prepare it as well as you do," Grandma had often told her.

It had been so long since Aloka had made the dish that she wasn't sure she could measure up to Grandma's exacting standards anymore. It would be a shame to disappoint the dear old lady on her birthday. Now Aloka prodded the cheese tentatively with a fingertip. To her immense relief, the spongy mass yielded and sprang back when she removed her finger, proving she had achieved the right texture. So she hadn't lost her touch after all.

Time to start thickening the milk. Sujata had promised to help, but there was still no sign of her. Aloka counted the days—only three more before she returned to the States—and still Sujata had made no attempt at reconciliation. In the back of her mouth Aloka tasted the bitterness of always having to be the responsible one. Sujata owed her the nicety of making the first move this time.

Aloka shifted her gaze to the lowest shelf of the cupboard and selected a heavy, oversized pot that had served generations of Guptas and was thoroughly, endearingly blackened from use and age. It reminded her of those halcyon days when her uncles and aunts and Pranab's parents would come over for dinner regularly, twenty-five or so people flowing in and out of the brightly lit house, the convivial bustle generating energy and warmth, and this same vessel had accommodated them all.

With sure fingers she set the pot on the stove, then adjusted its position over the burner so it received an even distribution of heat. At the sound of flapping sandals with a hurried quality, she knew Sujata had arrived. She turned toward the door.

Sujata rushed in, a trace of urgency enlarging her eyes, and headed straight for the kitchen counter, rolling up the sleeves of her tomato-colored sweater as she went. A silver *bindi* glittered between her slightly elevated eyebrows, but her lips were makeup-free, for a change. That was just as well, as the orange-shade lipstick she usually dabbed on didn't do much for her looks. A cherry color would be much preferable. Sujata bumped into a stool kept in one corner, which caused her arm to slide on the counter, and she almost knocked the cheese over.

"Sorry I'm late," she mumbled.

Aloka pushed the bowl over toward the wall for safety. A touch perturbed, she announced, "The *channa* is done. I'm just starting the *payesh* part."

"Couldn't you have waited for me?" Sujata grumbled in that direct curt manner of hers. "I'd liked to have seen how it's made."

How like Sujata, to turn her tardiness into a shortcoming on her sister's part. They weren't exactly making the right start. Aloka pulled out a container of milk from the refrigerator. Trying to maintain her self-control, she clutched the container to her chest and stepped over to the stove. "You weren't here on time and this takes quite a while to do it right."

"So, we've got the whole afternoon. What's the next step?"

"The milk has to be reduced." Aloka poured twelve liters of milk and a dozen cardamom pods into the pot. Eyes on the frothy surface, she switched on the burner. "That's the longest part of the recipe. Once the milk's been thickened somewhat, I'll add the sweetened cheese and some extra sugar and stir some more. The mixture will then need to be chilled. Finally I'll garnish it with pistachio and rose petals. Are you going to stick around?"

"You seem to think that I won't."

Aloka swallowed. Was there any way of reaching Sujata?

"How long does it take for the milk to thicken?" Sujata asked.

"It has to be stirred for about an hour."

"An hour!"

Grandma, shrouded in white, her dark eyes glittering, poked her head through the door. "Are you two arguing?"

"We're only trying to decide who'll stir the milk, Thakurma," Aloka tried to placate the matriarch, who might be trying to take a nap.

Grandma waved a hand in dismissal. "Can't you even agree on that?" She hobbled toward her room without waiting for an answer.

Aloka picked up a cooking spoon. "Why don't you stir for a while?

Slowly, like this." She demonstrated a clockwise circular movement interspersed with an occasional figure eight on the surface of the milk. "Get into a rhythm. And don't forget to scrape the sides and the bottom every so often. Otherwise the milk will burn and we'll have to start over." Pausing, she held out the spoon to Sujata.

"Okay." Sujata clutched the spoon tightly, as though it were a weapon to fight off an intruder, and began her mission. Stationing herself at the other end of the counter, Aloka worked some sugar into the fresh cheese, glancing over occasionally at Sujata. So much unfinished business to discuss, yet such iciness between them. At last, unable to bear the tension any longer, she said, "Did it bother you that Thakurma and I went to lunch?"

"No surprises there. You've always been her favorite. All I ever heard was, 'Aloka is so beautiful, so personable, so kind.' During *mela* you always got the bigger doll."

Aloka kept slicing the cheese into tiny pellets. "Funny you should say that. We did discuss the will. The tea plantation—which she is giving to you, by the way—is much bigger in value than the house."

Sujata clanged the spoon on a spoon rest. Bubbles of milk from the back of the spoon drizzled over the counter. "I don't suppose it occurred to you that the plantation also comes with bigger problems? Like losing money for the last seven years?"

The milk came to a rolling boil, white clouds threatening to overflow the sides of the pan in a revolt. Aloka caught Sujata's eyes and pointed. "Stir!"

Sujata picked up the spoon with a careless hand and stirred without enthusiasm. She stood sideways to the stove, steam misting her right cheek.

"Do you know we're both acting terribly childish?" Aloka set the cheese pellets aside. "I don't care if Thakurma gives you more property. That's not the point. I come home in a world of pain from a failed marriage and I don't get even a word of consolation from you."

"You took Pranab away from me and you want my sympathy?"

"It was this way long before Pranab, ever since we were kids. You never seemed to care about me, you didn't talk to me, you wouldn't go anywhere with me. I had many friends then, but it used to crush me to think how my own sister acted like a stranger to me."

"I felt like I was behind you in every respect, Aloka, and I thought less of myself because of it. How could you expect me to be close to you when all you did was make me feel inferior? I still can't walk in your venerable shoes, nor do I have the patience to stir milk for an hour, but I have other strengths now. In any case, if I seemed to have neglected you these past few days, don't take it personally. It's because I, too, have a lot on my mind. The thought of taking over the tea plantation is really intimidating. And then there were issues with Mreenal. . . ."

"He wasn't too tickled about the tea estate, was he? Well, he is a city boy, after all. I understand both sides of that issue."

"But do you really understand a single woman's problems? After all, you were married for a number of years."

"You have the nerve to say that, knowing how my marriage turned out? Thanks in no small part to you, I might add!"

"Would it have lasted if I hadn't been around?"

Her words, like a large, ominous bird, swooped down on Aloka and startled her. She stepped toward the window and stared out blankly into the vast space beyond. Sujata had cut straight to the center of the issue. Her incisive observation had merit, though Aloka could only curse her for it.

"Oh, Aloka, please forgive me—I had no right to say that. I've caused you enough grief already."

Aloka took a few moments to gather herself. When she sneaked a look at Sujata, it shocked her to see the crumpled face. Sujata bit her lip, squeezed her hands, and flexed her feet inside her sandals, like she used to do as a child when she was upset. Aloka felt a surge of affection toward Sujata, the usually tough woman, suddenly so vulnerable.

"When Thakurma asked me if I'd help you in the kitchen, at first I had reservations. Then I thought if we spent some time together we could resolve our differences. . . ." Sujata's voice trailed off.

"I've always thought that we're very different, too, but maybe we aren't. After all, we both fell in love with Pranab."

Sujata laughed ruefully. "You know, it wouldn't have worked for me, either."

"Pranab thinks he's still in love with you."

"He doesn't seem real to me anymore. All that went on between us is just memory."

"I know practically nothing about what went on between you two."

"Do you really want to know, Aloka?"

"I do, once and for all. I don't want any hidden issues standing between us, so we can start with a clean slate and be real sisters. Besides, I have a right to know."

"You were away on that spring day when it started," Sujata began haltingly.

Aloka learned that the lovers kissed each other three times when they met, that the kisses signified love, everlasting love, and love only for each other, and that they had many secret "love nooks." Sujata appeared to speak from a tearful interior, her voice still so young, and her hand sadly expressive in the way it made shorter and shorter circles over the milk, finally stopping altogether.

Aloka took a jerky breath. "Did you two ever talk about me?"

"Oh, yes! You were in our minds constantly. Pranab gave you the name Sundari, the beauteous." Sujata recounted how they called Aloka gorgeous and foolish behind her back. Aloka never came between them or cast a shadow over them; she was more like an abstract figure of speech, a symbol of their transgression. They'd even made plans to elope, leaving behind only a note for Sundari. "This is to inform your beauteousness that . . ."

The words struck her like bullets. Aloka kicked the stool and made a dash for the door, but Sujata rushed after her, arms outstretched, and clasped her in a desperate embrace. It took Aloka a moment to come back to the present and feel the poignancy and regret in Sujata's trembling body. Then, abruptly, Sujata let her go. "Oh, no. The milk is burning."

That announcement and the acrid smell escaping the pot dissipated the sisterly closeness. Aloka hurried over to take a closer look, one hand turning off the stove with an emphatic click as she went. Sure enough, the edges of the milk had begun to turn deep brown and the skin on top had taken on a paper-like crispness.

"You haven't been stirring, that's why. What a pity. Now we'll have to throw it out and start all over again." Aloka concluded with, "Just what I was afraid of."

Sujata, visibly embarrassed, seemed to shrink in stature as she stepped aside. "Once again I've made a mess of things, it seems."

Aloka emptied the pot into the sink. The steaming liquid sizzled as it hit the stainless steel surface. She began scrubbing the pot furiously, listening to the *tap-tap-tap* of the dripping faucet, as she tried not to dwell on the difficulty of removing burned milk residue from a metal surface. Her inner arm began to ache from the strain. By the time she finished, her fingertips were pink and crinkled from the long immersion in hot water. How terribly wronged she felt.

"Please try to forgive me, Aloka, if that's humanly possible."

Inwardly Aloka struggled to muster every bit of kindness and understanding she was capable of. Forgiveness, as she knew from previous experience, was often a liberating emotion, a rainbow of hope, relief, and sorrow. It would not come all at once, but rather in numerous small acts of daily life. From now on she would trust Sujata with her confidences, be genuinely glad to spend time with her, offer her support when she needed it, lend her the cherry lipstick that they had fought over as children. With that notion clearing her head, Aloka added fresh milk and cardamom to the newly cleaned pot, turned on the stove, and began to whisk. The repetitive motion helped calm her. Another revelation dawned on her.

"You can finally rid yourself of the guilt you've been carrying, Sujata. In the final analysis you did nothing wrong. I was the one standing in the way of a great love."

Sujata's eyes were filled with gratitude. Her face glowed for an instant, then became softly reflective. "Yes, great love is what I truly felt for Pranab. But in retrospect, I don't regret being forced to leave home. Unhappiness would surely have come to me if I'd stayed. In a way I'm grateful it was you who married Pranab."

Sujata's confession had rendered the atmosphere heavy and still. And yet truth has a way of freeing one's energy. Aloka busied herself cleaning the counter with a rag, then went back to stir the milk vigorously.

"I admire you for being such a big-hearted person, Aloka. You've listened to my story without hitting me or screaming. I wouldn't have been so understanding."

"We'll never know, will we, *bontee*? Now, would you mind stirring for a while?"

"I promise not to take my eyes off it." With a confident hand, Sujata made perfect circles on the surface of the milk, breaking the film on top and dipping down to the bottom. The churning sound seemed to entertain her. When the milk came to a rolling boil, she lowered the heat and stirred quickly like an expert till the foaming subsided. She radiated the contentment of a sailor navigating a calm waterway.

"You have mastered the art of *payesh*, it seems." Aloka smiled with satisfaction at having passed this bit of know-how to Sujata.

"When I walked in," Sujata said after a while, "you seemed like an empress of the kitchen, handling everything perfectly, and I started to feel inferior all over again. And you know I still feel like I can never measure up to you."

"Don't be silly. You're about to take on a tremendous responsibility. You *are* accepting Thakurma's offer, I assume. When are you going to give her the good news?"

"On the eve of her birthday."

"Oh, and by the way, I was always a bit envious of you, too, Sujata. You were so far ahead of me when it came to tea. That being our family business, I was threatened as well."

Sujata seemed to be taken aback by this admission. "Really? I had no idea you felt that way."

Just then Reenu glided in, her eyes darting from one sister to the other, as though taking the temperature between the two. With obvious trepidation, she turned to Sujata. "Pranab-*babu* is here to see you." She said this meaningfully and watched for their reactions.

"Can't you see I'm busy cooking right now?"

"Let me take it over." Aloka reached out with her hand, and for an instant they shared the spoon handle. The two pairs of eyes met knowingly. It had taken all these years and much unpleasantness to achieve this degree of understanding, to feel this sisterly intimacy.

"I'll be along in a minute," Sujata replied to Reenu, and waited till the maidservant was gone out of sight. Then she turned to face Aloka and relinquished the spoon to her. Aloka extended her arms, embraced Sujata, and stood clinging to her, the way she'd wanted to for a long time.

"It won't be easy." Sujata released her sister and began rinsing her hands under the spigot. "But I'll have to tell Pranab one last time not to come to see me anymore. The servants will be told not to let him in."

"He'll feel totally lost, I'm sure." Aloka held out a plush hand towel. "He's always had one or the other of us to fall back on. Now it's time for him to get his life together on his own. Will he able to handle that? We'll just have to wait and see. He'll have some serious thinking to do, that's for sure."

"So, you don't want to see him at all?" Sujata asked.

"If I were to run into him again somewhere, I'd say hello, maybe chat for a couple of minutes, and then be on my way. When a love has ended, there's really not much to say."

Sujata returned the towel to the towel rod and straightened its sides. "A long time from now, Pranab will probably look back and think about both of us. He'll see my relationship with him as a little poem scribbled on a scrap of paper that the wind has blown away. But he'll see your life with him as a treasured book that he somehow managed to lose. He'll realize he made by far the bigger mistake with you."

"My very articulate sister," Aloka sighed. "You'd better go see him now. He's been waiting a long time."

Sujata nodded in agreement. "I'll be back. Watch the milk for me, will you?"

forty-seven

As she entered the living room, Suzy could barely make out Pranab's features. His buff-colored cotton jacket faded into the background. Sitting in
a meditative posture by the bookcase in a shadowy corner of the room, he
was contemplating a bunch of long-stemmed blue irises in a vase. She
weighed the subject she was about to bring up and almost stumbled, as one
of her shoes snagged at the edge of the carpet.

He must have heard her, for he rose eagerly. "Ah! It's you, Sujata! Reenu
said you were in the kitchen."

With the odor of burned milk still lingering in the air, the subject of
cooking provided an opportune conversational gambit. She sniffed the air
with mock exaggeration and flopped into a seat across from him. "Aloka
and I are cooking together!"

"Well, I don't want to keep you away from the fun in the kitchen. I came to see you one last time. I'm leaving this afternoon."

"You're not staying for Thakurma's birthday?"

"No, I really can't." He reached over and handed her a small box gift-wrapped in silver paper. "It's time for me to go."

"You caught me by surprise."

"It was a difficult decision. . . ."

Suzy set her eyes on him, wondering.

"A decision that Aloka helped me make. She straightened me out over breakfast the other day. I had gotten it all wrong. I should never have had that affair with you. Both Aloka and you prospered from it, became stronger—look at you two now—but it ended badly for me. I've squandered years of my life; now I'll have to start all over again. At first I dismissed what she had to say. Only days later did it all make sense. She really became my guiding light, my *alok*. So, now I'm going back to New York."

"I thought you hated New York."

"It's ugly and gross, but over the years it has become an easier place for me to exist. No one there cares where you come from, who you are, or what you do. I sought friends like I had here and only met with hostility or disinterest. Curiously, being shunned like that gives you the space and solitude to grow. And New York offers more than one chance. Maybe I'll find some other line of work. That's the upside of a humongous city like that."

The words that came in a burst had certainty in them. So, his years in the States hadn't been a complete loss. He was finally pulling it together. He appeared stronger than the last few times she's seen him, more in control. For a fleeting moment, he became the man she had fallen in love with right in this room, a king on that afternoon, his words her command to obey.

Then Suzy noticed that Reenu had tiptoed in and was hovering just inside the door. Sensing that she was intruding, the maidservant turned, as if to go back the way she came.

"Were you looking for me?" Suzy asked.

"The florist is on the phone," the maidservant whispered. "Should I ask him to call back?"

"Please."

Suzy appreciated Reenu's tactful handling of the matter. Oddly, now that it had become clear she might never see Pranab again, she wanted to linger a bit. She finally saw him for who he was, neither a giant nor a despicable man, but rather an ordinary being, whose openness and humility inspired fondness; a man who had difficulty controlling his impulses, but ultimately was one struggling to make a decent life for himself.

"I want to thank you belatedly," Suzy said, "for what you attempted to do for the tea plantation. My elders didn't listen to your advice about paying attention to the tea workers' grievances. They didn't understand why you were so interested in labor rights, what you were trying to achieve with that protest march. In retrospect, I can see that you had the situation figured out. Had you been able to steer my father in the right direction in a peaceful manner, he'd probably still be alive and we'd have fewer problems with labor unions now."

"I didn't handle things well, young firebrand that I was. When my high ideals failed me, there was nothing left but emptiness. I couldn't pull out of that. Maybe I reached too high, maybe we're not all capable of greatness. From now on, I'm going to concentrate on small activities, like getting some young boy excited about Sanskrit literature. Perhaps it's enough to influence one mind, not hundreds. As I get older, I am finding more satisfaction in simple pleasures. I guess I've finally accepted being ordinary."

He rose from his chair. Then he seemed to reach an impasse, for he fell silent, and only after some deliberation said, "I wish you every happiness, Sujata."

As she looked on, he gazed at her face wistfully for a long disquieting moment. Then he turned and quickly slipped out the door.

Now that the *channer payesh* was done to her satisfaction and the bowl was tucked away in the refrigerator, Aloka drifted out to the back lawn for some fresh air. The heat of the kitchen and the long preparation time had exhausted and somewhat disoriented her. Much to her elation, Grandma was standing at the back fence, looking out over the glen just beyond the house. Hearing Aloka's footsteps, the wispy woman turned. Her white sari flapped in the wind and caught around her legs. In her eagerness, she stood taller. "I'm just surveying your property," she said mischievously.

Leaning against the fence, Aloka breathed in through the aroma of earth and wood and let it settle into her chest. Through the diffuse violet light of sunset, Mount Kanchenjunga loomed above them, massive and purple-black, its upper reaches still cloaked in snow. Just beyond the lawn where the conifers were wreathed in damp gray mist, a sunbird jumped out of its nest and poured out a jumble of clipped melodic notes.

"Remember when you and Sujata used to play out there?" Grandma indicated an area off to the far left that had become overgrown and junglelike.

Grandma was hinting at the need for constant upkeep of this huge property that Aloka would have to undertake long-distance. The clever woman was doing her best to make sure that Aloka stayed involved with the family on a regular basis. Aloka squeezed Grandma's hand gently to reassure her in that regard.

Soon Grandma began to tire of standing and they settled into a couple of wicker chairs plumped with throw pillows. A crow rose up from the bushes and circled overhead, cawing raucously as if wanting to participate in their conversation.

"Did it surprise you that Pranab left for New York?" Grandma said. There was a barely concealed sarcasm in the way she enunciated the question.

"Not for long." Aloka stooped to gaze in wonder at the intense magenta of a bougainvillea blossom that a gust of wind had deposited at her feet. "To be honest, I was relieved. All this time I've felt guilty for having dragged him to New York. Now he's going back there on his own!"

"I'm sure, Aloka, you've drawn some conclusions from this."

"Yes, one of them is that Pranab wouldn't have made it here, even if we'd never left the country. He didn't have the strength to deal with adversity."

"He didn't have the character. Do you remember, Aloka, how in our Bengali society *charitra* used to be an important word? When a marriage proposal came for someone in the extended family, the first question asked was, 'Does he have good *charitra*?' We're losing that. Now it's only: How much money does he make? Which neighborhood does he live in? Is there potential to go abroad? Can the family afford a big wedding? I wish I'd relied more on my hunches and warned you about Pranab's character."

"I wouldn't have listened, Thakurma. I was young and had to learn the hard way. We were taught that the heart is never wrong and, when in doubt, follow your heart and not your head. Since then I've found out that's not entirely true. I followed my heart when I went with Pranab, and look what that led to. Had I joined my heart and mind to make that important decision, I'd have been better off. Now I realize that although our hearts want us to feel, and fully express our emotions, we must not take blind actions because of those emotions. There's where I went wrong."

"Still, you've come a long way, *amar sona*. You've risen above many difficulties."

"Not soon enough and not well enough. I don't mind saying that Sujata's the one who deserves most of the credit. She's come a longer way. She's done the best of the three of us."

Aloka's eyes followed Grandma's to the undulating magnolia tree limb and the crow bouncing on it. The love triangle that had originated in this house and shaken the family tree had finally resolved itself. It amused Aloka to consider that she had never cared for drawing triangles in her geometry class in school; she'd always preferred the geniality of circles. Now she could almost see before her the broken sides of a triangle, a few straight lines in space in a state of movement, no longer connected to form a prison for the restless souls.

The wind bathed Aloka's face in a refreshing coolness. A long outgoing breath carried some regrets with it, leaving her feeling light and airy. Soon it would be time to escort Grandma inside. Soon the currents of life would blow them each again in different directions.

forty-eight

In the evening, with shadows creeping up the wall opposite the window, Suzy gave Grandma's frail feet a gentle massage with her fingertips. Grandma's dry scaly skin was veined like the intricate sweater patterns she once knitted. Suzy's finger pressure must have been just right, for from her reclining position on her bed Grandma gave a grunt of satisfaction. Then she fell back into silence.

The custom of foot massage had been in the Gupta clan for as long as Suzy could remember. The loving practice improved circulation, stimulated the Ayurvedic pressure points, as well as conveyed respect to one's elders. Grandma had long ago tutored Suzy on how to hold the foot and how to apply the right finger pressure while making circular movements, and how to check for lumps or points where energy was obstructed.

Her imaginings still revolving around Mreenal, Suzy hid a long sigh. She wished she could sit with Aloka and empty every emotion—Aloka seemed so much more mature now and so willing to offer friendship—but how could Suzy bring up the subject of her breakup with Mreenal after acting so foolishly romantic so soon after meeting him. In any case, it would be difficult to get an hour of Aloka's time now, what with all the prebirthday activities going on around the house.

"I could just about fall asleep," Grandma said. "I appreciate your doing this, my child."

"We have to get you well rested for tomorrow."

Grandma had no idea how huge the event would be, how many people she would have to greet. The whole crew at the tea estate, some two hundred people who served in various capacities, had been invited. Unbeknownst to Grandma, her three college friends from Calcutta had arrived and checked into a nearby hotel. Relatives from other states were pouring into the town as well. This would be the biggest celebration in the Gupta home in everyone's memory.

"Have you thought about my will, dear?"

"Yes, I have. I'll accept your offer, Thakurma. It's a most precious gift."

"Oh, Sujata." Grandma lifted her head, beamed, and let her head drop back on the pillow again. "Now I can send a prayer to my ancestors and tell them that the estate will remain in the family. They'll see that I've done my job."

She closed her semitranslucent eyelids and her lips trembled in silent prayer. In joyful quickness, her eyes flew open again. "Are you happy, Sujata?"

"Yes, Thakurma. It's my wildest dream come alive. I'll own the most organic tea garden in Darjeeling and be able to distribute the finest product to the North American market. Many tea drinkers there still don't recognize quality leaves. I'm trying to come up with a marketing strategy. I am also checking into natural decaf processes. Decaffeinated tea is popular there, but a fine decaffeinated Darjeeling is still rare."

"I'm so glad you have your own reasons and are not doing it just for me."

"Oh, no! This opens up great new possibilities for me. There are potential tea markets just about everywhere on this planet. I'll be traveling to new places, even occasionally make a stop to see my friends and colleagues in Victoria."

"How fortunate we're to have you back. As you'll find out, there aren't very many family-run tea estates left in Darjeeling. The few that are still in existence pray for a male heir, so that their daughters will not inherit the property. Not me. Never once did I think that I needed grandsons when I had girls like you and Aloka." Grandma swiped at a trickle of tears flowing down her cheeks. "I'm sorry. I haven't had very many days like this lately. As you grow older, the years cheat you, wear you out, give you wrinkles and joint aches, but don't bring you an equal amount of satisfaction in return. By the way, the tea workers have a special celebration in mind the first day you go and sit in your father's office. And they're waiting to hear your ideas."

"I have so many new ideas! Like producing green tea. Like growing cardamom and oranges as additional crops. But first things first, we have a birthday to celebrate."

The massage now finished, Suzy laid Grandma's feet gently on the bed and drew the jacquard cover up over her. A beatific smile spread over Grandma's face. "Have you told Mreenal yet?" she whispered conspiratorially.

Sujata rose, moved over to the bedside table, and began rearranging the items there. Then, in as normal and even a tone of voice as she could manage, she answered, "Yes, I have."

"I can't wait to see that chap tomorrow. I have a tea quiz ready for him. Before he can ask for your hand, he'll have to pass the quiz. And don't you dare help him."

"I promise." Suzy forced a laugh as she returned to the bedside. "I'll do your hair right after breakfast. Then I'll line your feet with *aalta* and set out a brand-new pair of sandals."

"Good shoes are an old woman's best accessories. Her spirit manifests itself in her walk."

Suzy adjusted the cover around Grandma's halo of white hair one last time. Peace and repose had smoothed her forehead. She shut her eyes and parted her lips in a blissful smile. As Suzy looked at her lovingly, she found that her own unhappiness had receded into the background.

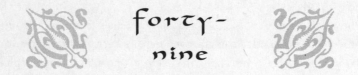

forty-nine

Relatives swirled in the entranceway just like the day Aloka had arrived. Standing on the porch, on her way out, Aloka bent down and picked up her suitcase. Images from Grandma's birthday, which had taken place only yesterday, replayed before her eyes. Grandma sitting upright in her half-moon chair—she was the only one in the family who could sit so regally. Members of the extended Gupta clan and friends surrounding her devised apt testimonials in their own words and conveyed thanks to her for what she'd brought to their lives. While tasting a spoonful of *channer payesh*, Grandma brushed aside any hint of reverence and asserted that in her heart she still thought of herself as a poor ugly village girl, cursed to bear unusual difficulties, but who treated any bliss that life handed her, like this ambrosia before her, as though it had been hand-delivered by the gods. After another taste, Grandma laughingly added that she perceived life as one of those grand epic plays that, as everyone knows, doesn't always end on an exalted note. One's only satisfaction, she concluded, might lie in having the good fortune to be present.

Now Aloka considered it her good fortune to have been a witness to that remarkable occasion.

Down by the car the driver cleared his throat to indicate he was ready. Aloka's fingers became as taut as the coarse rope that bound the suitcase. She had rehearsed these last few minutes in her mind many times. There should be no tears and no promises as to when she would return. Her life, after all, was in New York, where Jahar was waiting for her, and where, as Seva, she had the job of mending a thousand hearts.

Facing Uncle Umesh, Aloka fumbled for words. Her voice cracked a bit as she found herself promising that she would be back the same time next year. She had her sister, her grandmother, and a home here, a sanctuary where she could rejuvenate. Uncle Umesh only patted the corners of his eyes.

Turning, Aloka overheard an elderly uncle whispering to his brother, "Can you imagine a woman running a tea estate? Do they have the stamina or the temperament? In my opinion they do better as mothers. What a mistake."

Before Aloka could retort, Sujata edged her way forward with a thermos bottle and a Tiffin box for the four-hour car ride. "Your favorite *luchi* and *halwa* are in there," Sujata offered. "And tea, yesterday's harvest. It doesn't get much fresher."

Even as Sujata smiled in pride, the dark shadows on her face bespoke her loneliness. She had given up Mreenal and her cozy existence in Victoria, yet there was dignity and a firmness of resolve in her carriage. In the last few days Sujata, already assuming the role of new family matriarch, had greeted hundreds of guests. Under her care the household had functioned smoothly—meals served on time, rides arranged for the elderly, servants given a bonus, children escorted to the playground. Through all this she'd made sure that shipments from the tea factory left on time for the auction in Calcutta.

"You've got what it takes," Aloka assured Sujata. "But don't hesitate to call me if you ever need me."

"I will," Sujata replied warmly. "Be sure to send me clippings of your writing."

Aloka looked admiringly again at the brave new Sujata standing before her. How far she had come; how much farther she would travel. They stood in silence for a moment, gazing into each other's eyes, entering what Aloka believed was a realm of understanding beyond the verbal.

The driver signaled again, this time with an impatient hand gesture.

With a last, longing look at the crumpled faces, Aloka descended the front steps and hopped into the car. They were waving at her now, hands drooping in sadness, like a flock of uncertain birds about to take flight. Sujata and Grandma stood in the forefront, their eyes making desperate attempts to hold her in sight.

The car lurched down the winding tree-lined street away from the house.

Every journey, it dawned on Aloka now, is a quest for what we've been missing in our lives.

This trip had been to find Sujata.

READING GROUP GUIDE

1. Is Aloka hurt more by Sujata's betrayal or by Pranab's?

2. Did Sujata really love Pranab or was she just interested in hurting Aloka?

3. Was Pranab really interested in helping the workers on the tea plantation?

4. Who is the real Pranab—the immigrant or the revolutionary?

5. Why did Aloka settle into life in the U.S. so much more easily than Pranab?

6. Why does Aloka feel she needs so many secret identities?

7. Will Jahar make Aloka happy?

8. Is Aloka Nina's favorite? How does this affect the relationship between Aloka, Sujata, and Nina?

9. What part does Mreenal play in the novel?

10. Would Sujata and Pranab have been happy if they'd stayed together?

11. How does Pranab change by the end of the book?

12. Do you think that Aloka and Sujata can ever have a close relationship?

Rediscover how sweet life can be...

A NOVEL OF DESSERTS AND DISCOVERIES

BHARTI KIRCHNER

SUNYA IS THE
OWNER OF PASTRIES, a cozy Seattle bakery,
and her world has begun to crumble. With her business threatened and her
relationship ending, Sunya schedules a trip to Japan to get back in touch
with her one great love—baking.

NEW IN HARDCOVER · St. Martin's Press